Daddy's Girls

He was blocking my way to the front door. He was six foot two and played rugby. I was five foot three and didn't play anything if I could avoid it. I might have admitted defeat (for the moment) and gone to the kitchen. But he reached out and pushed my shoulder.

I went wild. I charged at him, I tried to knock him over. I knew I would get the worst of it, but he shouldn't have pushed my shoulder.

He stood between me and the front door. He was a rock and I was a futile little wave. He even smiled. His head was slightly to one side and tilted back in scorn. I could see up his nose. I imagined being sucked into one of his wide nostrils and back into his head and swallowed. His pale, blond-fringed eyes were lit up with challenge as if he had forgotten I was his fourteen-year-old daughter and thought I was another man wanting a fight.

By the same author
**available from Mandarin Paperbacks*

*Here Today
*Closing
Benefits
Stand We At Last

Zoë Fairbairns

Daddy's Girls

Mandarin

A Mandarin Paperback
DADDY'S GIRLS

First published in Great Britain 1991
by Methuen London
This edition published 1992
by Mandarin Paperbacks
Michelin House, 81 Fulham Road, London SW3 6RB

Mandarin is an imprint of the Octopus Publishing Group,
a division of Reed International Books Limited

A CIP catalogue record for this title
is available from the British Library
ISBN 0 7493 0581 9

Printed and bound in Great Britain
by Cox & Wyman Ltd, Reading, Berks

Acknowledgements

Elsbeth Lindner is a very fine editor. Her professional expertise, patient encouragement and generous friendship were invaluable to me during the writing of *Daddy's Girls*. I thank her.

I also thank many other friends and loved ones, relatives and colleagues, not to mention one or two total strangers, whose wit, wisdom, random remarks, reminiscences, research assistance, kindness and hospitality so often helped me on my way. They include Giles Ellis, Polly Fairbairns, Anna Petherbridge, James Petherbridge, John Petherbridge, Helen Sands, Vicky Schankula, Kate Sinar, Michael Thomas and Catherine Wood. Needless to say, none of these people bears any responsibility for the content of the book – some of them may not even have known how helpful they were being – but I thank them anyway.

Lines from *The Old Grey Squirrel* by Alfred Noyes are quoted by kind permission of John Murray (Publishers) Ltd.

A brief note on the genesis of the novel appears (because it gives away part of the story) at the back.

Christine

I

When my father realised that the ban-the-bombers would be marching past our house, he got out his Union Jack and hung it from the highest window. As they started to appear, he put *Land of Hope and Glory*, played by the band of the Royal Marines, on the radiogram. He turned the volume up to FULL and opened the sitting room window as far as it would go.

He walked out into the front garden to check that the flag could be seen and the music could be heard.

He strolled pugnaciously down the path. He stood guard at our gate with his arms folded and his grey eyes narrowed into scornful slits. Occasionally he half-smiled beneath his pale blond silky moustache, shaking his head as if at a private, sad thought. He looked as if he wanted the marchers to ask what the private, sad thought was, but they didn't.

They didn't need his good opinion. They didn't care what he thought, or what records he played. They had music of their own. They spread across our road and kept on coming till evening. Long after my father got tired of rushing into the house to move the needle back to the beginning of his LP, they were still marching.

They thrilled me. They had come from all over the country, and all over the world. Some of their banners were black and white with short, grim slogans ('Disarm or Die'; 'Thou Shalt Not Kill'), others had gorgeous colourful pictures of trades unionists united in brotherhood. The marchers played guitars and held hands, they carried bright yellow Easter daffodils, they were old and young, there were thousands and thousands of them, and they were singing.

I wanted to sing with them but I didn't know the words. I wanted to give them something but I didn't know what they would like.

I picked flowers for them from our garden but my father told me to stop. I asked my mother if I could make them cups of tea. She asked my father who said I could but the cost would be deducted from my pocket money, including electricity and wear and tear on the kettle.

It was Easter Saturday. They would be spending the night in Bleswick before moving off again in the morning from Bleswick Common. They would be sleeping in tents and church halls and schools, including my school.

My father was outraged. He didn't even want the marchers to walk on Bleswick pavements and breathe Bleswick air, never mind sleep in our schools. The council, he said, must be stark staring bonkers. Acts of immorality would take place in my school to which he must, as a parent, object. If it weren't for the atom bomb protecting everybody's freedom, marchers wouldn't be allowed to march in the first place. They would be sent to the salt mines. And he would bring the matter up at the Parent Teacher Association.

The next meeting of the Parent Teacher Association wouldn't be until next term. That night the marchers slept in my school. I lay in my own bed two miles away and hoped they were having fun.

When I woke in the morning, I wanted to join them.

At the very least I wanted one last look at them before they marched away and Bleswick returned to normal. I tried to slip out of the house.

My father asked where I was going.

'Just for a ride on my bike.'

'Would you like a piece of news?'

'What?'

'You are not going for a ride on your bike. Breakfast doesn't make itself. Help your mother.'

'It's always me,' I said. 'Why can't Janet?'

'Janet can help too. A holiday should be a holiday for everyone.'

'Are you going to help?'

'What a comedian you are, Christine.'

'*Are* you?' Rage boiled in me. 'Or not?'

'Have as many teenage tantrums as you like.' He hissed the t's, *Tseenage tsantrums*, mimicking the way he said my friends spoke and I would speak if he didn't keep my accent under control. 'But have them in the kitchen and *help your mother*.'

He was blocking my way to the front door. He was six foot two and played rugby. I was five foot three and didn't play anything if I could avoid it. I might have admitted defeat (for the moment) and gone to the kitchen. But he reached out and pushed my shoulder.

I went wild. I charged at him, I tried to knock him over. I knew I would get the worst of it, but he shouldn't have pushed my shoulder.

He stood between me and the front door. He was a rock and I was a futile little wave. He even smiled. His head was slightly to one side and tilted back in scorn. I could see up his nose. I imagined being sucked into one of his wide nostrils and back into his head and swallowed. His pale, blond-fringed eyes were lit up with challenge as if he had forgotten I was his fourteen-year-old daughter and thought I was another man wanting a fight.

I kicked but I couldn't reach anything worth kicking. His arm was longer than my leg and he was holding me back by my face. The finger and thumb of his hand closed round the soft flesh of my cheeks, squeezing it against my jaws and teeth. It hurt.

It hurt especially because it was my face. He grabbed it as if he owned it. He twisted it into a mask with his finger and thumb. The piece of his skin that connected his finger to his thumb pressed against my front teeth and I bit it.

'Oho,' he said. 'I didn't know pacifists bit people.' His tone of voice suggested that he thought he'd scored a point. If he had, it was lost on me because I wasn't sure what a pacifist was or why they weren't supposed to bite people who got hold of them by their face.

He slapped my face hard, twice, this way and that. I buried my face in my hands and pretended to cry to put him off his guard. It didn't work. When I made a sudden lunge towards the front door, he was ready. He got me by the wrists, backed me away from my escape route and threw me against the stairs.

I went down in a heap. I tasted the dust that had gathered

where the stair-carpet met the stair and checked where my limbs were. One of my arms had got itself wound round the cracked banister. I hadn't cracked it, it had always been cracked. My hand clung to the damaged wood.

My other hand was under my breasts, protecting them from the hard edge of the stair. I was proud of my breasts and I didn't want any harm to come to them.

I lay still and wondered what to do. I had never been in this situation before.

I had been hit before. I had been slapped and beaten often, by both my parents. Admittedly things had changed for the better since I became a teenager. My mother knew that if she hit me I would hit her back so she had given it up. And my father had given up bending me over and beating me that way. He seemed to think it was more decent to hit me around the face and head, so he did that instead. I preferred it.

This, though, was new. This was the first time he had knocked me down.

I lay still. The whole house was still. You'd never have known there were four people in it, waiting to see what was going to happen next.

2

His feet came towards me. His navy blue sailing shoes were inches from my face. Through a hole in the canvas I could see part of his big toenail, and a few hairs like pale silvery-gold threadworms.

I closed my eyes to shut him out but when he said, 'Don't smile, your face'll crack,' my lips twitched against my will.

'She's smiling!' His knee joints clicked as he squatted down and felt my limbs like a first aider. I wriggled my body in an almighty shudder to get rid of his hands. He said, 'No bones broken,' and backed away.

After his feet came my mother's. They filled her sandals. It was her habit to wear ankle socks and school sandals even though Janet and I begged her not to.

'Upsie daisy, let's have a look at you.' She sounded embarrassed. I supposed it must be a bit embarrassing for her. She might feel she had to take sides.

The briskness in her voice had nothing to do with which side she had taken. It was her normal response to minor injuries and illnesses. All illnesses and injuries in our family were minor as far as she was concerned. She used to be a nurse.

'What's this?' She prodded my arm and tried to uncurl my fingers from the banister. I hung on. I had a fellow feeling with the banister. It was damaged and no one could be bothered with it. I imagined her ticking off in her mind all the things that couldn't be wrong with me if I could keep such a tight hold of the banister. I couldn't have broken my arm. I couldn't be unconscious.

'You're not hurt,' she said. 'So let's have a bit less of the high drama.'

Away strode the sandals with my mother in them. Janet was

next. She was wearing socks and sandals as well, but chubby-legged little ten-year-olds were supposed to.

'You're crying wolf,' she said, in her bossy, pernickety, form captain voice, 'aren't you?' She sounded hopeful. I didn't see why she was so interested. It wasn't as if she was likely to be next. She hardly ever got hit. She took care not to risk it. She watched what I did, and did the opposite.

She was wrong in any case. I wasn't crying wolf. I wasn't even trying to get in the way. I was glad to have embarrassed everybody but that wasn't the reason why I went on lying there.

The reason I went on lying there was that I was embarrassed too. I didn't feel as if I'd been seriously injured, but I didn't know how to get up. I didn't know whether I was expected to get up and apologise or get up and be apologised to, or both, or neither. I didn't know whether to go to my room and sulk, or laugh as if it had all been a joke, or pretend it hadn't happened. So I stayed put and listened to the sounds of breakfast being prepared.

My father brought a tray from the kitchen with a cup of tea, a slice of toast and a boiled egg with its shell dyed blue for Easter. He set the tray down on the stair by my head.

My mother came storming after him and snatched the tray away. 'If she wants a meal, she can sit at the table like a normal human being.'

'I think she prefers to lie on the stairs, and thanks to the atom bomb she's free to do so.'

'That's all very well,' said my mother, 'but somebody's going to kick that tea cup over and who'll have to clear up the mess?'

'You.'

She stood over me. 'You've made your point. Why don't you go upstairs, have a wash, take a few deep breaths, come back down and have breakfast with us? Wipe the slate clean.'

Had I dirtied the slate? I supposed I had started the argument. Did that make it my fault, rather than his? He wasn't on the floor, I was. I decided to stay there.

After breakfast they gave Easter eggs to each other. 'I'll put Christine's in her room,' said my mother in a loud voice, stepping over me on her way upstairs, with a rustle of foil and cellophane. Then they got ready to go sailing.

This was an exhausting business, even for me lying on the stairs. Just listening to them wore me out. They thundered backwards and forwards, yelling at the tops of their voices, digging ropes and sails and kit bags and buoyancy bags and other junk from winter hiding places and carrying it all out to the back yard.

In the yard, everything had to be loaded into the baskets and the panniers on the bikes. This was a job in itself. My father was longing to get a car, but he kept failing his driving test. He had failed it four times already. He said he could not tolerate sitting in a confined space being told what to do by an officious little man.

My mother made a picnic. She said, 'Will you be coming with us, Christine?'

Janet said, 'Don't try to persuade her. We don't want her if she's going to be in a horrible mood.' In her arms were three bright orange life-jackets, and I wondered why I had never got around to cutting a hole in hers, in a secret, important place.

Not that I wanted to go sailing. It was the last thing I would ever want to do. Being able to give up sailing was another advantage of being a teenager, along with having my beautiful breasts and being hit by my father in a way that allowed me to look him in the face while he did it. I was no longer forced to sit in our wet, cramped dinghy, and goaded and ridiculed into pretending I was enjoying myself.

That was what happened when I was younger. If I looked as frightened or as bored as I felt, I would get a constant stream of 'Cheer up, Christine' and 'Look at the baby ducklings!' If I made the mistake of smiling at anything or looking relaxed, this would change to 'I think she's growing to like it.'

That was the expression they used: 'growing' to like it. And even now they talked as if the only reason I didn't like sailing was that I wasn't old enough yet to appreciate what fun it was.

I stayed where I was. My mother came and looked down at me. 'Have you made up your mind whether you're coming with us or are you going to spend the whole of Easter lying on the stairs?'

I let go of my banister and offered her my hand to shake. 'How do you do. My name's Christine, I'm your daughter and one thing you obviously don't know about me is that I never go sailing.'

I thought this was quite witty but it was wasted. She walked away saying, 'I'll leave your picnic on the kitchen table.'

My father called his crew together and carried out a kit inspection. Everything was found to be satisfactory. He said above me, 'You're on your honour not to go on that march.'

I shrugged, moving my shoulder against the stair-carpet.

'Sure you won't come with us, Christine?' my mother began. 'You might have grown to – ' I put my fingers in my ears. This shut out her words, but not the crashing thud of the front door. The stairs vibrated underneath my body.

I listened as my family rode away with shouted conversation and laborious creaking of pedals. In the silence they left behind, the phone began to ring. I hauled myself to my feet. I was stiff and I was glad of the excuse to get up.

3

It was Pam MacLeish. She wanted my father, but I didn't mind. I was glad to hear her voice. She was more than a friend, she was an inspiration to me. She was the only person I knew who stood up to him.

She was twenty-six and came from New Zealand. Two years ago she had set off from there to hitch-hike round the world on her own. She had got as far as London, fallen in love with it, and stayed.

She kept meaning to go to America, but in the meantime she worked as a temp and lived in Earl's Court, in various flats and bedsitters.

When she got tired of Earl's Court, she came to us for weekends. She helped my mother in the house, listened to Janet boasting, told me about her adventures and gave my father driving practice, if any neighbour was fool enough to lend him their car.

I couldn't imagine any of these activities being more exciting than spending a weekend in Earl's Court, but Pam said even Earl's Court got lonely at times and it was nice for her to have a family to visit.

The reason she had phoned today was that she had found a new flat and wanted my father's advice about the rent and the lease. My father was a surveyor, and whenever anyone in the family wanted to move house they came to him and he told them what to do.

Strictly speaking Pam wasn't a member of our family but we thought of her as one. Liking Pam was one of the few things we agreed on. Janet had a crush on her. My mother thought she was 'a fun girl' and my father said she had a lot of spunk in her. He said she was 'good value', which was high praise from someone whose job was to do valuations.

I told her he wasn't in, and said I would get him to call her back. I asked her when she would be coming to see us again. She said, 'When I'm invited.'

'You don't have to be invited.'

'Oh yes I do. I know what you poms are like.' She teased us a lot about being poms and standing on ceremony with icicles up our backsides.

We teased her about being a kiwi and a colonial, or at least my father did. He thought it funny to pretend to think she was Australian. When she reminded him that she was a New Zealander he would say, 'Same thing.' He liked to mimic her accent and that really was embarrassing because he was no good at accents. He thought he was brilliant at them, but in fact he had one all-purpose accent which he used for mimicking Pam, pretending to be a cockney or doing all the parts in a story about a Scotsman, an Irishman and a Welshman.

Pam laughed it off. She said she had been warned, back home in New Zealand, that if she came to England she would meet people like my father. It was lucky that she was so tolerant. I wouldn't have wanted to lose her friendship just because my father was a narrow-minded, embarrassing show-off.

Her voice went up instead of down at the ends of sentences, and she had a surprising, clipped way of pronouncing certain words. She said 'Janutt' and 'tickutt' instead of 'Janet' and 'ticket'. She called me Chrissie, which I liked even though it sounded a bit soppy. I sometimes called her Pammie in return. Her 'yes' sounded more like 'yiss', and her pronunciation of words like 'how' and 'now' sounded as if she had her tongue in a knot, but apart from these points her accent was hardly noticeable, and I hated it when my father made her sound crude and silly and common.

'Will your dad be at home tomorrow?'

'Probably not. He'll probably be going sailing.' With great sarcasm I added the words 'for a change' and at the same time Pam said, 'Oh, that'll be a nice change for him.' We giggled, and she said, 'What about you?'

'What about me?'

'All on your own again?'

Her concern took me by surprise. I didn't expect to be pitied for being left by myself. It was my choice. I was free to go sailing if I wanted to.

'Are you all right, Chrissie?'

'Yes, why?'

'You sound a bit funny.'

My body went weak, as if it suddenly remembered how it felt to be thrown against the stairs, to be knocked down on purpose.

I felt afraid.

I wanted to shout *NO! I'm not all right. He hurt me and then he got everyone to pretend he hadn't.*

I couldn't say that to Pam. It was too shaming. She might have thought we were a peculiar family with a violent father. She might have rung up the NSPCC, or the police. She might have stopped being our friend.

She might have thought of me as a silly little girl who deserved to be smacked.

'I wanted to go on the ban-the-bomb march and he wouldn't let me.'

She made a sound that was scornful of him and sympathetic towards me. 'Why not?'

'I'm never allowed to do anything. He's such a hypocrite. They both are. Every so often they feel guilty, they say, "Christine, if there's anything *you* want to do at weekends, tell us and we'll arrange it." Now there is something and they say, "Oh no, you can't do that."'

'I guess ban-the-bomb marches weren't quite what they had in mind. How about the Victoria and Albert Museum?'

'That's the most boring place in the world, outside Bleswick.'

'What's wrong with Bleswick?'

'It's a dump. The only exciting thing about it is that the marchers go through it. They've gone now and everything's closed for Easter and all my friends have gone away and I don't blame them.'

'You do sound fed up.'

'I am.'

'Come to lunch tomorrow.'

'With you?'

'Why not? I'm at a bit of a loose end myself.'

I said, 'Yes, please!' though I couldn't understand how anyone could be at a loose end in Earl's Court. My father called it Kangaroo Valley and said the day was fast approaching when English people would need passports to get in. That was what I liked about it. I wanted to meet people from every country in the world, and being friends with Pam MacLeish was a good start.

We made our plans. I would get a train from Bleswick Junction after breakfast. Pam offered to meet me at Paddington, but I said I would make my own way. I liked the idea of going on the underground and arriving in Earl's Court by myself. I would pretend I lived there.

It was only after I had put the phone down that it dawned on me that her invitation might have been in code. She probably knew that the march was due to end tomorrow with a rally in Hyde Park. She had probably meant, *Come up to London and use me as your excuse. We can go sightseeing. Hyde Park's a sight. If we happen by some strange coincidence to find ourselves at the rally, you can put the blame on me, an ignorant colonial who knows no better.*

4

I prowled around the house, looking for something to do. There was plenty that needed doing in the way of housework, but I didn't mean that. Housework was pointless, but I wouldn't have minded being able to do odd jobs. I rather fancied the idea of myself efficiently changing washers on taps, getting rid of damp patches and persuading doors to close that had never closed before.

No one else in our family did odd jobs. My father was a great procrastinator. He called it 'problem solving by inactivity'.

He was a member of the Procrastination Association. It actually existed, in America. He had seen an article about it in the *Reader's Digest* and had written off to join. They didn't reply for eighteen months. They invited him to an International Procrastination Convention, on a date to be announced.

He thought it was hilarious.

Being in the property business made him even worse. He was always talking about contractors he knew who would come to our house and fix up this or that little job. They would do it as a favour to him, so of course they could not be pressed for particular dates. This left him free to get on with his hobbies; rugby in the winter and sailing in the summer.

I hadn't got any hobbies, though Janet had. Janet was hobby-mad. Her room was like a museum. Every shelf was carefully set out with china horses, foreign dolls, glass animals, plaster-of-Paris models of Lady and the Tramp, interesting matchboxes, boring matchboxes, stones with holes in them, stones without holes in them, autumn fruits, signs of spring (depending on the time of year), tickets and programmes, wrapped sugar lumps, beer mats signed by our father's boozy friends, menus, photographs of people who had changed schools or moved house and left her grieving, feathers, sea shells, birds' eggs, and empty perfume bottles. As well as scavenging for all this rubbish, listing it in notebooks, dusting it, arranging it and showing it off to selected friends, she wrote poems and stories, sent them in to writing competitions, won more often than not, went riding, worked for her Brownie badges, went sailing, wrote to her penfriends and still found time to come top of her class.

All I wanted to do was go on the Aldermaston March. I wanted to go now. Tomorrow was too far away.

On my bike I could catch up with them easily. I wondered if I dared. My father had put me on my honour not to. He loved putting people on their honour to do this and not to do that. He was a great believer in honour.

There was a family promise that went back to his childhood: 'Honourable Heart'. Janet and I had learned from an early age that Honourable Heart promises were absolutely unbreakable, and so had all our Toms cousins.

No true Toms could go on lying after an Honourable Heart challenge. I certainly couldn't. I wished I could, but whenever I tried it I got frightened. I blushed or my hands shook. So if I went on the march, my father would find out. He wouldn't need a spy. He would find out from me.

I ate an Easter egg and wondered how brave I was. Some people in the ban-the-bomb movement had been to prison. I didn't think I would mind that as much as I minded being thumped by my father.

I decided to eat my picnic. It consisted of two rounds of roast beef sandwiches, a tomato and some fruit. I took the food out into the garden in the hope that it would feel more picnicky, but it just felt embarrassing. I went back inside.

I listened to the special Easter Sunday edition of *The Billy Cotton Band Show*, followed by *Life with the Lyons*. I got my bike out of the shed. I wheeled it along the passage to the front garden and leaned it against the hedge. Then I went back inside to get ready.

I was already dressed to march. I had my new blue jeans on and a jersey which showed my bust to good advantage. I had a nice figure, I didn't know why. I hadn't inherited it from my parents.

My mother was always fat or slimming or both, and my father looked ready to get down into a scrum at a moment's notice. So did most of his relations, including Janet.

I had never had a boyfriend and I thought it was about time someone appreciated me. Some of the marchers had been quite good-looking, particularly the beatniky ones.

I started to do my face. I didn't want to look as if my father had just hit me. I didn't want to look as if I had anything to do with him. I didn't think there was any resemblance – he had fair hair, I was dark like my mother – but people were always talking about the Toms family likeness and I didn't want to take any risks.

His face was square, mine was more of a triangle. I sucked in my cheeks and drew shadows with dark foundation. I was naturally pale, ivory-skinned. I always looked as if I were not very well and being terribly brave about it. This suited me fine. If I were ill, someone might want to look after me one day. My mother had bright pink hockey-field cheeks which Janet was inheriting. My father's complexion was sallow and sickly. I put Pale And Interesting Liquid Foundation on my cheeks and forehead, and toner on my cheekbones.

I added pale powder. I back-combed my hair, sprayed it with lacqueur and moulded it forward. His short back and sides emphasised the squareness of his head, his broad nose, his wide-open eyes, his big white teeth when he laughed or shouted. My mother's hair waved naturally and looked permanently windblown. Neither of my parents got any protection from their hair. They probably didn't need it. They had each other. I built my hair into a nest in which my face could feel safe.

He had grey eyes, hers were brown. Mine had nothing to do with theirs. They were blue with a greenish tinge. I drew thick lines of green Smoke Gets In Your Eyes eyeshadow. I relaxed my face muscles and let my eyelids droop. My parents were open people. They told the truth, yelled it at the tops of their voices if they felt like it. They clattered about. I wanted to be more mysterious. I whitened my lips and practised the look that said I had secrets to keep.

I stared at my beautiful sultry face and wondered when I was going to stop kidding myself. It was still me and I was still a coward. I could blot out my father's face from my face but I couldn't stop him from knowing what I did.

I listened to *Movie Go Round* and *Pick of the Pops* with Alan Freeman. I moved the dial to 208 to see if Radio Luxembourg had started yet, but all I got was a lot of hissing and an American talking about God.

I put a pile of my own records on the radiogram and turned the volume up to full. I swayed before the glass front of the bookcase and sang along. '*Poor Me, oh-oh-oh-oh-oh-oh* – ' My reflection looked as if I were on television.

I couldn't think what kind of programme would have a star like me singing against a background of *The Children's Encyclopedia* and World Books, so I moved them.

When my family came home at seven o'clock, my mother said, 'Have you spent the entire day messing up the book shelves?'

'Yes,' I replied.

She said, 'I suppose it's better than lying on the stairs,' and everybody laughed except me.

My father said, 'Have you been out anywhere?'

'I didn't know I was allowed out.'

'Your bike's in the front garden.'

'Is it?'

'I repeat my question: have you been out anywhere?'

'No.'

'Honourable Heart?' He gave me a steady look. I mumbled, 'Honourable Heart,' and dropped my eyes. I was telling the truth, yet I felt shifty. 'Pam rang up.'

'Pammie MacLeish?' He said it with an accent. 'What did *she* want?'

'You. She wants you to look at some lease or other.'

'That girl is always on the scrounge.'

'She is not,' said Janet, going pink.

My mother said, 'You must learn to take teasing, Janet.'

My father agreed. 'Janet should have had an elder brother.'

My mother said, 'That was up to you, dear. The sex of the baby depends on the sperm.' My father's sperm was something I preferred not to think about so I put on some more records.

My father glanced irritably at the mess in the hall where sailing junk had been dumped in a heap with the other day-to-day junk that had been there all along. He rubbed his hands together and said heartily: 'We've had a lovely day and so let's pull together and play the game and not leave all the clearing up to poor old Mummy.'

I wasn't falling for that one. I hadn't had a particularly lovely day. I walked off, saying over my shoulder, 'By the way, I'm going to Pam's tomorrow.'

I waited for Janet's howl of jealousy, but my father said, 'We're going to Salthaven tomorrow.'

'Since when?'

'Since we arranged it.'

'I didn't know,' I said, peeved.

'You should wash your lug-holes out.'

'I bet you arranged it when I wasn't there! I bet you discussed it on the boat!'

'We discussed it in your presence, madam. You probably chose not to hear because it would have disproved your theory that we never do anything you'd enjoy.'

My mother said, 'I think the grannies will be quite disappointed if you don't come, Christine.'

'I should hope so too,' I said, trying to sound flip. In fact I knew I would be even more disappointed. I couldn't let Janet have Salthaven all to herself, she was spoilt enough already. 'I suppose I'd better not snub my fans, if they're expecting me.' I thought of something else. 'Could Pam come with us?'

My mother said, 'She's probably busy doing something else.'

'She isn't. She told me she was at a loose end.'

'I can't understand it. An attractive girl like that. What do you think, darling?'

I refused to plead, but Janet said, 'Can we ask her, oh can we? Please, Daddy?'

He put on his giving-in face, but he said we ought to ring the grannies first to find out how they would feel about having an extra mouth to feed. 'They're not running a soup kitchen for Antipodean spivs.'

5

We met Pam at Victoria, outside W H Smith's. We saw her before she saw us. She was short and stocky with a slight stoop. My father blamed this on too much rucksack-carrying. He said she would have a spine like a kirbigrip by the time she was forty.

She had tartan trews on, and a grey duffel coat. Over her shoulder was an Indian tapestry bag, picked up on her travels. She had wiry red chin-length hair. She wore it in thick bunches. Her jaw was tough and her face looked a bit fierce in repose, but when she saw us she grinned and her green eyes brightened.

Janet ran into her arms, plaits a-flutter. They kissed. I wasn't a kissy person, so I just said, 'Hullo.' My mother and Pam exchanged pecks on the cheek. My father said, 'Morning, MacLeish. Straighten your shoulders.'

She told him to sod off, and we got on the train.

Pam dipped into her bag and passed round a box of small Swiss Easter eggs in gold foil. Everyone except my mother said, 'Ooh,' and, 'Thank you,' and took one. My mother said, 'You're a naughty girl, Pam.' Then she took one.

Janet sat next to Pam and gave her a mark-by-mark account of last term's achievements at school, and a splash-by-splash report of yesterday's sailing. Pam pretended to be interested. She said, 'You *are* clever, Janet!' every time Janet paused for breath. Not that this was very often.

Janet produced her *New Guide Table Book* and demanded to be tested.

I wondered when I was going to get a word in. I wanted to talk to Pam on her own.

The train pulled out of Victoria and crossed the river. Greenish-black water swirled round the struts of Grosvenor Bridge. Above us the chimneys of Battersea Power Station puffed out plumes of smoke, grey and sickly white. We went slowly through the slums of Vauxhall and Wandsworth and Clapham. My father called them slums. He always had something insulting to say about other people's houses. I thought the long grey terraces looked neat and cosy, and the Nissen huts and prefabs were romantic. I thought they were probably lived in by gypsies, who made clothes pegs and sold them door to door. The huts seemed to belong in the countryside and to have found themselves in the city by mistake. The countryside had come to join them. They were surrounded by blackberry bushes and wild flowers and weeds.

He said they were structurally unsound and unfit for human habitation. He said the houses near the railway line would have been better off if they had been flattened by the Luftwaffe, not that their occupants would be much better off in the new blocks of flats that councils were building to replace the ones that the Luftwaffe had managed to flatten.

The war had ended before I was born, but it had left so much of itself behind that it seemed to be part of my experience.

I couldn't remember the bombing, but I remembered broken windows and cracked walls and my mother being too busy fixing things up to play with me.

She sat me in the seat on the back of her bike and took me to furniture auctions. The furniture was dark brown and belonged to people who had died. In the corners of the drawers they had left dust and rubber bands and sweet wrappers.

The dead people had had sweets. For me sweets were rationed. I ate hard pears from the tree in our garden. My mother said, 'They're just as nice.' Advertisements in her magazines said, 'Back in the shops again! Full Cream Toffee Dreams are now on sale all over the country!' Pictures showed plump-cheeked boys and girls chewing as they played with new toys in neat playrooms with new furniture. Their mothers smiled and wore high-heeled shoes.

Balloons came out of the children's mouths. 'My Caramel Toffee Dream has come true!' 'My Mint Toffee Dream was well worth waiting for!' Toffee Dreams never made it to Bleswick. Now and again I got a bar of Standard Blended Chocolate. It tasted of fish oil.

By the time Janet was born, everything was off-ration. According to my father, this explained the difference in our personalities. I was bitter and twisted because I had been born under a Labour government. My first words had been 'I want'. Janet, on the other hand, had popped out of the womb under the Conservatives, taken one look at the world of unrationed prosperity and declared, 'That's mine'. Hence her sweet nature.

We finished Pam's Easter eggs and changed trains. Pam escaped from Janet and her table book and sat between my parents.

My father said, 'I know what you're after, MacLeish.'

Pam appealed to my mother. 'Do you know what he's talking about?'

'Hardly ever.'

'I thought you wanted my professional opinion on your lease?'

'Not now. It's your day off.'

'So?'

'Some time when it's convenient.'

'It's always convenient. Service is my middle name.'

'We must be related; it's mine too. Or perhaps you don't want any more driving practice?'

The train set off towards the sea which was just visible through a dip in the downs. Pam gave my father a typed document. He said, 'I notice you brought it with you. Day off indeed.' He didn't like what he read. His face took on an expression of doom. He said 'Tsk, tsk.'

'What's wrong?' asked Pam.

He didn't answer.

We stopped at a halt. The sound of milk churns being loaded into the guard's van competed with my father's sharp intake of breath. 'Dear oh dear oh dear.'

Pam tried to read over his shoulder. He said, 'Am I doing this, or are you?' She moved away. He read on and chuckled to himself. 'Good God. Still trying that one, are they?'

At Salthaven we got out and walked across the footbridge. It had a good view of the sea and the town and the downs beyond. I tried to delay Pam by pointing out the sights.

'That's where my mum went to boarding school and became the genius she is today. One of the places.'

Pam said, 'It looks as bad as mine.'

'It was great fun,' said my mother. 'I can hardly remember a thing about it.'

'And that's the Essoldo, or at least it was.' I pointed out the tower of the old cinema. 'That's where my dad used to take her in the back row of the stalls.'

'It's a lie,' said my father.

'And in the interval an usherette would walk up and down spraying everybody with a Flit gun.'

'You're getting a rather partial picture, Pam.' They moved out of earshot. I said quickly, 'When are you going to America?'

'Can't you wait to get rid of me?'

'Don't be stupid. It's about your flat.'

'Doesn't look as if it is going to be my flat,' said Pam. 'Your dad doesn't approve.'

'You don't have to do what he says.'

'If there's something wrong with the lease – '

'He always finds things wrong with leases. Lesson One of his surveyor's course was "If you can't think of anything horrible to say, don't say anything at all."'

She smiled. 'I'll probably be gone by Christmas.'

'Perfect!'

'Gee, thanks, Chrissie,' said Pam. 'You say the nicest things.'

'It's not that.' I gave her a push. 'It's just that I know someone who might want to take your flat over from you when you go.'

'Not up to me, Chrissie. It's up to the landlord.'

'But you could recommend a friend.'

'Is it somebody I know?'

'It's somebody *I* know,' I said. 'Somebody who wants to live in Earl's Court.'

6

Grandma Toms was little and elegant. It was hard to believe that she had given birth to my father, not to mention his three elder brothers who were all great oafs like him and always had been if the family photographs were anything to go by.

They had big, pompous Christian names that sounded more like surnames: Rutherford, Kennington, and Humphrey. My father had the worst name of all: Sandringham. It shortened down into Sandy, but even so.

Each of the brothers had married a woman with a tiny little name: Kay, Sue and Gwen. My mother had the smallest name: Jo.

Grandma greeted us in the grey oak doorway of her house on the edge of the downs. She hugged my father who said, 'Ma, this is – what was your name? Pam MacLeish.' He stage whispered behind his hand, 'Latched on to us on the train. Couldn't get rid of her.'

Grandma brushed him aside, winked at Pam and shook her hand. 'I'm very pleased you've come, dear.'

'Thank you for inviting me, Grandma.' She pronounced it *Grendma*. However she pronounced it I was afraid Grandma might think her a bit familiar, but she didn't seem to mind, probably because Pam was foreign. Also Pam had brought Grandma an Easter egg, which helped.

I found it reassuring when people took to Pam, as they always seemed to, in spite of her unconventional ways. I had a feeling I was going to be fairly unconventional myself, and it would have worried me if I had thought I would have to pay for this by being hated.

Grandma gave me a big hug. She smelt of perfume and wood smoke. I could feel her bones through her soft grey twinset. She said, 'Christine, you get prettier every time I see you.'

I said, 'Grandma, so do you.'

She turned to Janet. I could see her struggling to find something nice to say about how Janet looked, but she couldn't lie so she said, 'I've been hearing great things about your school report.'

Even if this were a lie, it was at least a safe bet. Finally she hugged my mother who was waiting humbly at the end of the queue. 'Don't you look nice, Jo? How you manage to be so well turned out when you have a young family to look after I do not know!' If Sue or Kay or Gwen had been there, she would have said the same to them.

We went into the long lounge with the polished wooden floor and Persian rugs. Grandma told my father to serve drinks from the trolley. He did it like a lamb. He even had to give me and Janet pepsi-cola, despite his long-standing ruling that pepsi-cola was common.

While he was doing the drinks, Pam gave Grandma her life story. She was an only child. She had grown up in a small town in the north of New Zealand's North Island and gone to boarding school near Auckland before returning home to work as a secretary in her father's farm machinery business. Her father wanted her to marry someone who would take the business over.

'At which point,' she said, 'I decided it was time to get the hell out. If you'll excuse me putting it that way, Grandma.'

It wasn't usual to say *hell* in front of Grandma, but she didn't seem to mind. 'I'm sure you made the right decision, dear. If you tie yourself down too soon, you'll only get restless.'

'You can say that again,' said my father with a laugh.

'You certainly can,' said my mother with a louder one.

Pam got the guided tour. My father showed her his old playroom, his old toys and some photographs of himself and his brothers having a jolly time with their old father before he died of drink. He told her about the grand party that had been given at the end of the war to celebrate the fact that although all four Toms brothers had been in the services, not one of them had been killed. He didn't tell her that the Toms brothers had been celebrating their own existence ever since, under the pretence of enormous Christmas parties that drove my mother up the wall, or picnic parties, or parties to go to rugby internationals or test matches, or boozy business do's to which wives were not invited.

Grandma called a taxi and we all set off for the Burlington Cliff Hotel where we were meeting my mother's mother, Gran Woolgar, for lunch. She was waiting in the lobby in a smart Jaeger frock. She gave my mother a tense smile and said, 'You've forgotten to put your lipstick on.'

'I have not.'

'Where *have* you been? I thought you'd had an accident.' We were her only family and she didn't like having to share us with Grandma, who had so much already. The rivalry between the two grandmothers suited me and Janet very well, because we got lots of presents. I liked both of them equally, and tried to allocate myself with fairness. I had already been with Grandma, so I sat next to Gran.

She said, 'And how's school?' which was disappointing but predictable.

'All right. I'm leaving at Christmas.' I had a policy of saying this as often as possible in front of my parents, as long as we were somewhere safe. I wanted them to get used to the idea. The bit about going to live in a flat in Earl's Court would come later.

'What do your parents have to say about that?'

'A great deal,' said my mother grimly.

Gran took my side. 'You don't have to be at school to be educated. You're learning all your life. Christine could do a lot worse than to become a first-class personal secretary.'

'She could do a lot better.'

'Don't snap at me, Jo. There's such a thing as being over-educated.'

My father became hysterical. 'Over-educated! Christine!' He gave me a smile with a threat in it. 'Could we not have this conversation now?'

I didn't care whether we had it or not. I had made up my mind. Once I was fifteen I was going to be out of my school so fast that it would forget I had ever been there. If my parents thought they could make me stay on, they might as well start stocking up right away on chains and handcuffs.

The waitress came to take our order. Gran Woolgar took charge and said, 'Have whatever you like.'

My mother licked her lips. 'Mmm, steak and kidney pie.'

'Fattening, Jo.'

'Oh shut up, Mummy.'

'It's no concern of mine.'

'You're right about that.' My mother said sadly to the waitress, 'A cheese salad please.'

My father and the two grannies each ordered roast beef. I asked for chicken. Janet waited for Pam to choose so that she could have the same. They settled for lamb because it had probably come from New Zealand.

Beyond the wide, salt-stained windows, the grey sea reared up into mountainous waves. As they broke against the sea wall, the thuds came up through the floor of the restaurant and the chandelier swayed. Spray and pebbles spattered the windows.

'This is what's known as an English seaside resort,' said my father to Pam.

'I expect it's lovely in the summer.'

'It's very similar to how it is now, I'm afraid,' said Grandma Toms.

Gran seized the chance to contradict her rival. 'It's not; we have some fine days. You must come and stay.' She made it sound as if she herself would arrange for the days to be fine, and Pam said, 'Thank you, Gran.'

For pudding everyone had either sherry trifle or ice cream, except for my mother who had a green apple on a plate with a bone-handled knife. Coffee followed and Gran Woolgar took out her cigarette case. I knew she wouldn't pass it my way when my parents were looking, so I contented myself with sniffing the air.

We walked out of the hotel into the howling gale. My mother put her face blissfully into the spray and said, 'Who's coming for a lovely walk? Christine?'

I made a face. 'Too windy.'

'Pam? Sandringham? Janet? Grandma? Mummy?'

'Not today, Jo,' said Gran. She patted her own back and winced. 'Rheumatism.'

'It's because you don't take enough exercise that you get rheumatism in the first place. And because you smoke.'

I linked my arm through Gran's and while everyone else strode off to scale the South Face of Salthaven Head we went on the pier. After we had lost all her money we walked home to her flat in Westminster Bank Chambers.

It was a cosy flat with lots of lovely furniture and ornaments from Gran Woolgar's days out East. There were photographs of the second of my two dead grandfathers, and also of my mother out East as a tiny little girl, looking an absolute fool in a huge sun hat. She looked an even bigger fool in the uniforms of the various boarding schools she got sent to in England.

Everything was polished and sweet-smelling. Gran said, 'Has your mother pulled her socks up yet?'

By pulling her socks up, Gran meant straightening out the house. I didn't want to discuss it. I made a noncommittal sound. Gran said, 'You're getting to an age when you'll want to bring boyfriends home. They'll take one look at your mother's housekeeping and worry that you'll turn out the same.'

'Have you done your pools yet?'

We did her pools, and spent the winnings. Then we rolled some cigarettes, looked at the latest additions to her Agatha Christie collection, and put the television on. I loved television. My parents wouldn't have one in the house, because they said I would become addicted. I was addicted already. I watched horse racing and smoked a cigarette while Gran got the tea ready.

When Janet got back with the others she wanted to watch television as well. Our parents scoffed and Grandma Toms looked as if she didn't quite approve, but Gran said we could have our teas on our laps and watch *Rin Tin Tin*. Soon we were all watching it.

'If you go to America, you'll be able to watch this sort of rubbish all day long,' said my father to Pam. 'And they have advertisements on the wireless.'

Rin Tin Tin ended and the news came on, with newsreel of the ban-the-bomb rally in Hyde Park. I was surprised. I had forgotten all about it. I wasn't really a serious person. I felt rather guilty and thought how lucky it was for CND that they didn't have to rely on people like me to get the bomb banned.

7

My summer term started a week earlier than Janet's. I set off for school in a filthy temper because she was going swimming.

My school was Bleswick County Girls, which was a secondary modern school. Janet's was the Convent of the Forty Martyrs, which was a snob school. It was the snobbiest school in the borough. The reason its terms started later and finished earlier than everyone else's was so that the whole world would know that Forty Martyrs girls needed less education than anyone else because they were so brilliant already.

I knew all about the Convent of the Forty Martyrs because I used to go to it myself. I spent six years in its junior school which specialised in getting you through the eleven-plus and on into the senior school which was a grammar school.

My parents made a great many sacrifices to send me to the junior school at the Convent of the Forty Martyrs in the hope that I would pass my eleven-plus. Now they were making a great many sacrifices to send Janet.

I came out of our front garden and cycled the hundred yards to the T-junction where our road, Manor Road, met Bleswick Avenue. Bleswick Avenue was a trunk road, taking you towards London airport and London if you turned right, and central Bleswick, Reading, Newbury and the West Country if you turned left.

I went left but I cut across the common to avoid the town centre. I had to ride past a few CYCLING PROHIBITED signs, but that was better than getting killed. The common divided Bleswick into two. When I was little I thought it was called the common because that was what the people were who lived on the opposite side of it from us, in the council houses.

My father said the council houses should never have been built.

He called them a desecration of the Green Belt. I didn't remember any Green Belt being desecrated to build the houses; on the contrary, I remembered an American air force base, with holes in the ground, barbed wire, and slabs of concrete. Not that it mattered all that much. The houses were of such a low standard of workmanship that they would probably have to be pulled down in a year or two.

My best friend Stella lived in one of the houses. She didn't know it was doomed and I hadn't the heart to tell her. It didn't look doomed. It looked modern and well-kept and I knew that inside it was a great deal more modern and well-kept than the Toms residence.

The trouble with our house was that my father couldn't get the idea out of his head that it was a bargain. For all I knew, it might have been a bargain when they bought it. The ancient furniture was probably a bargain when they bought that too, and so was the end-of-the-roll wallpaper. But those were the days of rationing. Those were the days when we were poor and he was doing his Articles. Now he was brilliantly successful, or so he said. Why we couldn't move house I did not know.

Number 79 Manor Road was 'a character property built to last', according to him. Built to drive my mother round the bend was more like it. She hated housework, and this was a house that needed more work than most. Her idea of heaven would be not to live in a house. She would rather be a cave woman and do no housework at all. Or move into a houseboat, cut the ropes and sail round the world, living out of tins.

I stopped my bike at the kerb, rang my bell and waited for Stella to come out. I wondered what she would be wearing.

Uniform was optional at Bleswick County Girls. At least, it was for Stella and other people who had normal parents. I had to wear uniform because my father thought uniform promoted good order, *esprit de corps* and a sense of belonging. It was quite funny that he wanted me to have a sense of belonging to Bleswick County Girls, because he sent me there in the first place as a punishment. 'If you act like a guttersnipe you can go to a guttersnipe school,' was what he said. 'And see how you like that.'

He was quite surprised when I did like it, or at least liked it more than I had liked the Convent of the Forty Martyrs, which wasn't saying very much. I got better marks at Bleswick County Girls than I ever had at the Convent of the Forty Martyrs, but that wasn't saying much either.

It was part of my father's idea of honour that if you belonged to something you should belong to it fully, and that included guttersnipe schools. (He stopped calling Bleswick County Girls that once I actually went to it, but I knew that was how he thought of it, particularly when it did things like having ban-the-bombers to stay.) And that was why he made me wear uniform.

Summer uniform consisted of a red and white cotton check dress with a white cotton belt, a grey cardigan, a grey blazer, white socks and Noddy sandals. The red of the dress was dark and brownish. Stella called it scab-red. It was all very well for her to be disgusting about the colour, she didn't have to wear it. She was wearing a blue skirt with a stiff petticoat underneath and a pale pink three-quarter-length raincoat. Her blonde hair was done in a beehive with a silver slide at the back. She carried her books in a patent leather shoulder bag which I hadn't seen before and which matched her shoes.

I wheeled my bike and told her my news. 'Pam's got a new flat.'

'What's it like?'

'It's a basement. It's in Earl's Court Terrace, just round the corner from the underground. You can look up and see people's feet going by – '

'Fabulous,' said Stella.

' – And their suitcases,' I added dreamily. One of the things I liked about Earl's Court was that you could always see at least one person with a suitcase. It was a place of arrivals and departures and I liked to guess what everybody's story was.

Stella was more interested in the rent. I told her what it was and what my father said about it, which was that Pam could pay a lot more and get a lot less.

Stella said, 'That's good, isn't it?'

'It's very high praise.'

'How many rooms?'

'Sitting room, bedroom, bathroom. The kitchen's in the hall.'

‘Only one bedroom?’

‘We could have a folding bed in the sitting room.’

‘Bags I the bedroom,’ she said. ‘When’s Pam going to America?’

‘She says she’ll be gone by Christmas.’ We turned the corner and saw our school and sighed. Stella said, ‘Tell her not to go till we’re out of this dump.’ The blocks of classrooms were huge matchboxes made of stone and glass, arranged like a perspective diagram on the wall of the art room. If you continued the lines, they’d meet. I imagined a bird swooping down onto the meeting point, getting hold of the lines in its beak and pulling till the whole school collapsed in tiny tight pleats.

After registration we lined up to cross the playground to the main hall for assembly. We were supposed to walk smartly and silently in twos but most of us preferred to wander and chat. We would be leaving this year or next and the teachers knew there was no point in making an issue out of every single rule. I kept a lookout for smashed windows and the trail of general litter and filth which I had been told would have been left behind by the ban-the-bombers but I didn’t see anything.

The headmistress welcomed us back for another term and hoped we were all rested and refreshed and ready to resume working hard and playing hard which was the secret of successful school life. I rolled my eyes at Stella and she rolled hers back at me.

Our first lesson was English. Stella offered me a shilling bet that we would have to write a composition called ‘What I did in my Holidays’. I didn’t take the bet because I thought it would be ‘What I did in my Holidays’ too, and it was. We looked at each other and nearly burst. Miss Roper said ‘Stella and Christine have obviously had amusing holidays and I shall look forward to reading two amusing compositions. Let’s hope they won’t have to be written in detention.’

I opened my rough book.

‘Dear Chris,’ I read. ‘I hope you won’t think I’m taking too much of a liberty but I couldn’t resist reading your rough book.

‘I had a look at some of the others but I liked yours best. You’ve got quite a sense of humour, haven’t you?

'I've got to do something. It's three o'clock in the morning and everyone's snoring except me. I don't want to sound ungrateful, but your school's floors aren't much for sleeping on, are they? Not that you'd know. If you're anything like I was when I was at school, you fall asleep at your desk.

'Are you and the other girls for peace? We're marching for you as well as for ourselves.

'Write back, I dare you.

'Yours fraternally, Walter Benfold.'

8

'Dear Walter,

'I was so shocked to find your letter in my rough book that I couldn't stop laughing and I got a detention.

'Sorry our floors were too hard for you to sleep on but that's typical of my school, it's no good for anything. I'll be leaving as soon as I'm fifteen – roll on Christmas.

'I've never been to Southampton but it's near where I go for my summer holidays with my family (i.e. my father who's a surveyor, my mother who's a nurse and my little sister who's a show-off). We stay in a coastguard's cottage at Larcher's Point and we can see the ships coming out of Southampton Water.

'I'm for peace but I'm the only person in the school who's interested in things like that. I don't know what else to say so I'll sign off. I'm sorry if my letter's boring, but it's pretty boring being in detention.

'Yours truly,

'Chris Toms.'

I looked the letter over while I waited for the detention hour to end. I was starving.

It wasn't quite true to say that my mother was a nurse. She had been a student nurse but she gave up her training to get married. I supposed she was a housewife, but 'housewife' didn't seem a very nice thing to call anyone, let alone my own mother. 'Housewife' was a word that I could only imagine being written in one colour: grey. My mother had a grey book called *The Housewife's Guide to Successful Home Management*. It had been given to her by her mother as a hint.

I knew parts of it off by heart in the way I thought a condemned man might remember the exact words of the death sentence:

7 am. Rise, wash, apply light make-up, brush hair, put on fresh housecoat. Wake husband with early morning tea and draw his bath. Whilst he is in the bathroom, strip bed and lay out his clothes for the day.

7.30 am. Go through house opening all windows. (Weather permitting: use common sense here.) Make and serve breakfast, the table having been laid the night before.

8 am. (Or as soon as your husband has left for work.) Clear breakfast, put dishes in sink to soak. Sweep out sitting room fireplace, re-lay fire, re-fill coal bucket. Plump cushions, empty ash trays, dust ornaments, wipe woodwork, vacuum carpet –

8.30 am. –

I couldn't remember what was supposed to happen at 8.30, but it didn't matter because I thought it was probably a misprint. No one could get all those things done by 8.30. My mother certainly couldn't, so it didn't matter what she was supposed to do afterwards.

I asked her about this. She laughed at me. 'Don't take things so literally. Mummy was only getting at me when she gave me that book. It's a counsel of perfection.' She made perfection sound like something to be avoided at all costs.

After my detention I felt grumpy and indignant and faint with hunger. If I had fainted it would have served the school right, but Stella had left a Five Boys bar for me in my blazer pocket in the cloakroom and I ate it in the nick of time.

I went to her house to thank her.

'Your mother rang up,' she said.

'What about?'

'"Where's my darling little girl?"'

'You didn't tell her, did you?'

'I said you were at choir practice.' She took me into the kitchen, which was modern and labour-saving with a neat white water heater on the wall. She gave me a glass of pepsi with ice cubes from the fridge, and a Wagon Wheel. We went into the sitting room and watched *Wyatt Earp*.

I showed her the letter I had written to Walter. She said, 'Why don't you tell him what you look like?'

'I don't want to put him off.'

'You know, you could be quite attractive.'

'"My best friend says I could be quite attractive."'

'Send him a photograph,' she suggested.

I looked for one when I got home, but the camera belonged to my father and he only ever took pictures in the boat, so there weren't any of me over the age of about ten. I pointed this out to my mother who was on her knees in front of our ancient Excella boiler at the time, locked in combat. Her face and hands were black with soot and coal dust and she said, 'You really do look for things to sulk about, don't you?'

I heard on 'BBC Announcements' that the Ministry of Health were going to run refresher courses for married women who used to be nurses. The courses would start at 10 am and finish before 3 pm so that children wouldn't have to go home to empty houses.

I wouldn't have minded going home to an empty house if it meant I could walk down the street with my mother in nurse's uniform. I told her what I had heard. She said, 'It's probably for qualified people.'

'He said "trained or partly-trained".'

'I've forgotten everything I knew.' She spoke more to herself than to me.

'You've still got your books,' I reminded her. Her nursing textbooks had red covers with her maiden name (Jo Woolgar) written in faded ink. The people in the illustrations had old-fashioned clothes and hairstyles, and some of the instructions were a bit gruesome, but I preferred her nursing books to her housework books.

> *The nurse should position herself in such a way as to ensure that the patient cannot, at any stage in the procedure, see the leech.*
>
> *For ease of identification, paint gentian violet over as wide an area as possible of the limb that is to be amputated.*

Plug the rectum, and in the case of a female the vagina, with brown cotton wool and then white. Pack and label all personal belongings for collection by relatives.

'Did you ever lay out any dead bodies?'

'Dozens of times.'

'Was it horrible?'

'Depended what they'd died of. Have you made your bed today?'

It was impossible to have a normal conversation with my mother. She always brought the subject round to housework.

'Yes.'

'Honourable Heart?'

'Are you going to send off for details?' I asked.

'What of? How to get you to make your bed?'

'*Nursing*.'

'I'll discuss it with Daddy. I'm going upstairs in a minute and your bed had better be made.'

'There's a form in the *Radio Times*. I'll fill it in for you.'

'There's no need to fill anything in. I know exactly what they're looking for, they're looking for perfect housewives whose children help and co-operate.'

I made my bed.

I wondered if I ought to have a little talk with Janet about us helping and co-operating more but I decided against it. Janet was in Sister Dolours' eleven-plus class, and, having been in it myself, I knew that it provided the perfect excuse for not doing housework.

I didn't want to end up helping and co-operating on my own.

When my mother complained about housework, my father would say, 'My job, on the other hand, is a continuous round of fun and excitement.'

'At least you have variety. You don't survey the same building day after day and write the same report.'

'I would if I thought I could get away with it.'

'That's right, make fun.'

'I am being absolutely serious when I say I'd love to be a housewife.'

'Done!' cried my mother at the top of her voice.

'I'd whip through the housework in the mornings and in the afternoons I'd go sailing.'

'I'm looking forward to seeing that.'

'You won't be around to see it,' he said. 'You'll be on the 8.24 from Bleswick Junction to Paddington. Morning after morning. You'll be doing my job. Won't you?'

'I'm thinking of going back to nursing.'

'Thanks to the atom bomb, you're free to think whatever you like.'

'So you don't approve?'

'Some days,' he said, 'you don't even find time to clear away the breakfast.'

She bit her lower lip like a child who'd been caught out. 'That's because there's no reason to.'

'Only sluts leave breakfast on the table all day. How's that for a reason?'

She said calmly, 'All right, I am a slut. I'm lazy and disorganised and I have no self-discipline.'

'God's gift to *Emergency Ward Ten*.'

'I'd get myself organised if there was something I had to do, something I wanted to do, somewhere I had to be by a certain time. It would be like a kick in the pants.'

'Any time you want a kick in the pants, apply to me. There *is* something you have to do. Look after the house, look after me and bring up our children.'

'For the rest of my life?' My mother was on the verge of tears. 'You're working your way up. You can change your job. You've got different people to see, lunches to go to, secretaries bowing and scraping. What have I got?'

'What you wanted.'

I had heard that some parents tried to avoid having rows in front of their children, but it might have been a rumour. Anyway, my parents certainly weren't that sort.

I had witnessed hundreds of arguments. None of them had made me feel as sick and cold as this one did. I kept my eye on the *Radio Times* but the nursing coupon stayed where it was. I had to face the ghastly fact that she was obeying him.

I had been to weddings and heard wives promising to obey their husbands. I had always thought of it as a bit of a joke. Now it sank in that it wasn't a joke at all.

I felt humiliated and desperate to escape. Was escape possible? At least I hadn't promised to obey him. If I obeyed him it was only because he hit me when I didn't. He didn't hit her, or at least I didn't think he did. So why did she obey him?

Was it normal? I had a terrible feeling that it might be.

Why was I the only person who could see how unjust it was?

Would my mother have to go on obeying my father until one of them was dead?

Was that the reason why she called him 'Daddy'?

9

Shortly before the end of the summer term Walter Benfold wrote back.

'Dear Chris,

'I didn't know what to think when your letter came. You'd been on my conscience ever since the march because I know schools can be funny places and I didn't like to think of you getting into any kind of trouble because a strange man had written things in your rough book.

'Then you wrote and told me you'd had a detention on my account. But you seem to be able to see the funny side.

'You'll have to forgive me. I'm always doing daft things. My wife says I should grow up. I tell her I'm sorry but this is as grown-up as I'm going to get. I'm thirty-four and I drive my own taxi. We've got twin boys aged ten and a daughter about your age, and they're all teasing me unmercifully about you. They say next time we go on a march they're not going to let me out of their sight.

'Seriously, the next one for us will be on Hiroshima Day (August 6th) in Southampton. We'll be planting a commemorative cherry tree and laying a wreath. If that's when you're going to be on holiday, why don't you join us?

'I know where Larcher's Point is, though I've never been there. I assume you and your family are keen sailors, going to a place like that.

'Anyway, Chris, that's all for now, so cheerio and good luck and thanks for being such a good sport about the detention.

'Yours fraternally,
'Walter Benfold.'

Left to themselves, my parents and Janet would have hired an ocean-going yacht for their holidays. But I would have refused to set foot in it. Larcher's Point, being dry land, was a compromise.

It had sea on three sides and a great deal of wind. It had its own lighthouse, a castle to scare away the Spanish Armada, and coastguards' cottages for rent. The cottages were hundreds of years old and falling down. We rented the one that had the furthest to fall, but even it had cracked windows and tiles coming off the roof. Its floors were covered with a jigsaw of slimy lino. Its furniture had been taken off ocean liners in ship-breakers' yards. The beds felt clammy as if they'd come from the bottom of the sea.

There was no electricity. We used candles and calor gas. The water supply was a rain tank on the roof. The lavatory was an Elsan bucket, which had to be emptied by my father. He preferred us to pee on the beach. He offered bribes. He called himself 'Dan, Dan, the Elsan Man,' putting on sea boots and rubber gloves and striding off to dig a hole in the shingle. The important thing, he said, was to remember where you buried the last lot, otherwise you might find it again.

Sometimes a small ferry brought workmen or trippers out to the point and back again, but usually the only way we had of getting to the mainland was on foot or in the sailing dinghy that my father rented from a nearby boatyard.

I walked by myself along the two-mile spit that connected the point to the mainland. It was a mild breezy day. It was August the fifth, Hiroshima Day minus one. My feet clanked in the shingle. On my left, liners and tankers rode the waves of the open sea. On my right, in the more sheltered waters of Larcher's Bay, my family were sailing.

They were far from me but I could see that Janet was at the helm. She looked like an overgrown orange insect, with her enormous life-jacket and her solid legs, bare under her shorts. Sailing was one long fidget. Even at this distance it got on my nerves. Her plaits flicked across her shoulders and streamed behind her in the wind as she glanced this way then that. She looked at boats coming towards her to make sure she wasn't going to hit them, she looked at boats going away from her to make sure they hadn't hit her. She looked up at the burgee to check the direction of the wind. She looked to my father for approval.

This wasn't given lightly, even to Janet. My father was even bossier in a boat than out of it. He was as critical and pessimistic about people's sailing abilities as he was about their houses and their leases. But he loved teaching people to sail, and he loved them for allowing themselves to be taught. I had seen it in his eyes with Janet, with my mother and even with Pam.

He had tried to teach me, but I didn't want to learn.

I wondered what they were talking about. I seemed to remember that there was always time for a bit of conversation, in between all the 'Lee-ho' and 'Steady about' and 'Cheer up, Christine, look at the seagulls.'

I wondered if they ever discussed me. They probably said what a bore it was that because of me they were deprived of the pleasure of plunging through the Bay of Biscay in a gale. They probably made plans for cruising to the Galapagos or crossing the Atlantic on a raft once I had left home. Little did they know that their bluff was soon to be called.

Perhaps they forgot I existed and then had a nasty shock when they saw me again.

I wondered how Walter Benfold's children felt about being taken on ban-the-bomb marches in a family group. Perhaps one of them was rebellious, and refused to go, and demanded to be taken sailing instead.

I walked along the beach as they were hauling the boat out of the water on rollers. My mother handed me her purse and a list and told me to go to Mrs Barclay's and make a start with the shopping.

Strictly speaking I shouldn't have had to do housework while Janet was doing things concerned with sailing, but I decided not to make an issue of it, just this once. I went to the shop.

Mrs Barclay and I had filled three bags with groceries by the time my mother arrived to tell me I had got it all wrong. 'We always have Golden Shred on holiday,' she said, 'it's traditional.'

Traditional meant it was what my father and his brothers had when they were boys. My mother handed back the jar of Chiver's Chunky. 'And these are the wrong sardines,' she said. 'I'm sorry to put you to all this trouble, Mrs Barclay.'

'That's all right, my dear.' Mrs Barclay found the right sardines. No one apologised for putting me to trouble, so I walked out of the shop, pushing past my father and Janet who were leaning over the refrigerator cabinet choosing ice creams.

I crossed the road to the bus stop and looked at the timetable of buses to Southampton. I shivered and squealed as my father sneaked up behind me and pressed a choc-ice to my neck. Eating his own choc-ice, wearing his sailing shorts, he looked like photographs of himself as a schoolboy. His pale hair was full of salt, which made it look nicer than when it was full of Vaseline hair oil, crisp and clean and slightly wild. He had a tan, with white smile-lines round his contented eyes. He was nicer on holiday than he was in real life, partly because of the Elsan and partly because he could sail all day every day without the interruption of having to go to work.

He looked where I'd been looking. 'Fancy a trip to Southampton, do you?'

I shrugged. 'I might go one day.'

'We could all go.'

'I wouldn't want to keep you from your sailing.'

'Christine, sarcasm is the lowest form of wit.'

'I wasn't being sarcastic.' For once this was true.

'This is your holiday as well as ours,' he said. 'If you want to go to Southampton, we'll make a family trip of it.' He beamed with the pleasure of having found something that he thought I would enjoy. 'You're getting a bit fed up with coming here for holidays, aren't you?'

'There's nothing for me to do. I'd rather go abroad.'

'Where abroad?'

'I don't know.'

'You can't just "go abroad". Abroad isn't a place.'

'I'd like to hitch-hike round the world, like Pam.'

He laughed. 'That bum.' He sat on the kerb. 'I'm not letting you hitch-hike. But have a think about where you'd like to go and we'll discuss it for next year.'

I looked at my feet and at the line on the ground where the shadow of the bus shelter ended and the bright air began. I was too surprised to speak. I was embarrassed.

'There are schemes,' he said. 'Exchanges. You could go and stay with a French girl and she could come and stay with us.' He paused. 'It would be a good way of brushing up your French, especially if you were going to, er, stay on at school and see if you could pick up a few GCEs.'

I was furious. He never missed a trick. I walked out of the bus shelter. He came after me saying, 'Can't we discuss it? Please?'

'We've discussed it loads of times. I don't want to take exams.'

'Sit down.'

I sat, crossly.

He looked at the ground. 'What happened about the eleven-plus is forgotten about. You know that, don't you?'

I knew nothing of the kind. I knew he would never forget that I had cheated and neither would I. I never told people. I told them I didn't pass, or that I went to a secondary modern school, and left them to assume that I had failed.

He and my mother preferred people to think I failed, but I didn't fail. I didn't want to fail so I didn't give myself the chance. I took my table book into the exam with me and used it during the mental arithmetic paper.

The place was crawling with invigilators. I wouldn't have got away with it in a million years. I didn't remember thinking about getting away with it. I didn't remember thinking anything. Perhaps I just didn't like the idea of someone I had never met deciding I had passed or failed, so I decided not to do either.

I was caught, disqualified and expelled from the convent in less time than it took my fellow candidates to do their hundred sums. I was driven home in the school secretary's car with my gym blouse and my shoe-bag.

I thought my mother was going to kill me. She yelled at me for fifteen minutes, slapping any part of me she could reach, too furious to aim properly, too furious to hurt. She left the hurting to my father. He bent me over and beat me with calm coldness.

'*Cheat*,' he said. '*Cheats, I hate 'em. Ugh.*' I put my hands out as a shield but he told me to move them out of the way. My small hands wouldn't have provided much protection against his hands, but he waited for me to move them out of the way and then he hit me.

If I moved under his blows he told me to keep still. He waited for me to be still and then he hit me again. '*Cheats, I hate 'em. Ugh.*' He wanted me to know that I had done the worst thing that I was capable of doing. There was nothing more. I had fired my last bullet and might as well surrender to the sheriff in the white hat.

He wanted me to know that he was in command, of me and of himself. He wasn't hurting me because he had lost his temper. He was hurting me because he hated cheats.

Now, though, he was saying: 'One mistake shouldn't ruin your whole life. It would be a pity if you felt you couldn't face exams. Qualifications are what get you on in life.'

'What about Mummy's nursing?'

He licked the paper of his choc-ice. 'I'm not going to force you to stay on at school. But I think you'll be making a big mistake if you leave at Christmas, and I wouldn't want you to do it because of some little problem that could easily be put right another way. Don't leave school just because you're fed up with family holidays and want to go abroad. If you can come up with a reasonable sounding idea for a foreign trip for next year, I'll finance it for you.'

10

We went to a pub. I joined my father in the saloon bar and drank a half of shandy while he had several pints of Hampshire Ale. He was teaching me to drink. He preferred that I should learn from him rather than from somebody unscrupulous.

My mother ate crisps in the garden with Janet and got impatient. Then we had a picnic lunch and looked for blackberries. The ones we found weren't ripe but Janet ate them anyway. We found a horse in a field and fed it.

'Let's have a competition,' suggested my mother, 'to see who can find the most wild flowers.'

'Hark at Brown Owl,' said my father.

'To whit to whoo,' said Janet.

We all laughed.

'Seriously,' he said. 'I want to be back on the water.'

My mother said to me, 'Why don't you come with us? It's ages since you've been sailing, you might have grown to like it.'

'I'll go on the ferry, thanks.'

'Oh, Christine – '

'Can I have the fare money?'

'Why won't you come with us?'

I put out my hand to my father, who gave me half-a-crown. I said, 'Gee, thanks, sugar daddy,' and sauntered off towards the jetty where Steve the ferryman was starting up his motor.

My mother called after me, 'Tell Steve we need another cylinder of calor gas. And if you get back before us, start collecting firewood for the barbecue.'

The ferry was filling up with afternoon trippers. I sat apart from them. I hoped they would realise, from my request to Steve about the calor gas, and from the fact that I knew his name and he knew mine, that I wasn't visiting Larcher's Point, I lived there.

Steve said he would bring a cylinder on his first trip tomorrow morning, at about nine o'clock.

'Will you be going straight back?' I asked him. He said he would, and I said, 'Can I go with you?'

He nodded, which meant that the first part of my plan was sorted out. He would get me to the mainland in time to catch the bus for Southampton. This left me with the problem of how to dissuade my family from coming with me. I wondered if I should be as horrible as possible so that they wouldn't want to come. The trouble with that approach was that my father was quite capable of saying, *You're not going at all, full stop*. Even without knowing the real reason why I wanted to go, he could do that, if I made him angry enough.

The alternative was to be very nice indeed between whenever they got home and supper time, which was when plans were usually made for the next day. By the time I got as far as saying, 'I prefer to go on my own', they would be so fond of my new charming self that they wouldn't dream of going against my wishes.

Steve decided his ferry was as full as it was going to get, and put me in charge of undoing the mooring rope and jumping into the stern with it as we moved off. This wasn't difficult but it impressed the trippers. I wondered if my parents were watching. I knew they couldn't understand why I was quite willing to help Steve with his boat but I wouldn't go anywhere near theirs. It seemed simple enough to me. Steve's boat was a motor boat.

My father could talk till he was blue in the face about wind and tide, and how if I took the trouble to learn about the laws that controlled them I would understand that sailing was the safest form of transport yet invented by man. I preferred the strong throb of the motor, laying down the law about where the boat was to go, and taking it there.

We surged on ahead of the dinghy which was tacking into the wind with my mother at the helm. Janet waved. I ignored her. I was overwhelmed with fidgety irritation as I watched my mother steering the boat backwards and forwards and not getting anywhere. The fuss that went with sailing was out of all proportion to the achievement. And that frightened me, because it reminded me of housework and my mother's whole life. I preferred her to my father, but I didn't want her life. His seemed safer.

We had barbecues practically every night. My mother loved them. We couldn't have too many barbecues as far as she was concerned. They were as near as she got to not doing housework. Crumbs and rubbish got blown away on the evening gale, which was what Nature intended should happen to them. And my father cooked because he thought it was manly to cook in the open air. We washed up in the sea.

The only trouble with barbecues was collecting firewood, which was a task that went on and on. We collected it off the beach in the warm evening. The tide was out and all around us sea creatures clicked and bubbled under wet sands scarlet with sunset. A couple of yachts rode at anchor, showing red and green lights. Another sailed its stately way across the darkening horizon.

Birds called through the salty, velvet air. Steve's ferry was taking away the last of the day trippers. We owned the point, the castle, the lighthouse and the cottages. We owned everything.

'Isn't this *lovely*?' my mother cried, dragging an enormous log.

My father went to help her. 'Aren't *you* lovely?'

'I'm not, don't be silly.'

'You are. I love you when you're all brown and salty and windblown.' He kissed her.

She kissed him back with great passion. 'I love *you* all the time.'

'This was how you looked the first day I took you canoeing. You didn't capsize the canoe, so I thought, that's the girl for me.'

Janet and I made puking noises.

In the far distance the chugging of Steve's ferry grew fainter. 'He'll be bringing the gas in the morning,' I said. 'And I'll go back with him.'

My mother looked up from her kiss and said, 'You don't want to go to a horrible stuffy city when you could be here.'

'You don't have to come with me.'

'Oh, but we want to. Don't we, everybody?'

Janet said, 'I don't,' which united our parents against her. 'You do,' they said together.

I said, 'Wouldn't you rather be on the water, Daddy?'

He gazed over my mother's shoulder and out to sea, at the slow, graceful movements of the yacht in the gathering darkness. My mother stroked his back. 'Missing a day's sailing wouldn't kill us, would it, Sand?'

'It might,' he said.

He cooked sausages and chops and baked potatoes. Janet helped him and I pretended to.

My mother wrapped herself in jerseys and sat on a log by the fire to sew up a tear in a sail. She used an enormous bodkin and a special thimble that was made of leather and covered half her hand. She finished sewing and wrote postcards to all my father's brothers and their wives and families. He said, 'Put "having a wonderful time, wish you were here",' and she said, 'No fear.'

When it was too dark for writing she sent me into the cottage for binoculars and started identifying stars. 'Janet! Christine! Come and look at The Little Bear!'

'To whit to whoo!' muttered my father.

I looked through the binoculars, though I knew from past experience that I wouldn't see anything remotely resembling a little bear, and I didn't. I wasn't convinced that Janet did either, in spite of all her knowledgeable nodding and intelligent questioning and careful filling in of dates and times in *I Spy the Sky at Night*.

We ate our barbecue. My mother drank cider, Janet drank orange and my father and I had pale ale. For pudding we passed round an enormous tin of fruit cocktail, taking it in turns to spear a bit of fruit with a fork. This was another tradition. You were allowed one stab per turn. And if you sulked about getting a pineapple chunk when you had been hoping for a cherry you were a bad sport and not a true member of the Toms family.

We sang 'Ten Green Bottles' and 'De Camptown Races' and 'One Man Went to Mow'. My father put on a high voice and did an imitation of the nurses' choir at my mother's old hospital singing 'Nymphs and Shepherds'. This sent my mother and Janet into hysterics, and I laughed too, probably because of the pale ale.

Our singing and laughter seemed to swoop off into the chilly August darkness, fly round the lighthouse, bounce off the walls of the derelict cottages and the castle and come back, echoing. Everything was ours, even the air, and we filled it with our noise.

We stopped. There was no reason for our silence. Nothing had happened, no signal had been given. Each of us seemed to know that it was time to be quiet. We listened to the noises of the night, and even the sound of our breathing was an intrusion.

My father took my mother's hand and nodded at the darkness. 'Fancy a stroll?' He helped her to her feet and they walked off. His arm was round her waist. Her head was on his shoulder.

Janet and I sang 'True Love' after them at the tops of our voices but they didn't sing back so we stopped and put the fire out. We fetched saucepans of sea water and poured it on the flames. Steam shot into the air. Hot stones cracked with loud reports. We added more water to be sure, then kicked away the wet black charcoal and buried the remains of the fire under more stones.

I thought of the people of Hiroshima, going to bed on this night all those years ago, not knowing what was going to hit them.

11

They always went for a swim at sunrise, however cold it was. The shrillest, iciest wind had no chance against my mother's heartiness, my father's years in public school, and Janet's fear of him calling her a sissy. They said the morning bathe was the only way of keeping clean but it wasn't. While they were suffering in the sea, I boiled a kettle and had a strip-wash at the sink. By the time they came back with blue flesh and chattering teeth, I was dressed and dainty and warm.

While we were having breakfast, we heard the familiar chug of Steve's ferry coming out from the mainland. 'He's early,' I said, finishing my food. 'I'd better go.'

My mother said, 'Go where?'

'Southampton.'

'Go another day. I'll get organised and come with you.'

I ignored her and set off with my father who was coming to collect the gas cylinder from Steve. We arrived at the jetty by the castle as Steve was steering his boat alongside. The boat was full of workmen. I thought they were probably from the Ministry of Works or Trinity House and had come to do repairs to the castle or the lighthouse.

My father said, 'You're right to be independent. You can't explore a city properly with your family in tow.'

'You used to like wandering about on your own when you were a boy, didn't you, Daddy?'

'As a matter of fact, I did. What time do you think you'll be back?'

'I'll get the last ferry. I hope you have a nice day's sailing.'

'It is rather perfect.' He smiled at the windblown sky and the choppy, sunlit water. He looked grateful, as if I had given them to him. He handed me a pound. He took the rope that Steve threw him and moored the ferry with an expert knot. Steve passed up the gas cylinder while the workmen unloaded their tools and equipment.

I stood to one side, and the workmen looked at me. One of them wolf-whistled softly. My father looked amused. The one who had wolf-whistled was young and handsome, with blond hair and sexy eyes. He smiled at me and I smiled back.

He got out of the boat and I got in. One of his friends said, 'Just your luck, Terry. She's going.'

'Out of harm's way,' said my father, paying Steve for the gas.

Terry's friends were egging him on. He called to me, 'Are you coming back?'

'Might be.'

'When? Where are you going?'

'Southampton.'

'What do you want to go there for?'

'Don't know. I've heard it's a nice place.'

'It's not very nice today. It's full of ban-the-bombers.'

My father still had the look on his face that said he was pleased to see me getting chatted up. It didn't change.

He leaned forward as if to kiss me goodbye.

He said through his smile, 'Are you going to get out of that boat of your own free will, or am I going to have to come aboard and get you?'

He pushed me into the cottage. My mother looked up brightly from the sink. 'Did you forget something?'

'I forgot what a deceitful little bitch this one is!' He backed me towards a chair.

'Let go, you're hurting!'

'Not as much as you deserve!'

'Hit me then!'

He looked as if he would like to but he pushed me down into the chair instead. I thought of crocodiles, not eating you at once but storing you away for later. Janet picked at the threads of her tea towel and dried a plate with great concentration.

I didn't dare get up but I shouted at the top of my voice, 'Why am I deceitful?'

'Guess where she thought she was going, Jo. On a march!'

'So what if I was?'

'So this if you *was*. You are *not* – ' he put his mouth close to my ear – '*going on marches*.' The loud rasp of his voice, gruff but with a shrieking edge, pierced my ear. It hurt as much as a blow. Was I too old now to be hit in the face? Was the latest punishment to turn me deaf?

Janet said fearfully, 'Please, Daddy, don't shout.'

'Mind your own business! Get out of here!'

She fled. My mother stayed. She said, 'You shouldn't tell lies, Christine.'

'Name one lie I told! I said I was going to Southampton and I was. Where's the lie in that?'

She looked to my father who had no answer.

'You're wrong, you see, you both are, why do you always take his side?'

'You know we don't approve of you going on marches.'

'Why?'

She didn't know the answer to this either so she handed over to him. He said, 'Because believe it or not we care about you and we don't want you crushed underfoot in mob hysteria.'

'Name one time that's happened!'

'You're too young to remember the Nuremberg Rallies.'

I had never heard of them. 'This is a *service*! It's religious! You let Janet go to her Brownie parades! There'll be priests from every religion, and whole families, little children and babies and everyone will be planting cherry trees and laying wreaths to remember Hiroshima – '

I wouldn't have thought I could make things worse, but that was the effect of the word *Hiroshima*.

'Remember Hiroshima?' I had never seen him so angry. I thought that this must be how he had looked when he was fighting the Japanese. Perhaps he thought I was the Japanese. Perhaps he thought the finger he was stabbing towards my face was a bayonet. 'I was on a frigate in the Pacific. You know what our favourite job was? Hosing bits of Jap off the deck after a kamikaze attack. Remember Hiroshima? Wreaths? Ha bloody ha. We danced on the decks, we thought, thank Christ for that, perhaps we can go home now.'

My mother said, 'I thought the same. I thought, perhaps they'll let him come home to me now.'

'Ten thousand times as hot as the sun, they told us. Not hot enough, we told them. And why stop at Hiroshima?'

'They didn't.'

'Should have gone on till the whole bloody empire was up in smoke, not that those evil little yellow slant-eyed nips would have lain down even then – '

Tears rolled down my cheeks. My mother remembered we were on holiday, and tried to make peace, summing up for and against. 'On the one hand, Christine, you shouldn't tell lies, but – '

'I *didn't*!'

'Let me finish.' She turned to my father. 'On the other hand, Sandringham, you must admit that the purpose of fighting the war was to defend freedom of – '

'Freedom *under the law*, Jo. I cannot condone law-breaking.'

'Neither does CND,' I said.

'What about all this sitting down?'

'That's the Committee of One Hundred.'

'Oh, that's the Committee of One Hundred, is it?' His sneering sarcasm was almost as bad as his blows. 'Word of advice, old thing. Never join an organisation that's divided against itself. Be like me. Stick to the Tory Party, the Church of England and the Royal Institution of Chartered Surveyors.'

'As soon as I get home, I'm going to send off and join CND.'

'Don't push your luck, little girl.'

I looked at his tanned, salty, boyish face and thought what a nasty little bully he must have been at school. Beyond his shoulder, the alarm clock on the mantelpiece told me that the Southampton bus was moving off from the bus stop opposite Barclays' Stores.

I wiped my eyes. My voice was calm and so was I. 'I'm going to join and if you try and stop me I'll leave school.'

12

It worked.

At the time he blustered and harrumphed and said if I insisted on cutting off my nose to spite my face that was all right with him. But when we went home and the new term started, so did the Be Nice to Christine Policy.

That was what I called it. He called it treating me like an adult in the hope that I would behave like one.

'Behaving like an adult' meant staying on at school till the summer after next and taking GCEs. In exchange, I could stop wearing uniform from Christmas onwards and have a holiday in France next summer. Also, I would be allowed to join CND, though not to go on marches.

I sent my name and address and a sixpenny stamp to CND's head office in Carthusian Street. They sent me the address of my local group, and a badge which I put on at once. Before I had a chance to get in touch with the group, it got in touch with me. Someone called Adam Preston rang to invite me to a meeting of the Youth Group.

He sounded old for a Youth Group. His voice was deep and upper-class. 'It's on Tuesday. We always meet on the first Tuesday of the month at my place.'

'What time?'

'7.30. Do say you'll be there.' He made it sound as if the meeting would be cancelled if I couldn't make it. 'We're having a speaker.'

I didn't know whether having a speaker was good or bad or different from what they usually did, so I waited and he explained.

'It'll be Professor Burton from Atoms for Peace. He'll be talking about how atomic energy can be used to generate electricity for use in the home.'

'What's the address?'

'17 Percy Street. Bring your own coffee cup.'

When I told my parents, my father said, 'We'll have to meet him first.' I laughed because I was sure it was a joke but it wasn't.

'*Meet him?*'

My mother said, 'I agree with Daddy. We discussed it years ago, long before you had any interest in boys. We agreed that we'd give you and Janet as much freedom as possible when the time came but we'd want to meet any boyfriends before you went out with them.'

'I AM NOT GOING OUT WITH HIM.'

'How do you know there'll be anyone else at this so-called meeting? You might end up being shipped to Buenos Aires under the white slave trade.'

'That would be better than being kept prisoner here.' I tried to storm out but he stopped me.

'Where do you think you're going?'

'Buenos Aires.'

'Stay here and listen to what we've got to say.'

'I don't want to!'

My mother said, 'If he's a decent chap he'll understand. He'll think all the more of you for having parents who care. If not – '

'I AM NOT GOING OUT WITH HIM.'

'Even so,' said my father. 'Before you go to his house we want to meet him.'

'May I go to my room? *Please?*'

'Of course you can,' said my father, speaking sadly and tolerantly as if he were the misunderstood one.

I stamped as hard as I could on each stair and dust rose like puffs of smoke. I slammed into my room. Four or five dirty coffee cups rang in their saucers. The door of the old brown wardrobe swung on its hinge. On hooks and hangers in the darkness my clothes trembled.

I took a pile of clean washing off my bed and flung it on the floor. I lay down, clenching my fists and drumming my heels. I was trying to get rid of any anger. It wouldn't go. What could I do with it, what could I do? I was supposed to be against bombs but I felt as if I had become one.

My mother's feet on the stairs sounded almost as loud as mine, but she wasn't angry, at least she wasn't at the moment. She was just energetic and fat. Her fat was like her housework. She hated it, she raged at it, she fought it, but it settled around her and she was never free of it. I wondered if she wanted to be. She tapped on my door. 'May I come in?'

'It's your house.'

She came. I got off the bed and backed away. I wasn't afraid of her in the way I was of my father, but I didn't want her kidding herself that she was welcome in my room. She spotted housework, and her eyes lit up. She collected the coffee cups. She reached behind a pile of my *Mirabelles* and found a cereal bowl with a spoon stuck down with Weetabix and milk gone dry. 'Are you thinking of opening a china-and-glassware shop up here?'

'Ha ha.'

'I've come to suggest a compromise. Or rather, two.'

'What's the point? First I can join CND, then I can't. First he wants me to behave like an adult, then the two of you treat me like a little baby.'

She said, 'It's because you're growing up so fast that you have to be so careful and Daddy and I want to be careful of you.' My stomach heaved with embarrassment but she went on. 'You *can* join CND, you *have* joined. The problem is that we didn't realise they'd have meetings in people's homes. We assumed they'd be in a public hall, somewhere safe – '

'So somewhere public is somewhere safe?'

'More or less.'

'Why can't I go on marches then? They're public.'

'The first possible compromise is that – '

'WHY CAN'T I GO ON MARCHES? THEY'RE PUBLIC.'

' – is that I could come with you to the meeting at Adam Preston's house.'

'It's YCND, Mother. Y for Youth.'

'Yes, that's what Daddy said you'd say. The second possible compromise is that Bleswick YCND could have its meetings here.'

'*Here?*'

'Your friends are always welcome here. You know that.'

'Oh sure. And have him walking in making remarks. Rule Britannia. I fought a world war for you lot.'

She formed the crockery into a neat, portable pile. 'I've made two constructive suggestions. Take them or leave them. I expect you'll leave them. I expect you prefer to sulk.'

'You still haven't told me why I can't go on marches.'

'On that I agree with Daddy.'

I let out a shriek of exasperation, then burst into song. I made the song up. The tune was the same as 'I belong to Glasgow'.

'I agree with Daddy

'I agree with Dad.

'There's nothing the matter with Daddy

'It's just that he drives you mad.'

My mother said, 'Don't show off. And heaven help you if I ever come in here again and find clean washing on the floor. You can do your own in future.'

My own what? I thought. *Compromising, problem solving, agreeing-with-Daddy, washing, tidying, housework?* It was all the same to her. I was her housework and she hated it.

Adam Preston rang up and said, 'You didn't come to the meeting.' He couldn't have sounded more hurt if we'd had a date and I'd stood him up. He asked me to the next meeting. A solicitor would be there, speaking about Civil Disobedience and the Law.

'I won't be able to come to that one either.'

'Ah.' He waited. His silences were almost as sexy as his voice. 'Do I detect parent trouble?'

'My parents are completely ignorant, they think you're all communists.'

'That's an exaggeration.'

'They think you're going to ship me to Buenos Aires.'

'What for? No, don't tell me, Chris. I'll be shocked.'

'Anyway, I'm not allowed to march and I'm not allowed to go to meetings.'

'What *are* you allowed to do?'

'Nothing.'

'Have you got a bike?'

'Yes.'

'Are you allowed to ride it?'

'Now and again as a special treat.'

'Are you free on Saturdays? We're looking for someone to deliver *Peace News*.'

I wondered what objection my parents would come up with to that.

Oddly enough, they approved. Or at least, they couldn't think of any good reason to disapprove of me riding my bike round Bleswick, a thing I did anyway.

'Just make sure you don't go into anyone's house,' they said.

'Rightio.'

On Saturday morning I ate my breakfast quickly and went to get my bike out while everyone else was still at the table, including Pam who was staying with us for the weekend. As I wheeled my bike past the kitchen window my father opened it and said, 'Your tyres need pumping.'

I knew they did. I hated pumping up my tyres, so I had decided to risk it but now the risk was a double one. If I came home with a flat tyre, after having been warned, he would be so smug.

Pam said, 'Why don't you pump them up for her, Sandy?'

'Oh, sure.'

She made a face. 'What a lousy father you are.'

'Do you realise she's going off to distribute communist – '

'Wherever she's going, it's no more than your paternal duty to pump up her tyres. My dad used to pump mine.'

'That's probably because he couldn't wait to get you out of the house and under the nearest bus.' Chuckling at his own wit my father came outside and pumped up my tyres. I watched with my mouth open. He called Pam out to feel the tyres. 'Hard enough for you?' he asked, and she said, 'I should say so. What do you think, Chris?'

'They'll do.' I cycled off in a state of utter astonishment.

I hadn't realised that the Be Nice to Christine Policy included having my tyres pumped up. I put it down to my father's Honourable Heart. If you joined something, you should join it fully, pull your weight, be a good sport, keep your end up, help and co-operate and generally play the game. This seemed to apply as much to CND as it would have if I had joined the Young Conservatives.

13

Adam Preston's house was detatched, with its own garage and a well-kept garden. The woman who opened the door looked well-kept too. She must have been at least forty but she had a Millicent Martin hairdo, a nice figure and high heels. She wore a tight skirt and a waist-length floral overall. She seemed to know who I was. She called Adam and he came clattering down the stairs.

He was a bit of a disappointment. From talking to him on the phone I had pictured him as suave and lanky but he was shorter than I was. He had fair, shaggy hair and big, studious, Hank B. Marvin spectacles. He wore a check shirt, darned socks, no shoes, and grubby grey trousers that looked as if they might once have been pale blue.

If I had seen him in the street I wouldn't have looked twice. I couldn't connect him with his sexy voice, but there it was. 'Hullo, Chris. This is awfully good of you. Will you come up?'

He took me to his bedroom. The air was thick with smoke and the ash trays were full. His unmade bed was covered with banners and paint tins and glue. A Roneo duplicating machine stood on the dressing-table. The dressing-table mirror was spattered with a fine mist of bluish-black ink. *My mother ought to see this*, I thought. *It would make her appreciate me more.* His bookshelves sagged under heaps of 'A' level science books and *Eagle* annuals. A poster stuck to the wall with yellow masking tape showed President Kennedy and Mr Krushchev eating the world with knives and forks.

I narrowly avoided treading on a tube of ink which lay on the floor with its lid off. I picked it up but there was nowhere to put it. He looked at it in surprise. He seemed to think I'd brought it with me and he was trying to work out why.

He left me holding it while he counted copies of *Peace News* and wrote addresses on them from a list. 'I've drawn you a map,' he said. 'If I can find it. Do you smoke?'

'Yes please.'

'You'll find a packet of Perfectos somewhere. Light me one as well, would you?'

There were Perfectos packets everywhere but they were all empty.

His mother put her head round the door. I supposed she was his mother, though she didn't act like one. She seemed quite calm about his room. Perhaps she supported CND herself and regarded his room as a cross she had to bear. She took the ink tube out of my hand, found a top for it and put it in a box. She said, 'Adam, why don't you ask your friend if she'd like a cup of tea?'

This annoyed me because I thought she could just as easily have offered me one herself, instead of using it as an excuse for teaching Adam to mind his manners.

'No thanks, Mrs Preston. I don't want anything.'

'Sure? It's Mrs Jennings, by the way.'

'Got any fags, Mum?'

'Yes, thank you.' She made a face, went away, came back and threw him a packet. 'They'll stunt your growth,' she warned.

Seeing my puzzled look, Adam said, 'They're divorced. Jennings is my stepfather's name.'

I had never met a divorcee before. Adam passed me her cigarettes. I took one and he lit it. I tried to smoke it in a sophisticated way.

We sorted out the papers. I said, 'Are you still at school?'

'Just,' he said. 'Till Christmas.'

'Shake.' I put my hand out.

'What?'

'I'm leaving school at Christmas as well.'

'I'm in the third-year sixth at Bleswick Grammar,' he said. 'I'm doing Oxbridge. If I don't get in I've got a place at Durham.'

'Oh.'

'What about you?'

I laughed and blew smoke in the air. 'Nothing like that. I'm thick.'

'What school do you go to?'

'BCG. Like the injection.'

'Eh?'

'Bleswick County Girls. I didn't pass my eleven-plus.'

'Doesn't mean you're thick. It's the system that's stupid, not you.'

'I bet you passed.'

'All right, I did, but it doesn't mean anything.'

'That's easy to say.'

'Perhaps it is. Sorry. *Would* you like that cup of tea?'

I didn't want a cup of tea but I wanted to go on talking to him so I said yes. He called to his mother and she brought us a tray. I told him about finding Walter Benfold's letter in my rough book, and what my father said when he found I was trying to go to the Hiroshima Day march.

Adam said, 'Your father is quite wrong. The Japanese were ready to surrender *before* the bombing. The bombing was a show of strength by the Americans for the benefit of the Russians. It was the first shot of the Cold War.'

This sounded good and I hoped I would be able to remember it.

Adam explained how an atom bomb worked and how a hydrogen bomb was different. Then he told me why CND should be working for the return of a Labour government. Mr Macmillan and the Tories would never bring about nuclear disarmament, and even with Labour in power it wouldn't happen at once because of right-wing Labour MPs with vested interests.

I nodded.

He stopped talking now and again to ask me for my opinion but I hadn't got one. He was like a teacher, the sort of teacher who isn't exactly nasty to you but who can't believe you don't know everything they know. I kept expecting him to test me.

On Monday Stella wanted to know all about him. 'Is he good-looking?'

'Mmmm. Dishy.'

'How tall?'

'He's got lovely eyes. He's going to Oxford next autumn.'

'Oh jolly good show old bean. Has he asked you out yet?'
'Never you mind.'
'That means he hasn't.'
'Why ask if you know the answer? It's not like that, anyway. It's politics.'
'In his bedroom? What were you doing in his house, anyway? Without letting Mummy and Daddy inspect him first.'
'I know,' I yawned. 'It's amazing I got out alive.'
I sat through three more Saturday morning lectures before he finally said, 'Chris, would you like to go to the pictures one evening?'
'With you?'
'No, with Clarence Entwhistle.'
'I'll see.'
'Don't do me any favours.'
'It's just that my parents won't let me go out with anyone they haven't met.'
Adam shrugged. 'They can meet me.'
'But my dad'll say something awful and my mother will do something stupid.'
'I don't want to go out with your awful father or your stupid mother,' he replied. 'I want to go out with your sweet self.'
I reported this to Stella, who said, 'Chris, I'm really happy for you.'
'But what am I going to do?'
'What about?'
'Going out with him.'
'Go out with him.'
'I mean, my parents.'
'You take him to your house,' said Stella patiently. 'You say, Mum, Dad, I want you to meet Adam. Adam, these are my parents, that one's my mum and that one's my dad. Then you run for it.'
'My father'll stick his thumbs in his waistcoat and say, "Can you keep her in the style to which she's accustomed?" I can just hear him.'
'Go out with him in secret, then,' said Stella, losing patience. 'Say you're with me, I'll back you up.'

I wondered if I dared.

I couldn't make up my mind, but it turned out not to matter, because having asked me to go to the pictures with him Adam promptly forgot about it. He forgot about everything except catching the train to London to stand outside the American Embassy and the Russian Embassy with a 'Hands Off Cuba' banner in his hand. He even stopped going to school. He said there was no point. World War Three was about to start and he would be a fool to study to go to Oxford or Cambridge when there wasn't going to be an Oxford or a Cambridge for him to go to.

14

My father said we should keep our nerve. As long as President Kennedy stood firm, everything would be all right.

I kept thinking about all the things I wanted to do, and all the things people around me wanted to do, and how we might never be able to do them. I wouldn't be able to go out with Adam, Pam wouldn't travel to America, Stella and I wouldn't move into her flat in Earl's Court, my mother wouldn't lose weight or go back to nursing, Janet wouldn't pass her eleven-plus. She wouldn't even take it. She would have learned her tables and practised her verbal reasoning with Sister Dolours and it would all have been wasted. Even this thought failed to cheer me up.

I didn't know where Cuba was. Alone in the classroom after school, I took the cold metal globe down from its shelf and had a look. I twirled it on its axis. Beyond the classroom window the autumn sun was flaming red. I remembered something about *ten thousand times as hot as the sun*. I remembered my father saying, *Not hot enough*.

I twirled the world. I slapped my hand down to stop it. The oceans were pale blue and dry. The North Pole and the South Pole were white and still. England and the sunny countries of the Commonwealth were as pink as a poisoned finger. I couldn't find Cuba. I set off for home, cycling across the common in the bloodstained sunset.

As I wheeled my bike past the kitchen window I saw what was on the table for tea: raw carrots, apples and a box of Energen rolls. I could hardly bear to go into the house.

When I did I noticed two more things to depress me: the latest edition of the Convent of the Forty Martyrs School Magazine being read by my mother, and Janet looking pleased with herself.

Nothing brought out the Toms family likeness in Janet's face more powerfully than a moment of achievement. Her calm, proud eyes stared straight at me, and, through me, at everyone else in the world who would never have their name in lights.

My mother passed me the magazine and I saw '*Dartmoor Days* by Janet Toms, Prep IV'.

'It's Janet's story!'

I could see that. What I couldn't see was why my mother was behaving as if there were something unusual about Janet having a story printed in her school magazine. It happened year after year. Her first story had appeared when she was five and in Kindergarten One. Since then, it had been as if no editor dared produce the magazine without a Janet Toms story in it, for fear that readers all over the borough would storm the convent and demand their money back.

A quick glance told me that *Dartmoor Days* wasn't about criminals, as I'd hoped from the title, it was about ponies. If it had been about criminals I might have read it, but three pages of ponies were more than I could take.

It was the longest story in the whole magazine. Janet's stories were getting longer by the year. I blamed Pam for this. She had given Janet a copy of *The Young Visiters* by Daisy Ashford. At first Janet had been thrilled to have a book with spelling mistakes in it because they made her feel superior, but now that she was nearly eleven – two years older than Daisy Ashford had been when she wrote her novel – I guessed she was starting to worry that she might be past it.

I slung my coat over the back of a chair and waited for my mother to say, *Hang it up properly*. Instead she said, 'Aren't you going to congratulate Janet?'

'Congratulations, Janet.'

My mother took an Energen roll out of the box. 'You might sound as if you mean it.'

'It doesn't matter if I mean it or not. We're all going to die.'

'I don't think so. I agree with Daddy. As long as President Kennedy stands firm . . .' Her knife sliced into the roll. It was round, like the globe. It collapsed in on itself as she cut. It became a plateful of wispy crumbs which she stuck together with butter.

'I'm not talking about that, I'm talking about dying of starvation; isn't there any cake or anything?'

'There's no justification for cake.'

'Bread then?'

'Have a carrot, they're very nutritious.'

'I don't want something nutritious, I want something to eat. Can I go out and get a Penguin?'

Janet chomped on her carrot like a furious little horse. 'If she's having a Penguin, I want a Toffee Yo Yo.'

'Honestly, you two. Two minutes in your mouth, two hours in your stomach and the rest of your life on your hips.'

'I'll take the money out of your handbag, all right?'

'If you can find it.'

I couldn't. No one ever could. I found bits and pieces of small change lying around the house. I took them to the shop and bought a Penguin, a Yo Yo and an *Evening Standard*. As I walked home I licked my Penguin like a choc-ice. I kept my eyes on the paper because I was afraid that if I looked up I would see a mushroom cloud.

On the front page were photographs of battleships, planes taking off, the United Nations building in New York and President Kennedy who had been making another speech. 'We will not prematurely or unnecessarily risk the consequences of worldwide nuclear war. But neither will we shrink from that risk any time it must be faced.'

I wanted to shrink from it but he wasn't asking me what I wanted.

Chocolate coated my tongue. Soon it would be in my stomach and then it would spend a lifetime on my hips, but that might not be very long.

There was no point in doing homework but my mother insisted. There was something comforting about her insistence so I did it.

I was interrupted by a phone call from Adam. He said, 'Chris, can anyone hear you?' His voice was shaking.

'I don't know.'

'Don't say anything then. Listen. Things are looking bad.' His words chilled me even more than the wireless and newspaper reports. I had a feeling that he had special secret knowledge. 'A group of us are going to Galway.'

'Where?'

'In the west of Ireland. It's safer. Eire's neutral, they might leave it alone. If we're lucky with the wind we might escape the worst of the fallout . . . there'll be seven of us. Eight with you. I don't want to go without you, Chris. If I thought you were dead, I wouldn't want to live. You're not saying anything.'

'I can't.'

'Will you come? Talk in a normal voice, say yes or no. Say yes.'

'I don't know.'

'Will everyone in your house be asleep by midnight?'

'No.'

'One o'clock?'

'Probably.'

'We'll be there, Chris. We'll park outside your house at one o'clock and wait till five past. Synchronise watches.'

'Pardon?'

'The exact time now is six forty-five – '

'Precisely. Pip, pip, pip.'

'Chris – '

'Sorry.'

'If you haven't come out by five past one . . . but you will, won't you?'

'I don't know.' He had told me to talk in a normal voice, but I was shaking more than he was. This was real.

He said, 'I've frightened you, I'm sorry.' He became angry. 'They've frightened me and I'm passing it on. You're the first girl I've ever really, you know, and what am I offering you? Why can't we just go to the pictures together on Saturday nights?'

He was right. He had frightened me, and not just with his talk about fallout. I was worried about defloration. I had been worrying about defloration ever since reading a book in my father's secret dirty book collection called *The Second Sex*. It had been written by somebody French and translated. It had dreadful stories in it about virgins bleeding and screaming when their hymens broke. I had always tried to put the worry from my mind as something that would be all right on the night, but now I realised that Adam and his friends were probably planning to restart the human race, and if I went with them the night might be tonight.

15

Pam came home with my father. She had phoned him at work because she was frightened. He had said she could come and stay with us until Kennedy sorted out Krushchev's nonsense which wouldn't take long.

'The colonies turn to the mother country for protection,' he crowed. 'As usual.'

She didn't laugh. 'Mind you,' he said, pouring her a drink, 'you might have been safer to stay put. Who'd waste a perfectly good atom bomb on Earl's Court?'

Over supper he told us all that we should have been on convoy escort duty in the Western Approaches if we wanted to know what war was all about.

'We don't,' said Pam. She looked round the table. 'Do we?'

'I thought they were supposed to breed 'em tough down under.'

She looked away from him as if he were a tiresome child. She said to my mother, 'It was the civilians here who had the worst of it last time, from what I've heard.'

'It was nothing much,' said my mother. 'You were too busy to worry about it.'

I helped wash up and hoped nobody would be too surprised. It gave me the chance to take some cheese and some tins up to my room. I packed them into my rucksack along with warm, waterproof clothes. I hid the rucksack under my bed. I had a bath, and wondered when I would have another one. I dressed in slacks, thick socks and a flannel shirt. I put my nightdress on over the top in case my mother came in to kiss me goodnight. I didn't know whether I wanted her to or not. If she did, she might notice how hot and nervous I was. If she didn't, I might never see her again.

I got into bed. She didn't come up. She was too busy. I could hear her clanking about. Pam was in the sitting room with my father, listening to his classical records and then to the radio.

'This is the BBC Home Service. Here is the eleven o'clock news. In Washington today, President Kennedy repeated his warning . . .'

I wished Pam hadn't come. Her presence was a sign of her fear, and her fear increased my own.

'. . . by a power hostile to the United States to break the blockade of the island of Cuba will be met with the utmost . . .' She would take my place in our family in the last days of the world. They would give her my bed to sleep in. '. . . hope that reason would prevail. At the United Nations . . .'

Pam might die in my bed. '. . . the end of the news. The BBC Home Service is now closing down for the night.' The National Anthem played. I shuddered and wondered where I would die.

I heard Pam come upstairs to wash. My father followed shortly afterwards and pretended to complain about the time she had spent in the bathroom. They chatted on the landing and he lent her a pair of pyjamas.

My mother stayed downstairs to put the finishing touches to the day's housework. She riddled the boiler, which shook the house. Sweeping sounds followed, and the chink of china.

Midnight approached and passed. I was soaking in sweat. At last I heard my mother's careful, heavy footsteps. Her slow tread told me she was carrying a tea tray. She took it into her and my father's bedroom.

If the stories in *The Second Sex* were true, then every married man I knew had hurt his wife in that cruel, embarrassing way, and every married woman had been hurt by her husband. I couldn't understand how they could go on talking to each other. She boiled the kettle from the light switch by their bed and made tea. She chattered brightly to my father who replied in grunts. It was twenty to one by the time all the lights were out.

I prayed for them to be asleep. I waited as long as I dared. It was four minutes to one when I began to tiptoe downstairs.

I held my rucksack in my arms and felt my way with my feet. I couldn't see anything. I underestimated the number of stairs. I turned my ankle on the last one. I gasped as sickly pain snaked up my leg. I toppled forward. The rucksack thudded to the ground but I kept hold of it and it broke my fall. I staggered towards the front door. I undid a bolt. Upstairs a light went on.

I opened the front door. It caught on the chain, which I had forgotten about. I undid it and ran out onto the front path. The van was on the other side of the road. Its back door was open. Adam beckoned. He saw me limping and came to help.

A beam of light swept the dark street. My mother was shining a torch through the window and trying to read the van's number with binoculars.

My father appeared in the front doorway in his brown dressing gown. 'CHRISTINE! COME BACK HERE THIS MINUTE!' His voice seemed to turn me to stone. I couldn't have been more scared if I had heard the bomb going off. I stood in the middle of the road. My father pursued me from one direction. Adam was coming towards me from the other.

A voice called from the van, 'Leave her, Adam, if she doesn't want to come.' It was a girl's voice and it filled me with jealous rage. Who was she to tell him to leave me? I ran towards the van. The pain in my foot was nothing. My rucksack was light as a leaf. Adam took my hand. I was free.

I was free for one second. Then my father's fingers clamped round my other wrist. He hauled me towards the house. With his other hand he hauled Adam. The van revved up and drove away, changing gear at the T-junction. My father got me and Adam into the house. He kicked the front door shut but he didn't let go of us.

'Would you please take your hands off me, sir?'

'I might have said the same to you with regard to my daughter!'

Adam sat down on the bottom stair. The movement was so unexpected that my father let go of him, and of me, and stared.

Adam blinked back through his thick lenses. He looked composed and unconcerned. He was neatly wrapped in his duffel coat, sixth-form scarf, jeans and desert boots. My father's dressing gown was fastened on the wrong buttons and his shoelaces were waiting to trip him up. On the end of Adam's scarf was a 'Hands off Cuba' patch. It dawned on my father that he had a sit-down demonstration in his own home. He let out a strangled cry and raised his fist.

'Sandringham! Don't hit him!' My mother stood at the top of the stairs. I had never heard her tell him not to hit me. She tied her dressing-gown cord in a huge double bow and said, 'I think we should all go into the kitchen and have a cup of tea.'

'Cup of tea! We don't even know who this fellow is!'

'Adam Preston, sir. From Bleswick YCND.'

'I didn't think you were from the League of Empire Loyalists. I suppose you know Christine's not sixteen yet? Not by a long way.'

Sitting calmly on our bottom stair, Adam said, 'Nuclear weapons don't ask how old their victims are, sir.'

'Don't get clever with me, sonny boy. Either you give me a full and proper account of your actions or you give it to the police.'

Janet was next to appear. 'What's happening?'

'The bomb's gone off, what's it look like?'

'Has it, Mummy?'

'Of course not, Christine's being silly.'

My father pointed at Janet with a furious finger. 'If you're not back in bed in five seconds, I'll make you wish it *had* gone off.' He stabbed the air. She ran. He looked relieved; someone still obeyed him.

'Could we please go to the kitchen,' said my mother, 'before we wake the whole of Bleswick?'

'And how do you propose to get this fellow to move?' He prodded Adam with his foot.

'I'll move wherever you like, Mr Toms, Mrs Toms, if I can have Mr Toms's word that there won't be any violence.'

'Don't you set terms in my house. Get into that kitchen or you'll be down at the police station so fast you won't – ' My father stopped as if reason had failed. He dialled the first two nines of 999. He didn't get to the third nine because Pam came out of the spare room in his pyjamas.

Their bagginess flattered her figure. She could have stepped out of a *Looks Even Better on a Man* poster. Her hair was loose. Her feet were bare. She rubbed her eyes like a sleepy child. Then her easy manner took over. 'I didn't know you had visitors.' She advanced down the stairs towards Adam.

I saw how attractive she was and I was afraid.

'I'm Pam MacLeish,' she said. 'I'm a friend of the family. Since no one's going to introduce us.'

'How remiss of you, Jo. What on earth has happened to your social graces, neglecting to introduce Lady MacLeish to the fellow who's been caught in the act of trying to kidnap our daughter.'

'He wasn't,' I said.

'If I can explain,' said Adam.

'Doesn't look like kidnapping to me,' said Pam with a nod at my rucksack.

Adam said, 'I take full responsibility for – '

'Tell it to the police, sonny boy.'

'Where were you *going*?' My mother sounded close to tears.

'Ireland,' said Adam.

'Why?'

'To get away from the fallout.'

'"To get away from the fallout."' My father mimicked Adam's voice, cruelly and stupidly, making him sound like a queer. 'Of all the wet-wopped, lily-livered – ' He turned again to the telephone.

Pam said, 'Does that mean "shit scared"?'

'What?'

'I'm from the colonies. We're not too bright down there. Does "wet-wopped, lily-livered" mean "frightened?" That's the crime, is it? That's what you're going to tell the police? That your daughter and her friend are quaking in their bloody boots? Make that her two friends. I'd have gone to Ireland with them if they'd asked me.' Dark spots of anger glowed on Pam's cheeks. Her eyes were lit up and mocking. I had never seen her like this, and I didn't think my father had either. She might almost be threatening him, except that I couldn't think what she could threaten him with.

Her voice softened. She spoke as if she and my father were the only people present. 'We can't all be tough and fearless like you.' She took the receiver out of his hand as she might take a carving knife from a baby. 'Don't smile, your face'll crack.'

His lips twitched. 'Just because I'm laughing, doesn't mean I'm not – '

'*Jolly cross*, I know, but you don't really want Chrissie getting involved with the police, do you?'

'I suppose it would be a bit hard on them.'

Everyone laughed. The laughter went on and on. No one wanted to be the first to stop. We were embarrassed. There had been a crisis. People had made fools of themselves. But it was over. There wasn't going to be a war.

Adam rose cautiously to his feet. He kept an eye on my father as if he were a large unknown dog that hadn't wagged its tail yet. 'If you'll all excuse me – '

'Count yourself lucky I wasn't in a bad mood.'

'I do, sir.'

'If you take my advice you'll concentrate on your studying and leave politics to the politicians.'

'I'll keep that in mind, sir.'

'They know what they're about. There won't be a war. They've set their faces against any kind of appeasement. We all know what happened with appeasement last time.'

'Yes, sir. If you're right – '

'I am.'

' – and there isn't a nuclear war, would it be all right if I took Christine to the pictures?'

Pam made a snorting sound and covered her mouth with her hand.

My father's jaw dropped. 'Words fail me, Jo, but I have to admire his nerve. What do *you* think?'

My mother replied, 'Well, we can't say we haven't met him.'

16

'Ah, Chris. Let me.'

The floor was covered with junk from his bed. We lay on the patchwork counterpane and President Kennedy and Mr Krushchev looked down at us from their cartoon. They were carving up the world with knives and forks. Adam was trying to undo my bra.

'Don't.'

'Why not? They're beautiful.'

'Are they?'

'I'm getting all steamed up.' He took his glasses off. He put them on his bedside table, dislodging an ash tray with two burning cigarettes. He rescued them and knocked his lamp over. I laughed and he looked stern. 'Do you know what Reich says about women who laugh during sex?'

'This isn't sex. Is it?'

'I don't know what else you think it is.' He stroked me through my clothes.

I didn't try to guess whether Reich was a friend of his or somebody famous. I was bound to be wrong. 'What does he say?'

'He says that they . . . hang on a sec . . .' He looked it up in a book. '". . . have a serious lack of capacity for surrender which requires undivided absorption in the sensations of pleasure."'

'What's that in English?'

'It probably means that a girl once laughed at him in bed – when he took his glasses off – and he's never forgiven her. I'm *serious*. I'm going to have to do something about all this laughing.'

'Yeah? You and who else?'

'Who else do you want? I only meant I'd have to kiss you to shut you up.'

I had no one to compare him with but I thought he was quite a good kisser. He made my lips tingle and my stomach turn over even though he wasn't touching me anywhere near my stomach.

His hands went up inside the back of my sweater again. He fiddled with my hooks. I wriggled free. 'Christine Toms, you're a rotter. You've got those dear little breasts and you won't share them.'

'"*Dear little*"!'

'Ha! I thought that would get you going, you vain creature.'

'They're not too small, are they?'

'I can't tell. I'd have to examine them more closely.'

'This is exactly what my parents said would happen.' I swung my legs onto the floor. 'I'm going back to the meeting.'

'They can manage without us. They've got the living room, they've got the agenda, they've got their cups of coffee.'

'But my parents will ask me what it was about.'

'It's about "After Cuba – "' he kissed me and I lay down again. '" – The Way Forward."'

I had made up my mind about my way forward. I would stay at school and take GCEs in French, English, Geography and Commerce.

Stella had been looking forward to leaving with me at Christmas and going to live in Earl's Court. Now she was furious. 'We agreed! You promised! We had it all worked out.'

'I've changed my mind,' I muttered.

'Well I haven't.'

I tried to soothe her. 'Pam's not going to America yet, so we wouldn't have been able to have her flat.'

'It's not the only flat in the world.'

'I want to get my O-levels.'

'What for?'

'I just do.'

'It's that stuck-up boyfriend of yours, isn't it?'

There was no point in denying it. When he became a student at Oxford University he wasn't going to want a girlfriend who was a shorthand typist or a shop assistant. I didn't know what else I could be but I owed it to him to try and become something interesting.

'He'll laugh at you,' Stella warned.

'You're just jealous.'

'What of? He's probably laughing at you already. He's got time on his hands till he goes to college, hasn't he? He'll make use of you and then he'll chuck you for a bluestocking with BO.'

'Meow, meow, meow.'

He wasn't making use of me.

It was more that he had read things in books and I was giving him his first chance to try them out. I was trying them out as well. Even if he wanted to make use of me, I wasn't going to let him. I set limits. I rationed him, and myself.

I let him take off my bra. I liked the excitement of wondering when he would do it, and I liked telling him off for clumsiness when he fumbled with the hooks. I liked these things almost as much as I liked the tender, tickly feeling of his flat hands moving slowly over my breasts. He squeezed my nipples till they almost hurt. I liked that too.

I loved the look that came into his eyes when we were doing this. I might have called it religious if that hadn't sounded so soppy. His eyes glowed. He half-smiled. He was like a stranger, but at the same time he was like somebody I had always known, and always would know.

Because I knew him so well I let him take off all my clothes above my waist. He took off his own clothes above the waist too, and we got under the bed covers. We lay with our chests pressed against each other. His was thin and bony with hairs round his tiny nipples. He said, 'You'd never think we were the same species, would you?'

I couldn't believe this was me. The done-up buckle of his trouser belt pressed against my stomach and I knew I was safe. I wanted to laugh and cry. I wanted to dance with happiness, I wanted to go to sleep. I felt grown-up and babyish and full of wants.

I want were my first words, according to my father, but now I was satisfied. Even wanting was satisfying. I wanted something but I didn't really know what. What I was getting was so lovely, I couldn't understand why people went further and took risks when this was enough.

It wasn't enough for Adam. He pressed himself against me and under the hardness of the buckle I felt the hardness of him. I knew what an erection was and I knew what it meant.

We *were* a different species.

He undid his fly buttons and put my hand inside. I felt his underpants. I took my hand away.

He said in this throat, 'Stroke me. Chris. Please.'

'Do your buttons up first.'

He stared. 'Why?'

'Do them up.'

He did them up. He said huffily, 'It's not such a terrible sight.' He sounded mortally offended, but it wasn't the sight of it that I was worried about.

The tiniest drop of sperm could ruin my life. It was dangerous stuff and I wanted it safely buttoned away.

17

'This sort of thing was all very well when we were dewy-eyed newly-weds with babies – ' Christmas was coming and my mother was bellowing like a bull ' – but four middle-aged adults and six great clodhopping teenagers in a house this size for a week is no joke, and neither will the state of the lavatory be!'

'Don't exaggerate, Jo. I'm sure Sue doesn't get worked up like this when it's our turn to go to them.'

'Oh, the sainted Sue. Glory alleluia I'm a bum.' All my mother's sisters-in-law were thorns in her side, but Sue dug deepest. Sue was a perfect housewife. Sue was always beautifully turned out. Sue went to evening classes. Sue had produced four children, three of whom had managed to be boys and all of whom had passed the eleven-plus. 'They're your bloody family! You organise it!'

'And are you going to do my job?'

She put her hands in her hair and tugged. She helped herself to a third Weetabix. She had a grubby lilac jumper on that I was sure had done service as a bath-cleaning cloth, and a calf-length skirt that wouldn't do up round her waist. It was fastened with a blanket pin. 'I'm worn out,' she said.

'From doing what?' he sneered. 'Eating?' He took the Weetabix away.

'Couldn't we compromise?'

He mimicked her. '*Couldn't we compromise?*'

'I don't mind them coming just for Christmas Day,' she said. 'I'll give them a super day. All the trimmings. No holds barred. And then they can bugger off home.'

'You didn't mind going to stay with them last year.'

She said reasonably, 'When we go there, we have to stay because we haven't got a car.'

'I thought it wouldn't be long before you threw that in my face.'

He was getting ready to go to work. 'We'll cancel the whole thing. I'll ring Humphrey and tell them Christmas is off. Sorry, girls.' He gave me and Janet what was supposed to be an apologetic smile. It was the first sign either of them had shown of being aware of our presence at the breakfast table since the row had started.

'Why won't you *listen* to me?' my mother shrieked after him along the hall. Her face was purple with fury. 'Why won't you *discuss* it?'

'Discuss it? With you in full cry? Cancel it!'

'I don't want to cancel it.'

'You don't know what you do want. Bye, bye, girls, I can see you're going to have to lovely day.' He banged out of the house.

She banged after him. She yelled along the street, 'What about the cards?' Her voice was loud enough to stop traffic, and Janet and I cringed at each other. We didn't hear his reply but I knew what it would be. *It's all in hand.* He insisted on sending cards from some charity for worn out rugby players. Each year he left it later and later to buy them.

She came back in, sighing. I said, 'Why don't you choose your own cards and leave him to send his?'

'He'd never send any.'

'So?'

Janet looked up from her table book. 'Are we having Christmas or not?'

'Of course we are. But you girls are going to have to help me.' My mother glared as I got to my feet. 'Cue for Christine to make herself scarce.'

'Don't you want me to go to school?'

'Make sure you bloody well come straight home afterwards.'

'I can't wait.'

Unfortunately for Janet, the Convent of the Forty Martyrs had already broken up. She said, 'What can I do to help you, Mummy?'

At this time of year, not even being a poisonous prig could protect her from my mother's wild, lashing fury. 'That's *not the point* and you know it!'

Janet looked astonished. She still expected our mother to make sense. She said, 'Why isn't it?'

'It's your attitude as much as anything. I want you to be a willing helper.'

'I am!'

'There's so much to do!' My mother munched cold toast and wept. 'And you're not capable of any of it!'

Janet said in a small voice, 'I could make a crib.'

'That's right!' My mother's clenched fist came down on the breakfast table. Her coffee cup fell over and the cups and cutlery rang. 'Take the easy jobs!'

Stella didn't even bother to come in to school for the last morning. She was still sulking. We hadn't spoken to each other for three weeks but I had heard that she would be leaving Bleswick soon. Her parents had drawn the line at letting her live in a flat on her own, but she had a married sister in Epping whose husband had a record shop. She was going to work there and live with them.

I didn't suppose I would ever see her again. She wasn't really my type. She was a bit immature. I preferred adults, like Pam and Adam.

School ended at mid-day and I went to look for him. He was delivering the Christmas post. We climbed together to the tops of blocks of flats, stopping half way for cigarettes and kisses. It was a cold, dry, grey day with air smelling of snow.

'What would you like for Christmas?' he asked.

'Me two front teef.'

'Seriously.'

'"Sherioushly."'

He stared at me from under the mail bag which was almost as big as he was. I explained. 'That's what my father says when he's drunk. "Sherioushly."'

'Are *you* drunk?'

'No, but he will be, all over Christmas. Him and Humph.'

'Him and whom?'

'His brother.'

'Coming to stay with you?'

'Yep.'

'Who else will be there?'

I counted on my fingers. 'Humphrey, Sue, Vernon, James, Kevin, Julie, Sandringham, Jo, Christine, Janet, Mr Thomas Cobley and various others.'

Adam finished his cigarette and we climbed the next flight of steps. Casually and without looking at me he said, 'Will Pam be there?'

I stopped and stared after him. He had been fascinated by Pam, ever since the Cuba crisis. He had wanted to know where she came from and how we knew her. He kept asking after her. How was she? Had we seen her lately? Once he had called to collect me when she was there. He hadn't been able to keep his eyes off her, and I had decided not to let it happen again.

Now he said, 'Isn't Pam an honorary Toms? Won't she be with you for Christmas?'

'Yes, as a matter of fact. I suppose you'll want an invitation.'

'Not particularly.'

'Why, what's wrong with us?'

'Would I be right in guessing that your mother gets a bit excitable at this time of year?'

'She's dancing like a dervish,' I said with feeling. 'She's got the house looking like a cross between the Quartermaster's Stores and World Refugee Year. Come round and see what I mean.'

'Do I have to?'

I sighed. 'No, but I do.'

He pushed the last few envelopes through a letterbox. 'Come home to tea at my place and butter my crumpet.'

'I can't.'

'I want to give you your Christmas present.'

It was half past three. I said, 'Shc's going to kill me as it is.'

'So why not experience what I have to offer before you die?'

I didn't dare. I went home.

From three doors away I could hear her shouting at Janet. 'These are the *wrong potatoes*!' I opened the front gate and walked gingerly up the path. 'I never buy this kind! You know I don't! Mr Short knows I don't! They've got bitter skins, they're full of eyes and they don't roast! What was he thinking of, to give you these? Did you say, "They're for Mrs Toms"?'

I didn't hear the answer, just a rather piteous mewing sound, but I gathered it was no.

'Well, I give up! I ask you to do a simple bit of shopping and this happens! Why don't you listen? When will you girls understand that you're *no help to me* if you don't do things the *right way*?'

Poor old Janet. She went to all that trouble to be different from me and still ended up being spoken to as 'you girls'.

18

My mother wrenched open the front door. 'Oh what an honour. Lady Muck has deigned to come home.'

'Good afternoon, Mother. May I wish you the compliments of the season?'

'Ha bloody ha. Where the hell have you been?'

'If you must know I've been helping Adam deliver the post.'

'You'd help the whole world before you'd help me.'

I walked past her into the kitchen. Janet looked forlorn among her spurned potatoes. I was hungry. There was nothing to eat, though the house was full of food. It was all raw or dried or tinned, or not to be touched till the guests arrived.

'Give me a job,' I suggested to my mother, 'and I'll do it.'

'I can't think of one off-hand.'

'So why does it matter that I went out with Adam?'

She yelled, 'Are you going to be a barrister when you grow up? You'd make a bloody good one! You put words into my mouth! You pick on every little thing I say!'

'Which do you mean?'

Janet said, 'Don't, Christine.' She sounded uneasy. She probably thought our mother was going to burst a blood vessel.

I tried again. 'Why don't I go and buy us some crumpets?'

'There's no justification for eating a meal in the middle of the afternoon.'

'Crumpets,' I said. 'Not a shin of beef.'

'Have a raw carrot.'

'All right,' I sighed and hunted in the vegetable box. 'There aren't any.'

My mother said, 'Did you buy any carrots, Janet?'

'No.'

'Why not?'

'You didn't ask me to.'

'You shouldn't have to be asked! I need a constant supply of carrots! You shouldn't expect to have things spelled out! It's all very well for you girls insisting on having your cousins to stay for Christmas but it all makes work and I've got to have some co-operation!'

She sent me out to borrow blankets from her friends. I went via Adam's house. It seemed so quiet I felt I ought to whisper.

His mother was out shopping. We prepared a tray with tea and crumpets and took it up to his room. We ate the crumpets and lay down. He licked butter off my chin. 'You may not want to see me, Chris,' he said seductively, 'but I'd love to see the rest of you.'

'Why?'

'Let's have these down.'

'Don't.'

'All right, all right.' He gave up trying to roll off my roll-on. He smoked and ignored me. Where his hand had been, my flesh felt shrivelled and miserable. I waited humbly.

He stubbed out his cigarette and crept his fingers up under my skirt. He unhooked my suspenders, one by one. He rolled down my stockings and caressed the insides of my thighs. I didn't dare stop him. He might ignore me again. He slipped his fingers inside my knickers. I gasped and twitched. The feeling was embarrassing and surprising. I couldn't make up my mind whether the surprise was nice or nasty.

It didn't matter anyway. I was sure that once he discovered how wet I had become, he would be so disgusted that he would stop. But he didn't look disgusted, or particularly surprised for that matter, and he didn't stop. His fingers crept and played. 'Is that it?' he said.

'Is what what?'

'That should feel nice, Chris. Does it?' He made circles in my wetness. I was shocked but all I could think of was thick cream being stirred slowly with a smooth new wooden spoon. 'You like that, don't you? Do you ever do it to yourself?'

'No!'

'You can now. This is called your clitoris. Oh, don't move away . . .'

'I didn't.'

'Well, it did. Here it is again.' Golden syrup threaded its way into the cream. 'It's a Greek word.'

'Who cares?'

'It means tickler. Its sole function is to give you pleasure. Tell me which gives you more pleasure, *this* – ' his finger went round and round ' – or *this*.' His finger did something else. His face hung above me like the moon. His expression was tender and devilish and I wanted to stop saying no. I wanted him to undress me and overpower me and do everything, even hurt me if he wanted to, as long as it wasn't too much.

I closed my eyes. It was nice to shut out everything except feeling, but I panicked. I had to keep an eye on him.

I saw him looking as if he were doing an experiment and I was it.

Thc sweet, creamy feeling went away. I was sore. I moved his hand.

'Did you come?' he said.

'I've got to go.' I sat up. 'I'm supposed to be borrowing blankets. Have you got any spare blankets? If you have, don't tell my mum, she'll have them off you before you can – '

'*Chris*. Did I do that right?'

'I don't know. You're the expert.'

'I can't be much of an expert if you're running away. Let's try something else. Would you like me to kiss you?'

'It's so embarrassing.'

'Don't be embarrassed, it's natural.'

'Anyone would think we didn't have blankets of our own.'

'Chris, would you like me to *kiss* you? There?'

I was so amazed by what I thought he meant that I put my clothes back on at once. He watched sadly. He opened his mouth a little way and poked out the tip of his tongue. He moved it backwards and forward across his lips. It left a glistening trail.

'Think about it,' he said.

'I've got to go. I'm supposed to be making mince pies. Or beds or paper-chains or something.'

'Stay.'

'No.'

'Why? What are you scared of?'

'Housework.'

'*What?*'

'Babies, I said.'

'You're not going to get babies from anything we've done.'

'I know, but you know.'

'You think one thing's going to lead to another.'

'Well.'

'I should hope it would,' he said. 'But not yet, we've got lots of other things to try first. See what I've got you for Christmas?'

It was a second-hand book with flimsy grey pages. *Modern Woman and Sexual Joy* by Dr Prudence Laburnum. 'It's a first and only edition,' he said. 'It was published in 1932, and banned in 1933.'

The diagrams reminded me of my mother's nursing books. 'I know all this.'

'You know about the plumbing, but this is about the psychology, the techniques, the perfect understanding that casteth out fear.'

His use of the word *fear* embarrassed and confused me. He was my boyfriend, my steady, so it was up to him to protect me from what I feared. He was my boyfriend, he wouldn't do anything to harm me. But it was exciting to think that he could.

I put on a tough look. 'I'm not afraid of *you*.'

'I should think not.' He laid his naked arm alongside mine, comparing the muscles. I wanted him to be big and strong but he wasn't. He said, 'If it came to a fight I bet you'd win but I'm not going to fight you. You've got enough to do with fighting yourself. Read Chapter Four, "The Omnipresent Parent". It'll interest you. Dr Prudence reckons frigidity in women is caused by subconscious – '

'If it's got words like that in it, I'm not reading it.'

'The reason you hold back from pleasure – your own and mine – is that you think your father's standing at the end of the bed watching you. I'm not sure how he finds the time, mind you. His own seems fairly fully occupied, with his wife and his mistress.'

I stared at Adam in amazement. 'Didn't you realise?' he said. 'Surely . . .'

'I realised you couldn't keep your eyes off her!'

He sighed and put his shirt back on, as if he thought I wouldn't listen properly if I had his bare chest to look at. 'It was the two of them I couldn't keep my eyes off. Flirting and playing the fool. He runs rings round your mother, but one word from – '

'You've got a one-track mind, you stupid idiot. Pam's a friend of our family!'

He shrugged. 'You said her name, I didn't.'

I finished dressing without another word. He tried to put *Modern Woman and Sexual Joy* into my bag but I dashed it out of his hand. I had had enough of his tricks.

I had read articles in magazines about things boys would say to get you to go all the way with them, but I had never heard of the line that went, *Your father's doing it with one of your best friends so you can do it with me.*

Janet

19

'*Wakey wakey*!'

'I'm awake, Daddy, thank you.'

'Can I come in? Are yer decent?'

'Yes.' I was still in bed, doing last-minute revision by the light of my bedside lamp. Outside, in the dark sky of the February morning, the moon still shone on the snowy roof tops. Beams glittered through the frosty ferns that had formed on the inside of my window. Eerie light fell on the white china bodies of my horses, grazing on the white shelf above my bed. My breath made shapes in the cold air. I imagined theirs doing the same.

He loomed over me in his long brown woolly dressing gown. With his golden hair, his golden eyelashes curling round his twinkly blue eyes, and his warm smile, he looked like a giant toy – a teddy bear or a cuddly lion. He cuddled me sometimes, but never enough. He did it less and less often as I grew older, and, whoever started the cuddle, he was always the one to end it.

This morning we weren't even going to start. He had brought me my early morning tea. When he saw my table book he looked worried. 'How long have you been awake?'

'Not very long.'

'What you don't know now, you'll never know.' He put on his Gran Woolgar voice. 'You're learning all your life. There's such a thing as being over-educated. Nine sevens?'

'Sixty-three, pence five and three.'

'Jolly good. Four thirteens?'

'Fifty-two, pence four and four.'

'You'll walk it.' From the pocket of his dressing gown, he brought out a box of new HB pencils, his stopwatch and a packet of glucose tablets.

'You'll need these,' he said.

I was particularly pleased with the glucose tablets. All my

friends took glucose tablets for energy, but my mother said this was silly. She said I got all the glucose I needed from my balanced diet.

Downstairs, something came through the letterbox. From the bedroom next door, her voice said, 'Ooh, post,' in tones of delight. Her feet made a cantering sound on the stairs as she rushed to pick up the letters. She sighed. She was always disappointed by post because it was never for her. I didn't know what she expected. 'It's all for Janet.' She thudded up the stairs and threw a pile of envelopes on my bed. She said crossly, 'What are these?'

'Glucose tablets.'

She looked as if she were going to say something but he put his hand over her mouth. 'Come off it, Jo. What's a packet of glucose tablets against a lifetime of school fees?'

'Fine, if she wants her teeth to drop out.'

I opened my good luck cards. One was from my parents themselves. Another was from Pam. Others had come from relatives, including my grandmothers.

Grandma Toms's card had a ten shilling note pinned to it. The message said, 'Gran Woolgar and I decided to club together to send you a little something as a reward for doing your best (which we know you will!) so this is from us both.' But Gran Woolgar had sent a ten shilling note of her own.

Mummy said, 'You'll have to send one of them back.'

Daddy looked amazed. 'Why should she?'

'They've obviously sent two by mistake.'

'More fool them,' he said.

'More fool them,' I agreed.

'Don't talk about your grannies like that.'

'He said it.'

'He didn't. Anyway, upsie daisy.'

'Can I have the fire on?'

'It's not cold,' she said.

'Course it's not,' said Daddy, looking out of the window. He scraped frost from the pane with his fingernail and made *uv-uv-uv-uv* shivering sounds. He winked at me. 'Take a few deep breaths and eat a raw carrot. Have a heart, Jo. Today of all days.'

She fetched a paraffin stove, filled it and lit it. She said, 'You wouldn't have lasted long at my boarding school.'

He said, 'I don't suppose she'd have wanted to.'

'Nonsense, it was great fun.' She looked in my drawer and found I hadn't got a clean blouse. She rushed off to iron one.

I went down to breakfast. It was kedgeree. I tried to eat but my mouth was dry.

'Have some butter on it.' She put an enormous dollop on her own plateful.

Daddy said, 'Is Lady Precious Stream out of the bathroom yet?'

Mummy shouted up the stairs: 'Christine! Daddy wants to come in there!'

Christine yelled back, 'Can't he speak for himself?'

'Come out!'

'I do live in this house too, *Mother*!'

'Daddy's got a train to catch.'

'Fine, he can catch his train and I'll to go school looking a complete fright!'

He gave me a severe look. 'That's no way to talk about your sister.'

'I didn't say anything.'

'You did. You said, "She looks a complete fright anyway, most of the time." Didn't she, Jo?'

'Don't be silly the two of you. Eat your breakfast.' She and Christine resumed their shouting match. 'Come out now and you can go back in when he's finished!'

'Pooh! No thanks!'

When Christine did come down she was wearing a tight skirt and a V-necked jersey which showed the line between her bosoms. Daddy wolf-whistled and sniffed the air. 'Has someone set up a hairdressing salon around here?' He tiptoed out of the room with his hands over his head as if he expected Christine to hit him.

She looked as if she couldn't be bothered. She picked at her kedgeree. 'Has this got fish in it?'

'Of course,' said Mummy.

'What kind?'

'Cod.'

'I hate cod.'

'Since when? Have some butter.'

'No thanks. I want toast.' She pushed her chair back and stamped out to the scullery.

Mummy looked anxiously at how little I had eaten. 'Do you want some toast, Janet? Christine, make an extra piece.'

'I'm not making toast for the whole world.'

'No one's asking you to, but how about a piece for Janet as it's her eleven-plus today?'

Christine appeared in the doorway and gave me a horrible smile. 'Today?'

'You know perfectly well it's today. It wouldn't have killed you to get her a card.'

'What does she need a card for? She hasn't passed yet.'

'Make her some toast and don't be unkind.'

Christine held a piece of toast just out of my reach. 'Eight twelves?'

'Could I have my piece of toast, please?'

'Answer first, toast afterwards.'

My eyes stung. I looked at Mummy who said, 'Christine, shut up and give her her toast.'

'Toast isn't going to help if she doesn't know what eight twelves are.'

'I do know, I do!'

'Tell me, then.'

'You don't have to, Janet.' My mother got hold of Christine's wrist and twisted it until the toast dropped on to my plate. Christine said, 'Of course you don't have to, particularly if you can't.'

'I can, I can!' I spread the toast with butter and marmalade and took quick bites. 'Eight twelves are ninety-six, pence eight shillings!'

'That's a clever girl,' said Christine. 'Let's hope the other ninety-nine questions are as easy as that.' She poured herself a cup of tea. 'By the way I borrowed one of those ten bob notes, is that OK? You'll get it back.'

I started to choke on my toast. Mummy patted my back and said, 'Of course she hasn't touched your money.'

Christine shrugged and looked mysterious. 'I haven't then.'

'Honourable Heart?'

'I don't have to say Honourable Heart to you.'

I put down my toast and started for the door. 'I'm telling Daddy!'

'Go ahead.'

I rushed upstairs. Through the bathroom door came the smell of burning, as he set light to toilet paper in the lavatory pan. It was his way of getting rid of the smell.

'Christine's taken my money!'

'What did you say? I'll be out in a second.'

I went into my room and opened the secret drawer of my desk. My ten shilling notes were where I had left them, inside my post office book. They brought my total savings to £16. 4. 3d.

I put the money in my pocket with my glucose tablets. I would keep it with me until I could pay it in. It was against the rules to take large sums of money into school, but I could always explain that I was afraid of Christine stealing it. The nuns would understand. They had expelled her so they knew what she was like.

20

The first snow had fallen at Christmas. Since then there had been more blizzards and no thaw. Dirty mounds of hard grey ice reared up in the gutters like Arctic icebergs that had lost their way. Cars spattered me and my mother with grit as we hurried along the pavement, stepping over slippery slabs of new snow on old snow.

The Babies' playground was dotted with snowmen. They had been there for weeks, neither melting nor changing. The Babies seemed to have forgotten they were there. They ignored them as they rushed towards the snug cottage that was the kindergarten. Sister Jude beamed from the doorway, calling them by name to leave their mothers and come into the warmth where she was.

I envied them. I wanted to follow them into their milk-smelling world of pinafores, plasticine, and hundreds, tens and units. I almost felt I ought to. The kindergarten seemed to be where I belonged. How could I be taking my eleven-plus today? I didn't know enough.

Mummy walked with me as far as my classroom block and straightened the ribbons on my plaits. 'Good luck.'

'Ssshhh.'

'Why?'

'We're not allowed to say "good luck".'

'Twaddle.'

'Sister Dolours says it's superstition and blasphemy.'

'We don't believe,' said my mother, 'in a God who makes a fuss over every little thing.'

'Can I come home to lunch?'

'You don't really want to.'

'I do.'

'But it's so cold and horrible. Brrr.'

'Can I?'

'I suppose so, but don't expect a five-course banquet. Look, there's Eva with her sisters. Coo-ee, Eva!'

My mother's *coo-ee* was loud and piercing, and I tugged her hand. 'Don't, Mummy, shhh.'

Eva was the first girl I had ever made friends with. She was a Catholic. We had sat next to each other in Kindergarten One, and measured each other's plaits. Since then we had taken it in turns to come top at everything.

She looked up from sharing break money out among her sisters and waved to us. She shooed the little girls off towards their various classrooms and came over. She was my height, but whereas I had heavy bones and puppy fat, she was broad and flattish. Daddy said she was like a playing card. He said that if you looked at her from the side you wouldn't see her.

'Hello, Janet. Good morning, Mrs Toms.'

'Hello, Eva. Nervous?'

'A bit. Are you, Janet?'

'A bit.'

'You've no need to be. Either of you. If you two don't pass, who will?'

'That's what *my* mother said.'

'Well then. Off you go. Good lu – ' Jokingly, she put her hand over her mouth and looked as if she expected Eva to tell her off. 'Sorry, Eva.'

When she had gone, I searched my pockets for my glucose tablets and gave one to Eva. I must have owed her hundreds.

As we entered the cloakroom we heard a sound like the buzzing of rather frantic bees.

'Twelve inches one foot, three feet one yard, five and a half yards one rod, pole or perch.'

'Sixteen ounces one pound, fourteen pounds one stone, eight stone one hundredweight.'

I wanted to get my own table book out, but Sister Dolours was against last minute revision. She said it scrambled the brains. I imagined my brains, churned up and burnt, like eggs left too long in a saucepan.

I glanced at Eva and wondered if she were thinking what I was thinking. She was form captain, I was vice captain. We were expected to enforce school rules, not break them.

We were expected to pass.

Not everyone in our class would pass, but we would. No one doubted our ability, so what right had we to our doubts, our panic?

She gave me a glucose tablet and we went upstairs from the cloakroom to the classroom. The humming sound was there as well.

'Once seven is seven, pence seven pence. Two sevens are fourteen, pence one and two.'

Eva did the altar. She took down the semicircular vase from its place at the feet of Our Lady and picked out the snowdrops that were dying. Her lips moved in prayer. She was probably praying for strength and wisdom, for me as well as for herself. She often prayed for me, for my health and happiness and general intentions, and also that I would be guided to become a Catholic.

I knew she wasn't praying for success in the eleven-plus. We had been warned against praying for success. To pray for success was to treat God as a labour-saving gadget.

I dusted Sister Dolours' desk, opened her register at the right page and topped up her inkwell. I had just finished when she appeared in the doorway.

She was the most youthful-looking of the nuns. She couldn't have been all that young because she was always telling us about girls she used to teach coming back as grown women to thank her, but she had smooth, pale skin, gleaming black eyes, silky eyelashes, and a heart-shaped mouth. Daddy said he could see why some of the nuns had become nuns, but not Sister Dolours – she was a smasher. Besides which, he said, she was the only one without a beard.

She pinged her bell. 'Good morning, Prep Four.'

'Good morning, Sister.'

'The community said a Mass for you this morning. That will have done a great deal more good than all this muttering.'

'Yes, Sister. Thank you, Sister.'

'Before we stand for prayers, has every girl got everything she needs to take with her to the hall? Has every girl got at least three HB pencils with points that are sharp but not too sharp?'

'Yes, Sister.'

'Show me. Has every girl got a watch with a second hand?'

'Yes, Sister.'

'Has any girl got anything she should *not* have?' I felt myself blush. Christine's disgrace lived on in the memory of the school. 'Has any girl got any books in her pockets, or pieces of paper with anything written on them?'

'No, Sister!'

'Turn out your pockets. Get into twos and check one another. Anyone can make a mistake.'

I wondered if Eva would feel obliged to report me for my ten shilling notes. They had nothing written on them, but having them with me was against school rules. From her own pockets she took out a handkerchief, a shilling and a silk envelope containing her rosary and her veil. On the other side of the classroom Sister caught Alison Jones with a stuffed rabbit's foot on a silver chain. Sister's voice trembled with wrath and disgust. 'Alison, what is this?'

'I don't know, Sister.'

'How did it come to be in your possession? What sort of example is this for a girl from a good Catholic home to be setting to the little non-Catholics?'

'I don't know, Sister.'

'Put it in the wastepaper basket this minute. I shall have it burned. Make an Act of Contrition. Tell your mother to send your uniform to the cleaners. Janet Toms, why are you crawling around on the floor?'

'I've lost something, Sister.' I had lost my money. I had searched all my pockets.

'What have *you* lost?' She sounded as if she took it for granted that, whatever it was, it would be something even worse than a stuffed rabbit's foot.

'I don't know, Sister.'

'You don't know either! If you don't know what you've lost, you won't miss it. I think we had better say our morning prayers and make our way to the hall before it turns out that nobody knows anything!'

21

The junior hall was as old as I was. Work had begun on it in the year I was born, which was the year Christine started school. It was built on the site of the old chicken run. During the war and afterwards, while eggs were in short supply, the nuns had kept chickens, but when eggs came off-ration the nuns had got rid of the chickens and built the junior hall instead.

In the years before I started school, Christine used to bring home stories about the building of the hall and the death of the chickens. She said that Sister Jude, the kindergarten teacher, had wrung their necks with her bare hands.

As Babies, we had used the junior hall for rest hour. We lay on mats on the floor after lunch. We competed to see who could keep quietest for longest. I worried about the chickens. When we left the kindergarten, we stopped having rest hour and only went to the junior hall for assembly and school plays.

Now the hall was set out with desks and chairs like a classroom. We filed into our places and sat down. I looked at the stage and remembered how spotlights could illuminate one corner or one actor and make you forget the rest of the stage, the rest of the hall, everything. That was what I must do now. I must forget about my lost money. I must shine the spotlight on my eleven-plus. I must do a hundred sums in forty minutes.

Sister Dolours whispered to the outside invigilator. He whispered back. They gave out the papers. He gave me mine, though I didn't want him to. I didn't know him. His knuckles were hairy. A scabby scratch on his thumb had a raw look as if he had been picking at it. I wanted to receive my paper from Sister Dolours' delicate white hand. I wanted to put my own hand back into my pocket and find two ten shilling notes.

I must not think about the ten shilling notes.

My eleven-plus paper was a thin booklet with a pale blue cover.

I must not turn back the cover yet. Anyone who opened their paper before the signal would be disqualified. I wrote my name. I waited. I stared at my desk, focussing on the knot in the wood which marked the exact spot where the first question would be when I opened the paper. Once the signal had been given I must not waste time focussing my eyes.

In my right hand my pencil was ready. In my left hand my thumb waited to push the switch on Daddy's stopwatch. My stomach made a whirring sound. I was tense as a bowstring. I was the arrow. The knot in the wood was my target. Soon I would be released. I was excited.

'Girls, you have forty minutes. You may begin.'

The first question made me blink.

3 × 3 =.

I thought I might have something in my eye. I rubbed it but the question was still 3 × 3 =.

I could have done that in Kindergarten One. I could have done it before I started school. There had never been a time when I didn't know what three threes were.

I wrote 9 but it didn't look right. I read the question again to see if there might be some complication that I had missed. Perhaps the examiners wanted me to turn the answer into shillings and pence.

It was impossible. The answer would be ninepence.

3 × 3 = 9.

I had started my eleven-plus. I had answered the first question and I was certain that I had got it right. Daddy's stopwatch ticked away the seconds. I was losing seconds and I had none to lose. I must move on. But I couldn't take my eyes away from 3 × 3 = 9.

The girl in front of me turned her page. She too had written, 3 × 3 = 9. She had written a great many other things besides. She had done a whole page and I had only done one question.

I heard footsteps. I froze. The outside invigilator was standing behind me and I was looking at another girl's paper. He would have been warned about me. *That's the sister of the girl who cheated.* I waited for his hand to descend on my shoulder. I lived through everything. I would be led from the hall. Eva would look up, shocked. Then she would return to her paper. Sister Dolours would scold me until I cried. In tears I would be sent to the office. My satchel and my shoebag would be fetched. I would be sent home. My mother would slap me and shout at me and send me to my room to wait for my father who would give me a proper beating. '*Cheat*!' he would say, from the back of his throat where phlegm gathered and bubbled in disgust. '*Cheats! I hate 'em. Ugh*!'

The invigilator walked by without stopping.

I returned to my sum. 3 × 3 = 9.

It couldn't be right.

Sister Dolours had never given us questions as easy as that. I looked for her. She was pacing between the desks. Her lips moved. Her fingers clutched her rosary beads, daring them to click. Her eyes were alert. They met mine. *If a question is too difficult*, they reminded me kindly, *move on and come back to it*.

She had never told us what we were supposed to do if we got stuck because a question was too easy.

Wildly I turned the pages.

1½ cwt potatoes @ 3d per lb.

I recognised avoirdupois, fractions, pounds, shillings and pence. I wrote the answer, £2 2s 0d. This was what I had been trained for.

My pencil flew from sum to sum.

'Pencils down,' said Sister. 'Check that your name is on the front of your paper and hand it in.'

I didn't need to check. I remembered writing my name in that faraway time when my eleven-plus was something over the horizon, something over the page. The invigilator took my paper. In the moment it left my desk I seemed to know that, however old I lived to be, I would never again be expected to do a hundred sums in forty minutes.

I rushed to the cloakroom and plunged my hands into my coat pockets. They were empty. At the next peg, Alison Jones said, 'Wasn't it hard? I bet I failed.' No one took the bet. Sister shooed us all outside. Eva and the others gathered shivering by the milk crates.

I remembered giving her a glucose tablet on our way into school. I had got it out of the same pocket where I had put my ten shilling notes. We had been standing outside the classroom block. I hurried there. I searched around in the grimy snow. The wind caught a piece of reddish-brown paper. It bowled along the path by the stations of the cross. I caught it at Jesus Falls a Second Time. It was a Crunchie wrapper.

Sister blew a warning whistle. Everyone made their way back to the hall. Eva beckoned urgently. I followed. As I passed by the Babies' bungalow I heard the sweet, breathy sound of them chanting their two-times tables.

The first half of the English paper was punctuation, vocabulary, grammar and parsing:

Write the plural of ox, tooth, sheep, roof, wolf, penny.

Is a sturgeon a kind of doctor, fish, soldier, house or foreign currency?

Turn the following into direct speech: Mrs Jones told Grocer Brown that he had given her too much change. He asked her what she meant. She replied that –

They were all about money. Everything was about money. Money was so hard to get and so easy to lose. It wasn't that I wanted to buy anything. On the contrary, I hated buying things. I liked to have things bought for me but I didn't like buying them myself. I liked to keep my money. Money was something I liked to have.

I must not think about it. I must not allow myself to be distracted. Money was arithmetic. This was English. What were two ten shilling notes against a lifetime of school fees? I should be starting my composition.

One of the subjects was 'What I Would Do If I Had Five Shillings'. I looked away in disgust. The alternative was 'An Exciting Journey'. I could do that. I wrote a story about a heroic girl who sailed her father's dinghy across the English Channel during the war and helped to rescue the soldiers from Dunkirk.

22

We returned to our classrooms and prayed. We thanked God for helping us to do our best in the first two papers. We asked the Holy Ghost to guide the minds of the examiners who would be doing the marking.

'In the name of the Father and of the Son and of the Holy Ghost, Amen.' Sister beamed as if she were pleased with us. 'Good afternoon, girls. I hope you will enjoy your lunch.' The girls who were staying to lunch looked as if this were not very likely. 'A sum of money has been found on school premises – '

Alison said eagerly, 'How much, Sister?'

'Have you lost any money, Alison?'

'Well, I don't know, Sister. I might have.'

'If you had lost *this* sum of money, you would be in no doubt. But you all know the rule about bringing money, so I doubt whether it belongs to anyone here. It has probably blown in from the street. Run along and have your lunch, you have earned it.' She paused. 'I doubt whether the sum of money has been earned. Anyone who had had to earn it would have taken better care of it. It has probably been dishonestly acquired.' She walked over to the Crusade of Rescue box. A picture on the side showed a fireman on a ladder saving children from a fire. *TO THE RESCUE WITH YOUR PENNIES*! 'Since nobody has claimed the money,' she said, 'we will give it back to God.'

I went home for lunch. The breakfast things were still on the table and Mummy was at the sink, washing sheets. I thought she ought to have a washing machine, but whenever I suggested it she said, 'You show me the machine that can get things as clean as a conscientious housewife working with her bare hands!'

Grunting, she wrung out the sheets and forced them through the mangle. Between grunts she said, 'How did you get on?'

I said, 'All right,' which was what Christine always said when she didn't want to talk about something.

She laughed. 'You get more like your sister every day.'

'I do not.'

'How many of the sums did you do?'

'Only ninety.'

'Only! Ninety sounds enough to me.'

It wasn't enough. Only a hundred would have been enough. But there was no point in trying to explain that to her. She wouldn't understand, any more than she would understand about getting tripped up by questions because they were too easy.

To change the subject, I said, 'What's for lunch?'

'Oh, cheese.'

I made a face. Cheese wasn't lunch. 'Can we have fish and chips?'

'We had fish for breakfast.'

'Can we?'

'Fish and chips are a bit starchy.'

'Can we?'

'Go on, then. Find my handbag.'

I wished I hadn't spoken.

When I was about seven I had written a story called *The Runaway Handbag*. Daddy had laughed his head off; Mummy had said, 'Ha ha ha.' She couldn't stand the way she was always losing her handbag. Neither could I. It had all her important things in it, and she never knew where it was.

'*Do please* find my handbag,' she begged, and I scuttled off to hunt for it. It could have been anywhere. The only place I didn't bother to search was my own room. I always knew exactly what was in my room, which I kept clean and tidy so that nothing could find its way in there by mistake and get buried in the way things were always getting buried in other parts of the house.

The handbag turned up in her and Daddy's bedroom, under the covers of the bed which had not been made. 'I knew it must be somewhere,' she said, pleased, unzipping all its different pockets and rummaging for her purse.

'Why don't you have a special hook to keep it on?' I suggested.

'One of these days I will,' she said.

'Why not now? Then you'd always know where it was.'

'It's not as simple as that, Janet.' She finished unzipping and looked disappointed. 'I must have forgotten to go to the bank.' I couldn't understand this. If I could go to the bank and be given money whenever I felt like it, I would go every day. She said, 'Could you pay for the chish and fips with your own money? I'll give it back this evening.'

I whispered tensely, 'I can't.'

'You can, you're the richest person in the family.'

'I'm the poorest.'

'Go on with you. What about your pound?' I looked at the floor and didn't answer. She said, 'You haven't spent it already? You haven't lost it?'

I wanted to say I had paid it into the post office, but I didn't dare, in case she said, *Honourable Heart*?

I told the truth instead, starting with my fear that Christine would steal my money if I left it at home and finishing with it going into the Crusade of Rescue box.

Mummy was outraged. 'Crusade-of-Father-Goswell's-beer-money, you mean!'

'It's for the poor children.'

'They turn them away if they're not Roman Catholics. Explain to Sister Dolours that you made a mistake and you want your money back.'

I wondered what her school days had been like, if she really thought it was possible to talk to a teacher like that. To change the subject I said, 'Why do you *always* forget to go to the bank?'

'Because I am not perfect. I wish I were, but I'm not. What would you like, cheese on toast?'

'Yes please.'

'I can't stop. You'll have to do your own.'

I fetched a lump of cheese from the larder. She said it was the wrong lump so I took it back and fetched the right one. She chose the right knife for me and showed me the right way to slice the cheese. She told me to be sure and put the cheese on toast at the right end of the grill pan. I asked her if she wanted any and she said, 'No, this will be a good opportunity for me to miss a meal.'

But when I had cooked mine and was sitting down to eat, a look of longing came into her eyes. 'Can I have a bite?'

'Oh, Mummy, don't.'

'Just a taste.'

She bit off a large chunk, leaving toothmarks in my melted cheese. She chewed and swallowed and turned the grill back on. 'It's no good,' she said. 'I'll have to have a piece myself. It's all your fault.'

While she was cooking, the second post came through the letterbox. We raced each other to pick up the letters. She won, but they were all for me.

'Not fair,' she said, pretending to cry.

'If you want letters,' I told her, 'you ought to write some.'

'One of these days I will.'

'You could have a special time each day for writing letters. That's what I do.'

'That's a counsel of perfection.'

Smoke rose from the grill pan. She rushed to put the fire out and I opened my post. I had a letter from a pen friend, two more good luck cards, a Butlin's brochure and a letter from the Pallas Press which said,

> 'Dear Miss Toms,
>
> 'The Editorial Board have now considered your novel, *The Dungeon Beneath the School*, and I am writing to tell you of their unanimous opinion that this is an exciting and original piece of work by a bright new talent.
>
> 'We are delighted to accept it for publication, and a prompt response from you will guarantee its inclusion in our autumn list.
>
> 'As you are doubtless aware, publishers' overheads are high and rising, and the market is not always as receptive as it might be to genuine literary talent such as yours. A certain element of financial risk is always involved. In your case, however, we believe the risk to be small.
>
> 'We are therefore offering you specially favourable terms, and asking only for an initial deposit of £20. Our

contract is enclosed, and we look forward to its return together with your signature and your remittance.

Yours faithfully,

'E. J. Hawthorn, Managing Director, the Pallas Press.'

Mummy said, 'What is it?'

I hid the letter. I needed time to think. I said, 'Something from Butlin's.'

'You and your Butlin's.'

'I like Butlin's.'

'One of these days you'll find you've booked a holiday and you'll have to go.'

23

I remembered writing my first story.

I was three. I used the first piece of paper I could find. It was the fly leaf of *The Just So Stories*.

My mother smacked me. 'Don't scribble on books!'

'I wasn't scribbling! It's a story.'

'Is it? Well stop making that noise and read it to me.'

It was about a girl called Ann who went for a walk and met another girl called Susan. Susan took Ann home with her for a drink of orange. Susan's mother gave Ann a beautiful doll. That was the end of the story.

My mother said it was a very good story. 'Very realistic,' she said. 'Have you ever gone into someone's house when you didn't know them?'

I shook my head.

'Has someone you don't know been giving you presents?'

'No.'

'So it's not a true story?'

How could it be a true story? I didn't know anyone called Ann. 'I made it up.'

'Good.'

My next story was true. I wrote it when I was four and in Kindergarten One. It was about a naval parade that Daddy had taken us to in London. We saw the Queen and thc Duke of Edinburgh, and sailors marching and fainting. Christine liked the fainting, but otherwise she was bored. I wasn't bored. I thought the whole thing was wonderful. Nobody told me to write about it, I just did: 'A Visit to the RNVR'.

I wrote it in an exercise book so that I wouldn't get smacked. My parents said I was an infant prodigy. 'Apart from the spelling,' said my mother. 'What's a "dyook"?'

'The Queen's husband.'

'Oh, I *see*! Dy – ook! Lovely!'

'Don't laugh, Mummy.'

'Go on with you. You have to learn to take teasing. Show it to Sister Jude, see what she says.'

Sister said, 'You're a great girl!' and took the book away from me.

One day, when I was in Kindergarten Two, a girl from the sixth form came into the classroom and talked to the nun in charge. The nun nodded and pointed at me. The sixth former came over to my table.

'Are you Janet Toms?'

'Yes.'

'I've got something to show you.'

It was the school magazine. It had my story printed in it: 'A Visit to the RNVR, by Janet Toms'.

I stared at the black words.

The sixth former said, 'Are you pleased?'

She wanted me to be pleased so I said, 'Yes', but I was puzzled. I didn't understand how this could have happened.

My story had been more than a page long when I wrote it. Now it was still the same story, but it had shrunk. It filled only a tiny space. There was room on the page for other stories by other girls. The other girls were from higher classes. Mine was the only story from the kindergarten.

It was the only one to have written above it in italics, *This is the unaided work of a little girl of five. It is printed exactly as written.*

I said to the sixth former, 'I was four when I wrote it.'

'Four, were you?' She laughed in a tinkly way. 'Sister, we've made a terrible mistake. Janet says she was four when she wrote it.'

'But you're five now,' Sister pointed out. 'A big girl.'

Out in the Babies' playground at break time I wandered in a kind of dream, clutching the school magazine, looking at my story. I wondered if Christine would come over from the junior playground to see me.

A big girl whom I didn't know put her arms round me. She was hairy and smelt of perfume. She said, 'We sometimes go on the *rinver* too.'

I glared at her. I knew there was no such word as *rinver*. She was talking down to me, like people who said *bow-wow* and *choo-choo* to babies. I knew she was laughing at me, but I didn't know what the joke was.

'We go on the rinver in a boat,' she said.

I moved away from her arms and her smell. 'Do you mean the river?'

'No, the rinver, like you've got it in your story.'

'That's the RNVR,' I said. 'The Royal Naval Volunteer Reserve.'

'Oh, is it?' she said, 'I thought it was another of your spelling mistakes.'

That evening I asked my mother if there were any other spelling mistakes in the magazine. She searched, but couldn't find any.

I must have looked wistful. She explained. 'I don't suppose it means everybody except you is a brilliant speller, Janet. The editor probably corrected other people's.'

'Are there a lot of mistakes in mine?'

'A few.'

I said, 'It's not fair.'

She said, 'Go on with you. You're lucky to be published at all. If they'd corrected your spellings, people might not have believed how young you were.'

I realised that my spelling mistakes were a joke. That was what *printed exactly as written* meant.

Since then I had always had the feeling that people who praised my writing were really laughing at it. I didn't mean laughing at the jokes – I wanted them to do that. And I didn't mean laughing at the spelling. I was a good speller by now, and old enough to have what mistakes I did make corrected. I meant laughing at the sheer ridiculousness of me writing anything in the first place.

Even when I had a story read out on *Children's Hour*, I heard a tinkly laugh in the broadcaster's voice.

When Pam gave me *The Young Visiters* I felt a wave of fellow-feeling for Daisy Ashford. I guessed that the people who had published her book had thought it would be funny to leave in all her bad spellings. They hadn't even corrected the title. *Visiters*. There it was like a banner, a hand beckoning, pointing, *Look at this silly girl who thinks she can write a book and can't even spell. Isn't she sweet, cute, stupid?*

There was a preface by J. M. Barrie, the author of *Peter Pan*. He said things like, 'It seems to me to be a remarkable work for a child, remarkable even it its length and completeness, for when children turn author they usually stop in the middle like the kitten when it jumps.' He drew attention to her mistakes with sneering inverted commas. And he was rude about Daisy Ashford's portrait. He described her face as 'complacent' and 'smug'. I thought she just looked pleased.

I hated J. M. Barrie on Daisy Ashford's behalf. I thought jealousy had probably made him spiteful. Even if she was only nine when she wrote *The Young Visiters*, it was still much better than *Peter Pan*.

E. J. Hawthorn at the Pallas Press wasn't sneering at me, or being spiteful. He had sent a contract. All I had to do was sign it and send twenty pounds and my book would be published. I had £16 4s 3d in the post office, and £1 in the Crusade of Rescue collecting box.

I went back to school. Everyone in my classroom was practising verbal reasoning. 'Excuse me, Sister. You know the money you put in the Crusade of Rescue box.'

'I do know, Janet.' Her blackbird eyes bored into mine. 'What about it?' She was going to make me say it.

'It was mine, Sister.'

'You mean you have lost some money? How much?'

'A pound, Sister.'

'A pound note?'

'Two ten shilling notes.'

'I see.' At least she believed me. 'How did you come to have two ten shilling notes, Janet?'

'My grandmothers gave them to me, Sister.'

'That was kind of them. Is it your birthday?'

'No, Sister, it was to wish me luck, I mean – '

'Why did you bring the money to school?'

'I thought Christine might steal it if I left it at home.'

'We should never blame others for our own disobedience. The

money is in the Crusade of Rescue box now. It will be sent to help the poor children.'

'Yes, Sister.'

'Do you want me to take it out?'

'Yes please, Sister.' Everyone was listening. I avoided Eva's eyes. Sister looked as if it didn't surprise her in the least that a person whose grandmothers believed in luck should want to raid the Crusade of Rescue box. She took out her key ring and gave me a tiny key.

Everybody watched as I opened the box, tipped out all the coins and rescued my ten shilling notes. Sister stood over me as if she thought I would take more than my due if I were given half a chance.

CALF is to COW as KITTEN is to MILK/CAT/MOUSE/BEEF?

Which of the following shapes are identical?

I struggled with my verbal reasoning but my brain would only do arithmetic.

£20 take away £16 4s 3d = £3 15s 9d.

£3 15s 9d take away £1 = £2 15s 9d.

£2 15s 9d = 55-and-two-thirds shillings.

Even if I could save a shilling a week, it would take over a year.

Six boys, Tommy, Pip, Billy, Andrew, Jack and Fred, go to the sweet shop. They all buy humbugs . . .

I wanted to say, *Don't waste your money, boys! Give it to me, lend it!*

My parents wouldn't give me money just because there was something I wanted. They would say, *If it's worth having, it's worth saving up for.* Anyway, I wanted my published book to be a surprise.

I wondered if Pam would lend me £2 15s 9d.

. . . but only Pip buys bullseyes. Licorice Allsorts are bought by each boy except Tommy, who buys wine gums, and the boy who bought bullseyes . . .

Daddy might give me money for passing my eleven-plus. But would the Pallas Press wait that long? And would I pass? *Write the name of any boy who bought sugar sticks but not bubble gum or bullseyes.* My mind was blank. I used to know how to do these but I had forgotten. I must think. I must remember. There was something about drawing a frame and putting the names of the boys down the side and the names of the sweets across the top.

I tried it. It didn't look right. Perhaps God was punishing me for taking my money back from the Crusade of Rescue and leaving the children to burn. Those poor children. There were too many of them to be a family. The fire must have broken out in a children's home. I thought how unlucky they were, to have been in a home in the first place, and then to have it catch fire.

I might write a story about them one day. I might have it published by the Pallas Press. It could be a sequel to *The Dungeon Beneath the School*. I wanted so much to be a published author. I wanted it even more than I wanted to pass my eleven-plus. Perhaps God knew this. Perhaps He was taking me at my word.

24

On Saturday I went with my parents to Twickenham for the Welsh match. It was my first International. Until now, I had been too short to see anything.

My Uncle Humphrey, my Aunt Sue and my cousins Vernon, James, Kevin and Julie lived near the rugby ground, and they had invited everybody for a pre-match lunch. Kennington and Kay were there with their sons Antony and Jeremy, and so were Rutherford, Gwen and their sons Theodore, Nicholas, Sebastian and Chapman.

Apart from me, all the daughters had stayed at home because of the cold weather. Humphrey was annoyed about this because he had gone to a lot of trouble to get the tickets. Even his own daughter Julie, who was thirteen, said she would not be coming to the actual match.

Daddy commiserated with Humphrey. 'Bad form to cry off at the last moment.' He looked at me with pride, and asked of his brothers in general, 'How come your daughters are so wet?'

'Excused games,' said Humphrey.

'Time of the month,' said Kennington.

'Frail and feminine,' said Rutherford. 'Talking of which, where's the delectable Christine?'

'She won't be up yet.'

'Heard she was having it off with a communist. That true?'

Daddy said, 'Would that it were. You should see what turns up on the doorstep nowadays. A Dago.' Christine had been going out with Miguel since the New Year. She had met him at a party. When Daddy first met him he said, 'Come back, ban-the-bomb, all is forgiven,' but Christine had shown no sign of forgiving Adam for whatever he had done to offend her.

The mothers rushed off to the kitchen. Julie went with them

but I stayed with the men. They drank pints from a pipkin of ale. I had orange.

My boy cousins were all older than I was and ignored me, but my uncles twinkled down at me as if I were a pet. They were tall and broad like Daddy, with the same open faces and big features. But they were older and darker. Uncle Rutherford was the eldest, and rather pompous. He and his wife Gwen were the only ones we had to call uncle and aunt. His black hair and black beard had grey streaks, and he wore horn-rimmed glasses. He worked in insurance, and had a permanently gloomy look, as if he were always thinking of what could happen.

As head of the family he liked to be kept informed. When he asked me, 'How did the eleven-plus go?' I had a feeling he would file the answer away for future reference.

'All right, thank you, Uncle Rutherford.'

'Too easy, wasn't it, Janet?' said Daddy.

I wished I hadn't told him about that.

Humphrey had last seen me at Christmas when I was revising like mad. Now he said, in a loud voice for Daddy to hear, 'Does your father know that we bought Julie an *expensive new bike* when she passed hers?'

'Bribery,' said Daddy. 'Janet doesn't need to be bribed.'

'I do.'

'You're too late, mate. Anyway, you've got a bike already.'

At the other end of the room, Pam was helping Sue to lay the table. I shivered with the pleasure of seeing her and wished she would come and talk to me, and leave the laying of the tables to thc aunts.

Anyone would think she was trying to be one, as she trotted helpfully backwards and forwards. She couldn't be one. She enjoyed herself too much. And she was too young. She wore her hair in bunches. She wore trousers with stirrups, thick socks and no shoes. She wore a man's jumper and no make-up. She didn't seem to belong to any age group. I wanted her to belong to mine. Or did I? I liked having her as a friend who was grown up. But was she grown up? I didn't know. When she saw me and waved and came over and kissed me, I didn't care either. She had a fresh, soapy smell, and her red hair gleamed.

Daddy said to her, 'Gidday, cobber.'

Pam said to me, 'How was your verbal whadjamacallit?'

'Reasoning. All right, thank you.'

Humphrey said, 'She's sick of the sound of it, especially now her father's told her there's no payoff. How mean can you get?'

'Sandy can get a lot meaner than that,' said Pam.

Daddy put out his tongue.

Pam said, 'What a nice coat.'

He said to me, 'Why is everyone so rude to Daddy? You're not rude. Give Daddy a kiss and tell him what you'd like for your payoff.'

'Money please.'

'Money!' Everyone laughed. I didn't know why. I didn't think I had said anything funny. Money was a serious business when you had hardly any, and your only hope of getting more was if someone gave it to you. Daddy said, 'That's all my daughters see me as. A bank. You're the richest person in the family, Janet. When you're not having your pockets picked by Mother Mary Helpyourself.'

'She didn't.'

Sue brought in a roast chicken. Kay, Gwen and Mummy followed with other dishes. There was an enormous beef casserole as well as potatoes in their jackets and four kinds of vegetables. Mummy said, 'Sue, you're a marvel. You put me to shame.'

'Nonsense, Jo. Look at that marvellous Christmas you put on.'

'Oh, but I was so bad-tempered about it.'

'You see?' said Daddy to his brothers. 'She's well aware of what she's like. So why doesn't she improve?'

Afterwards there was a choice of baked apples, fruit salad or a steamed fruit pudding. The steamed fruit pudding had been made according to a family recipe which had been passed on to the daughters-in-law by Grandma. Mummy said, 'Her recipes never make sense to me. I'd better try a piece to find out how Sue does it.'

After the meal we wrapped ourselves in thick jerseys and coats and made jokes about how nothing would do up after all the food we had eaten. We put on gloves, scarves and woolly hats and set off for the match. The pavements were crowded, but within the crowds the Toms's were separate. We were a strong, tramping, buttoned-up army. I was the youngest and the smallest but I had all these chunky men and tall boys and mothers to look after me, not to mention Pam. We were alike. The strong, square family likeness was evident in every face. Even the wives had it. Even Pam looked like a Toms.

We spread out and spilled across the road. Cars slowed down for us. In the crowds round about, people were talking with Welsh accents, which Daddy imitated. 'Indeed to goodness, boyo.' We all laughed.

Men were selling pink and green newspapers, hot dogs, and white rosettes with pink wax roses in the middle. Daddy bought a rosette and pinned it to my coat. He offered to buy Pam one but she said she would be supporting the Welsh.

I went with my cousins through the Schoolboys' gate. Inside the ground there were four stands, North, South, East and West. North, East and West were under cover. South was in the open air. We went to South.

Pam said, 'I wouldn't want you to think I was complaining.'

Daddy said, 'Perish the thought.'

'Perishing right, mate. What's so special about us that we have to stand in the open air?'

Mummy said, 'I've been asking myself the same question throughout most of my married life.'

My aunts said they had too. The uncles chuckled and Daddy said, 'You get a nicer class of spectator in the South Stand.'

Pam rolled her eyes and shivered. 'The weaklings and the lower orders die before half-time, I suppose.'

The South Stand was like a riverbank made of wide concrete steps and packed with people in thick coats. Their breath rose above them in a white cloud. They shifted and fidgeted, gave each other friendly punches, stamped their feet. They blew on their hands and passed round bottles, chocolate bars, cigarettes, thermoses and hip-flasks. They barked with laughter and burst into song. Welshmen were singing *Bread of Heaven*. Daddy conducted his brothers in a roaring version of *Rule Britannia*, until *Bread of Heaven* died away.

We found a place for ourselves with a clear view. Daddy

perched me on a crush barrier and gave me a programme. He put his arm round my waist to save me from falling off, and I put mine on his shoulder. Some people behind us complained that they couldn't see with me sitting there. Daddy gave them a scornful look and said, 'Move somewhere else, then, she's only eleven.' The other Toms's clustered round. They were my guards, my courtiers. I was the queen.

On the far side of the sea of heads in front of me a band was marching across the green, frosty pitch, playing music I couldn't hear because of all the singing and roaring and cheering and stamping around me. Two men ran round the outside of the pitch carrying a huge hairy green and white leek made of paper.

The leek was as tall as they were. They set it against one of the H-shaped goal-posts. They knelt before the leek and worshipped it. A grinning policeman led them away. In the stands the roaring rose like the sea, then broke into different sounds – singing, stamping, conversation, echoes – and rose again as the players came out, two lines of fifteen men running in step, the English players in snow white shirts, the Welsh in scarlet.

The noise was more than noise. I could see it, taste it and smell it. I could reach out and touch it. I knew it came from the throats and feet of thousands and thousands of people, but it seemed to exist on its own, like a granite cliff or electricity or thunder.

It was importance. I was part of the importance and it was part of me. By coming to the match on this bitter afternoon, I had earned something that Christine and my girl cousins would have to do without. I had earned my share of this importance, even though the importance was nothing to do with me.

The noises faded as the players posed to have their photographs taken. I realised how tense my body was and I shivered. 'Cold?' said Daddy, hugging me tight.

'No.'

'I am,' said Pam.

'I'm not hugging *you*,' said Daddy.

'Don't say that, you'll break my heart.'

Humphrey said, 'I'll hug you, Pam, when Sue's not looking.'

Sue yawned. 'Help yourself, Pam.'

'I won't, thanks. I'm trying to give it up.' She looked wistful. 'It's summer in New Zealand.'

Daddy said, 'Go back there then.'

'I just might,' said Pam in a tone that sounded as if she wanted somebody to say, *Oh, don't*.

'Oh, don't.'

'For you, Janet, I won't. I can't think of any other reason to stay.'

'Bloody colonials,' Daddy muttered. 'Coming over here whingeing.'

The players finished having their pictures taken and stood to attention for 'God Save the Queen'. Silence fell over the stands, and Daddy helped me down from the crush barrier so that I could be at attention too. When the Welsh National Anthem started I thought he and his brothers would try to drown it with their own singing but they didn't. They kept quiet and looked pained but tolerant.

25

I couldn't see what was going on so I read the official programme. I looked at the photographs of the players and gave them points for handsomeness.

'Enjoying it?' said Daddy.

'Yes!'

'Understand what's going on?'

'Yes!'

'What did you think of that decision, eh? About the line-out?'

I was saved from having to answer by the whistle blowing for half time. People started moving off towards the bars and lavatories.

Pam said, 'Can you get a cup of tea round here?'

'TEA?' Daddy scoffed, and his brothers joined in.

'Tea drinking's a disgusting habit.'

'Curse of the working classes.'

'Neither cheers nor inebriates.'

'Ruins your liver.'

'Even so,' said Pam, 'I'm going to die if I don't get something hot inside me.' The men made some more jokes which I didn't understand, and Mummy said, 'Behave yourselves. Honestly.'

Pam said, 'You'd like a cup of tea, wouldn't you, Janet?'

Daddy said, 'You'll stand in a queue for an hour. You'll miss the second half.'

I said, 'Yes please, Pam.'

Pam said, 'Is anyone else coming? Jo?'

'No, I'm all right and I agree with Da – I agree with Sandy, by the time you've stood in a queue it won't be worth it.' She gave Pam half a crown to buy my tea.

When we were out of sight, Pam said, 'Honestly, your mum. As if I can't afford to buy you a cup of tea once in a while.' She gave the half crown to me.

'Thank you. I'm going to save it up.'
'What for?'
'Something.'
'OK. You don't have to tell me.'
'I want to tell you.' I wanted to tell her and nobody else. I wanted everyone else to find out by chance. I wanted them to see my book in a shop window and be amazed.

We walked through the crowds and found a tea bar beneath the West Stand. It was indoors but the queue stretched into the open. We joined the end. 'Do you want to know what I'm saving up for?'

'If you want to tell me.'
'It's a secret. You're not to tell anyone.'
'OK.'
'You know my book?'
'Which one?'
'The one you typed.'
'Which one?'
'*The Dungeon Beneath the School.* It's going to be published.'
Cheers and stamping shook the West Stand above our heads. The second half had started. Pam's face was bright with surprise. 'Janet!'

'If I can get the money,' I said. She gave me a long look which embarrassed me. I didn't want her to think I was hinting. I wanted her to offer me the money without my having to hint.

She said, 'What money?'
'Twenty pounds altogether, but I've got most of it. I only need two pounds fifteen and nine.'

Some people in front of us gave up queueing and went back to the match. We shuffled forward and came under cover. It wasn't much warmer inside than out but at least we were nearer the tea.

Pam blew on her mittens and said gently, 'Who is this money for?'

'Mr Hawthorn.'
'Who's he?'
'He's the man at the publishers.' I wished she would stop looking as if I had done something wrong. 'I *sent* him my *book*.'

'Don't shout!' She patted me. I hadn't realised I was shouting.

'Have you met Mr Hawthorn, Janet?'

'No. He wrote to me.'

'Does he know how old you are?'

I shrugged.

'Have you signed a contract?'

'Not yet.'

'But he's sent you something to sign?' I wished she would stop looking so worried. She thought of something else. 'Have you sent him any money?'

'No.'

'Maybe we should ask you dad's advice before you do.'

I was angry. 'It's a secret. You promised!'

We reached the front of the queue. Pam bought two teas in thick white china cups, and two slabs of fruit cake. We stood by a shelf that was wet with spilt tea and soggy crumbs. We warmed our hands on our hot cups and listened to the roaring overhead.

She said, 'I worked for a publisher once.'

'Mr Hawthorn?'

'No . . . but I've still got some friends where I worked. If you sent me your contract, I could show it to them. I could ring them up. You wouldn't mind that, would you?'

'What for?'

'People in business quite often know things about other people in the same business. Maybe we could find out what this Mr Hawthorn's up to.'

'Why should he be up to anything?' I felt protective about Mr Hawthorn and I didn't want Pam's friends saying the bad things she obviously expected them to say about him.

She said, 'I'll keep my promise about not telling your mum and dad. Will you make me one in exchange?'

'What?'

'Will you promise not to send this Mr Hawthorn his twenty pounds until I've had a chance to show the contract to my friends?'

I shrugged crossly. 'I haven't got twenty pounds.'

'Janet?'

'All right.'

'Good. Thank you, sweetie.' She drained her cup. 'Shall we go back to the match?'

I would have preferred to stay where it was warm, but I could tell she wanted to go, so I followed her out into the frosty, roaring air of the late afternoon and the second half.

A couple of weeks later she telephoned me to say she had some good news and some bad news. 'Which do you want first?'

'The bad.'

'Miss Delbarco says you shouldn't touch the Pallas Press with a barge pole.'

I had known she would say that.

'It's a swindle, Janet. That twenty quid is only the first payment. They'd have been after you for instalments for the rest of your life. They're what's called Vanity publishers. They're not real publishers at all. They're only interested in money.'

'Are they?'

'Real publishers don't expect the author to pay. They pay the author.'

'That would be better.'

'Of course it would. Do you want the good news now? When's half term? I've got an open invitation to take you in to Delbarco and Wilde any time you like. I'll give you the guided tour and you can see what a real publisher's office looks like. Miss Delbarco suggested it herself. She was impressed that someone as young as you could finish a novel and get as far as sending it to a publisher.'

'She can read it if she wants.'

'Um . . . she didn't – '

'I've still got the carbon copy.'

'I think you should keep that one, Janet. Don't let it out of your sight.'

'It's all right, I don't mind.' I couldn't wait to get off the phone. I had heard of Delbarco and Wilde. I had some of their books, pony novels and school stories and some classics. The address was inside the cover. Delbarco and Wilde Ltd, 48 Bedford Terrace, London WC1. I copied the address on to a large envelope and sent the carbon copy of *The Dungeon Beneath the School* to Miss Delbarco.

26

He took me on the 8.24 from Bleswick Junction. He knew a few people in the carriage, and he told them that I was his daughter. He seemed half proud, half embarrassed.

He opened his *Daily Telegraph*. His eyes reminded me not to talk. I read *Elizabethan* and pretended I was going to town on business.

I was in a way. I had received a postcard from Miss Delbarco. 'Delbarco and Wilde acknowledge receipt of your manuscript which is receiving attention.' It would have received her attention by now. I was dressed in my best, in my grey pleated skirt and my viyella blouse.

I turned to the competition page. This month they wanted poems about picnics. I started to compose one.

Pam met us at Paddington. She was wearing a skirt and nylons and high-heeled shoes. She had swept her hair back into a loose french pleat. I wasn't sure about this change in her; she didn't look quite right, or comfortable. Daddy wolf-whistled and said, 'Good God. Legs.'

'Isn't he uncouth, Janet?'

'Yes.'

'He's sulking, isn't he, because he's got to go to work today and we haven't.'

'Yes.'

'How come you're not adorning someone's typewriter today, MacLeish? Won't anyone have you?'

'I have to have a day off now and again to spend all the money I earn. Come on, Janet, let's go and look at the bright lights.' She took my hand.

He walked off towards the red and blue underground sign. I felt sorry for him. He looked left out. The further he went from us the more he seemed like all the other men in dark coats and trilby hats. They were a river that carried him along. The river broke over the steps that went down into the underground. He disappeared.

Pam said, 'Have you had breakfast?'

'Yes, thank you.'

'So you don't want to go to the Ole Riverboat?'

'What is it?'

'If you're not hungry, you won't be interested.' We turned a corner outside the station and came to the Ole Riverboat Pancake House. I read the menu with amazement. Words like *blueberry, waffle, maple syrup*, danced from my eyes to my tongue. There were no words like that in Bleswick. My salivary glands came on like taps. *Fudge brownie, chocolate chip, cheesecake.*

'It's American,' said Pam. 'There's one of these places in every town in the States.' I tried to imagine such a country. I could imagine only too well why Pam would want to go there. I felt like dragging her away from the Ole Riverboat so that it would lose its power to lure her, but she opened the door and took me inside.

I breathed the sweetish smell of coffee and something even sweeter but slightly strange, maple syrup probably. The waitress brought two plastic menus and two table napkins. She also gave us glasses of water which we hadn't asked for. Pam said, 'They always do that in America.' The water had ice cubes in it. 'Choose whatever you want, sweetie.'

'What are you having?'

'I shouldn't really have anything.' She patted her stomach and my heart sank. 'So I'll make do with a toffee and banana pancake with whipped cream.'

'I will as well.'

'Why don't you have something different? We can taste each other's.'

I had blueberry muffins with ice cream and chopped nuts. Afterwards we went down a moving staircase into the fusty yellow air of the underground. Pam walked with the quick step of an expert, always knowing which turning to take. I stared at a poster advertising Start Rite shoes. Two toddlers were setting off along a tree-lined road. The trees got closer and closer together and met at the horizon. 'Children's Shoes Have Far To Go.' It was the sort of picture that looked as if you could step into it.

I held Pam's hand. I was afraid of getting lost, and embarrassed by my fear. This was the capital city of my own country and I was relying on a foreigner to show me round it.

She explained about the different coloured lines on the maps. It wasn't enough to find the right line, you had to know whether you were 'Northbound', 'Southbound', 'Eastbound' or 'Westbound'. The words sounded grand and distant as if we were going overseas.

On the far side of the platform was another of the Start-Rite posters. It reminded me of the picture of the Cat That Walked by Himself in *The Just So Stories*. The road was long and tiring but safe. All around was wilderness. Next to it was a cartoon and long poem about how Polar bears kept warm in blizzards. 'There Is No Substitute For Wool.'

Warm wind whooshed out of the tunnel, rattling the litter on the platform. The red tube train hurled itself towards us out of the darkness and slid to a halt. Its sides opened and we got in.

I didn't want to think about how far below the ground we were. We rattled through tunnels whose sooty walls were close enough to touch. I could hardly remember how daylight looked or fresh air tasted. The man next to me lit his pipe. Above his head two men looked out of the corners of their eyes at a woman who was looking straight ahead. 'Somebody Isn't Using Amplex.'

The smell of tobacco smoke mingled with the sourish-sweet aftertaste of ice cream on the back on my tongue. At last Pam said we should get off. We stepped on to a platform under the gaze of a girl on a poster wearing nothing but a shirt which only just covered the tops of her legs. 'Looks Even Better On a Man.'

Delbarco and Wilde had their office in a cobbled alleyway, between an antique shop and a pub called The Flying Fish. In the wall was a window like a glass case, with books in it. I recognised a book that I had at home, *The Pony Party* by Lucy Morecambe.

Lucy Morecambe might have stood where I was standing. She

might have walked into the entrance where Pam and I were now walking. We went up in a lift that was barred like a birdcage. It creaked and lurched and stopped in a shadowy corridor. The shadows were cast by bookcases. Bookcases were everywhere. Their shelves sagged like hammocks under their overflowing loads. More books were piled high on the floor, as if queueing up for their turn in the hammocks.

In reception, two girls sat on straight-backed chairs looking nervous. A young man was ignoring them as he put typed manuscripts into envelopes. When he saw Pam his face went bright in a way that was hard to describe. I had seen it before. People were always glad to see Pam, at least men were.

'Hello, stranger,' he said.

'Ferdy,' she replied warmly.

He looked at a list pinned to a clipboard. 'Your name's not down.'

'Eh?'

'She's interviewing for a new secretary today.'

Pam laughed and pretended to back away. 'Don't look at me. This is a social call.' She giggled. 'What happened to the old secretary or needn't I ask?' She put her hand over her mouth and winked at the girls sitting nervously on the chairs. 'Don't let me put you off. She's fine once you get used to her. Anyway, Ferdy, she's expecting me and Janet.'

'She didn't say anything to me.'

'Janet's an author,' said Pam.

'Pleased to meet you,' said Ferdy.

The girls on the seats stared and stared. One of them giggled. I didn't know why, but the moment seemed to freeze. Everyone was looking at me. Their look went on for ever. I squirmed inside. I was out of place. Pam had betrayed me. She didn't really think I was an author. She had brought me to this place so that people would laugh at me. I shouldn't be here. I was a child in a world of adults. I didn't know why I made the adults uneasy when I only wanted them to admire me. I didn't know if I were bad or good. I just knew I was funny.

'So she's forgotten we were coming.' Pam sounded irritated but not very surprised.

'Her diary's full,' said Ferdy.

'How about that, Janet?'

'It doesn't matter,' I said quickly. I had changed my mind about wanting to meet Miss Delbarco. She sounded rather frightening. Yet she had my manuscript. It was receiving her attention.

Pam was saying, 'She definitely said I could show Janet round the office.'

Ferdy shrugged. 'Go ahead.'

We walked through a door marked PRODUCTION into a long, light room. Like everywhere else, it was full of books, but this time they were shiny and new. A man with a bow-tie kissed Pam on both cheeks. Pam called him Roger. She said, 'This is my friend Janet. She wants to be an author. She is one.'

Instead of laughing, he looked as if he knew already. He looked as if he knew all about me. My spirits rose. Perhaps my book had already been published. Perhaps that was what 'receiving attention' meant. I glanced around in hope and fear, half expecting to see it.

He said, 'What kind of books do you like, Janet?'

'All kinds.'

'Any favourite authors?'

'You like Lucy Morecambe, don't you, Janet?'

'Yes.'

'That's lucky,' said Roger. 'She's got a new one coming out. Here, look.'

It was called *A Pony Alone*. The picture on the front showed a frail-looking pony in a swirling grey mist. 'I'll tell Lucy you're a fan. She'll be so pleased.' He knew her. He knew me too, now. He pointed at the book in my hand. 'Smell it.'

I thought he was teasing, so I hesitated. He snatched the book, opened it and buried his nose between its pages as if it were a bunch of flowers. 'That's the smell of a new book, I could get drunk on it.'

I breathed in the smell of paper and chemicals. I tried to hand the book back, but he said, 'Keep it. It's not published yet so don't let anyone see it unless they're a reviewer.' I agreed not to. I held the book tightly in my hands. It felt special and delicate, like a baby that had been born too soon and couldn't be allowed out yet, into the world and the open air.

27

We watched a copy editor at work. He was going through a manuscript, making marks for the printers and correcting the author's spelling mistakes. I pointed out one that he had missed, and he said, 'Thank you, Janet.'

We met an accounts clerk, a press officer and a sales representative who was on his way somewhere else. They all talked to me for a few moments, but I noticed Pam hurrying the conversations along as if she didn't want anyone to have their time wasted.

'That's about it,' she said as we made our way back to reception. The nervous girls had gone. 'I hope it's been interesting for you.'

'Yes, thank you, Pam.'

'It's a pity Her Ladyship couldn't – ' Pam stopped. A door had opened on to the corridor. We were being watched by a tall, distinguished-looking woman in a navy blue jersey dress. She was older than my parents, but not as old as my grandmothers. She looked distracted and rather angry, but when Pam said, 'Good morning, Miss Delbarco,' Miss Delbarco's expression changed to a sickly sweet smile with a glimmer of gold teeth.

She looked straight at me as she said, 'Thank goodness I caught you before you left.' I shivered with excitement. 'When they told me you were here,' she said, 'I thought, my prayers are answered. Why don't you come into my office for a few moments?' She beckoned. I followed. Pam came too.

It was like a cave full of books, some old, some new. A mist of dust rose from the books, with sunbeams dancing. Her desk was piled high with manuscripts. I couldn't see mine. It must be somewhere special. She said, 'When are you coming back to work for me again?'

I didn't understand. I began to say, 'I beg your – ' She lit a cigarette and looked past me at Pam. The smoke entered her voice, which seemed to be on the edge of coughing but she didn't cough. She said wistfully, 'It's been chaos since you left, Pam.'

'Doesn't look like it to me,' said Pam. 'We've had a fascinating morning, haven't we, Janet.'

'I wish I could say the same.' Miss Delbarco sighed and blew smoke.

'Roger was very good, he explained about galleys and page proofs, didn't he, Janet, and – ' Pam gave me an encouraging look and left the sentence for me to finish.

I wanted to speak. I wanted Miss Delbarco to speak to me. But she wasn't interested in me. She interrupted and carried on with what she had been saying before. 'On second thoughts, I suppose it was rather fascinating to see what turns up at interview these days, seriously expecting to be employed.' She seemed furious. 'Some of those girls couldn't even type, Pam. Never mind be of all-round assistance to me in the way you were. And as for their grammar, why can't they be like you? Your grammar's perfect, and you're not even English.'

'It's very nice of you to say so, Miss Delbarco.'

I didn't think she was nice. I thought she was rude. She seemed not to have noticed I was there. If she had, she probably thought I was just some child whom Pam had brought with her.

'I'll pay you more than you're getting now,' she said, and my heart fluttered, and went back to normal again.

'You're very generous, Miss Delbarco.'

'*Generous*.' Miss Delbarco scoffed through her smoke. 'Nothing to do with it. I *need* a secretary and I'll pay what you're worth.'

'I'm not looking for a permanent job at the moment.'

'Why not? You're wasted, temping.'

Pam smiled and said, 'Thanks,' but I could see she wasn't going to give in.

Miss Delbarco went on complaining. 'Not one of those girls this morning could name a single book we publish.'

'Janet could,' said Pam. 'She's a great admirer of Lucy Morecambe.'

Miss Delbarco glared at the book in my hand. 'So I see. Where did you get that?'

'Roger gave it to her.'

'Oh did he.'

'We won't take up any more of your time, Miss Delbarco.' Pam signalled that we were going but Miss Delbarco seemed suddenly to realise that one way of getting round Pam might be to suck up to me. She gave me a vague, fidgety smile and said gruffly, 'Is this the child who nearly got taken for a ride by Hawthorn?'

'Yes. This is Janet Toms.'

'Hullo, Janet.' She sounded as if she were trying to imitate Uncle Mac. 'Never pay for publication, dear. When the time comes, we pay you. If it comes.'

'Thank you, Miss Delbarco.'

She tinkled.

'Well,' said Pam, 'we'll be off.'

'But my book.' My voice cracked with the strain of trying to be polite, trying not to shout.

'What about it?'

'Are you going to publish it or not?'

'I don't know what you're talking about, dear.'

'I sent you my book. You sent me a card. You said it was receiving attention.'

'I did?'

I took the card out of my shoulder bag and showed it to her. She gave me a long, solemn look. She said, 'Excuse me just one moment.'

She left me and Pam alone in the office. Pam said, 'I didn't know you'd done that.'

'I wanted to.' I felt a sort of frenzy inside myself. I wanted to kick something, perhaps somebody.

Miss Delbarco came back carrying my manuscript and a loose sheet of paper with typing on it. 'Ferdy was just about to send it back to you. You've saved us the cost of a stamp.' She sounded as if she thought I would be pleased. She remembered she was supposed to be buttering me up. 'The reader had a lot of nice things to say.' She read from the loose sheet of paper. '"Although derivative in places, and, at 47 pages, an impossible length, *The Dungeon Beneath the School* is an imaginative story, skilfully written. The author has a good ear for dialogue, and constructs her story well. I would guess she is still quite young – about sixteen – and might produce something fairly interesting if left to mature." Praise indeed, dear!' said Miss Delbarco.

Was it? To me it sounded like J. M. Barrie's preface to *The Young Visiters*.

She said, 'Do you go to a boarding school?'

'No.'

'You seem to know a lot about it.' I knew about the good things from my mother, who was always saying what fun she had had. I had made up the bits about the dungeon. 'I expect you read a lot of school books,' said Miss Delbarco. 'That's what "derivative" means. Some of your ideas don't seem to come from you.'

'I didn't copy it.'

'I'm not saying you did. I'm sure our reader is right. In a few years, you're going to be a very interesting writer and I want you to send me your first novel.'

'It *is* my first novel.'

'Your first adult novel, dear. I shall read it. I promise.' She sighed. 'If I'm still alive, that is.' She gave Pam another of her sweet and wistful looks. 'Which I probably won't be if I don't find a decent secretary in the meantime.'

Pam and I had lunch at a Golden Egg and spent the afternoon at Madame Tussaud's. We looked at Kings and Queens, Famous Sportsmen and Figures from World Literature. Pam said, 'You'll be here one day, Janet.'

In the Chamber of Horrors we drew back the curtain that you weren't supposed to look behind unless you were over eighteen. A man was hanging with a hook through his stomach. The front of his white robe was caked brown with blood and bits of his guts. Pam went, 'ugh,' and I did too, but it didn't bother me all that much. It didn't seem nearly as real as the slot machines. By putting sixpence in the slot, you could set off a clockwork movement of wooden dolls which started with a judge pointing at a man in the dock, and ended with the man having his head cut off.

The slot machine gave me a queer feeling in my heart, as if I were responsible for the man's death. If I hadn't put my sixpence in the slot, the beheading would not have happened. The other man had the hook through his stomach whether I looked behind the curtain or not.

I thought I might write a novel about a girl in the olden days whose father is a judge. He has the power to sentence people to terrible deaths, but she pleads with him to let them off.

At five o'clock we went to Daddy's office so that he could take me home. Pam asked for him at reception. The receptionist said, 'What name is it?'

'It's his daughter,' said Pam. 'And her friend.'

The receptionist told us to take a seat and said into the phone, 'Would you tell Mr Toms his daughter is here? And her friend.'

We waited, reading *The Estates Gazette* and *Country Life*. After about five minutes he came towards us out of the lift, wearing his raincoat and carrying his trilby hat, his briefcase and his *Evening Standard*. He looked tired, important and slightly self-conscious, as if he were in a play.

The receptionist said, 'Good night, Mr Toms, sir,' and he said, 'Good night, Linda.'

He said to Pam, 'As you've had her all day, I suppose the least I can do is buy you a drink.'

Pam said, 'What's she supposed to do, sit on the pavement? Why don't you both come back to Earl's Court? We can have a drink there and something to eat.'

'The day of miracles is upon us,' he said. 'MacLeish offering hospitality.'

She poked out her tongue and laughed. 'Don't come then.'

'Oh please can we?' I begged. I hadn't seen Pam's latest flat. 'It's half term.'

'What's Mummy going to say?'

'She won't mind as long as we tell her.' It was something she always said. *I don't mind you being late as long as you TELL me.*

'You take the blame,' he said.

On the tube to Earl's Court we had to stand. Pam and Daddy hung on to straps in the ceiling. I couldn't reach the straps so they held my hands to keep me from falling over. I felt as if I were their child.

Pam's flat was in a basement. It had two rooms and a cooker in the hall. The wallpaper was dingy and there was a dampish, fatty, gassy smell, but once she had drawn the curtains and turned on the lamps, it felt quite cosy. Daddy put shillings in the meter and lit the gas.

He took off his coat, and took it and mine and Pam's into her bedroom. He hung them in the wardrobe. He opened a cupboard in the hall and took out a bottle of beer and two glasses. He seemed to know where everything was. I supposed he must have visited the flat when he was checking Pam's lease for her.

I said, 'Is there a phone?'

He said, 'Second landing,' and gave me fourpence.

I told Mummy we were having supper at Pam's, and she said she supposed it was all right but she would have appreciated a bit more notice. When I got back to the basement, Pam had undone her French pleat and brushed her hair. It fanned out, glowing in the lamplight. She had changed from her smart clothes into patched jeans, a green and black check shirt, a floppy green cardigan and bedroom slippers.

She was cooking sausages and mash on the cooker in the hall. Daddy was sitting astride a straight-backed chair, drinking beer and telling her a complicated story about somebody he had seen today. This was unusual for him. At home, when he came back from work in the evenings, it drove him mad to be asked what he had been doing. He said, 'Let a man unwind, for God's sake,' and wouldn't talk properly for at least an hour. In Earl's Court, he seemed to unwind more quickly.

28

Sister Dolours had a pile of snowy white envelopes. She said, 'Will my form captain and my vice captain give these out, please?'

Eva and I divided the pile. The envelopes were addressed to everybody's parents. Sister said, 'These must go straight home, unopened. Any girl who opens her own envelope will be in very serious trouble indeed.'

I put mine in the zip pocket of my satchel. As I walked in a group to the bus stop, my satchel tapped at my left ribs, then my right ribs. My heartbeat tapped back, faster.

Alison Jones held her envelope up towards a light patch in the grey sky. The envelope flapped in the wind. She pretended to read. 'Dear Mr and Mrs Jones, I am pleased to tell you that your daughter Alison got a hundred per cent in all her papers – '

It didn't sound funny to me. It was what I wanted my letter to say. I glanced across at Eva. I could tell she was thinking the same.

' – She is the most brilliant, the most genius – '

Everyone cheered, booed and laughed. Alison curtsied and blew kisses. She said, 'I'm going to open it. If I've passed, they're not going to change their minds just because I open it, are they?'

No one answered, and Alison said, 'I don't see why we shouldn't.'

She had changed *I* to *we*. If she got into trouble, she wanted others to get into it with her. I moved away, but not too far. I wanted to know what the letter looked like.

I never saw. She tore the corner of her envelope, pulled out a corner of her letter and peeped at what it said. She probably thought that if she didn't quite open the envelope, she wouldn't have quite read the letter. She went very pink. She didn't speak. She pushed the letter back into the envelope, as far as it would go. She pressed down the flap. She walked away from us. We looked at our shoes. When the bus came, we called, 'The bus, the bus, Alison!' but she went on walking.

Mummy opened my envelope and showed me the letter that said I had the offer of a free place in the senior school of the Convent of the Forty Martyrs. I could stay until the upper sixth.

'You clever girl!' She patted my back and kissed my cheek. 'I don't know where you get it from; certainly not from me.'

I said, 'Are you going to give me anything?'

'That's the wrong attitude.'

'Are you?'

'If we were, what would you like it to be?'

'Money, please.'

'What for?'

'Something.'

'Let's see what Daddy says.' She picked up the phone and got through to his secretary. 'Hello, Miss Graves, Jo Toms here. Oh. Is he somewhere I can contact him with some good news? All right, I'll ring him there.' She rang another number.

He would be so pleased. And I would be relieved. The uncertainty would be over. I still felt uncertain. I had held the letter in my hands, I had seen what it said. I had seen my mother's pleased smile and received her congratulations. But somehow the success was not quite real until Daddy knew about it. Once he knew, it would be definite. Once he knew, there could be no doubt.

'Good afternoon,' she said into the phone. 'I'd like to speak to a Mr Toms who's having a meeting with your Mr Perrin. Well, I think you'll find he is. Well, perhaps I could have a word with Mr Perrin anyway. Hello, Charles, this is Jo. Have you got the light of my life with you?' There was a silence. Mummy looked puzzled. She said, 'That's funny.'

He wasn't there. He didn't want to hear my news. Why should he want to hear it? It was ordinary. I had passed my eleven-plus. So had thousands of children, Alison Jones excluded. So what?

She said, 'His secretary seemed to think he was with you, Charles. I *see*!' She chuckled. 'We *have* caught him out. He'll have to arrange his alibis in advance another time. You and

Dorothy must come to dinner soon.' She put the phone down and her smile faded.

'What's an alibi?'

'It's a joke. Daddy must have made a mistake. We'll tell him when he gets home.'

I wanted to tell him now. I wanted to hold on to my achievement. I saw it in my mind as a silver cup that had glittered for a moment in my hands before being taken from me and fading into darkness. I had longed for this moment and worked for it and now it had come and gone. I could hardly remember a time when I hadn't passed my eleven-plus.

It was ordinary. Everyone had taken it for granted that I would pass. Perhaps even I had taken it for granted. Perhaps I had only pretended to be anxious. Perhaps the eleven-plus had been easy. Certainly my good result had been expected. It wasn't enough. It wasn't enough for me. I had to achieve something unexpected, I had to win a glittering and glorious prize that would stay bright in my hands forever.

He came in at about seven looking weary and despondent. He put his hat on the kitchen table. She said, 'I've just polished that table,' and picked the hat up again. 'Where were *you* this afternoon?'

He gave her a cool glance. 'What's it to you?'

'You weren't where your office said you were.'

His pale eyes narrowed in his tired grey face. His blond hair had turned dark with Vaseline hair tonic and dust from the city. I wanted to wash all that dirt down the plug hole and feel his hair come up smooth and silky clean beneath my fingers.

He stamped past her. She sighed and called after him, 'Don't make an issue of it.'

'You're the one who's – '

'Charlie Perrin and I thought it was rather funny, that was all.' She laughed to show how funny she and Mr Perrin had thought it was. 'You'd used him as an alibi without telling him.'

'Alibi? Who's on trial? On what charge?'

'Take a joke. Don't be such an old cross-patch. Janet, tell Daddy your news.'

'I've passed my eleven-plus.'

His irritability disappeared. He put out his arms and held me close to his big chest. He cheered and danced me round the kitchen. 'What a brilliant lot we Toms's are.'

'Watch out,' said Mummy. 'She's expecting a payoff.'

'Of course she's getting a payoff. She'll be saving me a fortune. I'm going to get her a typewriter. That's what she needs if she's going to be an authoress.'

Mummy said, 'What a good idea.'

'We'll ask MacLeish to help us choose. If a shorthand typist can't tell a good typewriter from a bad, I don't know who can.'

Mummy seemed to think our cuddle was going on too long. It was her turn. She came up behind him, put her head on his shoulder and said in a wheedling voice, 'Tell us where you were this afternoon.'

'Where do you think? Go on, give me a laugh. Tell me how you think I spend my days.'

'I expect you were in the back of a car somewhere with a beautiful blonde.'

'I was in the front of a car with a halitosis-ridden oik with a Hitler complex.'

'Oh, a *driving lesson*.'

'A test. I didn't tell anyone because I got precious little sympathy last time.'

'But you passed this time?'

'Not according to Goebbels.'

He failed, I thought. *But I passed*. I felt guilty.

He threw a piece of paper onto the table. Mummy read it with eagerness, which I thought was unkind of her. He said, 'That bears no relation to what I actually did. He should count himself lucky I'm too busy to sue.'

She put down the paper. 'A few more lessons and you'll do it.'

'I don't need any more lessons,' said Daddy. 'I need practice.'

'I suppose we'd better ask Pam to come for the weekend soon.'

He sighed. 'I suppose we had.'

29

It was the weekend of the end-of-season party at the rugby club. This was a chance for players to say goodbye to each other for the summer, and to thank the wives for all the work they had done behind the scenes.

From early Saturday morning, Mummy was busy with preparations. We didn't get any breakfast because every available space in the kitchen was covered with flans and sandwiches, iced cakes, puddings, sausage rolls and *vol-au-vent* shells. She said, 'There's no need for breakfast.'

Christine stormed out of the house. She said she was going to El Toreador, which was the name of the restaurant where Miguel worked. 'They'll give me breakfast,' she said, 'even if my own mother won't.'

Pam said, 'What can we do to help you, Jo?'

'Nothing that I can think of, off-hand.'

Daddy said, 'She's impossible to help.'

'Hard though he tries, eh, Jo?' said Pam.

'Hard though he tries. He's quite right. I am impossible.'

'But look what you're doing for his bloody club!'

'If the end of the rugby season isn't worth celebrating, I don't know what is.'

Daddy said, 'Are you girls going to natter all morning, or do I get a driving lesson?'

He and Pam and I walked round to the house of the neighbour who lent us the car. He and the neighbour chatted while Pam and I tied on the L-plates.

I got into the back of the car, Daddy got into the driving seat and Pam sat next to him. I moved over to be behind her. She was wearing a soft fawn jumper. Her clean white neck rose out of its cuddly polo collar. Her bunches bobbed about as she moved her head.

I sniffed a sweet peachiness in the air. It was the smell of her shampoo, from a herbal shop in Earl's Court. She had once let me massage her scalp with it, and use it on my own hair. My mouth watered. I pretended she and Daddy were my parents, and enjoyed the peacefulness of being with them.

I knew not to say anything during the driving lesson. She didn't say much either, apart from, 'Good.' She obviously thought he was getting better. She said 'good' so many times that he turned to her while he was waiting at traffic lights and said, 'Are you taking the piss?'

'No, honestly. My money's on you passing next time.'

'How much money?'

'Perhaps not my entire fortune.' She nodded towards the lights, which had changed. 'Green means you can go.'

He drove us out to the by-pass and we had bacon, eggs, beans and chips at a lorry drivers' pull-in. The tables were dirty, and he said, 'Not a vitamin in sight. Don't tell your mother, for gawd's sake.'

After we had had our breakfast he drove us to Bleswick Office Supplies to choose a typewriter. I liked one in the window. It was neat and trim with gleaming silvery fittings and pale grey keys. It had a red and black ribbon and its own carrying case.

We went into the shop and Daddy asked the assistant to show it to us. The assistant fetched another one in a box. Daddy read the box and said, 'I wouldn't trust anything made by the Japs.'

Pam rolled her eyes and winked at me. She gave the assistant a look that said, *Take no notice. I'll deal with him.* 'As portables go,' she said, 'these are fairly good machines.'

'What do you mean, "as portables go"?'

'I'll show you.' Pam asked the assistant for a piece of paper. She rolled it into the typewriter, pulled up a chair and typed. *The quick brown fox jumps* – Her short strong fingers sped across the keys. Her clean pink and white nails were shiny with clear varnish. Soon they were moving too fast for me to see them. – *The lazy dog. Now is the time for all good men to come to the aid* – The letters changed from black to red. *Janet Toms is going to be a famous authoress . . .* She slowed down. The keys were like dancers, each one backing away to let the next one step forward. *And I will say I knew here when she was young.*

'Feels OK,' she said. 'But look what's happened.' Under the force of her fingers, the typewriter had slipped to the edge of the counter. 'It's going to be in my lap in a minute.'

'We can supply rubber mats, madam,' said the assistant.

Daddy made a scornful sound. 'What do you think we are, bedwetters? I think what's needed is a more substantial machine. What have you got that's made in England?'

'Well, sir – '

'Where they're made isn't the point. The point is what kind of machine would be best for Janet. Did you particularly want a portable, lovey? Mightn't an office machine be better?'

I didn't know. It hadn't been my idea to have a typewriter in the first place. I wanted money.

Daddy strode into the second-hand department and called back to the assistant, 'How about this Imperial?'

'Yes, sir. I'll get it down for you.' A great deal of huffing and puffing followed. In the meantime, Pam sat me in front of the little silver-grey portable and said, 'Try it.'

'Can I?'

'Course you can. It's for you.'

I tried to type J but it came out as j. Pam showed me how to use the shift key and I wrote JANET TOMS. I did it as gently as I could so that the typewriter wouldn't prove itself unsuitable for me by slipping about. Suitable or not, it was the one I wanted.

The assistant staggered towards us with the Imperial. It was black and greasy-looking, like a hunk of machinery on the floor of a garage. Above its long roller, the assistant's face was red and straining. Daddy cried, 'Mind your backs!'

I got up from my chair in alarm. For a terrible moment I thought the assistant was going to dump the Imperial down on top of my portable because he couldn't see it and couldn't bear the weight. Pam moved the portable out of the way just in time.

The Imperial had a royal crest on it, with the lion and the unicorn. *Manufactured by the Imperial Typewriter Company, Leicester, England.* 'This,' said Daddy, 'is what I *call* a typewriter.'

Pam said to me, 'You know how much I hate to agree with a word your dad says, but this one might be a better bet.' She put paper into the Imperial. 'Try it.'

I typed angrily with my index fingers. JANET FORBES MONTMORENCY.

'Who's Janet Forbes Montmorency?'

'Nobody.' It was a name I felt like writing. I didn't want to write my own name on the second-hand Imperial. I felt stupid.

'You won't damage that one,' said Pam.

'I wouldn't damage the other one.'

'Not on purpose, but if you only use two fingers you hit much harder than if you touch-type. With the portable, you'd always be chasing it round the room.'

Daddy asked the assistant whether the second-hand machine had a guarantee. The assistant said no, and for a moment I thought I was going to get the portable after all because Daddy was very particular about things like guarantees. But the assistant went on, 'No guarantee if you take it as it is, sir, but if you'd like us to overhaul and recondition it for you it'll be guaranteed for twelve months, parts and labour.'

'How long would that take?'

'Twenty-one days.'

'Sounds fair enough.' He raised an eyebrow at Pam. 'What's the expert's opinion?'

Pam shrugged. 'I think Janet still wants the portable.'

'Doesn't know what she's talking about.'

'It's her present.'

Daddy said to me, 'What Pam doesn't know about typewriters isn't worth knowing. And I'm not completely ignorant on the subject myself. But it's up to you. Which is it to be?'

'I'll have the Imperial.'

'Well, look a bit cheerful about it!' he commanded.

The assistant gave him some papers to sign. He read them first, with suspicion in his eyes. The assistant said, 'What name?'

'Toms'.

The assistant wrote 'Mr Toms' on a label and started to tie it to the typewriter.

'It's Janet Toms,' said Pam. 'It's hers.'

The assistant said, 'Sorry, Mrs Toms,' and wrote another label.

30

It was getting dark when we reached the club house. Daddy parked the car as close as he could so that we wouldn't have to wade through an ocean of mud in our party shoes. He fetched a couple of planks to make a causeway, and Mummy, Pam and I walked along it with trays of food.

The club house looked like a huge garden shed. Daddy opened the door and waved us inside.

'Wo – ho!' cried a man. 'Why does Toms get all the most beautiful women?'

Daddy beamed. The man took a chicken *vol-au-vent* off Mummy's tray, swallowed it whole and said, 'They can cook as well.' Daddy said, 'Pipe down,' and the two men went to the bar.

In the main club room a three-piece band was setting up its instruments. Their name was on their drums: Lennie and the Linesmen. A man on a step-ladder was arranging balloons round a portrait of the club's founder. A woman was pinning up clues for a treasure hunt.

Mummy led the way to the kitchen. It was about a quarter of the size of our kitchen at home, and it was full of wives unloading trays of food. They exclaimed over ours.

'Jo, you put us to shame!'

'You *have* pushed the boat out!'

'Abandon diet ye who enter here.'

'*You* don't need to diet.'

'Have you ever thought of taking it up professionally?'

Mummy said, 'What can we do to help?'

I didn't like the sound of 'we', and Pam looked as if she didn't either. We went to the Ladies.

The lavatory was an Elsan bucket and we agreed to put off using it for as long as possible. We hung up our coats and Pam brushed my hair, which I was wearing loose with an Alice band.

The band was white to match my socks and the smocking on the front of my lemon yellow dress.

'Your hair's so long now, Janet. And you're getting to be so pretty.'

'Honourable Heart?'

'What, lovey?'

The moment had passed and I didn't say it again. I couldn't bear to. I didn't want to risk her answer. Who was I to get compliments from her? Who was I to fish to have them repeated? She would cut me down and I would deserve it.

She looked gorgeous. She had a slinky black evening dress on, with chiffon sleeves and a silver brooch. Her nylons were sheer, her heels were high and her hair was loose. She had just washed it and it fluffed out round her head. It was thick and glowing. I could imagine how it would feel if I plunged my fingers into it. It would be warm and living, like sand on a beach at the end of a sunny day.

She dabbed perfume behind my ears and on to my wrists. She took a little ball of cotton wool out of her handbag, soaked it in perfume and tucked it down the front of her dress and brassiere. She straighted the seams of her stockings and we went to look for Daddy.

The bar was foggy with smoke and packed with drinkers, mostly men in blazers or sports jackets and jerseys, tipping pints of beer down their throats and making 'Wo – ho!' noises. I knew a few of the Bleswick players but there were a lot of visitors as well, from other rugby clubs.

Daddy's friend Bixwell wolf-whistled at Pam and said, 'Where's the rest of the family, Toms?'

'Christine's out doing God knows what with her Dago waiter.'

'And the little one? Janet?'

'Janet's here.'

Bixwell beamed over the long slope of his grey-jerseyed stomach. 'This isn't Janet! This gorgeous grown-up glamour-pants isn't Janet! Janet's a little girl with plaits for me to pull!' He kissed my cheek and laughed. 'Wo – ho!'

Daddy said, 'I suppose you're expecting me to buy you a drink, MacLeish?'

Bixwell said, 'If he won't, I will.'

Mummy appeared out of nowhere in her flowery cotton frock and tapped me on the shoulder. 'Oy. Out of the bar.' She glared at Daddy. 'You're completely irresponsible. I'd have thought you'd worry about losing your license, if nothing else.'

'Don't be hard on him, Jo,' said Bixwell. 'He's a good boy really. Come here . . .' He gave her a hug. 'There's nothing I like more than a woman with a bit of flesh on her.'

'You can talk!' She didn't like Bixwell. She thought he led Daddy astray. She always referred to his wife as poor, unfortunate Lindsay.

Bixwell stroked his stomach with pride. 'It's all best bitter,' he said. 'What's yours, another little tadpole?'

Before my mother could reply, a stranger came pushing through the crowd. 'Pammie MacLeish!' he shouted. He was tall and had a very short crew-cut. He wore flannel trousers and a blazer with a crest on the pocket. 'Pammie, it is you, isn't it?'

At first Pam look puzzled. But then she gasped and smiled and said, 'Rusty!'

Rusty made a whooping sound. He picked Pam up and whirled her about. People stepped out of the way of her flying spiky heels.

'Put me down, you bloody fool!' She had her arms round his neck and was laughing.

'What are you doing in this godforsaken country?'

'Saving up to leave, mate. What about you?'

Everyone was laughing, apart from Daddy, whose eyes had gone narrow. 'I don't know who you are but you heard what she said. Put her down and get your hands off her.'

Everyone seemed to freeze. Slowly, Rusty set Pam on her feet. He turned his back on Daddy and said, 'Didn't hurt you, did I?'

'Only gave me the shock of my life. Let me introduce my friends. Jo Toms, Bixwell, Janet Toms, and the one with the bad manners is Sandringham, as in the Queen spent Christmas at. He's Jo's husband.' She said this firmly, and Daddy looked sheepish. 'This is Richard Nayle, my next-door neighbour from back home. Known to friend and foe alike as Rusty.'

Rusty said, 'We were childhood sweethearts. Practically engaged, then she ran away.'

'We were not.'

'Not for want of trying, eh, Rusty? Wo – ho!'

Mummy couldn't believe it. 'Did you say "next-door neighbours"?'

'"Next door" doesn't mean quite the same in New Zealand as it does here,' said Rusty.

'Seventeen or eighteen miles,' said Pam.

'Even so,' said Mummy, beaming broadly as if Rusty were her long-lost friend rather than Pam's. 'What a small world.'

Rusty said he had been in England for four months. He had known Pam was here somewhere but he hadn't got around to looking her up yet. He had joined a rugby club called the London Exiles. He had seen a notice advertising the Bleswick party and decided to come along. He was obviously glad he had, and so was Pam.

My mother seemed gladdest of all, she was cock-a-hoop, but that didn't stop her shooing me out of the bar and into the main club room for the treasure hunt and other games. I won a box of New Berry Fruits, a set of hair slides and a book token for ten shillings.

I took the prizes to the kitchen and gave them to Mummy to look after. One of the other wives looked rather disgusted because her child hadn't won anything.

The dancing began. Rusty brought Pam from the bar and they waltzed. Even in her high heels, she was tiny compared with him. I noticed the bend in her back that Daddy was always teasing her about, saying it came from her trying to do manly things like carrying her own rucksack. Now it added to her look of romance because she leaned forward on to Rusty's chest as if she were terribly tired. He supported her. She looked up into his brown eyes and long handsome face. He whispered into her hair and they smiled at some secret. I thought it was probably something to do with New Zealand, that faraway place that belonged to them and that I would never see and couldn't imagine.

I wondered if it were true about them being childhood sweethearts. I had never had a sweetheart. I was too serious.

In the bar the men were singing.

Caviar comes from a virgin sturgeon
Virgin sturgeon's a very fine fish –

I blocked the song out with the gentle music of the waltz. Pam and Rusty looked as romantic as film stars.

Virgin sturgeon needs no urgin'
That's why caviar's my favourite dish!

I felt like crying. It was a frightening feeling because I didn't know why I was so sad. I sat on a chair on the edge of the dance floor and stared at my lap. My hands fidgeted and plucked at the skirt of my dress.

He had loved her and lost her and found her again. He towered over her and held her close. He steered her gently in the dance. He would look after her. He would never let her go.

I had not thought of Pam as a person who needed to be looked after. I had thought she could look after herself, but perhaps she couldn't. Perhaps everybody needed somebody to look after them. In Rusty's arms she looked so little and happy and safe. He would carry her off. I thought it would serve us right for not looking after her better ourselves, when we had her in our family.

Lennie said, 'Take your partners for the fox trot.' The Linesmen struck up a new tune.

Mummy went to the bar and dragged Daddy out by his tie. He leaned back like a dog not wanting to be taken for a walk, and the men cried, 'Put him through his paces, Jo! Wo – ho!'

His hair was falling into his eyes, which had a clownish expression. He stepped on Mummy's feet. He pretended to fall over. Pam and Rusty and other dancing couples laughed at his antics, and moved off in the opposite direction.

Mummy looked as if she wanted to dance properly. She muttered angrily, 'You might at least try.'

A man with slicked-back hair and a shiny suit tapped Daddy on the shoulder, bowed to Mummy and asked her to dance. Daddy walked away, pretending to cry until he realised no one was looking.

In the bar the men sang:

We come from good schools, good girls are we
All of us keep our virginity –

He came towards me, swaying on his feet. His words ran together. ''njoying y'self, young Janet?' He was pretending to be drunk. I laughed. 'Yes, thank you.'

Our head prefect, her name is Jane
She only likes it now and again
And again and again and again and again and again –

He chuckled. 'Hope you're not listening to this.'
'No.'
'Wanna drink?'
'No, no thank you, will you dance with me?'
'I can't dance.' He did a few clumsy steps to prove it. 'Seriously, Janet. Would you say your old father was a talented dancer? He's brilliant at most things, but dancing? Sherioushly.' Pam and Rusty danced into sight, laughing at him. 'Only ponces dance. Look at that ponce dancing with – ' He stopped himself. 'Dancing with your mother.'
'*Please* dance with me!' I put my arms around him and my feet on top of his feet. We danced a few steps with his feet lifting mine.
Bixwell tapped him on the shoulder. 'Don't keep your beautiful daughter to yourself, Toms.' Daddy handed me over. Bixwell pressed me close to the scratchy grey wool of his jersey.
Daddy approached Pam and Rusty. He crept up behind Rusty as if he meant to tap him on the shoulder. Before he could do it, the fox trot music stopped and everybody clapped. Rusty gave Pam a quick kiss on the lips. Daddy went back to the bar.

31

He stayed in the bar for the rest of the evening. He didn't even come out for the Last Waltz.

Mummy danced the Last Waltz with the man in the shiny suit, Pam danced it with Rusty and I danced it with the rather stupid boy who had come second in the treasure hunt.

'Thank you very much, ladies and gentlemen,' said Lennie. 'Safe journey home.'

People got their coats, or stood around talking. There was a final burst of singing from the bar. Daddy came out clutching a half-full glass of beer. His hair was still falling in his eyes. Mummy tried to brush it back for him, but he dashed her hand away.

She nodded towards me and said brightly, 'I think it's somebody's bedtime.'

He looked puzzled, as if he had forgotten who we were. He focussed his eyes on the other end of the room, where Pam was chatting with Rusty and his friends. 'Look at her, flaunting her body among the kiwis. It breaks my heart to tell her she's going to have to drive us home.'

'*You* tell her it's time to go, Janet,' said Mummy, pushing me forward, trying to hold Daddy back. I hesitated on the edge of Pam's group and listened to the voices of her new friends. They spoke with a strange, slow, flat accent. I noticed for the first time that Pam had traces of it.

'Janet. How are you doing, lovey? You know Rusty. This is Keith and Rose and . . . sorry, everyone. I've forgotten your names.'

'Daddy says we're going home.'

Rusty looked as if he couldn't understand why Pam had to go home when my father told her to. He said, 'But you're coming to the party, Pammie.'

'Love to, but I'm staying at Janet's parents' and I'm the chauffeur.'

Daddy arrived, saying, 'Let's be having you, MacLeish. Bags and 'ammicks.'

'She wants to go to another party,' I told Mummy, who cried, 'Another party? With Rusty? Of course she must go!'

'"Of course she must go!"' Daddy imitated her. 'Of course she must go to the ball! Nymphs and shepherds! How do *we* get home? Walk? Or do I drive?'

'Certainly not. We'll call a taxi.'

'Fantastic,' said Daddy. 'Fan bloody tastic.'

Pam hesitated. I could tell that she wanted to go to the party, but she also wanted to be well-mannered. 'There's no need, Jo,' she said. 'I can miss the party.'

'But I don't want you to miss it! I want you to go! I insist.'

'"I want you to go,"' Daddy sneered. '"I insist."'

Pam gave him a cool look and turned away. She said to my mother, 'Is there someone else who'll drive you?'

'Lots of people! Lindsay Bixwell will. Janet, go and get Pam's coat. Stay as late as you like, Pam. Here's a key.'

'Give her a key, that's what all good hotels do.' Daddy drank more beer. 'Easy come, easy go.'

I fetched Pam's coat. The club house was emptying. Pam, Rusty and their friends were moving towards the door. Mummy was pushing them. 'Off you go! Enjoy yourselves!'

Pam said, 'I'll try not to wake you when I come in.'

'That's very considerate of you,' bellowed Daddy. 'Con bloody siderate.'

Bixwell was staggering out to the car-park, singing and waving, leaning on his wife. Mummy looked around for someone else she knew but they had all gone. She went to the call box in the corner of the club house. Daddy said, 'What is that woman doing now?'

'Calling a taxi.'

'Must be wonderful to spend money without having to earn it. I can drive home.' We went out to the car-park and he started to untie the L-plates.

Mummy galloped towards us, shouting. 'You can't, you can't!'

Daddy opened the door of the car. 'Get in, Janet.'

I sat in the cold darkness of the back seat, holding the L-plates and listening to their argument.

'You failed your test!'

'On a technicality.'

'This is irresponsible!'

'I'm *responsible* for that car! I'm not leaving it here for the night!'

'You're in no state to drive!'

'Oh the poor put-upon wife with the alcoholic husband! Why don't you and poor unfortunate Lindsay get together and write to Evelyn Home about it?' Daddy got into the driver's seat and started the engine. 'Are you getting in or not?'

Mummy said sulkily, 'Our trays and things are still in the kitchen.'

'Go and get them then.'

'Come and help me! It's your bloody club!'

'*Go and get them.*'

I said, 'I'll get them.'

'You'll stay there.' He looked over his shoulder as if he were a kidnapper and I were his victim.

We waited. Cars left the car-park, one by one. Daddy leaned his forehead on the steering wheel. By the time Mummy came with the trays, he was asleep.

'Sandy – ' her voice was full of fear and anger but she was forcing it to sound gentle. 'The taxi's coming.' She reached for the ignition key.

He took her hand and grunted, 'You drive, darling.'

'I can't.'

He opened his eyes. 'What? Oh no.'

'*Please* let's wait for the taxi.'

'You don't need my permission to throw my money away. Wait for whatever you like. *I'm* driving home.'

She got in. He drove slowly, making wide semicircles round parked cars. He went straight across a red light and Mummy drew breath through her teeth, making a loud *fffssst* sound.

'*Ffffssst!*' he mimicked.

She said, 'I'm going to have to learn to drive.'

'You do that before you start telling me how to.'

'I hope for your sake the police don't see us.'

'Liar. You'd love it.'

'Do keep your eyes on the road.'

Our house was dark. Daddy said, 'What the hell time does Christine call this?'

'She's probably in bed.'

'She probably is, but when's she coming home?'

'Be quiet in front of Janet.'

We opened the front door. I was relieved to be home and I rushed up to Christine's room. I didn't usually worry or even care where she was, but for some reason on this particular night I was anxious.

From the landing, I said, 'She's not here.'

Daddy flopped in the hall chair. 'Little whore.'

'*Sandringham*!'

'What's a whore?'

'Daddy's being silly. What time is it?'

'It's practically midnight. She's supposed to be in by eleven, as she well knows.'

'We weren't in by eleven,' said Mummy.

'These girls are running wild and you never back me up.'

I felt like pointing out that I wasn't running wild, but the front door opened and in came Christine. She unbuttoned her raincoat, flopped cheerfully down on the bottom stair and said in a funny voice, 'My feet are killing me.'

Daddy glared. 'Where is he?'

'Who?'

'The Dago.'

'His name's Miguel, actually.'

'And doesn't Meegwell-Actually have the decency to bring you home? Does he leave you to walk the streets like the streetwalker you are?'

'What?' Christine sounded bewildered.

Mummy said, 'Have you had a nice evening?'

'Until I got home. Why's he in such a horrible mood?'

'Where did you go? Anywhere nice?'

'We didn't go anywhere. I helped in the restaurant.'

'Well, I wish you'd help at home more.'

'I knew you'd say that.'

'*Don't cheek your mother!*' Daddy shouted so loudly that I ran round the bend of the staircase. I sat on the landing, out of sight in the darkness. I went on listening. '*Unless you want to be thumped!*'

'I didn't cheek her. Why do you always pick on me?'

'Tell your Dago boyfriend that in England it's customary to bring a girl home after – '

'He did bring me home, he borrowed the manager's car. I didn't ask him in because I knew you'd be drunk – '

'Oh we are a grown-up little girl, aren't we?'

'And I was right!'

She wasn't right. She wasn't. I clenched my fists. I wanted to run downstairs and punch her, knock sense into her head, make her understand that he was only pretending to be drunk. I wanted to knock a sense of humour into her, and then she would realise he was joking. There had been lots of drunk men at the rugby club, and he was imitating them, as a joke.

He said, 'Watch your mouth, little girl, or you know what you'll get.'

Mummy said, 'Stop this, both of you!'

'Both of us? He started it.' How could she say, *He started it*? That was what quarrelling children said. Didn't she realise he was her father? Our father. 'Did you hear what he called me?'

'He was only joking.'

Christine made a howling sound. 'I'm not staying here!'

'I don't know where you think you're going.'

'Anywhere as long as it's away from that drunken sod – '

'You asked for it,' he said. I heard a blow fall. I waited for the next. She was getting her beating. She was getting what she deserved. She was nothing to do with me. Yet I winced with pain and shook with fear.

Her pain and fear were nothing to do with me, nothing. I left them in the darkness on the landing. I ran to my room and put the light on.

Downstairs the front door opened.

Mummy shouted, 'You're not going out again, Christine! Come back here, you're not hurt.'

The house shook as the front door slammed.

I slammed my own door and leaned on it. My breath came quickly.

The house felt safer with Christine gone. I looked at my neat bed and my collections. My foreign dolls were grouped together by continent. My horses grazed in descending order of size. My stones, my birds' eggs and my butterflies were labelled.

My writings, published and unpublished, were in cereal boxes. *Novel in Progress 1. The Judge's Daughter. Novel in Progress 2. On the Shelf. Poems. Short Stories. School Mag. Elizabethan.*

The books in my bookcase were arranged alphabetically by author. I could find whatever I wanted. On the wall were my certificates of merit. No one had ever given Christine a certificate of merit for anything.

Downstairs, the front door opened.

I opened my own door a crack.

My mother was saying, 'You go after her. You're her father.'

Christine

32

I made for the T-junction at the end of our road. My feet hurt so I took off my shoes and carried them. I half ran, half hobbled.

I turned right along the trunk road. The air was orangy-yellow from the new neon street lamps. I followed signs for London and London Airport. The sides of my raincoat flapped like wings.

Panting breaths scraped across my tongue. My mouth tasted dry and sour. My nose was running. Bits of grit from the pavement ground holes in my nylons and burrowed up into the soft flesh of my feet. With each step they dug deeper.

A car overtook me. It slowed down and stopped. It waited with its engine running. The driver leered at me. He opened the passenger door. He beckoned. I dodged down a dark side street called Cambridge Avenue. It had tall trees and old fashioned lamp posts. The houses were detached, with wide gardens and long drives.

I hid in the shadow of a tree and watched the car. It revved its engine and sped away, hooting. The hoot hung in the air like a sneer, the sneer of my father saying *Dago*.

I leaned against the tree to get my breath back. I wiped my runny nose, which left a glossy dark smear on the back of my hand. I stared at the smear. I was fascinated. I wanted a closer look. I walked a few steps towards the nearest lamp post. Under its light the smear turned red and another blob trickled out of my nose and down my top lip.

The night began to spin.

Somehow I got myself into a garden. The windows of the house were blank and dark but there must be somebody who would look after me.

I slumped next to a privet hedge and put my head into the darkness between my knees to escape the dizzying white light that told me I was going to faint. More blood dropped out of my nose. I tasted the memory of his hand lashing across my face.

Upsie daisy!

I put my head back. The blood went down my throat.

Ninety-nine per cent of nosebleeds are caused by nose picking!

I leaned against the hedge. Between its leaves I saw the slow moving, wobbly light of a bicycle with a policeman on it. The hedge swayed under my weight but it held me. I closed my eyes.

Time passed. I opened them again. It was still dark. The inside of my nose felt solid and prickly. Drops of blood had caked on the front of my blouse. I buttoned up my raincoat, covering the mess.

I groped around for my shoes and put them on. I licked my hanky and wiped my face. I went on wiping until the hanky came away clean. I didn't feel clean. I felt foul, and cold to my bones. I combed my hair with my fingers and made my way back to the main road. I longed to turn left and go home to bed but I turned right.

The filling station was closed but the red Mobilgas horses on the tops of the petrol pumps glowed out a kind of welcome. There were slot machines with cigarettes, chewing gum and chocolate. Another one offered five different kinds of hot soup at sixpence a cup. I had never heard of such a machine. It was probably American. I wished I had sixpence. I didn't want soup particularly, I just wanted to try out the machine.

I looked on the ground in case anyone had lost any money. I felt a tickle deep in my nose and lifted my head up. A voice said, 'You're out late.' A policeman was watching me. He must have ridden across the forecourt from the road. He sat on his bike with his feet flat on the ground.

I said, 'I'm not doing anything.'

'What *are* you doing?'

'Trying to get some soup.'

'Can't you get soup at home?'

I imagined opening my raincoat and showing the drops of blood on the front of my blouse and saying, *That's what I get at home.*

'Not the kind I like.' I wiggled the Coin Reject button. 'It's taken my money, can you arrest it?'

'What's your name?'

'Do I have to tell you?'

'I'm trying to be friendly,' he said. 'And friends do generally know each other's names. I'm PC Tutsworth. And you're – ?'

He waited. So did I. He hadn't said I *had* to tell him my name. He'd dodged that question. I thought about a girl at school who said, *Once they've got your name, they always remember it.* She knew. She would know. She came from a family that was always in trouble with the police. But the Toms's weren't that kind of family.

He got off his bike and leaned the saddle against the side of his leg. I thought he was quite young and handsome. It was hard to tell because he had his helmet on and I didn't dare look too closely at his face in case he looked at mine and it still had blood on it.

'I've got to call you something,' he said. 'Give me a made-up name.'

'Chris.'

'I'm not sure I won't have some of that soup myself, Chris. Nice, is it?'

'Don't know.'

He took a handful of change from his pocket and sorted out two sixpences. 'What kind d'you want?'

'Spring vegetable.'

'I'll have tomato. Would you hold my bike?'

I wondered what he would do if I rode away on it. I wondered how far I would get.

As he bent towards the machine, light shone in his face. He *was* young. His eyebrows were blond. If it weren't for his uniform, anyone seeing us might think we were on a date. We could have been to the pictures together and he could be buying me a cup of soup before seeing me home.

The soup machine made complicated sounding noises inside itself, but he seemed quite at home with it. This depressed me because I realised he had probably used it before. He probably came here every night, to arrest girls. He handed me a steaming paper cup and took a gulp from his own. He spluttered and gasped and spat on the ground. 'It's hot!'

I read out what it said on the machine. '"Hot soup."'

'Remind me not to come to you next time I want sympathy.' He blew into his cup. 'When we've had our soup, would you like to come down to the station with me?'

'I haven't done anything.'

'I never said you had. But we've got a nice lady officer down there who you might like to have a chat with.'

'What about?'

'Whatever it is that's brought you out on your own at this time of night. Row with Mum and Dad, was it?'

I put my face into my soup cup. If he wanted to take that as a nod, he could.

'What about? Staying out late?'

He thought he was so clever. I wondered whether all the teenagers in Bleswick came here when they had rows with their parents about staying out late. I wondered whether the police had put the soup machine there themselves, to attract us, like a wasp trap.

He said soothingly, 'You haven't given me any reason to take you in if you don't want to come. You can go straight home if you prefer.'

I finished my soup and started walking.

He came after me, pushing his bike. 'The police station's that way.'

'I'm going home.'

'I'll follow you.'

'What for?'

'I want to be sure you get home safe.'

You mean you don't believe me. You think I won't go home. You think I tell lies.

'I'll keep my distance,' he said. 'You don't seem to me to come from the sort of family where they expect to have their daughters brought home by the police, and I don't want to make things worse for you.'

All I had to do was open my jacket and show him the blood. But I didn't, because I didn't know what would happen next.

I thought I would end up telling him the whole story as we walked together to the police station, and telling it again to the lady officer when we got there. Somebody would probably write it down, but when I tried to imagine what would happen after that my mind went blank.

Would my father be arrested? Would there be a trial? Would he be fined or sent to prison? Would I like that?

Would it be in the papers? Would I have to talk to someone from the National Society for the Prevention of Cruelty to Children? Was I a Child? Was it Cruelty? In our family we didn't know the answers to this sort of question.

PC Tutsworth said, 'If anyone bothers you, I won't be far behind. I'll see you safe to your door.'

33

I went round the back. The kitchen light was on. My mother sat at the table in her dressing gown. She ought to be distraught, wringing her hands, but she was polishing a brass candlestick with Duraglit wadding and reading *The Housewife's Guide to Successful Home Management.*

She had a pot of tea on the go and she had been at the bread bin. There was a half eaten folded-over marmalade sandwich on a plate. She tried to hide it but gave up when she realised I had already seen. She said with satisfaction, 'We're quits.'

'What?'

'You don't say anything about this – ' she nodded at the sandwich – 'and I won't ask where you've been.'

She made it sound as if I had got in a few minutes late from school. Was she mad, or pretending, or was she simply not giving me the satisfaction of knowing that she had been worried? Perhaps she hadn't been. Her face looked calm and scrubbed and ready for bed. Her brown hair was brushed back, her teeth were clean. Her brisk expression gave no hint that polishing brass wasn't her normal 3.00 am activity. Perhaps it was. I said, 'Where is he?'

'Who?'

'The thug.'

She laughed. 'Daddy's in bed, if that's who you mean. Where I'd like to be. Look at your stockings!'

We looked at my stockings. I said, 'Will you tell him never to hit me again?'

'He didn't hit you. Do you want a cup of tea before you go to bed?'

I pulled out a chair and slumped against its hard back. I ached all over. 'I want a bath.'

'You'll wake Daddy.'

'I've got to wash my feet.'

'Do them down here.' She spread newspaper on the lino. She tipped the washing up out of the washing-up bowl and filled it with hot water. She set it down on the newspaper.

I peeled and picked off what was left of my nylons. I lifted the heavy black lid of the boiler and put the bits in among the dead looking coals. She said, 'I'd rather you didn't put household rubbish on the boiler. It has to have proper fuel otherwise it goes out. It's been out once today already.'

'I hope it had a nice time.' I tested the water in the washing-up bowl with my toe. The washing-up bowl was actually an aluminium jam saucepan given to her by her mother, as a hint that perfect housewives made their own jam. 'It's too hot,' I said.

'It's not.'

'I hate it when he gets drunk.'

'You think you're so sophisticated, Christine, but when you say things like that you show how immature you really are.'

I said slowly, 'He . . . was . . . drunk.' I meant it as a statement but my voice went up and it came out half way between a sob and a question.

She answered the question. 'He wasn't drunk. Not really.'

I opened my raincoat. She said, 'Have you had a nosebleed or something?'

'He punched me in the face. You know he did.'

'It was hardly a punch. Let's have a look at you.' She got hold of the sides of my head and bent my neck until light shone into my face. She peered up my nostrils. She looked curious and impatient.

'That hurts,' I said.

'It doesn't. Open your mouth. Move your head from side to side. Nosebleeds always look worse than they are.' She let go of my head and picked up the candlestick and the Duraglit wadding. 'There are a lot of blood vessels in noses. Ninety-nine per – ' She stopped. A key was turning in our front door.

She put her finger to her lips. She switched off the kitchen light.

Feet went up the stairs. They sounded too polite to be burglars' feet. They entered the guest room. 'Pam,' whispered my mother.

The guest room door closed. My mother turned the kitchen

light back on. I was shocked at the sight of my raw, grimy feet in the scum-covered water of the jam saucepan. I was ashamed and I was glad we had hidden.

'She met someone she knew at the rugby club and they went on to another party,' my mother said. 'They seemed quite smitten with each other, I do hope it's Mr Right at last.'

'Oh, she went off with another man, did she? That explains it.'

She paused in her polishing. 'Explains what?'

'Do you think they're having an affair?'

'It's a bit soon for that but they certainly seemed quite smitten with each other.'

'I meant Pam and the thug. Pam and *Daddy*.' I spat the word.

'Honestly, Christine. The things you come out with.'

'I'm going to ask him,' I said. 'I'll ask him in the morning. First thing.'

She shrugged. 'Make as much of a fool of yourself as you like.'

'I'll ask Pam too. I'll ask both of them.'

My mother fetched two tea towels for my feet. 'Take that blouse off, I'll put it in to soak.'

'Adam thought they were having an affair.'

'Adam had a lot of peculiar ideas.'

She was right. Adam did have peculiar ideas. His ideas were what I had liked about him. I had liked them as long as they were only about nuclear disarmament and sex. Sex in general, that was, or my sexiness in particular. Saying things about sex between my father and Pam had been going too far. That comment of his had gone beyond the limits. There were limits. At least, I had thought there were.

I took off my blouse and handed it to my mother without a word. In my bra and skirt and bare feet I felt like a woman of the streets. I ought to be leaning over a balcony, somewhere hot.

I went to the bathroom. I closed the door quietly and peered into the mirror. My face was flushed and my hair had gone stringy, but the only bloodstains were inside my nose. I washed and went to bed. I tried to comfort myself to sleep by thinking about Miguel, his gentle cuddles and tender kisses in the car on the way home.

Miguel was much more gentle and tender than Adam, which was surprising, because Miguel was more manly-looking. He had a bristly chin and thick dark hairs on his muscular arms, but he wasn't very passionate. His way of kissing was completely different from Adam's. He kept his mouth closed and moved his hands up and down the outside of the back of my coat and that was about it.

Sometimes I thought I might end up going all the way with Miguel just to make a change from feeling his hands stroking my back through my coat, but he showed no sign of wanting to and I didn't know how to bring the subject up.

I closed my eyes. Stiffness crept into the muscles around my nose. I remembered how it felt to have Adam put his tongue in my mouth and my ear. He had wanted to put it everywhere. He had wanted to put everything everywhere, but I wouldn't let him. I had rationed Adam, and now I was stuck with Miguel who rationed me.

A voice hissed, 'Don't ask them!'

At first I thought I had been sleep-walking and was looking in the mirror again. The sickly light of very early morning shone on a face that could have been my own.

It wasn't my face. It had some of my features but that didn't make it mine. An eye was an eye, a nose was a nose. There were millions of eyes and noses in the world; they couldn't all be different.

This was my mother's face. It had lost the brisk, jolly look that it had had downstairs. I had wondered if it were hiding anything. It wasn't hiding anything now. It was bare and open with emotion. I was embarrassed. Seeing her face like this was like seeing her bare bottom. Her face was suddenly a private part that she was forcing me to look at. Her eyes blazed, her nostrils dilated, her lips were drawn back in a sort of frenzied, imploring snarl. 'Don't ask them, Christine. Promise not to say a word about it? Honourable Heart?' She gripped my shoulder under the sheet. Her fingers felt like the talons of an eagle.

'Does that mean it's true?'

'Don't shout, you'll wake them!'

I whispered, 'Does that mean it's true?'

Her grip loosened. The eagle had been shot. It sagged on the bed, defeated. I felt a little pity and a lot of distaste. A defeated mother was no use to me. She said, 'I don't know.'

'Ask him, then.'

'We mustn't. That's what I'm trying to – '

'I'll ask Pam. She's my friend.'

'Women like Pam are nobody's friend.' My big fat mother shrank into her dressing gown. She pleaded. 'If you ask her, if you say a *word*, they'll know that we know. They mustn't know that we know. It's our only chance. When a woman like that is scheming to steal a man away from his family, there are two moments when she might succeed. The first is when he has her for the first time. When she lures him into her stinking, putrid bed.' She was sitting on my bed but she wasn't talking to me. She was hissing at the window and the blotchy, lightening sky. 'Well, he's had her, and from the looks of things she was a bit of a disappointment because he hasn't gone to her, has he? He's still with us. He still prefers us. He still loves us.'

Dried blood itched in my nose. I stared at her through narrowed eyes. 'First it's not true.' I counted on my fingers. 'Then you don't know whether it's true or not. Now it is true.'

'Do you know what you should be when you grow up?'

'No, what?'

'A barrister. You twist my words. You pick on every little thing I say.'

'Which?'

'The second dangerous moment is when the husband finds out that the wife knows. That's the point when people say and do things that they'll regret. A slut's a slut, a bit on the side's a bit on the side, easy come easy go is the motto of girls like Pam. But if he thinks he's got to make a choice, he might make the wrong one.

'That's what's so clever about me, Christine. I'm saving him from making the wrong choice. I'm saving him from himself. They think they're clever but I'm cleverer. My cleverness is that I don't know anything. *I don't know anything*. See how nice I am to her? I give them no grounds for suspicion. Rusty could be the answer to our prayers. Let's keep our fingers crossed that he'll take her away. And in the meantime I'm going to do a blitz on the house.'

Slippers shuffled on the landing. He was going to the bog. My mother whispered fondly, 'We've woken him.' She kissed my forehead and gave me a secret smile. She seemed to think I had agreed to something.

She went to the bedroom. I heard her getting into bed.

He came out of the bathroom. I wondered how he was going to feel about leaving the bed empty and coming back to find it had my mother in it. I wondered if he loved her at all.

34

It was a point of honour with my father never to make a fuss about hangovers. Chap should take his drink and take his punishment.

He strode through the house, banging on people's doors.

> *'Wakey, wakey, rise and shine.*
> *You've 'ad your time, you've 'ad your time.'*

If there was one thing more embarrassing than my father doing imitations of Chief Petty Officer Pertwee, it was my mother doing imitations of his imitations. '*Show-a-leg, show-a-leg, show-a-leg-oh* – ' she boomed.

Janet joined in. '*'Eave-oh, 'eave-oh, lash up an' stow* – '

Pam came in on the chorus. '*GIDDOUTAVIT!*'

Outside my door he said, 'Is anyone still asleep?'

I covered my face with my sheet. 'Christine? Are yer decent? Speak now or forever hold your peace. I'm coming in.' He did. He loomed over me. '*Show-a-leg, show-a-leg, show-a-leg-oh* – ' I stayed under the sheet. He cleared his throat. 'I behaved like an oaf last night.' His voice was gruff. 'No excuse. Ashamed of myself. I apologise.' He bit the ends off his words. He waited. 'Can't say more than that. Do you accept my apology?'

I didn't answer because I didn't know what accepting an apology meant. I never had known. It seemed to mean pretending something hadn't happened when it had. How could I? I still had dried blood up my nose.

He said, 'Shake hands?'

I lay still with my hands under my body. He waited a few moments, then walked out. He was sighing with relief at being back in the right.

He shouted, 'Breakfast orders if you *please*, ladies and gents.'

My mother said quickly, 'I'll cook the breakfast, you'll only make a mess.'

'You're impossible to help but I'm going to help you anyway. All in favour of sausages, say aye.'

'Aye, aye!' piped Janet.

'Aye,' said Pam with a little more dignity.

My mother said, 'I won't have anything, this will be a good opportunity for me to miss a meal. I'll do a blitz on the bathroom.'

'All right, you men, get fell in. Captain to the galley. First officer to hose down the heads. Second officer on special duty: sulking in her room. Able Seaman to get the papers, Rating MacLeish to – '

'Jo,' said Pam. 'What can I do that will be of most help to *you*?'

I waited with baited breath for the reply, but there was nothing unusual about it. 'You don't have to do anything, Pam. You're a guest.'

Guest or not, Pam helped her clean the bathroom. I wondered if she would have been so keen to help if she had realised that this was the beginning of the blitz that was supposed to win back my father's heart.

I lay in bed and listened as they scrubbed and chatted. '*Wasn't* it a coincidence meeting Rusty again?' said my mother. 'Yes, wasn't it?' said Pam. My mother said, 'Did you enjoy the party?' and Pam said she had. My mother was a brilliant actress. No one could have guessed that there was anything behind her questions other than polite interest. It was a bit terrifying because it made me wonder what else about her was an act.

'Will you be seeing Rusty again?'

'I hope so.'

'Then I hope so too.'

I tried to work out what they were doing. From the sound of things, my mother was scrubbing the lavatory with the lavatory brush, and Pam was wiping the shelves in the medicine cupboard and rearranging bottles. I wondered why. I hadn't heard my mother asking her to do it.

I often wondered how women knew which housework to do next when there never seemed to be any particular reason for doing one thing rather than something else. They even seemed to know in other women's houses. Pam was behaving like every other woman I knew. She was behaving like my aunts. Whenever Sue, Kay or Gwen came to our house, their first words would be, *What can I do to help you, Jo?*'

My mother's reply was always, *You don't have to do anything, you're a guest.* Sometimes she would add, *Sit down and relax after your journey*, but the aunts never did. Their eyes narrowed, they sniffed the air like horses scenting home, spotted the nearest housework, got their heads down, rolled up their sleeves and did it.

The same thing happened when my mother went to their houses. There was a pattern. Women who went visiting offered to help. Hostesses told them they needn't. But the visiting women would always do housework anyway. And they would always do the right housework. Their mysterious housewifely powers enabled them to read the minds of the hostesses and discover the exact bit of housework that the hostesses would have asked them to do if they weren't saying that they didn't want them to do anything. And then they would do it.

To me, this was stupid. Even when I was told to do housework, I only did it under protest. Why do it when you had been told not to? Women seemed to expect other women to read their minds on this, and to know that yes meant no. I knew in my bones that if the visiting women didn't do housework, the hostesses would be furious.

'Jo! Would you ask Lady Precious Stream whether she wants breakfast?'

My mother said playfully round my door, 'Are you going to honour us with your presence at breakfast?' I turned away. She said, 'You'll feel much better if you get up and take a few deep breaths.'

I waited for her and Pam to go downstairs. I went to the bathroom, dropped a lily-of-the-valley bath cube into the bath and turned on the hot tap. Pipes hissed all over the house.

My mother opened the kitchen door and yelled up through a mouthful of breakfast, 'Are you running a bath?'

'I'm running a garden fête actually.'

'Pam and I have just cleaned the bath.'

'What for?'

'Pardon?'

'Am I only allowed to use it when it's dirty?'

She said in triumph, 'I don't suppose the water's all that hot anyway.' I felt the water. She was right, it was tepid. I swore. She went on, 'I don't suppose Daddy will have remembered to riddle the boiler. There's more to Sunday morning chores than frying a few sausages.' I wondered why she let him get away with things like getting drunk and thumping me till I bled and committing adultery, but went on and on and on at him about housework. 'You have to riddle the boiler as well.' She did it herself with thuds and thumps. The house shook. She shouted up the stairs, 'There'll be hot water in about half an hour.'

'Forget it!' I got dressed in old jeans and a sweater. I put a clean dress in a bag with clean underwear and make-up and some money. I ran out of the house through the front door and caught a bus to the public baths.

The baths had been built in Victorian times for people who lived in slums. They were next door to the swimming pool. I had always wondered what they were like inside.

I paid my 2/6 and the attendant gave me a key with a number on it, a small cake of yellow soap, two clean, knobbly towels and a disapproving look, as if she knew as well as I did that I had a perfectly good bath at home. I walked along a white tiled corridor that smelt of steam and disinfectant. I found my locker and an empty cubicle. I got undressed.

The baths were separated from each other by wooden partitions that didn't quite reach the ceiling or the floor. I could hear my neighbours. There seemed to be a whole family on my left. On my right, someone wallowed slowly. Whoever it was sounded old and heavy. They coughed till I thought they were going to die. When the coughing stopped, I heard a cigarette being lit.

I turned on the tap. Water gushed out in a white torrent, too hot and hard to touch. When it stopped swirling it settled down to a yellowish-green colour. I dipped the corner of a towel into the water, shaped it into a point and used it to clean dried blood out of my nostrils. At the same time I read a notice on the wall about Communicable Diseases.

I thought how funny it was that only a few hours ago I had refused to go to the police station with PC Tutsworth because it would look as if I came from a bad home, and now here I was at the public baths.

35

I put on clean underwear and stockings, and unpacked the dress I had brought with me. It was turquoise with a belted waist and a full skirt.

I did up the buckle of the belt on the tightest hole. The skirt fanned out. It was a summer dress and this was its first outing of the year. It had shrunk, or I had grown. The greeny-blue fabric strained over my flattened nipples.

The hairdriers didn't work so I did the best I could with a towel. I saw a trace of greyish yellow bruising round my nose and covered it with make-up. I slung my white Bri-nylon cardigan over my shoulders and walked out on high heels into the dazzling spring morning. The sun warmed my damp head. The swollen buds on the trees were ready to burst. They looked itchy and sore.

'Chris! Long time no see!'

'Hello, Mrs Jennings.'

'You're looking summery.' She picked up the milk from her front step. She was looking summery herself in her pale pink housecoat with a matching ribbon in her fair hair. 'Are you coming in?' she said. 'Adam's away.'

I followed her through to the kitchen. 'Two Way Family Favourites', was on the wireless and a chicken was roasting in the oven. Through the open back door I could see Mr Jennings sitting in a deck chair with a pot of coffee and the *Sunday Pictorial*.

'Georgie loves and misses you very much indeed,' said Jean Metcalfe. 'And he can't wait for the Christmas after next. He says the message is in the song, which is Johnny Burnette with 'You're Sixteen, You're Beautiful and You're Mine.'

Mrs Jennings put the milk into the fridge and said, 'So how have you been keeping, Chris? We've missed seeing your smiling face. Oh dear, spoke too soon.' A tear overflowed out of my eye, followed by another.

She sat me in a chair and gave me a tea towel to wipe my eyes with. I soaked it. She gave me a cigarette but my tears put it out. She gave me an encouraging pat on the shoulder. It wasn't enough. I clung to her. She hugged me back but she got embarrassed because we weren't related. She broke free and fetched a leaflet out of a drawer. 'That's where he is,' she said. 'He hasn't gone to the moon.'

He might as well have gone to the moon. He had gone to Birmingham. He was working as a volunteer for Construction Not Destruction. A photograph showed two students standing next to a cement mixer. The caption said they were building an adventure playground.

I hated the girl student for looking so pretty in her dirty dungarees. 'What's an adventure playground?'

'It's a place for having fun,' said Mrs Jennings, mimicking my gloomy voice. 'Nobody ever tells me anything and there's no reason why you should break with tradition, but the impression I got from Adam was that it was you who gave him his marching orders, not the other way round.'

Jean Metcalfe said, 'Tessa wants Lance Corporal Brian Garner in BFPO 47 to know that she's looking forward to September 17th because that's the day when she and Brian are going to – '

'I'm sure they are, but we don't need the details,' said Mrs Jennings, turning the wireless off. 'I won't say he hasn't found someone else, Chris, because I'd be the last to know, but he hasn't mentioned anyone. Are your parents going to haul me over the coals if I give you a drink?'

'Who cares? My dad's a drunk anyway.'

'He's not, is he?' She gave me a tiny glass of sherry and poured large gin and tonics for herself and her husband. She took one out to him and they discussed me in low voices while I drank my sherry. It was better than nothing. She came back in and invited me to stay for lunch. 'The chicken's a bit big for two and it's not unheard-of for Adam to ring up on a Sunday. Do you want to ring your mother and tell her you're staying?'

'She won't be interested.'

'Like that, eh?'

'They're all out on the boat.'

'So you were counting on having lunch here.'

'No, they always leave me a picnic.'

She got some new potatoes out of a bag and stood at the sink scrubbing mud off them. I wished we could have *Family Favourites* on again because the housework sound of her scrubbing was getting on my nerves.

'Can I help you, Mrs Jennings?'

'No, you're a visitor.'

Before I could guess what she really wanted me to do, the phone rang in the hall. She picked it up and said, 'Yes, I'll accept the charge. Hello, love. Fine, how are you? Guess who's here. Chris.' She paused for his answer. She said, 'Chris *Toms.*' How many Chrisses did he know? I didn't want to hear any more. I rushed to the sink and scrubbed potatoes as noisily as I could.

I went on scrubbing till they were bald and white. Mrs Jennings tapped me on the shoulder and pointed me at the phone. 'I'll be in the garden,' she said, going out and closing the door.

I wiped my hands and picked up the receiver. I didn't know what to say. *Hello* seemed a bit obvious.

'Hello,' he said in his deep, rich voice, and it was like the first time he ever rang me up to ask me to a YCND meeting.

'Hello.'

'Is that really you, Chris?'

'Yes.'

'What are you doing there?'

I didn't know what to say. I didn't want to talk to him on the phone, with all the operators between here and Birmingham listening in. Why should he be in Birmingham when I wanted him here? I hadn't seen him since before Christmas. That was my fault, but today I had come round specially, to apologise to him and tell him he had been right. And what thanks did I get? He was in Birmingham.

He asked again. 'What are you doing at Mum's?'

'Scrubbing potatoes.'

'Were you looking for me?'

'Not particularly.'

Very slowly, as if he were sounding me out, he said, 'You never gave me a chance to apologise for what I said.'

'You don't have to. It's true.'

After a long pause, he said, 'We can't talk about this on the phone.'

'No, we can't, can we?' *So why aren't you here?*

He said, 'Why don't you come to Birmingham?'

'What for?'

'Whatever you like. We need weekend volunteers. I'll send you the bumph.'

I cheered up. 'I'll try.'

'That's not good enough. Say you'll come, Chris. I've missed you.'

'All right.' I had forgotten how to talk to him. I was afraid I might cry again. 'Bye.'

I went to the bathroom to wash my face. When I came back Mrs Jennings was putting the potatoes on to boil. 'Sweetness and light?'

I nodded.

'None of my business,' she said, 'but why did you two split up in the first place when you're obviously potty about each other?'

'He said something.'

'Are you going to tell me what it was?'

'About my dad.'

'Adam should know better than to insult your parents,' said Mrs Jennings. 'You're quite capable of doing that, and he's got parcnts of his own.'

'He said my dad was having an affair with a so-called friend of our family.'

'I hope you told him to wash his mouth out.'

'He was right.'

She paused in taking salad things out of the lettuce crisper in her fridge. 'Are you sure? Just because Adam gets a bee in his bonnet, it doesn't necessarily mean – '

'My mum's sure.'

'Did she tell you she was?'

'Yes.'

Mrs Jennings sighed and sliced a cucumber. 'What's she going to do?'

'Nothing.'

'Isn't she going to tell the "friend" to bugger off, pardon my French?'

'She's pretending she doesn't know. She wants me to pretend I don't know. But I've told you now. So even if I don't know, you do.'

'It's not really any of my business.' *Chop chop chop* went her knife through the cucumber. She wouldn't look at me.

I said, 'Do you agree with my mother?'

'I hardly know her,' said Mrs Jennings. She was too busy with housework to look at me. Housework was dangerous. If she looked at me she might cut her finger off. 'I don't know your dad and I don't know the girl. But your mum knows all three, so she's probably got a fair idea of the right thing to do. It's not your responsibility in any case, so you shouldn't be worrying about it.' She finished slicing and gave me a bright smile. It froze. She said, 'Chris, is that a bruise?'

'Yeah, I fell off my bike. Are you saying I should mind my own business?'

'You could give your mother a bit of time. If these things are left alone they sometimes blow over. Will you help me lay the table?' She tossed a starched white cloth in my direction.

I unfolded the cloth in a great rage. I wanted to tramp over its whiteness in muddy boots. She claimed not to know my mother but she used my mother's words, my mother's tricks. It was a typical housewife trick to say, *No, you're a visitor* when I offered to help, and then, just when I was starting to relax, say, *Help me lay the table.*

She didn't mean, *Help me lay the table*, she meant, *Lay it.* But she would have been too embarrassed to give me an order, as if I were her daughter. Daughters were the only people housewives were allowed to order to help them. Visitors had to pick up hints and guess. Daughters were sometimes expected to guess too, and heaven help them if they guessed wrong.

Were housewives allowed to ask for help or not? If not, why was I always being ordered to lay tables and tidy rooms? If they were allowed to ask people to help them, why were they so roundabout and shifty about it?

Why should I lay the table while Mr Jennings sat in his deck chair like Lord Muck? Why should my father beat me for cheating and be given a free hand to cheat himself? Why should the very person he was cheating tell everybody else to keep quiet about it?

I laid the table but I only laid two places. This was to make a point. I wasn't staying. I would go home and eat my picnic, on my own.

I was used to *I agree with Daddy*. What I hadn't realised until now was that all Mummies lined up with other Mummies, agreeing with Daddies. I imagined millions of Mummies all over the world, agreeing with each other that they must agree with Daddies. Behind them were the Daddies, and they agreed too. Who could ever break through this wall?

36

Adam sent leaflets, and a love letter that said he was counting the days until he saw me again. 'Write back and tell me how many days I have to count.'

I got my mother on her own and informed her that I would be going to Birmingham for the weekend. She looked doubtful. I was surprised. It didn't seem to have sunk in that I could do whatever I wanted.

'What sort of weekend?'

'Construction Not Destruction.' I showed her a leaflet. It had ban-the-bomb symbols all over it. I didn't try to hide them. 'It's voluntary work.'

'Why do you have to go to Birmingham for that? I'm sure there's a great deal of voluntary work that needs doing in Bleswick, starting with your room.'

'Mother, you are such a wit.'

'You can't just go to Birmingham on your own.'

She still thought she could say things to me that began with *You can't*.

'I won't be on my own. Adam's there.'

She folded her arms. 'I thought you'd finished with him.'

'We're back together again.' It was time to remind her who was boss, and why. 'I told him he was right after all about Pam and – '

'*Shut up*.' I shrugged. She said, 'What about Miguel?'

'I've finished with Miguel.'

'Daddy *will* be pleased.'

'And you agree with Daddy?

You agree with Daddy.
You agree with Dad.
There's nothing the matter with Daddy,
It's just that he drives you mad.'

She ignored my singing and read from the leaflet. '"Floor space provided." That sounds a bit vague.'

'What's vague about it?'

'Do you know anyone else who's going to be there?'

'Adam. I told you.'

'"Bring sleeping bags." You haven't got a sleeping bag.'

'Will you buy me one?'

'I know what you're up to, young lady, but you're wasting your time. When Daddy hears about the sleeping arrangements, he'll put his foot down.'

'You'll have to persuade him to lift it up again.'

'Billy lives in Birmingham,' she said, throwing me on to the wrong foot because I didn't know who or what she was talking about.

I said, 'Who's he?'

'She. Fetch the Christmas card box.'

Light dawned. Billy must be a long-lost friend from her nursing days, or boarding school. She had quite a few friends like that, if you could call them friends. She never saw them. They exchanged Christmas cards saying 'We must get together in the New Year' and 'Why do we never have lunch?'

I looked through the cards but I couldn't find one signed 'Billy'.

'Of course you can't,' my mother said. 'That's not her name.'

'Eh?'

'She was Rosemary Billington so we called her Billy. She's Rosemary Carstairs now, Rosemary and Frank, that's what his name is – Frank.'

I went through the cards again and found one that said, 'When are you all coming for a weekend, we won't take no for an answer, love, Rosemary, Frank and the girls.'

My mother snatched the card, rushed to the phone, dialled for the operator and asked for the long-distance number. I could tell when she was through because she went pink and started to shriek as if she had gone quite mad. 'Billy? It's Jo. Jo Toms. Woolgar as was.' She hardly needed the phone and neither did her friend who shrieked for me to hear from the other end of the hall, '*Woolly*!'

'Billy!'

'How many *years*?'

'Where have they *gone*?'

'I've *kept* meaning – '

'I've *always* wanted – '

'Tell me everything!'

'What's there to tell? I married Sandy as you know and I've got two super girls, in fact one of them – '

The woman at the other end shrieked even more loudly than before. 'First let me sit down, then tell me how old they are.'

'Christine's fifteen – '

'*No!*'

'I'm afraid she is. Anyway, it's about her that I rang, she's very keen to – '

'And what about *you*, Woolly? Are you just the same?'

' 'Fraid so. Still in a muddle. Billy, this is a terrible cheek, leaving it all these years and then ringing you up to ask a favour, but Christine, she's my eldest, is very keen to take part in a voluntary work project in your part of the world and she hasn't got anywhere to stay.'

More mutual shrieking followed this lie. By the time the conversation had reached its end, Billy had invited not just me for the weekend, but our entire family.

When my father heard about it he was horrified. 'Not silly Billy!'

'Don't call my friends names.'

He said. 'You all used to call her that.'

'We didn't. Not really.'

'I'm not wasting a perfectly good sailing weekend trapped in a surburban semi in Birmingham, – ' he said it through his nose, *Berbiggam* ' – listening to that half-witted, jolly-hockey-sticks – '

'I think it's a pretty poor show when you won't share my interests. I share yours.'

'You can't call that woman an interest. I think we should each have our own interests and not inflict them on one another.'

'I'll remember that next time you want six dozen chicken *vol-au-vents*. Why can't we go as a family and stay with Billy's family?'

'And after that shall we have a family weekend with the Bixwells?'

'Not likely,' said my mother. 'Not after what happened last time.'

'I rest my case. Why don't you take the girls and have a weekend away from me?'

'What do you think I am, stupid?'

'What's *that* supposed to mean?'

'I mean it would be stupid for you to have to look after yourself. You'd never be able to manage.'

Janet piped up, 'I don't want to go to silly Billy's.' She looked to my father for approval and got it but my mother was furious. 'She's Mrs Carstairs to you, madam!'

'Well I don't want to go, I'm staying here with Daddy.'

My mother said with a sniff, 'I don't suppose he'll want you.' But he replied, 'Of course I want her. She can look after me.'

Janet said, 'We can ask Pam for the weekend, she'll look after us.'

My mother made a little gulping sound as she was hoist with her own petard.

My father groaned. 'That spiv? Must we, Janet?'

'She's not a spiv. Oh, *please*.'

It was brilliant. I almost respected him. Who could accuse him of anything? Who could blame him? It hadn't been *his* idea to invite Pam, it had been Janet's. What was my mother to do? Tell Janet that she couldn't invite Pam? Explain why not? Was she to insist on Janet coming with us to Birmingham? What reason could she give? More to the point, what would happen in Bleswick if the cat went off to Birmingham taking both her little kittens with her? Left behind, Janet could at least get in the way.

Was my mother to change her mind and say she didn't want to go to Birmingham herself? Again, what reason could she give? And what about me? This whole business had only started because I wanted to go to Birmingham.

My mother could hardly send me on my own to stay with Billy. I didn't even know her. I wanted to stay with Adam. I wanted to sleep in a sleeping bag on the floor of a church hall. So why didn't I do it? Why didn't I just go, reminding my mother that if she tried to restrict or punish me in any way I would give away her secret? I knew I could do that. What I didn't know was what might happen once I had done it.

She might call my bluff. She might say, 'Go on, then. Tell him.' What would I be telling him? That he was having an affair with Pam? It was crazy. He was the one who was doing something wrong, but he was the one who mustn't know that anyone knew about it.

What if he did know? What if I told him that my mother knew? Would he disappear into the sunset with Pam, as my mother feared and I hoped he would? Might he and Pam be pleased that they didn't have to keep it a secret any more?

Or might they break up, leaving my parents to have a glorious reconciliation? Might my parents unite against me, and not let me go to Birmingham at all?

Mrs Jennings had said, *It's not your responsibility. You shouldn't have to worry about it,* but I wasn't thinking of it as a responsibility. I wasn't worrying. On the contrary, I could see a chance to have a bit of power in the family.

But I only had power as long as the secret remained a secret. If I gave away the secret, I gave away my power. I decided to hang on to both.

37

'I'm very clever,' said my mother. 'He doesn't suspect.'

It was Friday evening. We were at Bleswick Junction, waiting for the train. I was giving myself a sight-test. I chose a single railway line and followed it into the gleaming silver tangle of rails outside the station.

'A wife who suspected wouldn't go off like this, would she?'

My railway line got lost among the other dazzling lines. I shaded my eyes against the early evening sunlight and squinted into the glare.

'A suspicious, nagging wife will drive a man away, Christine. The home should be a haven of peace.'

I couldn't find my railway line. I hoped that didn't mean I was going to need glasses. I would look horrible in glasses. I squinted at the lines till my eyes watered. Through the water a train came into view.

The announcer said, 'Oxford train. Change at Oxford for Birmingham.'

My mother said, 'I met Daddy in Oxford once.'

'Did you?'

'*My* Daddy. He and Mummy were home on leave. They got leave every three years, it was quite good. Lots of people didn't get nearly as much as that. He had to do some research at the Bodleian, so they took furnished rooms. Miss Dolby put me on the train at the end of term and Daddy and Mummy met me at Oxford. I ran the whole length of the platform and he picked me up.'

That seemed to be the end of the story. I followed her on to the train. It was crowded with people going home from work. They looked tired and fed up. They fidgeted with copies of the *Evening Standard* and the *Evening News*, ran fingers round the insides of grimy shirt collars, and looked out of the window with bleakness in their eyes.

I wanted them to know that tomorrow I was going to see my long lost boyfriend. I was wearing a new dress with red roses because my mother had insisted that I look respectable for Billy. I would have preferred to be wearing something a bit more CND-ish but at least I felt fresh and romantic.

'When he comes to his senses,' whispered my mother at the top of her voice, 'he won't hear a word of reproach from me.'

I begged her with my eyes to be quiet but she said, 'It's not his fault. It's not even her fault. She's a very, very sick girl. I pity her.' As the train picked up speed, so did my mother's pity for Pam. 'There's a certain type of girl, Christine. You can spot them at children's parties. Adorable little things. Rosebuds, with maggots inside. They make up to the little boys and they make up to the Daddies and they get extra pieces of cake. They get everything they want. It's a pity they can't be spotted at birth because that's when they should be strangled.'

'Shall I go and see if there's a buffet?'

'There should be institutions for keeping them out of harm's way. What do you want a buffet for, you're not hungry or thirsty. Nothing'll happen while Janet's around, will it? He wouldn't want to upset Janet, would he?'

'No.'

'I want him to have his fill of her. Have her till he's sick of her.'

'Janet?'

'*Pam*. The novelty'll wear off. He'll see her, warts and all.'

I wished she would lower her voice at least. To set an example I lowered mine. 'She hasn't got warts.'

'She probably has, and a great deal else besides,' said my mother with a mean snigger.

The tired-looking people in the carriage were perking up and listening hard. A man hid behind his *Evening News*, and shook.

I turned my face to the window and pretended to go to sleep. I stared at the gold insides of my eyelids. Silence fell over the carriage. I peeped at her through my eyelashes and saw her writing in her *Household Memoranda* book. I was glad she had stopped talking but there was something embarrassing about the way she chewed her pencil, stared into space and frowned with concentration, like a child doing homework.

I shut my eyes again. I tried to picture Adam's face. We were to meet at nine o'clock tomorrow morning at the headquarters of Construction Not Destruction. I hoped I would recognise him. I couldn't quite remember what he looked like.

'I'm not going to reproach him.' My mother's foot brushed my ankle. The train was slowing down. 'When he comes to his senses he won't hear one word of reproach from me.' We were arriving at Oxford and she was saying what she had been saying shortly before I fell asleep. I looked nervously at the other passengers and wondered if she had been doing Continuous Performances.

'Why should I reproach him? I don't know anything.' We got our things together. Beyond the window the towers and domes of Oxford glowed in the sunset. 'I don't know anything and I never have known anything. That's what's so clever about me.' We got off the train. 'The dreaming spires,' she said. 'I hope Janet will get into Oxford. I don't want her to end up like me.'

'Getting married, you mean? Who'd want her?'

We sat on a bench to wait for our connection. She said, 'Of course I didn't mean not to get married. I'd marry Daddy again ten times over.' Her voice was warm with love. I felt like puking.

'What did you mean then?'

'Nothing really.'

'What did you mean? Why don't you want Janet to end up like you?'

'I don't want either of you to. I want you to fulfil your potential, as I never did.'

'Why didn't you? Why don't you now? Why don't you go back to nursing?'

'Because Daddy – '

'Why don't you go to evening classes?'

'It's not as simple as that.'

'Why? Why isn't it?'

'There you go again. Christine Toms QC for the prosecution.' She opened her handbag and took a photograph out of her wallet. 'Billy,' she said, 'will meet with your approval. She got her SRN *and* her Midwifery. You'll be able to have a long talk with her about how hopeless *I* am.'

The picture showed my mother dressed in wartime nurse's uniform with another nurse at her side. The other one was a head taller than my mother and had a gawky arm round her shoulder. She had wispy hair, thick spectacles and a distinct look of Dilly Dreem the Lovable Duffer.

The platform was filling up. The Birmingham train was announced. My mother said, 'I'd better give you your ticket in case we get separated.' People started to push forward. 'Have I given you any pocket money for the weekend?' She stuffed bits of paper into one of my hands and the handle of my suitcase into the other. She said, 'I'm not the beast of burden.' We ran for the train. I seemed to be losing her in the crush but she mouthed, 'It's all right.' She signalled that she would go to the back of the train and I should go to the front. This doubled the chances of finding at least one seat. I found one, squashed between a nun and a city gent.

The train moved off. I felt uneasy without my mother, though there was no reason. This was normal drill. If my mother didn't find a seat, she would come looking for me and we would share mine. If she had found one she would sit in it and meet me at Birmingham.

The air in the compartment was sweet and stuffy. The nun's habit was touching my clothes. Nuns gave me the creeps. Sharp pain bit into my hand and I wondered if I might be getting a stigmata. What would she think of that? I realised what the trouble was. I was clutching my ticket so tightly that the corner of the cardboard was cutting into my palm. I loosened my hand and saw what else I was holding. I had the photograph of Billy, a pound note and piece of Household Memoranda paper with my mother's handwriting on it.

'Dear Christine,

I have decided to go home and catch them in the act as all this uncertainty is bad for our family life. Tell Billy and Frank that I have had to have a tooth out unexpectedly but we really must get together soon. From Billy and Frank's house phone home and tell Janet or Daddy or even the Slut if she has the temerity to answer our phone that we have arrived safely. They can settle in for the night all nice and cosy and never imagine that I am nearby waiting for my chance. Sorry for this note but I knew that if I told you what I was going to do you would argue and cross-examine me like the barrister you are at heart and could be if only you would apply yourself and go to university as I never did!

Lots of love from Mummy.'

38

The sun set. The sky went purple. The train pushed on and on through the countryside. Lights came on in snug farmhouses. The train carried me past them. Towns poked their fingers out into the fields. We went past bomb sites, building sites, gasworks and factories. Floodlights shed their pinkish yellow glare over acres of gleaming, identical cars with no number plates.

At Snow Hill Station a woman approached me. I recognised her from the photograph but I was surprised at how much older than my mother she seemed. She had lost her gawkiness and looked like a grown woman who might also be a nurse. She said, 'You must be Christine Toms,' and a man tried to take my suitcase.

I snatched it back. The woman said, 'Where's your mother? I'd have known you anywhere. You're her image.'

'I'm not.' I pushed past her. 'You've made a mistake.' I headed towards the exit and the dark city.

'Are you sure?' she cried, and I realised she was as silly as my father had said she was. I looked over my shoulder. She was looking over hers. Frank was looking too, and so was their daughter. I assumed it was their daughter. She had a surly expression. I liked that. If I had been dragged out at ten o'clock at night to meet and make friends with a total stranger just because her mother and my mother were nurses together once, I'd have had a surly expression.

I wanted to reassure her. *It's all right. You won't have to share your room. I'm not here.*

They were still looking at me so I hurried out of the station and found a phone box. I phoned Billy's home and was answered by a girl who I guessed was either another daughter or a babysitter. There was no danger that she would know my voice or my mother's, but I shrieked a bit to be on the safe side. I told her that I and my daughter Christine couldn't come after all because Christine wasn't very well. I tried to make it sound as if what Christine had wrong with her was something to do with her periods, so that the girl wouldn't ask for details. She didn't. She just said, 'They've gone to the station to meet you.'

I said, 'I'm so sorry for the inconvenience. We *must* get together soon.'

Opposite the station was a row of bus stops in front of a huge dark church with white gravestones. I looked at the timetables on the bus stops, but none of them mentioned the road where Construction Not Destruction was.

I took a taxi. We seemed to travel a long way through the shadowy city but it was hard to tell whether we were actually getting anywhere. We kept being diverted past roadworks and along one-way streets. I didn't blame my father for not wanting to come to Birmingham, it was all being dug up. Cranes and scaffolding towered above cement mixers and heaps of bricks on bomb sites. The square white beginnings of modern buildings peeped out of the rubble like the tips of new teeth.

We turned down a narrow street. The light from the few lamp posts was dim and greenish yellow. We could hardly read the numbers on the houses, which were small and huddled together in terraces. Their front doors faced straight on to the street. My father would have called them 'omes for the workers.

Some of the houses were boarded up. There were gaps in the tcrraccs. Thc houscs on cach sidc of the gaps were propped up by wooden struts shaped like lopsided letter A's.

One of the gaps had frames in it with dangling ropes. They looked as if they would come in handy for public executions. A sign read 'CONSTRUCTION NOT DESTRUCTION ADVENTURE PLAYGROUND'.

I got out of the cab and waited for the driver to turn into Birmingham's answer to PC Tutsworth and say he wasn't going to leave a nice young girl like me in a place like this. But once he'd taken all my money he drove off at high speed, as if what he really wanted to be was Birmingham's answer to Stirling Moss.

He left a smell of petrol in the warm night air where it mixed with soot and dog's muck and a faint hint of flowers.

Nailed to a tree in front of the adventure playground was a sign advertising a CND Poetry and Jazz evening, with today's date and the name of a pub, but no address. I thought that must mean the pub was nearby, and locals would know where it was. All I had to do was find some locals. I peered into the darkness around me but saw no one. I heard running footsteps and a shout of drunken laughter but they were some way off.

I chose a house with a light on. I knocked. A snarling dog hurled itself against the other side of the front door, shaking it till I thought it would give way. I ran.

I heard more drunken voices, and went towards them. I wandered a bit and found the pub. Everyone seemed to be leaving. I ducked into the Saloon Bar where the barmaids were collecting glasses and telling people to drink up. Their accents reminded me of Beryl Reid in *Educating Archie*. I made for the Ladies.

It was half way up a flight of stairs. From the top of the stairs came the sound of jazz, tantalising waves of music. I walked towards the waves and they engulfed me, making me tingle.

Smoke curled round a half open door. I peered in. The room was hot, and dark except for a spotlight on three jazz players with embroidered waistcoats and gleaming instruments. Cigarette tips glowed around them.

When the players got to the end of their music, a man wearing a bowler hat over long beatnik hair stood up to read his poem. He spent a lot of time shuffling pieces of paper, but when he got to the poem he seemed to be making it up as he went along. He sounded quite angry and kept saying 'fuck'.

He finished his poem and everybody clapped wildly, which he liked. He was a show-off. He reminded me of Janet. He looked as if he wanted to read us another poem but one of the barmen came up from downstairs and put the lights on. 'Thanks very much, ladies and gents.'

People stretched their limbs and rubbed their eyes as if they were coming out of hibernation. Adam was only a few feet away from me. I recognised him at once, even though his hair was longer than I remembered it and seemed to have gone grey.

He was wearing a frayed jersey and corduroy trousers with paint stains on them. His glasses looked different. The frames were thinner. He was talking to a group of people. Some of them were girls. One of the girls passed a packet of cigarettes. Everyone took one, including Adam. Someone brought out a lighter. They passed it round. Somebody said something that made them laugh. I didn't hear the joke, I just heard the laughter. I felt left out. The sound of the laughter told me that if Adam didn't recognise me I would walk out into the night and never be seen again. If he wasn't pleased to see me I would die. I wouldn't commit suicide, I wouldn't need to, I would simply disappear and die of natural causes.

It must have been a good joke because the laughter went on and on. He rolled his head around. His eyes met mine, went away and came back. He rushed over and hugged me. I hugged him. I didn't care who saw, I was so happy and relieved. He felt small after Miguel, but hard and strong, perhaps from all his building work. Suddenly I was shy. I tried to make the hug go on and on so that I wouldn't have to say anything, or look at him.

His hair smelt of sawdust and paint which explained the greyness and made me sneeze. He said, 'Bless you,' for the sneeze and then looked puzzled. 'I thought you weren't coming till tomorrow.'

'I'll go back then. If you don't want me.'

'Of course I want – but what about your mother and Bertie?'

'*Billy*. Can I have a cigarette?'

'Don't you buy your own yet?'

I took his cigarette and smoked it. He called, 'Jane, have you got a fag?' The girl tossed him one and he lit it from mine.

He said, 'Where's your mother?'

'If I'd known you wanted her, I'd have sent her instead.' I looked as sexy as I could and it worked. He smiled and shrugged and kissed me.

The room was emptying. The barman said, 'Thanks very much, ladies and gents,' put one hand on my back and another on Adam's, and pushed us towards the door.

Adam took my suitcase and we went down the stairs. We had a kiss on each stair. The barman rammed us in the ribs with a tray of glasses. 'Thanks very much, ladies and gents.' Outside the pub, other Poetry and Jazz people were kissing under lamp posts. I looked for Jane but I couldn't see her. Adam walked me into a shadowy corner and we kissed as if we had been starving and had found food. Every time he tried to stop I started another kiss because I didn't want him going after Jane.

•

39

The church hall was near the adventure playground. It reminded me of my father's rugby club, except that the people wandering about inside it looked as if they had brains. Student-type girls and men with beards came and went from the kitchen with mugs of coffee. Paper arrows on the wall showed where males and females were supposed to be sleeping, but no one was going to sleep. They sat on rucksacks, rolled their own cigarettes and had fierce arguments about the Labour Party. Two men were discussing something technical about one of their guitars. They passed the guitar backwards and forwards and strummed a few notes to make their points.

A fussy priest in jeans looked at me, looked at his clip board and looked at me again. 'Hullo! Who's this?'

Adam said, 'It's Chris, she's just arrived. Chris, this is Keith.'

'Pleased to meet you.'

'Chris what? Is she staying?'

'Toms,' I said. 'And yes.'

'The girls sleep up that end.' Keith bustled off.

Adam looked at my dress and my suitcase. 'You have brought a sleeping bag?'

'No.'

'Didn't I say to bring one?'

'I haven't got one.'

He looked at me. 'Has something happened?'

'Billy's children have got scarlet fever.'

'Scarlet – ?'

'The whole family's in quarantine. No one's allowed in or out. It's awful.'

He sighed. 'We'd better get you some bedding.' He took me up a flight of stairs to a store room full of broken pews and boxes of prayer books. On a shelf was a pile of grey blankets and grey pillows. He let go of my hand and scooped up an armful of the bedding. He looked as if he meant to take it downstairs but he stopped, changed his mind and dropped it on the floor.

He held out his arms to me and said, 'Please tell me why you're here.'

'If you don't want me, I'll go away again.'

'I do want you.'

We leaned against a broken pew, kissing. He tasted of paint and smelled of sweat but I didn't mind. I didn't mind my back getting uncomfortable either, but I pretended to. The more uncomfortable I seemed to be, the more he comforted me, and I needed a bit of comforting.

He admired my dress. I let him undo the zip.

Music and talk drifted up from downstairs. He took off my bra. He smiled as if someone had given him a present. He kissed the tip of my left nipple, then my right. They tingled and went hard. They were so hard they hurt. He soothed them. He ran his hands between my breasts and up and down the sides. They felt as if they wanted me to cry, because in all that time with Miguel they had never been properly appreciated and now they were being appreciated again.

He took off his glasses and his jersey. He pressed his hard, skinny chest against my soft, full one. *You'd never think we were the same species*. We were the same species now.

The door opened. A man and a girl stood there looking disappointed. They said, 'Oh, sorry.'

'Don't mention it,' said Adam into my neck.

The girl said, 'You might have put the sign on the door.'

There was a square skylight in the roof. Against its faint glow I could see the blank outline of his head. I couldn't see his features. He could have been anybody.

Anybody at all could have been unhooking my suspenders and rolling my stockings down. He didn't even smell right. Any paint-covered workman could have his hand inside my knickers.

I couldn't believe I was going to do this but I didn't think I was going to stop.

My eyes got used to the darkness. His face was white and devilish. Pews surrounded us like the bars of a cage but we weren't in a cage. We were free. We could do whatever we wanted. I knew what he wanted to do. I knew I was supposed to stop him. He wouldn't stop of his own free will, it was up to me.

He fiddled with the buckle of his belt. It sounded dangerous.

'Don't.'

'You mean I've got to keep my trousers on? What a rotter you are.' He left the buckle alone.

I don't know who's there, I thought.

'It's only me,' he said.

I must be safe with him if he can read my mind.

The talking and strumming from downstairs faded into silence. In the silence several hearts thumped. One was Adam's. The others were mine. My main heart had sent little hearts to different parts of my body to thump there. One was in my head. Another was in my stomach. A third thumped in the wetness between my legs.

It retreated from Adam's fingers and went on thumping in safety, deep inside, out of reach.

He said, 'Do you believe I can undo my belt and take my trousers down without using my hands?'

'No.'

'You're right, I can't.' He put his hands on the insides of my thighs. 'So if you can feel my hands, you know I've still got my trousers on.' He opened my thighs and put his face there.

I thought he was going to kiss me, which would have been bad enough. Bad enough for him. I didn't mind it. In fact I quite liked it. I thought he must be hating it, but he sort of settled down, as if he were about to have a good long drink from a river. A swamp was more like it. How could he? I was getting warmer and warmer down there, and up here my breaths were coming fast with little moans at the end of them. I didn't mean to let out those moaning sounds, but there they were. I was embarrassed by the moans and embarrassed by the disgusting thing Adam was doing. He didn't seem to have realised how disgusting it was but he soon would. And when he did, he would move away.

I didn't think I could bear that so I moved away first. I got hold of the sides of his head and pushed.

He looked anxious. 'Aren't I doing it right?'

'What?'

His eyes and teeth glowed up towards me. 'Why did you stop me?'

'Well.'

'Are you sufficiently aroused?'

He seemed to want an answer.

I tried out some in my head.

What if I said *yes* and I was wrong?

What if I said *no* and he got angry?

I didn't want to say *no*. I wanted his tongue back. I put my fingers where his tongue had been. They weren't as good as his tongue, but they weren't bad.

He threw his trousers and his underpants over a pew and lay on top of me. I tasted the dust in his hair and felt his penis. My fingers got out of its way, like pedestrians in front of a lorry. I still couldn't believe I was doing this.

He prodded me and made me flinch. That prod spoiled everything. I didn't want to do it after all.

I moved away. He came after me and gave me a long, deep kiss before trying again. He was trembling and gasping. I moved away again. He stopped me. 'I think you're supposed to come towards me. Sort of like this.' He moved his hips about.

'Why?'

'It says in *Modern Woman and* – '

'Why should I hurt myself?'

'If you want to – '

'I don't.'

'Oh.' He looked as if he couldn't believe it. He looked as if he were going to rape me. 'You mean not now? Or never?'

'How should I know?'

He turned away furiously and lit a cigarette. He didn't offer me one. The cigarette calmed him down and he said quietly, 'Either you do this with me now or you'll do it some other time with someone else or you'll be a virgin for the rest of your life. Do you accept my reasoning so far?'

Pompous git, I thought. I nearly said, *Save it for your clever girlfriends at Oxford*, but I didn't want him to save it for them.

He said, 'Is there anyone else you'd prefer?'

'No.'

'And do you want to be a virgin for – '

'No.'

'Well then.' He propped himself up on his elbows again and reared above me. I thought, *This is it*, but he stopped and said, 'There is another possibility. I think you can go to a doctor and have it done under local anaesthetic. Fancy that?'

'Not much.'

He leaned forward and my body gave way.

It hurt a bit but it wasn't nearly as bad as I'd been led to expect by the authoress of *The Second Sex.* Adam seemed to be having a much worse time than I was having. He heaved about, groaned and flopped on top of me as if he had just died.

The French authoress must have been unlucky with her defloration. Whoever had done it, it certainly wasn't Adam. He lit two cigarettes and gave me one. 'Best cigarette in the world,' he said.

I took a few puffs and agreed with him. I watched my smokestream mingle with his until there was only one. I could remember a time when I hadn't liked smoking very much and I wondered if sex was like that and you had to get used to it.

As if he had read my mind again, he said, 'Sorry.'

'It's all right, it was nothing.'

He sighed.

'It was lovely,' I lied. 'Especially before.'

'I should have kept going. I hope I'm not doomed to be a premature ejaculator for ever.'

'What's a premature – ?'

'Some men can go on for hours.'

I was glad he wasn't one of them but I didn't say anything.

40

He fell asleep. I lay with my eyes wide open. I had pins and needles, I felt sore and sticky between my legs, and I was wondering what had happened to my family.

I imagined my mother talking to herself on the train and getting out at Bleswick. She scurried home and hid in the garden. I wondered if she knew that the lilac bush provided the best hiding place. It had a good view of the house and gave off a nice smell.

She waited for darkness. The moon came out. She probably got a bit chilly. She watched to see which lights came on in which windows.

Janet's bedroom light came on first. Janet's going-to-bed routine took about half an hour. She folded her clothes, checked to see that I hadn't been interfering with any of her collections (as if I would), wrote a novel or two and said a thank you prayer for her day's achievements. She got into bed and turned out the light.

Which light would have gone on next? Or lights? If two lights went on – one in the double bedroom and the one in the spare – everything could still be perfectly innocent. But I had a feeling that only the double bedroom light had gone on. The window of the spare room stayed dark.

That would have settled it. I imagined my mother breathing faster and faster. In the window of her own bedroom, the light went out. She gasped with bitterness. They were nice and cosy. She was outside, alone with her jealous rage.

It would have been a rage to scorch the lilac leaves. It would have been a worse rage than any I had ever seen, and I had seen a few. It would be wilder than her Christmas rages, more furious than her slimming rages, or her rages when the boiler wouldn't light, or she couldn't find her handbag, madder than the frenzies in which she begged me to pretend not to know what I knew about my father.

There could be no more pretence after this. But what was *this*? What would she have done? Would she have climbed up the ladder to the bedroom window and caught them in the act?

The act. Adam lay with his head against my beautiful breasts. It was *our* act. I thought how lucky I was to have him, now that my home was about to become a broken home. If my mother had murdered my father and Pam, or burned the house down or something like that, Janet would probably be put into an orphanage, but I would stay here with Adam.

I woke by myself, itching from the blankets. I could smell bacon frying. I stood up. Wetness trickled like tears between my legs. I ran my hands through my tangled hair and over my face to feel whether it had changed. The skin felt dry but strangely soft. I walked round the store room, picking my scattered clothes off the pews.

I wanted a full-length mirror to look in, and a bath. I wanted Adam. I put my dress on over my naked body. I pretended it was a négligée. I took my sponge bag out of my case and opened the door of the storeroom. At the bottom of the stairs people milled about, rubbing their eyes and clearing up. They wore dungarees and paint-stained overalls which looked as if they had slept in them. I felt rather glamorous. Under my dress I was naked and I knew things. I would know those things for ever, whatever happened.

I followed the smell of bacon into the main hall. The sleeping bags had been cleared away and piled on the stage. There was a trolley with a tea urn and cups. Folding tables and chairs had been set out.

Each table had a catering pack of corn flakes, a pile of bowls and a big metal jug of milk. Through the hatch, I could see Adam in the kitchen with Jane. They both had badges on with the word ORGANISER, and chefs' hats with CND symbols cut out of them. She wore a pretty apron of purple gingham over tight trousers and a big grey home-knitted jersey. She was frying bacon. He was spreading margarine on slices of Wonderloaf.

I watched them for a long time but they didn't see me. I went to the Ladies. Girls wearing jeans and men's shirts were washing their faces and cleaning their teeth. They stared at me in my dress through eyes that hadn't had enough sleep.

I hadn't had enough sleep either but I had a reason. I had done it. Whatever happened for the rest of my life, I had done *it*. I looked into the eyes of the girl students and guessed which ones had done it and which ones hadn't done anything.

There was no bath so I held my face flannel under a tap, squeezed it out and took it into a cubicle to wipe between my legs. I wondered whether any of the girls had guessed what I was doing and why. I wondered if they disapproved. I didn't care if they did. I wanted them to.

Still barefoot and dressed like a woman of the streets, I went to the kitchen. I said loudly, 'Can I help?'

Adam jumped as if he had been doing something wrong. This made me even more suspicious that he had been. 'Good morning, Chris!'

'Morning.' I picked up a knife.

Jane said, 'You're a weekend volunteer, aren't you? You've got your own rotas.' She was pretending to be friendly but she was looking at the knife and she seemed nervous.

'It's all right.' I spread some margarine. 'I don't mind helping.'

'You don't have to, honestly,' said Adam. 'Have some breakfast. And er – ' he smiled – 'get dressed.' He said it as if he didn't want me to think he was ordering me about but he wanted me to do what he said.

Without a word I went back to the store room and put on jeans and a jersey. If he wanted me to look like everybody else, then I would look like everybody else. Last night he hadn't thought I was like everybody else. As I came back down the stairs I swung my hips in a sexy, automatic sort of way that I seemed to have learnt.

As I queued for breakfast, I felt empty and sad. Why should I queue up for him? I wanted him to be mine, as I was his. I looked at all the men. I wondered if they realised. I wondered if they were jealous of Adam. I tried to decide which ones I liked. There was one with black hair and a black beard and black curls peeping between his shirt buttons. I wondered what it would be like with somebody like him who was hairy and coarse.

I reached the front of the queue. You had to help yourself to slices of bread and hold them apart while Adam put bacon between them. He did mine very sexily. He gave me an extra rasher and a big smile. I thought he was going to say something but he turned to the next person in the queue.

I got myself some tea and sat with it and my bacon sandwich at one of the tables. The other people at the table were quite nice; they asked where I had come from and when I said Bleswick they pretended to have heard of it. But I couldn't take my eyes off Adam and Jane in the kitchen beyond the hatch.

My sadness had a sickly, familiar feeling. I seemed to know that this always happened after a girl lost her virginity, and it served her right.

I seemed to have done it dozens of times. I seemed to know what to expect. He had lost respect for me and I had lost him.

The priest from last night, who was wearing one of the ORGANISER badges, banged the side of one of the metal jugs with a spoon. He said, 'I'm not going to preach a sermon,' and the long-termers cheered. He said, 'Thank you. Remember that the whole point of Construction Not Destruction is to provide an answer to the challenge that is so often put to those of us who are against the bomb. What are you *for*? What is your alternative? This weekend, ***you*** are the alternative.

'Don't ram politics down people's throats. Some of them aren't interested in politics, and that's their privilege. Some of them oppose us, and that's their privilege too. Some of them think ban-the-bombers are sex-crazed drug addicts.' The long-termers cheered again, and Adam winked at me from the kitchen. Keith wasn't laughing. 'This is a serious matter. They've read it in the *Daily Express*, so it must be true. Once again, it's their privilege to suspect what they want, but it is not yours to confirm their suspicions. Remember, you are the ambassadors of the peace movement, and behave accordingly. If our personal behaviour turns people against us, we're wasting our time as far as building our movement is concerned.'

Adam was looking very, very solemn. I was sure I was going to giggle. I kept snorting and blowing my nose. Keith said, 'I'm not saying don't enjoy yourselves. I'm not a killjoy, God knows. But – '

'Make sure no one finds out about it, eh, Keith?' someone suggested.

'Make sure *I* don't find out.' He looked as if the joke had gone far enough.

41

I was down on the rota to do Slum Renovation with four strangers. I said to Adam, 'Why can't I be with you?'

'You will be.' He kissed me, but he was in a rush. 'Tonight.' He wasn't my lover any more, he was an Organiser, a long-term volunteer, a big shot.

'Why not today?'

'I'm staying here,' he said. 'Cleaning and catering.'

'I could do that.'

'Housework? You?'

I pointed at the rota. 'I don't know these people.'

He was completely unsympathetic. 'Get to know them. You're a big girl now.'

'You sound like my mother.'

'Which reminds me,' he said.

'What?' I edged away.

'Where is she?'

'Stop going on about that.'

'You still haven't told me why you changed your plans.'

'Look, do you want me to go on this rota or not?'

The others in my group were a fierce-faced Italian girl called Marcella who had a red hammer-and-sickle badge with Russian lettering pinned to her blue pullover, an engaged couple from Sussex University called Tim and Rachel, and Lawrence who was in charge.

Lawrence turned out to be the hairy one from the breakfast queue. He gave the orders while the rest of us loaded step-ladders, dust sheets, rolls of wallpaper and tins of paint into a van. We climbed in after them.

Lawrence drove and talked to us over his shoulder. 'We're going to see the Trentons. They're a problem family.'

Marcella said, 'It is the capitalist system that is the problem.'

'Yes, love. Have any of you done any painting or decorating before?'

'Of course.' Marcella sounded as if she thought Lawrence ought to know that she was an expert.

Rachel said, 'We've done a bit, haven't we, Tim? Only I wasn't very good.'

'What about you, Chris? Have you had any experience?'

I didn't answer. I was thinking about my own problem family, and how pleased my mother would be if a team of volunteers were to turn up and decorate 79 Manor Road, Bleswick. If she hadn't burned it down, that was.

Lawrence said, 'I don't think Chris is going to tell us whether she's had any experience or not. I think she prefers to keep quiet about it.' He chuckled into his beard and his eyes glittered at me in the driving mirror. He stopped the van, came round the back and opened the doors. He offered his hand to Marcella, who ignored it and jumped down by herself. I tried to do the same but he got hold of me round my waist and held on for much longer than he had to. Rachel was helped down by Tim.

We were parked in front of a terrace of sooty little houses in a windy street. Lawrence knocked at one of the doors, *bang-tiddy-bang-bang, bang-bang,* and a fat woman with bad teeth and lots of children let us in.

We carried our equipment into the house. The air smelt of nappies, fish and BO. The furniture was odd and old and broken, and frayed bits of carpet were sticky underfoot.

Lawrence showed us the work that had been done so far. Construction Not Destruction had put in a bathroom and an inside toilet, and had re-plastered one of the bedrooms. The bedroom now needed painting and wallpapering. Lawrence put Tim and Marcella in charge of this because they had experience. Rachel didn't look at all pleased about Tim being on his own in the bedroom with Marcella, even if the beds were covered with dust sheets. Lawrence said, 'Rachel and Chris can make a start on the kitchen,' and Rachel looked at me with dislike in her eyes.

'What do we do?' I asked him.

'Strip,' he said meaningfully. 'Rub down and make good.' The kitchen looked as if it would take all day to clear up, never mind decorate. Mrs Trenton said to Lawrence, 'I'm sorry, love, I'm all behind this morning.'

'We're here to help, Mrs T,' he said. 'You get your feet up.' He put his hand under her elbow and gallantly took her out of the room.

The sink and the draining board were covered with empty tins. Rachel carried them out to the bin in the yard. I started clearing dirty plates off the table.

'There's not much point in doing that,' said Rachel, with her hands full of tins. 'There's nowhere to put anything.'

'What shall I do then?'

She gave me the usual look of women who got exasperated when I didn't know what housework to do, but who weren't prepared to tell me. 'Can't you *see*?'

Stuck to the greasy wallpaper were picture postcards, family snaps and portraits of the Queen and President Kennedy cut out of magazines. I started to take them down, peeling back the sellotape. I thought that was one job I couldn't mess up.

I was wrong. A piece of sellotape brought a long strip of the soggy wallpaper away with it. I went on pulling and part of the wall came too, with stones and dust and chunks of plaster. Rachel said, 'You should have put dust sheets down before you started that. Why don't you help me with the washing-up?'

I would have loved to, but I didn't dare let go of the paper. If I didn't keep it pressed against the wall, the avalanche started again. I almost wished my father would walk in. He knew about walls.

'Help,' I said.

'Oh, honestly.' said Rachel. '*Lawrence!*'

He grinned at me. He said, 'You *haven't* done it before, have you?' He stood close behind me and took the wallpaper out of my hand. He didn't exactly stop the avalanche so much as leave it to subside. At least I wasn't responsible for it any more. I felt his breath on my neck.

Mrs Trenton looked in to see how we were getting on. The dust made her cough, and she stared in alarm at the hole in her wall. The wallpaper hung off it like skin round a wound. I thought she was probably thinking that it was all very well for us to spend a weekend smashing up her house when we had homes of our own to go to at the end of it.

The trouble was, I didn't know whether I had.

I said, 'Please, Mrs Trenton, can I use your phone?'

'What phone?' she replied, and Lawrence looked as if I should have known and shouldn't have asked. He said, 'Is it something urgent?'

'No.'

Mrs Trenton said, 'There's a call box at the shop.'

Lawrence said, 'I've got a better idea. My lodgings are just round the corner. There's a phone there.'

'It's all right. It doesn't matter.'

'Come on, love.' He put his hand on my shoulder. 'I'll take you.'

Rachel called after us, 'That's right, leave me to do everything.'

His room was at the back and the top of a tall house. It had a steep fire escape with missing steps. We had to keep stopping for breath.

'Home sweet home,' he said. He nodded at the phone. 'Help yourself.' I thought he might leave me to make my phone call in peace but there was nowhere for him to go. It didn't matter. There was nothing to listen to. The phone rang and rang in Bleswick but there was no reply. I got the operator to check the line. He said it was all right.

I waited and waited and gave up. I wished I hadn't tried. I wanted to go back to the Trentons and knock walls down. I wished I had the kind of face that didn't show things. I wished I could be casual, but I couldn't. I was in a panic, and Lawrence saw. He came over to where I was sitting. He took my hands in his hard, dirty ones and raised me to my feet. His arms went round me in a lovely strong restful hug. I supposed I shouldn't really be letting him hug me, but no one else seemed to be sympathetic. Adam was too busy with his precious Jane.

Lawrence sat me down on the bed. He kissed me fiercely, biting my lips. His breath was stale and his beard tasted of alcohol but I let him run it all over my face until I couldn't see anything except black hairy darkness.

I couldn't see what was happening so nothing could be. When he started to unzip my jeans, he didn't do it seductively or gently or mischievously as Adam would have done it, he did it casually as if they were his own jeans. Perhaps they were his. I didn't feel as if I had any right to tell him what he could or couldn't do with them.

His breath came in fast, sour, hissing gasps. He left my zip for a moment and fumbled with his fly buttons. This gave me a chance to start pulling my zip back up but he stopped me. 'You know you want it, love.' It sounded like a favour he was about to do me. I would be ungrateful to refuse. He opened the front of his trousers and let his penis out. It was the first one I had ever seen in daylight. I was astonished at how painful it looked, even for him, never mind what it would do to me while I was still sore.

I tried to move away. He said, 'You can't get out of it now.' It had stopped being a favour. It was a punishment, though I didn't know what for.

Outside, the fire escape was clanging as if an athlete or some other very energetic person were racing up it. A shadow appeared against the glass top of the outside door. I would have recognised the shape of the shadow even if I hadn't heard the vigorous footsteps. Lawrence said, 'Fuck,' and let go of me. I did up my clothes and opened the door to my mother.

42

She was wearing the same clothes as she had worn last night on the train. She was windswept, feverish and a little bit out of breath. She gripped my arm. She said, 'Ssh. Not a word.'

I leaned against the railings of the fire escape. I closed my eyes and had a quick fantasy of a mother who would say, *Thank God you're safe* or even, *Sorry I abandoned you on the train.* I let the fantasy go and said, 'Who to?'

'Anyone. Him.' She nodded over the balcony. Far below, Adam was toiling up the steps. My mother, who had run up them, said, 'He should give up smoking.'

'Mum. What is going on?'

'What's going on?' said Lawrence, looming out of the flat, scratching his beard and buttoning up his flies.

I said to my mother, 'Let's go.'

On the way down we met Adam, who was still having trouble with the steps. He patted his ribs and polished his glasses with his handkerchief. 'You found each other,' he gasped.

'Try a few deep breaths,' my mother suggested.

He looked at me accusingly. 'Mrs Trenton said you'd gone off with Lawrence.'

'I was only making a phone call.'

'Adam, would you excuse us?' my mother cut in. 'I need to talk to Christine on her own.'

'It's better if we don't say anything to anyone,' she said, as we walked down a sooty street near a gasworks. 'Forget the whole thing, it's all over.'

'What did you do, shoot them?'

'No need. Rusty was there.'

'*What?*'

'She'd brought him with her. Isn't that priceless? Rubbing

Daddy's face in it. I looked through the sitting room window and saw the four of them: Pam and Rusty, Daddy and Janet, playing Totopoly.'

'Was Janet winning?'

'Pam was in her bloody element, surrounded by admirers. Daddy with his nose out of joint, trying to be a good sport. I almost felt sorry for him.'

'Did you go in?'

'Haven't you listened to a word I've said, Christine? Do you think I'm crazy?' I didn't answer. 'I've been proved right in my tactics so far,' she said. 'Why should I change them? As long as they don't know I know – as long as I give them enough rope – things will take their course and they'll hang themselves.'

'What did you do?'

'I tiptoed away into the night. Left them to it. Stayed in a bed-and-breakfast under an assumed name.'

I thought how pathetic that was. There had been something rather magnificent about the idea of her opening up with a machine gun. But skulking in a seedy hotel a little way from home while she pretended to be somebody else was more in character. 'I caught the early train this morning,' she continued. 'I went straight to Billy's.'

'Oh.'

'Yes. Oh. "Where's Christine?" "Christine rang to cancel, though we thought we saw her at the station."'

'Yes, well.'

'"Yes, well, you can explain"? Good. You'll have to explain to your priest chappie too.'

'Keith?'

'If that's his name. Billy drove me straight to their headquarters, and your Keith was fascinated to discover that you didn't have your parents' permission to sleep there last night. Adam looked a bit green about the gills as well.'

'So you've told him?'

'I have told Adam nothing. He's interfered quite enough already in our family's affairs.'

I thought a bit as we walked along. I watched my feet stepping over the cracks in the pavement. I said slowly, 'I did have your permission.'

'You did not.'

'Yes I did.' I stood in front of her, folded my arms and spoke very deliberately. 'You said I could stay there whenever I wanted to. Have you forgotten? Try and remember. Then you can go back and explain to Keith that it was a misunderstanding.'

'You would never have my permission to stay in a place like that, and as for Daddy – '

'Oh, it's *Daddy* you're worried about, is it? Let's tell him, then, shall we? Let's tell him everything.'

Rage boiled up behind her eyes. 'You vicious, blackmailing little cow.'

'Sssh, don't shout.'

'You'd do anything to get your own way, wouldn't you? You'd even destroy my marriage.'

'We're in the *street*, Mother. Look. Trees. Houses. Lamp posts. *Stop shouting.*'

'I'm not,' she said in a normal voice.

'You were.'

'When?'

'Just now.'

'I wasn't. Not really.' She took a deep breath. 'I must say I was pleasantly surprised. Construction Not Destruction seems very well organised.'

'Oh, it is.'

'I didn't realise there'd be a priest in charge.'

'He's very strict about things.'

'What happens in the evenings?'

'We have educational discussions,' I said. 'It's the next best thing to being at university.'

'And you're sensible, aren't you?' she pleaded. 'I can rely on you to be sensible?' I didn't answer, so she answered herself. 'Of course I can,' she said. 'We'll tell Daddy you stayed at Billy's.'

'We've got to be sensible,' said Adam that night in the storeroom as we cuddled together among the blankets. 'We've got to get something.'

‘What?’

‘Well, um. A French letter or something.’

I had heard of them. I knew they were for birth control, but I didn’t know how they worked. I didn’t know whether the man had to swallow them or the woman. I didn’t want to think about it.

He read my mind. ‘We’re in the clear so far,’ he said. ‘Nothing can happen your first time.’

‘Is that in one of your books?’

‘I’ve heard it somewhere.’

‘Where do you get them from?’

‘I wish I knew. I’ve heard there are barbers’ shops where they cut your hair and take your money and say “Will there be anything else, sir?” They never say it to me.’

‘Aw, poor ickle fing.’

‘I’ll take care of it,’ he said. ‘I’ll take care of you.’ He gave me a big sloppy kiss and put his hand between my legs.

I flinched.

‘Sore? Sorry.’

He put his mouth there. I wasn’t quite so embarrassed this time. After all, he knew what it was like. Also, I didn’t have to worry that it might be a lead-in to going all the way because I knew it was.

It felt lovely. It felt as if I had a tongue of my own down there. I couldn’t remember the Greek name he had given it. It was a tongue. It tasted. A thread of golden syrup coiled round it. The syrup was warm. I thought of Tinkerbell, a beam of light that you couldn’t catch because you never knew where it would move to next. Adam caught Tinkerbell on his tongue, like a frog catching flies.

He crawled round and put his penis in my face. He lifted his own face long enough to say, ‘Will you kiss it?’

It was like kissing a dog’s nose. He pushed it against my lips. I thought if we weren’t careful, it would end up in my mouth.

43

On Sunday night I went home with my mother on the train. She talked all the way about her plans for winning back my father's love, now that she had been given, as she put it, 'another chance'.

'I'll do a blitz on the house,' she said. 'And on my figure.' She punched herself in the stomach and smacked her bottom.

'Lost cause,' I yawned. 'The house. Why can't we move?'

'Moving house is disruptive. I don't want him to be disrupted. And I'll curb that sharp tongue of mine. I do rather bite people's heads off, don't I? Be honest, Christine. Well, he's noticed it even if you haven't, and it's got to stop. I shall cultivate the soft answer which turneth away wrath.' She put on a serene look. 'And in August I'll see to it that he has the holiday of his dreams.' They were going on the Norfolk Broads. I was going to the South of France. She said, 'He's always wanted to have a proper sailing holiday, but we couldn't because of you.'

'Sorry to be a nuisance.'

'Oh, that's all right. If it weren't for you and Janet we'd probably have bought a cruiser and sailed round the world years ago.'

'Go ahead. Take Janet with you.'

'It's an idea,' she said. 'It would make him happy, wouldn't it? He's got the sea in his blood. It would keep him out of that woman's clutches. The trouble is, Janet's education.'

'She doesn't need to go to school, she knows everything already.'

'One of these days we'll do it. But we'll start with the Norfolk Broads. The holiday of a lifetime.'

'You mean because I won't be there.'

'I daresay that'll play its part in keeping rows to a minimum. I wonder if he knows anyone who'll Snowcem the outside of the house? Then I can get cracking on the inside.'

*

When we got in we found my father on his knees in front of the boiler, poking disconsolately at the dead coals. With challenge in his voice he said to my mother, 'I admit it, I've let it go out, don't start yelling.'

'What a nuisance for you,' said my mother. Calmly she took the poker out of his hand. 'Don't worry, I'll have it lit again in two ticks.'

Janet came running from her room with tears all over her face. 'They're going away for ever!'

'How soon?' My mother gripped the poker. Her knuckles went white and her face went pink. 'I mean, who?'

'Pam and Rusty.'

'Pam and *Rusty*?'

'He came with her for the weekend,' said Janet.

'Goodness.'

'They're going to America!'

'How wonderful,' said my mother, though I could tell she would have preferred New Zealand.

'Isn't it?' said my father. 'They've found another country they can leech off and complain about at the same time.'

His tone was his usual one for making cynical remarks about Pam – half joking – but I saw defeat in his face. It wasn't so much that his nose had been put out of joint, it was more that his nose, like all his other features, was starting to wonder whether it was as irresistibly handsome as it had thought.

Janet said, 'I think you're all horrible.'

My mother consoled her. 'We should be pleased for Pam. She's found someone to love her at last. She was getting to be an old maid.'

'We love her.'

'I mean in a special way.'

'I love her in a special way.'

My father was keeping a stiff upper lip. I thought of the kind of weekend he had had, and the kind I had had. I almost felt like telling him that I had been enjoying what he had had to whistle for.

In the weeks that followed I gloated as I watched him. He had been chucked, and he didn't even know that I knew.

He improved. Even I had to admit that. He was probably feeling guilty. Or perhaps he saw our home as the only one he'd got and any port in a storm. Whatever the reason, the Be Nice to Christine policy was suddenly extended to the whole family. It was even extended to people outside. When he failed his driving test again he spoke no harsh words against the examiner. He just booked another appointment.

He stopped staying out late with his boozy friends and his brothers – and Pam, of course. He came home to his darling wife and loving daughters. He took my mother out. He stopped complaining about my face, hair, music, room, clothes, political beliefs, boyfriend and behaviour; he stopped complaining about my mother's housework. He stopped making toilet paper bonfires in the lavatory to get rid of his smell. He used Air Wick like normal people. Most momentously of all, he hired a television. At first I thought it was just a guilt offering.

'Surprise for you girls,' he muttered. 'Thought you might like it.'

Janet flung her arms round him. He looked as if that was what he had done it for. He lifted her up and I said, 'Mind your hernia.'

They weren't listening. Janet was saying, 'Oh, thank you, Daddy!'

'Yeah, thanks,' I said. 'Does it get ITV?' It didn't, of course.

He told us we weren't to watch it all the time. At the first sign of addiction, he warned, it would go. He needn't have worried. The novelty quickly wore off and we only watched particular programmes, such as 'Juke Box Jury' and 'Z-Cars' and (in Janet's case) 'TV Top of the Form'. He was the one who got addicted. He came in after his day's work, planted himself in front of the screen, and that was him for the evening. It was him for half the night as well.

The television was more than a guilt offering, or perhaps I meant less. It was his way of being away from us even when he had to be with us. Behind his glazed eyes, he was no more in the room with us than the commentator on 'Sportsview'. He was outside, howling at the moon, licking his wounds.

My mother tried to lick them as well, without letting him know that she knew he had any to lick. She bought new dresses and went to the hairdresser. She brought him his supper on a tray. She didn't eat but sat with him, nibbling carrots, and saying, 'Look what I've lost.' She pressed her dress against her flat stomach.

'Jolly good. I bet you feel better for it too.' He eyed her up and down as if he had never seen her before. He cocked one eyebrow. 'You're getting to be not wholly repulsive. I can almost see why I married you.' He wolf-whistled through his teeth. He winked at me and Janet as if we were other men. When I reported this conversation to Adam, he said, 'Your father's such a bastard.'

'On the contrary,' I said. 'He was being nice.'

Adam said, 'It's all very well for your father resigning himself to your mum as the next best thing. Who's going to be my next best thing when you leave me and go to France?'

'Janet?'

'She has potential,' he said, and I thumped him.

I said, 'Why shouldn't I go to France?'

'I didn't say you shouldn't, but I don't want you to. Anyway, torture me. Tell me about these people you're going to stay with.'

'They're called the Godards.'

'You're joking! Is he a film director?'

'He's a businessman. Friend of Uncle Rutherford. She's a *femme de foyer*. Sounds better than "housewife" doesn't it? As if she gets time off to go to the pictures.'

'Does he wear dark glasses?'

'How should I know? They've got a flat in Paris and a villa on the Riviera and four *enfants*.'

'Names?'

'Charlotte, Maurice, Marie and Jacques.'

'Ages?'

'Charlotte's twenty-two, she used to be Rutherford and Gwen's *au pair*. Marie's fourteen. She thinks she's coming to stay with me next summer, in exchange. She's got another think coming.'

'Never mind Charlotte and Marie, how old are Maurice and Jacques?' He exaggerated the pronunciation, like my father saying *Meegwell*.

'Jacques is seven. Maurice is *dix-neuf*.'

Adam sighed. 'I knew it. You'll fall in love with this frog. Do you have to go?'

'Hark who's talking! What about when you go to university?'

'That's not abroad.'

'It'll be for months and months.'

'I'll come home every weekend.'

'This is for my education,' I said. 'I'm hopeless at oral.' He chuckled and I said, 'I didn't mean *that*.'

We were in his bedroom. He had come home for the weekend, officially to see his mother, actually to see me. We were lying on his bed, catching up on our news while we undid each other's clothes.

His mother had taken advantage of his absence in Birmingham to muck his room out and paint the walls. The duplicator and the banners had gone to live with the new chairman of Bleswick YCND. The books and magazines were in neat piles. It was like a hospital room.

He said, 'Speaking of things French . . .'

'Oh, have you got one? Let's see.'

It seemed to be made of tin foil, which I thought would either scratch or taste horrible. He tore the foil. Inside was something that looked like a flattened slug. He unrolled it until it looked like an ordinary slug.

'Oh I *see*.' I couldn't help giggling.

'What did you think? I've told you before about laughing during – '

'How are you going to put it on? It's all dangly.'

'So am I, and you're not much help.'

I stroked him and sucked him and somehow we got it on him. It fitted very tightly except at the end where there was a space full of air like a tiny puffed-up balloon.

'Now what?'

'Um, well, the business as before, I suppose.'

It wasn't as before. It was the worst time ever. The French letter was rough and dry and the whole thing hurt me even more than the first time we did it. I felt as if all my skin were being rubbed off. And it wasn't even worth it because the French letter broke. The ring round the top stayed where it was, half way along his penis, but the rest of it sort of disappeared into me and it was a devil of a business finding it and getting it out.

'Oh well,' said Adam.

'Oh well nothing. I'm not doing that again. I'm sterile, in any case. I had a serious illness when I was a little girl.'

'That's not all you should have had when you were a little girl if you told fibs like that. By the way, have you, er, since we, er – ?'

I said quickly, 'I'm always irregular.'

'Yes, but – '

'I never know when it's coming and when it isn't.'

'Oh,' he said.

'That's how I know I'm sterile.'

'Even so,' he said. 'I wish I knew what I was doing wrong. I mean, they must work. They go back to Ancient Rome.'

'No wonder they break. Doesn't your Doctor Prudence whatsit tell you what to do?'

'Not *really*. I mean, she's always going on about over-population and how there should be free birth control for the poor, but she doesn't actually – I mean, not as if she's ever had to put one on herself.'

'She hasn't.'

'You know what I mean. I tell you what.' He sat up. 'When I come to power and we have nuclear disarmament, we'll use some of the defence money to manufacture French letters and give them away free.'

I shrugged. 'Not much use if they break.'

'People will be taught how to use them so that they don't break.'

'At school?'

He thought about it. 'In the sixth form.'

'What about me? I'm not in the sixth form.'

'You're not, are you? You're jailbait.' Gloomily he cleared away the broken bits of French letter. 'They'll be better quality anyway. They won't be French.'

'You're as bad as my dad, he won't buy anything Japanese.'

'That's different. I've got a feeling in my bones about this *Maurice*.'

'So have I,' I said, to tease him.

44

Pam and Rusty would be flying to New York on August the 10th. We were invited to their farewell party in Earl's Court on the 9th, but we would all be away. Janet wanted to come back specially from the Norfolk Broads to go to the party. 'To do that,' said my father, 'would be to give MacLeish an undue sense of her own importance.'

Janet said, 'Can we send her a bouquet instead?'

'She wouldn't know what to do with it.'

'She would. We could have twelve white roses delivered to the plane.' Janet rushed off to Bleswick Blooms and came home with an Interflora catalogue.

'Who do you think I am, Lord Muck?' said Lord Muck, striking his forehead with the palm of his hand as he read the price list. 'That bum's had quite enough out of this family.'

'I agree with Daddy,' said my mother.

Janet tried me. 'Will you club together with me to send some flowers to the plane?'

'What hospital is it in?'

'For Pam.'

'Pick her some flowers from next door's garden, it's cheaper.'

'But they wouldn't be *delivered*.'

'Bung 'em in the post.'

'Oh *please*.'

'I haven't got any money,' I said.

'You liar, you have.'

'I've changed it all into francs. And I'm certainly not going to change any of it back again for someone who calls me a liar.'

She said with quiet dignity, 'You weren't going to anyway.'

I didn't kid myself that there would be any surprise bouquets from Janet waiting for me on board my BEA flight to Nice, but she made me a *Bon Voyage* card, and my parents gave me a satin sponge bag with a new flannel, soap, toothpaste and a dark brown bottle of suntan lotion with a gorgeous smell.

I was the first member of the Sandringham Toms family to fly, and my father marked the occasion by taking time off work to come to London airport with my mother and Janet to see me off.

In the taxi I felt sick with nerves.

The airport was a shock. It had grown and spread since I last saw it. I had been five years old and Gran had taken me there for a treat, to console me for the birth of Janet. There had been a fairground. I had driven a tiny car in a roundabout. This time I hadn't come to play. Perhaps that was why the airport seemed bigger. Long before we saw any planes it was reaching into the countryside with its wire netting and KEEP OUT signs. The air smelt of petrol fumes. They made me queasy and I asked the taxi driver to close his window. In the stuffiness I felt queasier still.

The afternoon sun glittered on hangars and warehouses, big as a block of classrooms at Bleswick County Girls. A petrol storage tank had a skull and crossbones on its side, and the bright red words INFLAMMABLE. NO SMOKING. The earth shook. A huge BOAC jet roared above our car. Its wheels went up into itself. Watching this was somehow embarrassing, like looking up the skirts of an old woman.

WELCOME TO HEATHROW. The road went into a tunnel with orange lights. My face in the mirror looked ghostly and sick, but so did everybody else's, and once I was inside the airport building I felt like a film star.

My heels tapped elegantly on the gleaming floor as I sauntered towards the BEA desk. I wanted people to think that I did this all the time, and that my father, who was coming along behind me with my luggage, was my servant.

The ground hostess looked at my ticket and said, 'Good afternoon, Miss Toms.' She tore out some of the pages which worried me until she handed it back and I was able to check that the return part was still there. She tied a label round the handle of my suitcase and sent it away on a conveyor belt. My father said, 'That's the last you'll see of that.'

I was early so we wandered around and looked at the magazine stands. I let my father buy me a copy of *Paris Match* and I made sure Janet saw me reading it. My parents held hands, intertwining their fingers. They were probably overwhelmed with emotion at the prospect of seeing the back of me.

In the privacy of the lavatory I had another look at Adam's letter.

> 'Darling Chris,
>
> 'It might as well rain until September. The next four weeks will be like four hundred years. Forgive me for not coming to see you off, I couldn't bear it. Have a wonderful time and learn so much French that you'll never have to leave me again. Phone the minute you get back, to end the suffering of,
>
> 'Your loving A.'

The words made me feel as if I were already in the plane, rising up in the great power of my lovableness and crashing down again with the knowledge that I was going to strangers who might not even like me.

I heard my flight being called. I thought if I waited here long enough I might be called by name, as if I were in a film, but I didn't dare. I left the Ladies and gave my father a quick hug to get it over with. After all, he was paying. My mother kissed me and said, 'We'll watch from the spectators' balcony.'

'Make sure your plane gets in the air,' said my father.

Janet started crying. I was astonished. She was actually sorry to see me go, or perhaps she was confusing me with Pam. In any case, I supposed there were worse sisters. While I was in France I might give some thought to starting a Be Nice to Janet Policy. In the meantime I hugged her and said, 'Goodbye, brat. Don't drown, whatever you do.'

In the departure lounge I was surrounded by people talking French and I actually understood some of it. I looked out of the window and saw a BEA plane that might be mine. I tried to believe that that huge, tiny thing was going to rise into the air with me inside it and put me down in a foreign country.

Signs in the Duty Free shop said that cigarettes and spirits could only be sold to people over seventeen, but no one tried to stop me buying two hundred Pure Gold. I felt too sick to smoke but I might want them later. I had heard that brandy was good for sickness, and was just wondering whether to buy myself some when an announcement said that BEA passengers for Nice should proceed to the departure gate. We should extinguish all cigarettes and not smoke again until we were airborne.

Airborne? I thought. *Me*?

But I soon was. I sat in a grey seat in a cabin that was like the inside of a rather luxurious bus, and felt the plane go faster and faster and upwards. My ears popped. I sucked a barley sugar but its sweetness only mixed with the sickly taste in my mouth till I couldn't tell which was sweet and which was sick.

The force of the take-off thrust me back in my seat. It was a thrilling feeling, and terrifying, and completely out of control. It reminded me of sex.

'Ladies and gentlemen, you may now unfasten your seatbelts and smoke if you wish. Your cabin crew will be serving you with drinks and refreshments. If Miss Christine Toms is aboard the plane, will she please make herself known?'

I didn't know how to make myself known. It sounded like taking a bow. I was embarrassed. I raised my hand and the air hostess brought me a rose in a box with a cellophane wrapper. It had drops of water on it, wet tissue paper round the roots and a card that said, 'With love from Adam.'

45

The air hostess gave me a plastic bag called a Discomfort Bag. I was sick into it and gave it back to her. She said, 'Thank you,' and gave me a glass of mineral water and a dry biscuit. Mineral water seemed a very French thing to be drinking. It tasted like water, but I knew it had health-giving properties. I drank it and sniffed my rose and my stomach settled.

I stared out of the window at the amazing, solid-looking clouds. I plucked up my courage to get out of my seat and go to the lavatory. When I moved I expected the plane to tip over, but it turned out that I wasn't that important. When I got back I found I could eat a little smoked salmon and brown bread. By the time the plane began to go down through the purple sunset sky towards Nice I had stopped feeling sick.

I got my first stamp in my new passport and waited for ages for my luggage. I went nervously towards Customs. I wondered if under-age cigarettes counted as smuggling. The customs men waved me through. I was a bit disappointed because I had wanted to see what would happen. I came face to face with the Godards sooner than I had been expecting.

I recognised Charlotte. I had met her a year ago, at Rutherford and Gwen's. She kissed my cheeks and introduced me to her parents, and to Marie who looked as boring in real life as she had seemed from her photograph and her letters. She was like a Gallic Janet without the brains and I was going to have to make friends with her. I wondered what had happened to Maurice.

Monsieur carried my suitcase out to the car-park. Madame chatted to me in slow, clear French which I more or less understood. She said that I was very welcome and that she hoped I would be happy at Menton. If there was anything I needed, I must ask for it.

I said, '*Oui*,' and felt a complete fool.

We drove along the road to Monte Carlo, which I had heard of. The signs said, *Menton, 30 km.* I multiplied by five and divided by eight. The road ran along the side of a mountain with sea twinkling far below in the darkness. Monsieur drove fast and pointed at fortresses. He shouted things over his shoulder at me about Napoleon, or it might have been the Romans.

'I feel sick,' I said. I didn't know what it was in French.

Monsieur swerved into a lay-by. I got out just in time and puked over a railing. Smoked salmon and barley sugar flowed down a slope towards the sea. Monsieur said it was *mal de la route.* Charlotte said it was *mal du pays.* She had felt the same when she first arrived at my uncle's house.

I stared up at the dark mountains and out to sea. Lights shone on boats. I thought of my family sailing away on their boat, round the Norfolk Broads or round the world, it made no difference. They went one way, I went another. I felt like crying.

I sat in the front of the car for the rest of the journey. My stomach settled but my throat still tasted of sick. The road sloped down towards the sea and the lights of Menton. It was an old town with cobbled streets, secret-looking passages and flights of steps that led into walls. Monsieur slowed the car to point out a church. It was called Notre Dame and he told me its history. I assumed it was history because it had a lot of numbers in it which sounded like dates.

We left the town and drove into a forest with sandy soil. Our headlamps lit up a square white villa with a balcony and green shutters. I got out of the car. The air had a clammy, sickly feeling and a rich, sourish smell. It was a mixture of wood and the sea. Far away a dog barked. It sounded enormous. Insects clicked and buzzed and bit me.

The Godards were fussing about with suitcases and keys. I took a few steps into the darkness. Madame called me into the house but I didn't want to go. I wanted the darkness to swallow me up.

I went into the house. They offered me food but I didn't want any. I was scared of being sick again. It was so embarrassing.

Charlotte showed me to my room. It had tiled floors, white-washed walls, and its own washbasin. I put Adam's rose in the tooth glass, unpacked a few things and went to bed.

I lay on my side, staring at the shadowy outline of the rose. *I'm abroad*, I thought, but I wished I were at home. The month stretched endlessly ahead, and I shed a few tears.

I felt better in the morning. I pushed back the shutters and looked down onto a sunlit verandah. Charlotte, Marie and Madame were laying the table for breakfast. I wondered how much housework I would be expected to do. I wasn't going to do as much as Charlotte had done when she stayed with Rutherford and Gwen, because she had been paid. But I didn't want Madame to hate me, so I hope she would tell me what she wanted.

I went to the bathroom for a shower. While I was at it, I had a go on the bidet. Back in my room the air was full of smells of coffee and baking from below. I peeped out and saw Monsieur sitting alone in a short-sleeved shirt, reading *Le Figaro*. Madame brought a pot of coffee and sat next to him. A younger man with fair hair joined them. I guessed this must be Maurice, so I put my shortest skirt on and my sexiest blouse and my war paint. I did my hair and went down to breakfast.

I was the last to arrive but no one seemed to mind. They said '*Bonjour*' and I said '*Bonjour*' back. Jacques, the youngest brother, giggled. Charlotte told him off and introduced the blond young man as Raoul, her fiancé. He said, '*Enchanté*,' and I ate a croissant.

I didn't say a lot but I found I could follow the Godards' breakfast table chat fairly well. They discussed how much better I looked this morning than I had last night when I had *mal de la route*. They said that after breakfast Marie would take me into Menton to show me the sights. I was to speak French all the time and Marie was to speak English.

I can't wait, I thought. *Je ne peux pas something.*

Jacques kept staring at me. To make conversation, I said, '*Où est ton frère?*' and he had hysterics again.

Madame looked apologetic. '*Maurice fait de la voile.*'

La voile? It sounded like, *Maurice has gone out thieving*, but that couldn't be right.

I looked at Charlotte who translated: 'Sailing. Maurice has got a little boat called *Elisabeth* and nothing can keep him from her, not even food.'

After breakfast, Charlotte, Marie and Madame jumped up and started carrying plates to the kitchen. I followed their example and nobody told me to stop. Once the washing-up had been done, everyone had another chore. Charlotte swept the kitchen floor. Marie rinsed the tea towels. I said, '*Puis-je vous aider faire le ménage, Madame?*' and she went into a long torrent of French which I guessed meant, *If you can't see for yourself what needs doing, Christine, it's probably quicker to do it myself.*

46

In the centre of Menton was a square with palm trees, cafés and shops, and buses revving their engines before setting off for romantic places such as Cannes and San Remo. I felt like jumping on the nearest bus and going wherever it took me, but Marie was a studious little person and wanted to show me the town hall. She said it was, 'Very interesting and very history.'

It had a Salon de Mariages with pictures on the wall by an artist called Cocteau. From the way Marie talked I could tell that she expected me to have heard of him, so I said, 'Ah! Cocteau!' in a wise voice.

The churches were very interesting and very history too, according to Marie, and there were about five hundred of them. When I had seen my four hundred and ninety-ninth, I started to suffer from *Mal de l'église,* as a result of all the bleeding crucifixes, crowns of thorns and stifling heat.

'*Café*,' I said firmly, pointing to myself. '*Je suis fatiguée.*' She gave me a look of contempt that was pure Janet and led me down some cobbled steps to a café by the harbour.

We sat under a parasol and I stuck my legs out to catch the sun, also to show anyone who was interested how much nicer they were than Marie's legs. She wanted a mineral water and I wanted a coke. She made me do the ordering. After that, conversation ran out so I bought some postcards. I wrote one to Adam and one to each of my grandmothers. There was no point in writing to my family because by the time the card reached England they would be of no fixed abode.

From the direction of the harbour a male voice called to Marie. A boy in a sailing dinghy was holding on to a ring in the harbour wall and waving. Marie went to talk to him. She seemed glad of the excuse to get away from me. I guessed it was her brother, Maurice. I hoped it was, rather than a boyfriend whom I would have to take off her. I gazed at him through my sunglasses. He was dark and bony, crinkly-eyed and curly-haired. He just escaped being too good-looking and managed instead to be the best looking boy I had ever seen.

I put Adam's postcard away in my handbag, slung it over my shoulder and sauntered towards him. Marie introduced us. He smiled at me and I said, '*Enchantée*.' I couldn't think of anything else. I wished that at some point in my French-speaking career I had learned how to say, 'Please will you take me sailing?' but it had never occurred to me that I would ever want to say such a thing.

I gazed at *Elisabeth* and made admiring sounds and gestures. Maurice said something in French to Marie, who translated. 'Do you want to go in the boat?'

I shrugged. 'I don't mind.' I lowered myself down the side of the harbour wall, trying to be modest in my short skirt while at the same time making the best of my legs. Maurice steadied the boat and showed me where to put my weight. I remembered my father saying to my mother, *This was how you looked the first day I took you canoeing. You didn't capsize the canoe, so I thought, that's the girl for me.* I tried to show Maurice that I wasn't completely ignorant on the subject of boats.

I sat to port and Maurice sat to starboard. Marie waved and went back to the café. Maurice hoisted the single sail. We skimmed over the blue, shiny water. Across the tiny boat our knees touched. His were hard-boned, brown and hairy. Mine were soft and white.

He seemed quite happy sailing his boat and smiling at me in spare moments, but I wanted to talk to him. I couldn't, because the only things I knew how to say in French were boring things. I wanted him to know that I was enjoying sailing with him even though I hated it with my own family, but explaining about me and my family was something I couldn't even do in English.

We headed towards the open sea and the waves got bigger. I hoped he would turn round soon. I didn't say anything because he might think I didn't trust his seamanship.

Slap, went the boat into the waves. *Slap, slap.* Spray drenched my blouse. My nipples hardened. Maurice grinned. I grinned back, there was nothing else to do. We were level with the end of the jetty. The *Elisabeth* was the smallest boat to have come out this far. The colour of the water had changed from blue to deep, blackish green. The waves got bigger.

My fixed grin unfixed itself. I leaned over the side of the *Elisabeth* and was sick. Yellow bile and brown coca cola foamed on the surface of the sea. '*Mal de mer*,' said Maurice. His lip curled with contempt.

I couldn't eat any lunch. I lay on my bed with the shutters closed and listened to the Godards as they lingered over their long meal on the verandah below. They were a very quiet family. They didn't seem to have rows at the table. My parents, on the other hand, didn't seem to think they had had a proper meal unless they had had a row to go with it. At least, that was how it used to appear, before my mother began her campaign of winning my father back through love.

I wondered if they would get through the business of packing for their holiday without returning to their old ways and going at each other hammer and tongs. It would be a testing time.

One by one the Godards came into the house, went to their rooms and slept. I wondered if they had left any food. I was feeling all right again, I was feeling hungry. This sickness was most peculiar. I knew exactly what my mother would say if she were here. *Mind over matter, Christine. Take a few deep breaths.* So that was what I did.

I went quietly down to the kitchen and found some cheese and salad. I sat on the verandah and wrote to Adam while I ate. I was feeling a bit miserable so I made it a funny letter. I told him about Marie and all her churches. I didn't mention Maurice, or homesickness or any other kind of sickness.

As the afternoon grew cooler the Godards got up and asked how I was. I said, '*Très bien, merci*,' and we walked down to the beach for an evening swim. The sea felt like warm velvet.

In the evening we went to a restaurant by the harbour and I ate a big dinner of fish and vegetables and fruit and bread. Our table was lit by oil lamps. Their glow was reflected in Maurice's eyes, but I could tell that a girl who insulted *Elisabeth* by getting *mal de mer* had no chance with him so I decided to be faithful to Adam.

Over the next few days I wasn't sick at all. I practically forgot about it. Then one morning at breakfast I had to get up and rush to the flower bed. After that Madame said she would take me to the doctor. She said what would my mother think if she knew I was ill and wasn't being looked after?

The only way to answer this question would have been to translate my mother's views on illness into French, so instead I let myself be taken to the doctor.

He was young and quite kind-looking. Madame told him that I had been airsick and homesick and carsick and seasick. He sent her back to the waiting room and asked me in English when my last period was.

'No idea.'

He waited. I explained. 'I've never been regular.' It was lucky that he spoke English. *French for Secondary Pupils* didn't prepare you for conversations like this. 'They come when they feel like it.' I sounded twittery and stupid but I couldn't stop. 'Sometimes I have it twice in one month, then I don't have it for months on end.' The air in the surgery felt muffled and white. It was like talking into a pillow. 'Sort of making up for it.' I laughed. This was so embarrassing. He was young and handsome and might have wanted to ask me out. Instead, I was going on and on about my periods.

'Why are you sick, Christine? Do you know?'

'*Mal du pays*,' I said quickly.

'You want to go home?'

I shrugged.

'When will you go?'

'End of August.'

He glanced at his calendar. It was the sixth.

'Three weeks,' he said. He looked relieved. He said quickly, 'Is it possible that you are pregnant?'

'Me?'

'Excuse me if I offended you.'

'No,' I said.

47

It was the eighth.

Tomorrow would be the ninth and the day after would be the tenth.

I packed a few things into a beach bag. I left my suitcase. I didn't want to draw attention to myself.

I waited for the Godards to start their siesta. I listened to their breathing.

I stepped out of the villa on to the hot sandy soil. Even the insects were quiet. I could have been the only person left alive in a world burnt up by the sun. I wouldn't have minded being the only person. It wouldn't have mattered. It was only because of other people that anything mattered, or this particular thing at least. It would have mattered enormously if there were the faintest possibility of it being true.

I walked down the hot road to Menton. A horse and cart went by me, loaded with hay. I looked casual. With a bit of luck the driver would know about mad dogs and Englishmen, and would put me from his mind.

There was a travel agent's in Menton. It had a BEA sign in the window, and Wagons-Lits Cook. I had always looked out for them because they made me feel patriotic. This afternoon, when I needed them, they were no use. The shop was shut.

It didn't matter. I caught the bus to Nice. It was easy, there was nothing to it. *Soon*, I thought, *when all this business has sorted itself out, I'm going to leave school and travel forever.*

I could do it now, I could disappear, I've disappeared already, nobody knows where I am. I'm a runaway, a film star, a round-the-world hitch-hiker.

I got to Nice in the early evening. It was busy and noisy and hot. I found another travel agent's with a BEA sign. I went in and showed the man my air ticket to London for 31 August. I told him I had to go today. He spoke English. He started to say it was impossible. I knew he was going to say that, and I knew it would be a lie. I was ready for it. I had a lie of my own. I told him that my parents had just been killed in a car crash in London and I had to go home to take care of my beloved little sister. Tears filled my eyes. I felt around in my handbag for the telegram to show him. I half-expected to find it.

He didn't wait for me to find it. He didn't want to know any more. He decided to do his good deed for the day. He picked up his phone and gabbled away in French. He wrote things on my ticket and stamped it loudly with a rubber stamp. He pointed at the airport bus and got rid of me.

I thought how easy it was to get what you wanted by telling lies to people who didn't dare to doubt what you said. It was a useful thing to know and I wondered how old my father had been when he found it out.

At the airport the ground hostess couldn't understand why my only luggage was a beach bag. I didn't bother to explain that people like me don't need luggage: we travel light.

I'm in a sort of trance, and it's not until the voice says 'Extinguish all cigarettes and fasten your seat belts in preparation for landing at London Heathrow,' that I realise what I've done: I've spoiled everything, I've wasted it.

My first trip abroad is over. I looked forward to it, and it's finished. I've run away from France and here's England coming up out of that darkness to meet me. We'll land at London airport and I'll go in through Arrivals. How can I be an Arrival, how can I be back? How can everything be over? I didn't buy any souvenirs. I didn't send my postcards. I haven't even got a proper tan.

The air hostess is checking that everybody's seat belt is fastened in preparation for landing. I don't want to land. I want her to take me back to France. She straps me in.

I remember something my mother said once when I was young and pestering her to know what I would be getting for Christmas. *Think how you'll feel on Christmas Day when Daddy and Janet and I and the Humphrey Tomses have lovely surprises and all your surprises have been spoilt!* When she said it, I couldn't imagine it. I can now.

I don't have to imagine – I know. I've had what I was promised and I've spoilt it. It's over. I can't have it back.

The plane lands and taxis towards the lit up buildings. Black rain beats in gusts against my port hole. I shiver in the stuffy air. I was warm in France but now I'm going to be cold again.

'Please make sure you do not leave any personal belongings on the plane.' I've left my personal belongings in France. How am I going to get them back? I didn't think of that. Why don't I think? Why do I always spoil everything? 'Thank you for flying with BEA. We look forward to welcoming you aboard again.' I take my cardigan out of my beach bag and wrap myself up in it. I step off the plane and down the wet steps. A bus waits. The airport is hideously familiar. I remember feeling like a film star. Now I feel like a refugee. I feel like a criminal.

'This way for baggage collection.' I've got no baggage to collect, unless by some crazy, magical chance . . . For one dazzling, dizzy second I think I see my suitcase lurching along the conveyor belt. I step towards it through the harsh, headachey air but someone else gets there first.

I haven't got a suitcase. How can I be back, how can it be over?

The customs men stare at me. I wonder if they'll search my beach bag. I would if I were them. I think I look like a very suspicious character indeed. Will they make me take my clothes off? Will they X-ray my body? Will they be able to tell?

They save themselves the bother. They wave me through. They can see at a glance that I haven't got anything.

Passengers from my flight wander like a little flock of sheep through the terminal. It's empty, apart from us and a cleaner with a mop. The banks and the shops are shut. Chairs are upside down on tables in the snack bar. Some of the passengers are being met by relatives with cars. My family don't know I'm here. They don't know where I am, and I don't know where they are. No Fixed Address, the Norfolk Broads.

People take taxis or make phone calls. *Phone me the minute you get back and end the suffering of your loving Adam.*

It might as well rain until September.

It *is* raining, it's still August, and I'm still jailbait. There's no point in getting him into trouble. I'll sort things out first and ring him up afterwards. We can have a good laugh about it.

I ignore the phone boxes and queue for the all-night bus to the West London Air Terminal, which is in Kensington. I know where Kensington is. It's near Earl's Court. People are always wandering around Earl's Court with suitcases, on their way to or from the West London Air Terminal.

You can look at them and wonder what their story is.

I reach Earl's Court at five o'clock in the morning and wonder if anyone is wondering what my story is. The beach bag slung over my shoulder has grains of sand in it from the South of France, but people looking at me can't know that.

The rain has turned to chilly, clammy mist.

I hurry through the smudgy dawn. Street lamps are going off. Newspaper shops are turning on the lights in their windows.

OVERLAND TO INDIA. 2 SEATS IN A BUS.

5TH AUSSIE GIRL FOR SUPER FLAT, £3 PER WEEK.

NEW TO THE UK? A WARM WELCOME AWAITS YOU AT THE EMPIRE AND COMMONWEALTH FRIENDSHIP LEAGUE.

LARGE CHEST FOR SALE. SMALL DRAWERS.

The other shops are still in darkness. Huge sausages droop from hooks in the dim windows of a delicatessen. A surgical goods shop has kidney dishes, bedpans and corsets, elastic stockings and finger stalls. TEMPS TEMPS TEMPS! says the blackboard in the window of the secretarial agency. 5 SHILLINGS AN HOUR!

I could do with that.

I turn the corner of her road. FOR SALE says a sign on a parked Land Rover. FOR SALE says the Dormobile behind it. I open the gate that leads to her basement. I wish I had my suitcase. I wonder if I've got a story. I wonder how it ends.

48

She rubs her eyes. She says, 'Chrissie? You're in France.' Her voice goes up at the end of the sentence. She yawns and lets me in. She's wearing a towelling wrap over men's pyjamas. Her feet are bare and her hair is loose. I follow her into the sitting room. Her pictures, her rugs, her ornaments, her souvenirs, have all been packed away. All that remains is the landlord's furniture.

On the sofa is a carrier bag full of LPs. It's her party tonight.

'I might be pregnant, Pam.'

At first it's difficult to say, but then it comes in a rush. It's a relief to reach her name. By the time I get there, I know she's going to help. I don't know how. I don't even know what help there is. I just know Pam is the person who can give it. I'm an outsider, but so is she. She breaks rules. She's been everywhere. She knows things. She must know people. She'll know what to do.

She's got her back to me. She's half way through opening the curtains. At the word *pregnant* she stops, then she finishes doing it. She turns in the grey light and stares at me. I look beyond her at two pairs of feet in lace-up boots striding along the pavement at the top of the steps. Whoever owns the feet is carrying a rucksack. I can't see it but I can tell from the feet. I wonder what's in the rucksack, I wonder where it's going.

She says, 'Why do you think you might be?'

'I keep being sick.'

'And? Shit, Chrissie, there's no point in telling me if you're not going to tell me.'

'I haven't come on for a while.'

'How long? How many have you missed?'

'About three.'

'*About*?'

'Yes.'

She says, 'You'll have to go to a doctor.'

'I can't, that's why I've come to you.'

'Me? What do you think I am?'

She doesn't want to be bothered with me. Her New Zealand passport and her TWA ticket are on the mantelpiece where she won't forget where they are. In the hall is a crate of beer bottles. She's going to America tomorrow, with her new boyfriend, to her new life.

I stand up to leave but she stops me. She says, 'I could take you to see my doctor.'

'What would he do?'

'She. Not what you're thinking. There's a law against it. But she might – ' Pam doesn't finish the sentence. I don't want her to. I don't want to hear that her doctor *might* give me the address of the National Council for the Unmarried Mother and Her Child. I can get that myself, out of Evelyn Home.

I say, 'I can't.'

'She's OK.'

'She won't be OK to me.'

'Why shouldn't she be?'

'I'm jailbait.'

'Don't name names.'

I'm so tired. I yawn. She yawns too. 'I'm not thinking straight. We can't do anything now. Get some sleep. I'll think of something.' She shifts the LPs off the sofa and tells me to lie on it. She covers me with an eiderdown. Beneath it my body still smells of the South of France.

I hear her go out and come back in again. She wakes me with a cup of tea at ten past ten. She's carrying a small flat yellow tin with a chemist's label stuck on it. THE TABLETS. TWO EVERY FOUR HOURS. MISS PAMELA MACLEISH.

'For you,' she says.

'Will they do it?'

It looks like a tin of cough sweets. She peels off the label. The lid says, LADIES' IRREGULARITY TABLETS FOR THE RESTORATION OF FEMININE FUNCTION.

'Where did you get them?'
'Doctor.'
I spill my tea all over the place. 'If you told her – '
'Relax, Chrissie.' She clears up. 'I told her I'd missed three periods and I was worried.'
I swallow two tablets with what's left of my tea. Nothing to it. 'Is that all I have to do?'
'They're not going to solve the problem. But they'll tell you if you've got one to solve. They'll bring on your period, if it's coming. If you don't want to go to a doctor and have a proper test, these are the next best thing.'
'*If* it's coming? What do you mean?'
'If you're pregnant they won't work. That's how you tell. You can't get rid of it with pills.' She looks as if she wishes you could. 'And you're not to fool around with knitting needles, either, or gin and hot baths. Promise me?'
I tip the pills out into my hand. 'What if I take them all at once?'
'You'll be sick as a dog and it'll make no difference.'
'What do I do then?'
'There may be nothing *to* do.'
'What if there is?'
'Take these and you'll know for sure by the time your parents get back from their holiday.'
And by the time you've gone to America.
'I'm not telling my dad.'
'It won't be as bad as you think. He thinks the world of you.'
'Sez you.'
'He'll harumph a bit but he'll help.'
'I thought *you'd* help.'
'Me?' she laughs sadly. Her voice changes. 'Can I help by telling you that – if it comes to it – there's nothing to get in a state about? Stay away from amateurs, please, Chrissie, I beg you, but there are private clinics. It's like having your appendix out. That's what they say they're doing, if anyone asks. It's what you say as well. They're clean and safe and – '
'How do you know?'
She thinks before saying, 'I've been myself.'

'When?'

'Year ago.'

'Was it Sandy's baby?'

She nods. She smiles sadly into her tea cup. Suddenly she freezes. She's realised what she's said. She glares at me. 'I walked into that one.'

She thinks I played a trick on her. *She* thinks *I* played a trick. She thinks I set out to trap her into admitting it. Why would I want her to admit it? Why would I want to know? I don't even know why I asked. The words seemed to slip out of my mouth without going through my brain.

I suppose if I'd said, 'Was it my father's baby?' or, 'Would it have been a little sister or brother for me and Janet?' she might have remembered to be careful with her reply, but I wasn't thinking about my father, I was thinking about my friend Pam and her boyfriend Sandy. I wasn't her boyfriend's daughter, she wasn't my father's mistress, we were just two girls gossiping about our uteruses.

Not sordid, she said.

It's the most sordid thing I've ever heard of: my father taking me to the private clinic where he took Pam, and for the same thing.

I don't care how clean or safe it is. It makes me want to puke.

Pam says, 'How long have you known? About me and . . . your dad?'

'Depends what you mean by knowing.' I stand up and start getting my things together. I put the tin of pills in my pocket. She says, 'Don't look at me like that.' I didn't know I was looking at her in a particular way.

She says, 'It's over between me and your dad. You can't blame two people for falling in love.' I wonder why she's pleading for me not to blame her. Why does it matter? Whether I blame her or I don't blame her, she's going to America tomorrow. Of all the people who know about this business I'm the youngest and I've had least say, so why does everyone keep acting as if I'm in charge of it?

I turn my back on her, slam her door and hurry up her steps. The sun has come out. It's drying the pavement. It shines on exotic fruits in boxes outside the delicatessens. I don't even know what the fruits are called, though I think the greyish green knobbly ones are avocado pears.

Negroes and Arabs and English people go to and fro with briefcases and shopping baskets and suitcases. There are music shops everywhere, they've all got their doors open and they're all playing Mersey sounds. At last England's got some decent pop groups. We can hold our heads up in the world. I swallow a Ladies' Irregularity Tablet.

It's dry and I have to stop and collect up some spit to help it down. A middle-aged man is prodding the tyres of a Land Rover, wondering whether to buy it. He looks sour and doom-filled, like my father surveying a house. He wants to find something wrong. He doesn't want the owner of the Land Rover to cheat him, but I wonder if he's a cheat himself. I've got a nice cheekful of spit by now, and I think of how surprised the man would be if he got it in his eye.

It would be a waste. I use the spit to get another pill down. I wonder if cheats like my father are in charge of everything. Not just boats and leases and Land Rovers and buildings and rugby teams, but everything there is. Laws and wars and aeroplanes, who goes to prison and who doesn't, who goes out to work and who has to give up their training and become a housewife, who has a baby and who doesn't, who gets waited on hand and foot, who goes to school and which school they go to, who obeys whom, who hits whom. Who's a criminal and who isn't, who's jailbait and who isn't, who can go to a clinic and who can't, what's cruelty to children and what isn't, who's a problem family and who isn't.

And what if making all those rules isn't enough for any of them? What if they're all like him, what if they all have to have an extra rule that says they can disobey any rule they don't like, even if they made the rule in the first place?

What if they tell everyone else that if they don't like the rules they should get them changed democratically, while they themselves don't bother to get the rules changed democratically because they like the rules the way they are? For other people. For them it's a different matter. They make the rules. They break them.

Down goes another pill. It seems to meet my anger on the way up and I go into a coughing fit outside an employment agency. I imagine the clinic staff when he turns up with me. *Another one, Mr Toms?* They smirk, then they cluck sympathetically when they realise I'm his daughter. I wonder what they're like. They're criminals, I suppose. Is my father a criminal? Who knows? Who decides? Who makes the rules? I cough and cough. A girl from the agency is changing TEMPS TEMPS TEMPS 5/– AN HOUR to TEMPS TEMPS TEMPS 5/6 AN HOUR. She says, 'Are you all right?' She brings me a glass of water. I get two more pills down. I make my way to the underground, and Paddington, and trains to Bleswick.

I don't care how clean and safe it is. I don't care if the Queen herself goes there. I'm not going. I'm not going to let him show off as the tolerant Daddy who helps his juvenile delinquent daughter no matter what she does because blood is thicker than water. He should know how thick my blood is. He's shed it. He's not shedding any more. I'll manage this myself.

Jo

49

The boat's name was *Katharine of Aragon* and she was a twenty-five foot sloop with gaff rigging and a loose-fitted jib. I had learnt these terms by heart from the brochure in case anybody asked. I couldn't have put my hand on my heart and sworn that I knew exactly what they all meant, but I knew as soon as I saw her that she was a jolly nice boat.

She had varnished timbers and her brown sails were stained with salt. I wondered romantically where she had been. There were two anchors, a quanting pole, and, for short trips, a tender with blunt ends and tiny oars. Below was a dear little galley, the heads with a washbasin, a main saloon and a fore cabin about the size of our understairs cupboard at home. This would be Janet's bedroom. Mine and Sandy's would be the main saloon; Mr and Mrs Hardy, the owners, demonstrated how the dining table opened out into a double berth. They made it look simple.

I exclaimed with delight over everything, and I was delighted to be here, but I was rather taken aback by the lack of space. Still, it was probably all to the good. The less there was of *Katharine of Aragon*, the less there would be to keep clean, or to prove inadequate at keeping clean.

Simplicity was the keynote. I would be like the prehistoric woman in *The Cat That Walked by Himself*: she scattered sand on the floor of her cave, lit a fire, hung up a horse-hair curtain and that was her housework done. If the cave got messy, she and her family moved on and found another.

Mr and Mrs Hardy said they would leave us to sort ourselves out. When we were ready to weigh anchor we should give them a shout and one or other of them would come a little way up river with us. I guessed that this was to check that we knew how to sail and Sandy considered it somewhat infra dig, but he didn't say anything.

I asked Mrs Hardy for directions to the nearest general store, which she gave. While Janet and Sandy began stowing away their kit and checking the boat's equipment against the inventory, I routed out my folder from my kit bag (needless to say, it had found its way to the bottom), unclipped Shopping Lists One and Two and set off with my string bags.

The woman at the shop was chatty and helpful, and gave me the benefit of her many years' experience of helping people to shop for boating holidays. For example she pointed out that a packet of Ryvita would be a better bet than a box of Energen Rolls because it would take up less space in the galley. There were lots of things like that, things that ought to have been obvious but which I had been too much of a fool to think of.

I made three proper trips, and one more little one because I had forgotten the Golden Shred. Sandy was very patient. We finally set off at about five o'clock, tacking eastwards into a light wind along the Bure towards Salhouse and Hoveton Broads. Sandy was at the helm and Janet took charge of the jib sheets. Mr Hardy just sat there. After about half an hour he said, 'I can see you know what you're doing, sir,' and let us put him ashore.

We cruised on alone into the sunset. The water was evening red. We nodded at other sailing vessels and averted our eyes from motor-cruisers, particularly the ones that had their fenders out, or TV aerials on the roofs of their cabins. One motor-boat skipper in a pretend sailor's hat was going much too fast, showing off to some girls he had aboard, zig-zagging, churning up a wash and calling remarks. 'Need a tow, old boy?'

'No thank you,' I retorted. 'Sailing is much more fun.'

The girls on the motor-cruiser laughed. Janet said, 'Sssh, Mummy.'

Perhaps my riposte had come out more loudly than I intended, but it amused me to know that I now had two daughters old enough to be embarrassed by me, instead of just one. I smiled at Sandy.

I had made the comment to please him. One of the main things he loved me for was that I shared his love of sailing. And during this holiday, I planned to be everything that he loved.

He didn't know that I knew about him and that little whore from New Zealand. Success wasn't exactly my middle name, but I had successfully kept that knowledge – the knowledge of *my* knowledge – from him.

The only other person who had the knowledge was Christine. That was unfortunate. It could have been disastrous. But Christine was a sensible girl at heart, and loved her father, whatever she liked to pretend. I had taken the right steps. I had talked things over with her in an adult way and convinced her that it was in the interests of the family as a whole that she should keep her trap shut. I thought she probably despised me for letting him get away with it, but it wasn't as simple as that. In letting him get away with it, I was getting away with it myself.

His unfaithfulness was, and his abandonment of me would have been, no more than I deserved. But we don't always get what we deserve in life, which is just as well for people like me.

The worst that could be said about him was that he was weak and too attractive for his own good. But granting all that, and granting the way Pam threw herself at him, I still couldn't avoid the question of my own failure. *Question* was the wrong word. I had no questions. Why ask questions when you already know the answers? I knew myself inside out. I was – had been – a rotten wife.

As a housewife, he had said once, when I pushed him beyond endurance, *you'd make a semi-competent No 4 stoker*. He was too kind. He overestimated my stoking abilities. On another occasion he had said, *If you must be a slut, for Christ's sake be a happy slut*. I couldn't even manage that. I was ill-tempered, sloppy, loud-mouthed, fat, shrewish. I wanted him to love me but I did nothing to make myself lovable.

That was what you had to do. I hadn't understood that, but I understood it now. I had been taught it in the nick of time – by Pamela MacLeish. Just because as a child you got loved by your parents no matter what – as my parents loved me, particularly Daddy – it didn't mean you could go on taking love for granted.

On the contrary. Love was something you had to go out and graft for.

Should I be grateful to Pam for teaching me this? I was the last person she would want to do favours for, but she had done me one. She had shown me what could happen . . . and withdrawn before it did.

It was as if she had flung me down a ravine . . . but just before my body smashed into the rocks she had tugged on the rope that had been attached all along. She had hauled me back, saved my life from her own threat to it. She had given me another chance. One day I might be grateful to her. Not yet though. Not until she had actually gone. Her flight took off from London airport seven days, fourteen hours and thirty-three minutes from now.

She was a girl who had known how to make herself lovable. To Sandy. To me she was about as lovable as dogshit on the carpet but that wasn't the point. I wasn't being asked to love her. And nor was anyone else, any more. Apart from Rusty. That was his job. I wished him joy of her. I really did. He had brought joy to my life by taking her out of it. This time next week . . . this time next week, plus a little while, they would be in the air. Then I wouldn't even have to hate her any more.

What a relief that would be. Hating was so tiring, especially when no one must know, and someone as sharp-eyed and untrustworthy as Christine *did* know. But Christine was far away now, in France, and by the time she came back Pam would be even further away. No more hating. I would save my energy and use it to make myself more and more lovable.

50

We took turns steering, getting to know *Katharine of Aragon* and her ways. Or rather, Sandy and Janet got to know them, I pretended to. I loved sailing but I was too much of a landlubber to grasp any sort of subtlety. I could feel that *Katharine of Aragon* was heavier and slower to respond to the helm than *Griselda*, our dinghy at home, but that was about it.

I preferred to place myself in Sandy's hands when I was on a boat, and do what he told me. After all, somebody has to be captain.

We found a mooring off the garden of a pub. Sandy took Janet for a drink while I stayed on board and put a kettle and two saucepans of water on the Calor gas rings. I lit the rings.

While the water was coming to the boil, I opened a tin of runner beans in salted water and ate them with a spoon. I looked out a broom and dustpan and brush and gave the galley, the main saloon and fore cabin a jolly good sweep. By this time the water was boiling. I used it to sterilise the loo, the cutlery and the plates and cups. This set my mind at rest.

In the course of doing my jobs, I mislaid my folder and so was unable to refer to Menu One. Rather than get into a fantigue, I breathed deeply until I was calm. I was fairly sure that tonight's supper was supposed to be curry. I decided that whether it was or whether it wasn't, that was what we would have.

I myself didn't like curry all that much but it didn't matter because I would only be pretending to eat. He liked curry, the hotter the better, and she liked whatever he liked.

He liked hot foods generally. I had seen him have competitions with his brothers to see who could eat the hottest things; they would eat whole chillis and spoonfuls of raw mustard until tears poured down their cheeks.

In London he liked to go for curry lunches aboard *HMS*

Carnation, the RNVR Training Ship on the Victoria Embankment. They reminded him of his navy days. I didn't kid myself that sailing with me on the Norfolk Broads made up for the navy, but I could make curry the way he liked it, and do other things the way he liked.

They returned from the pub with a bottle of cider. They had bought it for me so I pretended to drink some of it, but I poured it into the river when I could. Of all alcoholic drinks, sweet cider was the only one I would ever choose to drink, but I wouldn't choose it. If I were going to take in that many calories, I would rather have them in the form of a cream bun.

Pudding was Penguin biscuits, but I had a lovely apple. Sandy said, 'All hands to the galley,' so Janet did the washing-up. He took me for a walk along the towpath.

'Damn good scoff, Jo.'

'Oh, it wasn't.'

'All right. Wasn't then.'

I was bad at taking compliments, and this irritated him. Compliments confused me at the best of times, probably because I didn't get very many. I didn't deserve very many. When they did come my way, I treated them with suspicion. They might be jokes or sarcasms or lures. If I accepted them, I would be slapped down. As Daddy used to say, 'When did your trumpeter die?' If I were worthy of Sandy's compliments, what had he been doing with Pam? *Why had he let her in?*

'What d'you think of *Katharine of Aragon?*'

'It's lovely. I mean, she is.'

'Galley got everything you need?'

'Yes.'

What was this, an interview? An interrogation? Why couldn't we just be quiet? Why was he so afraid of silence? Did other couples twitter and jabber at each other like this? Did we always? Since Pam, I couldn't remember what was normal between me and Sandy and what wasn't.

Curlews called through night air that was warm as blood and smooth as cream and dark as the body's openings. We walked apart from each other but drew closer as the path narrowed. Our arms brushed. He took my hand. I glanced at his face and he smiled down.

He said, 'All right?'

I thought in exasperation, *What does THAT mean?*'

Does it mean, is it all right for me to hold your hand?

Does it mean, are you feeling quite well?

Does it mean, am I forgiven? Are we – you and I – all right for the next thirty or forty years?

Of course we are.

We have no choice. We made vows to each other, remember?

And even if I had a choice, I would still choose you and choose to stay with you, I would still choose to forgive.

'Yes, all right,' I said.

It seemed to come a long time after the question. It was only a sound, meaningless as a bird call.

Bird calls weren't meaningless. Not if you were a bird. They were mating calls, lewd and seductive. *To whit to whoo* or *pee-wit* could mean, *Come over 'ere, darlin'*. Or even, *I love you.*

I said, 'Shall we go back now?'

Janet was in her cabin. Her oil lamp cast her shadow against the curtain that separated her from our main saloon. She was sitting up in bed, writing.

We struggled to turn the dining table into our bed. It creaked a lot but it remained unmistakably a dining table. Janet called, 'What on earth are you two doing?'

'Come and show us then, clever,' said Sandy.

She came out in her pyjamas with her hair still in plaits. 'I think Mr Hardy undid this screw.' She undid it, and the table became a bed. 'Night-night,' she said.

We took turns to wash at the sink. He put pyjamas on, so I did the same. I would have preferred to be naked with him, but he decided when I was to be naked and when not. If he wanted me naked he would tell me. Or he would let me get into bed with my pyjamas on, and then he would tear them off me. There was always a chance of that.

We doused the lights and got into bed to a cacophony of springs and giggles. The air in the cabin was shimmery and whitish blue from moonlight reflected on the river and in through the tiny port holes. With his pale hair and gleaming eyes, he looked like a supernatural being. I bet I didn't.

In fact I knew I didn't, because he had the power to make me want to roll on my back and roll down my pyjama bottoms and offer myself, but I didn't have the power to make him want to take up the offer. He made a hopeless gesture in the direction of Janet's cabin, as if to say, *You must know we can't when she's there.*

It was a new one. I gave him that. It made a change from falling asleep in front of the television. I propped myself up on my elbow. I smiled down at him and tried to look teasing. I must not look serious, whatever I did. It had to be a joke that I was up and he down. He wouldn't like it as a serious thing.

If he didn't like it, why didn't he seize me, throw me on my back, rear over me, take me?

He lay there. I kissed him. He responded a bit but he wouldn't give me his tongue. I put my lips to his ear and sucked the lobe. It tasted of river and earwax. I whispered, 'Why didn't we send Janet to France with Christine?'

'Because we're daft. Come 'ere.' He chuckled and hugged me and let me go. 'Night-night.' The silence was awful. 'Don't want to traumatise Janet for life, do we?' he whispered. I didn't see why not. What about me being traumatised for life by not being made love to?

51

On the day Miss Pamela MacLeish was due to load her hot and squalid little body into an aeroplane and set off into the wide blue yonder, never (please dear God) to be seen again, I seemed to be the only member of *Katharine of Aragon*'s crew not incapacitated by grief.

Even the boat herself seemed to have given up the ghost. Considering her name, and considering how exultant its original bearer would have been had Anne Boleyn taken it upon herself to set off for the New World on the arm of some strapping new swain, I felt the boat was being a rather poor sport. I was in frolicsome mood. But *Katharine of Aragon* limped through the yellow, muggy air of the hottest, stillest day of the year, and, reaching the syrupy middle of Hickling Broad, promptly became becalmed.

Janet succumbed to an attack of the vapours, which she called sun stroke. I briskly informed her that nobody in England got sun stroke, not real sun stroke, but she retired below, helping herself to biscuits as she went. 'If you really had sun stroke,' I called after her, 'You wouldn't want to eat.' She took no notice. She lay on her berth, weeping and chewing and frenziedly writing her latest novel.

Sandy sunbathed. Sandy *never* sunbathed. Sandy held sunbathers in contempt; but today he was *in extremis*. His love was going. She was actually *going*. He knew it, I knew it. Naturally we did not discuss it. We didn't discuss anything. I made a few of my usual bright remarks to show there was nothing special about today as far as I was concerned; he did not reply. He did not want to talk to me.

He had managed the whole thing very badly. He ought to have arranged to be in a pub, surrounded by local yokels, preferably adulterers themselves with whom he could cry into his beer.

Instead the poor old thing was trapped with the missus on board a very small boat, surrounded by a great deal of water. So he took the only escape open to him. He stripped down to his pre-war swimming trunks with the appliquéd little man diving down his thigh, hauled his maddening golden body on to the roof of the the cabin and covered his face with the *Daily Telegraph*.

He looked like a sacrificial victim whose head had been removed in some awful rite. But if he were a sacrificial victim, who was the sacrifice being made to? Me? Was I the villain of the piece? Probably.

He would get over it. I supposed he would. But what were my suppositions worth, on adultery of all things? It was one of a great many subjects on which I was completely ignorant. I was a fairly simple soul as far as my marriage vows were concerned. I had made them and I had kept them. I thought others should do the same.

Poor old Sandy. It couldn't be pleasant to know that somebody you had thought you were in love with was flying off to the far side of the world with someone younger than you, freer, more potent. I felt like whisking away his *Daily Telegraph* and saying this to his face. But I didn't because I wasn't supposed to know.

I must not give any sign of knowing. I must not look at planes. I must not even look at the sky. If a plane appeared in it, an involuntary cry of triumph might burst from my lips. I wanted to look, but I didn't. I wanted to see evidence that it was actually possible for planes to fly and take people to foreign countries, far, far away.

I didn't want her plane to crash. I had considered it, but decided against it. Naturally I would have been quite happy for her to plunge into the sea and be painfully eaten by sharks or whatever other passing predators fancied chewing on a predator from another species. But I didn't trust anything in my life to be that simple.

If her plane crashed, I would bet my last shilling it wouldn't be into the sea. It would be into England, a soft bit. It would be into a mud flat on the Norfolk Broads. *Katharine of Aragon* would be sailing past at the time. It would be a miracle. Pam would survive, Rusty wouldn't. We would be back to square one.

No. I wasn't going to bother with plane crashes. Too complicated. This was simple, and it had been given to me. She was going of her own free will. That was all I wanted. I wanted her O-U-T. She could go wherever she liked in the world for my money (and I would have given her money, every penny I owned, if I had thought that was what it took) as long as it wasn't anywhere near my husband or me. I didn't want a confrontation or a drama. I was extremely proud of myself for having avoided both. I didn't want to discuss it. I wanted her to go away.

And she had gone. When finally we reached Potter Heigham (with the aid of the quanting pole; morale aboard the *Katharine of Aragon* was so low that even this indignity had apparently lost its sting) I raced off to the nearest phone box. Using coins I had husbanded for the occasion, and a phone number and flight number that were etched on the backs of my eyeballs, I rang the TWA desk at London airport and checked that the flight had taken off without mishap, and with its full complement of passengers. It had.

I leaned against the burning glass and metal sides of the kiosk. Tears of relief pricked my eyes as, very slowly, I breathed out all the anguish and terror and self-doubt that had been dumped into my life by Pam MacLeish. I choked. There was nothing to breathe in. The air in the kiosk was too hot, too dry. It was like being inside a pillow. I panicked, pushed open the door. Out in the open I breathed freely. There was plenty of air for everybody. I could hardly walk back to the boat. I was exhausted. I had lived through the ordeal of everyone who had ever agonised between life and death and heard the news they wanted to hear.

For some it might be, *No Abnormality Detected.*

For some it was *Not Guilty.*

For myself I couldn't think of any words more beautiful than, *Taken off with full Complement of Passengers.*

Aboard *Katharine of Aragon*, everything was quiet. There was no sign of Janet; Sandy was flaked out on her berth in her cabin, half naked, pink and sore-looking with sunburn.

The cabin's air was rich with the earthy stink of his sweat, fetid and delicious. One hand dangled at his side; the elbow of the other arm was bent over his eyes. His bare feet stuck out over the end of the bed. He didn't fit. This was Janet's bed, not his. He had no bed. He had a half share in a dining-table-cum-put-U-up. He looked like something that had been discarded.

He *was* something that had been discarded.

I pitied him.

Amid the bitterness and triumph in my heart, I found pity.

I thought that was rather Christian of me. I fetched my Nivea. I perched beside him, scooped out a cool white dollop and dropped it on his burning flesh. As I started to rub, he started to groan. Pleasure and pain were in the groans. By pressing harder or less hard, by moving towards or away from more darkly inflamed areas, I could control the groans, the notes of pleasure, the notes of pain.

Writhing beneath my fingers, he said, 'What are you up to?'

'Sunburn's a serious matter.' I went hard at a tender spot. He yelped. I laughed. 'See?'

'That's not what you told Janet.'

Bloody Janet. 'Where is she?'

'Gone for a walk. That *hurts*, Jo.'

Fancy that.

'Gently, Jo. Your poor patients.'

They got better. If only to escape my brisk ministrations.

'Stop it,' he said.

Make me stop it. My hands scraped and burrowed in his grilled flesh. When he seemed on the verge of having had enough, I became gentle. I caressed and tantalised. Then I hurt him again.

He reared up and rolled me over with his mighty strength. It was time for me to bow out. He took away all my choices, all my responsibilities, all my failings. He immobilised my vicious hands. I became the recipient of his justly vengeful, hurting, thrusts, lovely, lovely. His face loomed above me, lordly and meanly furious, possessive yet surprisingly kind. All was not lost if he could look at me like that.

He paused. 'I take it you've got the doings in.' He could take whatever he liked. 'Don't worry,' I said, and he prodded on, shafted me good and proper.

Don't worry.

Not *yes*.

Yes would have been a lie.

The doings were in the sponge bag.

52

When Janet got back everything was shipshape. I was cooking bangers and mash and singing *Red Sails in the Sunset.* Sandy was sitting at the dining table drinking a glass of beer and writing up the log. 'Are you going to put *that* in it?' I teased him.

Janet looked hot, distracted and depressed, which irritated me because, having made Sandy happy again I wanted to keep him that way. I tried to get her to join in with *Red Sails in the Sunset* but she went to her cabin and put her exercise book away.

I called after her, 'Did inspiration strike?'

'No.'

She was a clever girl, in which she was quite unlike me. But she took herself much too seriously.

After supper Sandy said, 'All hands to the galley,' so Janet did the washing-up. I said to him, 'Why don't we go to the pub?' which surprised him. He asked Janet to come with us, but she wouldn't. We left her sitting on the deck of the *Katharine of Aragon*, writing by the light of an oil lamp. She *looked* like a writer. She also looked a bit lonely, but that was up to her.

I held his hand as we walked along the towpath. We passed a few people and I said, 'Good evening.' He said, 'Do you have to?'

'Have to what?' I asked, astonished.

'Get into lengthy conversations with people you've never met.'

I apologised. When we reached the pub I put on a special bright smile. Pubs were very important to Sandy, and I had made up my mind that since he was making a special effort to be loving towards me I could make a special effort to take an interest in pubs. Some of these old Norfolk pubs were quite historic. I glanced interestedly at the beams.

He said, 'What are you having?'

'What would you like me to have?'

'Have what you want.'

'What *should* I have? As your wife? A beer, or a gin-and-tonic, or a Babycham or – '

'*Not* Babycham,' he said firmly. 'I draw the line at that.'

'There you are, you see. I didn't know. I don't know anything about it; educate me.'

He bought me a half pint of Old Norwich. He said that if I rolled it around my tongue in a particular way I would taste the hops.

I tasted something, I didn't know if it was hops, but on my next round I had a tomato juice.

We didn't talk much. I was still having my afterglow so I was happy enough, but in the normal course of events this was what I didn't understand about pubs and pub-going. You were thirsty, you went to a pub, you had a drink, fine. But *staying* there? Sitting on a hard bench hour after hour in a badly ventilated room, talking about nothing or not talking at all, pouring bitter liquid down your throat, and having to keep going to the lavatory? This was fun? Personally I would choose a doughnut over Old Norwich any day, but what would people think of me if I went out for an evening with a gang of girlfriends and all we did was take turns to buy each other doughnuts?

'One for the road,' said Sandy.

And then his brother Rutherford walked into the pub.

I thought, *Oh, no. Sandy's invited him to stay.*

But Sandy was as surprised to see him as I was. And in Rutherford's eyes there was a sort of haunted, horrified look.

He was the eldest brother, the responsible one. He was an insurance broker, working all day with risks and deaths and mishaps. His face was darkly bearded and permanently gloomy. Had our house burned down? Was Grandma Toms dead?

Sandy said, 'What are you drinking?'

'Nothing.' Rutherford put his hands on Sandy's shoulders, sat him back down next to me, glanced around to make sure nobody could hear and told us that Christine was dead.

My daughter Christine. Our daughter. Sandy's hand clutched mine. His grip was tighter than the grasps and clenchings of lovemaking. Our daughter. Our firstborn. Born first, dead first. First in, first out. Our firstdead child.

My baby, ours.

How?

'*How*?'

'Sssh, Jo.'

People were staring.

Pub people. Who cared what they thought? I didn't even know what I thought yet. I didn't know. '*Tell me.*'

Rutherford called over to the barman, 'Would you bring three brandies?'

'Certainly, sir.'

I didn't know you could do that in pubs. I thought you had to go to the bar. Were we special? Were we making a scene?

Sandy said, 'Tell us straight, Rutherford. Begin at the beginning.'

The beginning was a phone call he had received from Charlotte Godard in Menton to say that Christine had run away. Charlotte had rung him because she couldn't ring us. He couldn't ring us either, of course.

He had hummed and hawed a bit and phoned round the family. The consensus of opinion was that he should get into his car and drive over to Bleswick. No one was sure what for, but it was something to do. He asked our neighbours if they had seen Christine. One of them thought he had noticed steam coming out of our bathroom window some hours before.

Rutherford broke into the house. He found her in the bath.

'And – ?' Sandy looked steadily at his brother.

'And . . . unconscious. Pulled her out as best I could. Did what I could.' Rutherford cradled his brandy glass between his long, flat fingers. 'Called an ambulance. Too late. All I could do.'

Sandy said, 'You've left something out.'

'I'm telling you, man.'

'Get on with it then. Why was she unconscious?'

Rutherford said, 'Are you all right, Jo? Do you want another brandy?'

'I didn't want this one. I agree with Sandy. I want to know.'

'The ambulance chappies reckoned she was trying to give herself an abortion.'

'Knitting needles – ?' It was all I could think of. I felt a stabbing in my own womb, I wanted to bend double.

'Nothing like that, Jo. She'd been at Sandy's gin. And tablets of some sort. Threw up. Passed out in the hot water. Drowned. There'll be a post-mortem but that's what they reckoned. They've seen it before.'

After finding Christine, the next thing Rutherford had to do was find us. He had phoned round the family for ideas.

Humphrey suggested an SOS message on the BBC and volunteered to arrange it but of course we hadn't got a transistor, they were non-U.

Kennington and Kay had just received a postcard from Janet, showing Acle Bridge and mentioning the name of our boat. The postmark had enabled the brothers to narrow down the possibilities of how far we had got. They and their eldest sons got in their cars and drove to Norfolk. Since early this evening, Toms men had been plodding along towpaths from mooring to mooring, shining torches on to the name-plates of boats, shouting, 'Toms family?' and '*Katharine of Aragon*?'

That was how Rutherford had come upon Janet, who had told him where we were.

I had forgotten about Janet.

'Does she know?'

'Er, no,' said Rutherford. 'Not my place to tell her.'

I supposed that meant it was mine.

We walked in single file along the towpath. I led. Sandy held me tightly round my waist. He pressed himself against me, matching his step to mine. He was big and solid and trembling. Rutherford brought up the rear like a herdsman. As we neared the mooring, he said, 'I'll leave the three of you alone together. I'll be in the car-park.'

He left us, he escaped.

She was sitting on deck, staring into the darkness. Some sort of party was going on in the next-door boat, with people to-ing and fro-ing in tenders. She looked like the loneliest person in the world. She was an only child and did not know it. Her exercise book was closed in her lap. Her expression was one not often seen on Janet's face. She looked puzzled, unsure, afraid of something yet to be identified. Her open, confident, knowing, Toms features were only half open, half confident, half knowing. I knew a lot about half knowing. Knowing something's up, not knowing exactly what, preferring to leave it at that. 'Hello, darling.'

'Hello,' she said. 'Did Uncle Rutherford find you?'

'Yes.'

Sandy said, 'Yes he did, as a matter of fact.'

'Is he coming to stay?'

'No.'

'What did he want?'

'Shall we come aboard?'

'Where is he, why has he come?'

I stood full square before her. I put my chin up. *A guide sings and smiles under all adversity.* 'We're going to have to be very brave.'

'Why?'

'Christine,' I said, 'has had an accident.'

'What sort?'

I gave up. I let Sandy do it. I should have done it, but even in this I was found wanting. He took us below. He made Janet sit down. 'She's dead.'

As if correcting him, Janet said, 'She's in France.'

'She's in Bleswick and she's dead.'

She screamed, 'Don't be stupid, Daddy! Don't be stupid!'

He hugged her till she was quiet. 'It's true, old thing. We wouldn't make it up.'

'What sort of accident?'

I said quickly, 'We don't know yet.'

'We do, Jo.'

'We don't, we don't know it was that!'

Janet said, 'Don't know it was what?' She looked past me. She wanted her answer from him. He would not lie or conceal anything, he had an honourable heart. He said to me, 'She's got to know sooner or later. Everybody else will.'

'Wait until *we* know.'

He overruled me. 'Janet, do you know what an abortion is?'

'It's a sin.'

'What sort?'

'Mortal.'

'I mean, do you know what it . . .?' He was floundering now, he didn't know what she knew and what she didn't.

I had never told her about abortion.

Perhaps I should have. Obviously I should have told Christine more, though she always seemed to me to know everything.

I had told Janet about periods, but the best word to describe her reaction was *appalled* so why should I move on to abortion, how was I to know that something like this would happen?

He ran his hands through his hair. He cleared his throat.

'When a girl's not married and she's expecting a baby, girls sometimes do things to, er, make it go away. Bad things, dangerous things, you shouldn't ever, she should have told me, I would have – '

Astonished, I said, 'You would have *what*?'

Janet said, 'Was she expecting a baby?'

The juxtaposition of *was* and *expecting* made me gasp with pain. The past tense next to the future. Christine would never expect anything again, and nothing would be expected of her.

He was saying gently, 'Yes, Janet, it looks as if she was.'

Janet said, 'How?' and I realised she was at that stage when sexual intercourse is quite simply unimaginable.

'Young ban-the-bomb, I expect,' said Sandy. 'Saviour of the world. Didn't save her.'

53

The house was in a frightful pickle. The bath had overflowed, ruining the stair-carpet and the wallpaper in the hall. I was all for using this as an excuse for rolling up my sleeves and giving the place a jolly good blitz. Among other things we could get rid of the boiler. I had always suspected it of malice, and now it had killed my daughter. It had heated the water. It was news to me that Christine even knew how to light it.

The police wouldn't let us get rid of anything. They were gathering evidence. They found an empty yellow tin marked 'LADIES' IRREGULARITY TABLETS.' They asked if I knew what they were. I said that they sounded to me like a hormonal pregnancy test, or, more likely, a flour-and-water placebo. I explained that I had been a nurse.

They asked if I had ever seen the tin before. They put the same question to Sandy, and even to Janet. We all said no, of course not. They took the tin away for tests. They found gum on the lid, where a label had been peeled off. Inside, microscopic dust matched tablets found in Christine's stomach and her vomit. They needed to know how she had got hold of the tablets.

They asked our doctor, who hadn't seen her for months, and other doctors in the area. They enquired at local chemists' shops.

If Christine had acted alone, they said, it would be straightforward misadventure. But if anyone had conspired with her to procure an abortion, that person could be guilty of manslaughter. In addition, of course, there was the matter of unlawful sexual intercourse with a minor. Sandy gave them Adam's address and particulars.

Reverend Mother wrote:

'Dear Mr and Mrs Toms and Janet,

'Please accept the sincere condolences of the

Community following the tragic death of Christine. We are remembering her and you in our prayers. Our Convent and its chapel are open to you, should you feel that you can find comfort here.

'With the beginning of term less than a month away (and some local schools start even sooner than that) I feel it would be useful for the four of us to have a meeting as soon as possible to discuss Janet's future.

'I should be most grateful if you would telephone my secretary to arrange an appointment. May God bless and strengthen you in your grief.'

On the face of it, it was a perfectly reasonable letter. Kind, even. I couldn't find a single word in it that I could object to. But there was more to this epistle than the words it contained. There was a tone to the whole thing that I did not like.

It was smugness, a sort of Holy-Joe-ism. I supposed you could say if nuns weren't allowed to be Holy-Joes, who was? But what a time to pick. *Our chapel is open to you.* As I said to Sandy, 'Anyone would think we didn't have a church of our own.'

He said, 'They probably think we're ripe for conversion.' When Janet wasn't around, he said, 'Do you think they'll keep her?'

'Why shouldn't they keep her?'

'Dunno, just a thought. Why all this talk about "other schools in the area"?'

He had a point. In Roman Catholic terms, Christine had committed a mortal sin. Two mortal sins. According to them, she would be in hell. It might reflect badly on the school to have a pupil whose sister was known to be in hell.

But then Roman Catholics thought everyone who didn't belong to their faith was a heathen, and destined for hell anyway. It didn't stop the Convent of the Forty Martyrs accepting so-called heathens of all kinds as pupils, provided the fees were paid on the dot by their fathers or Bleswick Council.

We had on occasions been asked by friends why we sent our girls to the convent when we were C of E ourselves. I thought (and I made no bones about saying) that they were missing the point. The Convent of the Forty Martyrs was the best girls' school in the district. It was the only one with proper science laboratories, and its girls behaved beautifully in public. The religious aspect wasn't all that important, Sandy and I didn't believe in bowing and scraping and mumbo-jumbo. The important thing was to lead a good life, and Roman Catholics didn't have a monopoly on that.

I used to take Christine to church when she was little, but she didn't like it and I was always late with Sunday lunch, which led to rows. In the end I decided that I didn't want to believe in a God who put church attendance before a happy and harmonious family life, so I stopped going.

If that was blameworthy, I took the blame.

I took the blame for Christine's death, naturally. Why would a fifteen-year-old girl die like that if her mother hadn't failed her in some way?

But I was damned if I was going to allow the nuns to attach blame to Janet.

The three of us went forlornly to the convent. In his summer suit, Sandy looked tanned and brave, sad and noble and gorgeous. I wore a clean cotton frock and just looked tanned. Janet's plaits were too tight. Her face had the same stricken blankness that had come over it in that ghastly journey home from Norfolk in Rutherford's car. I had no idea what she was thinking, whether she missed her sister, anything.

We rang the bell at the convent entrance.

The grille opened and an old nun looked out. The grille was symbolic rather than real. These weren't enclosed nuns, they were actually quite worldly. Some of them drove cars.

I didn't recognise the old nun but Janet said, 'Good afternoon, Sister,' and I signalled to Sandy that we should let her handle the social graces side of things.

'May I introduce my parents, Sister? Mummy, Daddy, this is Sister Nicholas.'

'Good afternoon, Janet dear.' The nun beamed, and Janet almost smiled back. 'Good afternoon Mr and Mrs Toms.' She let us in to the marble-floored lobby. 'May God bless you. Poor Christine. It is a tragic loss.' No one would have guessed that they had expelled her. 'Reverend Mother is expecting you, please come this way.'

The school was closed for the holidays; we were taken into the convent area. There were a lot of gory sacred hearts about, as well as one or two pictures that looked as if they might be worth the price of a few loaves and fishes. The air smelt of polish and incense and cooking. There was also the usual trace of BO.

I had often wondered about this business of nuns having BO. I understood that they were supposed to have turned their backs on wordly vanity, but surely Christian charity should include consideration for others and therefore personal fastidiousness? Another thing they were supposed to have turned their backs on was the pleasures of the flesh, but I could tell that somebody not too far away from here was baking a cake.

Reverend Mother had one of those pale, ageless faces that made all nuns look the same. I couldn't make up my mind whether this effect was brought about by the habit or by virginity, always supposing they all were virgins. Some of them must have enjoyed a little experience of life before taking the veil, surely? Sandy always reckoned he could tell. I couldn't remember whether he thought Reverend Mother was or wasn't.

She absolutely terrified me, always had. But then so had Christine's old headmistress at Bleswick County Girls. She was a completely different kind of person, but the effect was the same. The combination of schools and authority figures unnerved me. I couldn't think why, because I myself had had such happy school days.

54

She served us tea and cake. I said, 'I shouldn't – '

'The Sisters,' she said, 'have been praying for the repose of Christine's soul – '

'Just a sliver, then.'

'And for you to be comforted.'

'Thank you,' I muttered, and so did Sandy, looking at the floor between his knees. Janet said, 'Thank you, Reverend Mother.'

'How are you managing?'

'Well,' I said. 'You know.'

'If we can be of any assistance – '

'Sister.' Sandy looked straight at her with an expression full of pain, boyishness, charm and naval officer power-of-command. 'If you don't want her back, just say.'

'I beg your pardon, Mr Toms?'

'We don't have to go through all this.'

'Mr Toms, I and the Sisters are looking forward to welcoming Janet back at the start of term.'

'Oh.'

'If I have not made that clear, then I am at fault.'

'No,' I said, swallowing cake. 'No, you're not, it's – '

He explained. 'When the boss calls you in for a chat about your future, you tend to assume the worst.'

Reverend Mother left us to our embarrassed twittering and spoke directly to Janet. 'You are a valued pupil in your own right, dear. We want you to stay with us – provided that is what *you* want. I am sure that a school like Bleswick Grammar would be as pleased to have you as we would be sorry to lose you. It is an excellent school in many ways – ' *And not in others*, she silently added. Janet heard and shook her head. Reverend Mother appeared satisfied. 'Then that is settled. Will you have some more tea? Cake?'

'This is awful of me.'

'Spoil yourself, Mrs Toms. Now we have a more delicate matter to discuss. Without wishing to anticipate the verdict of the coroner – '

'Sister, she was pregnant. It was a botched abortion. We know it, you know it, the whole world knows it.'

'Thank you, Mr Toms. My concern is for Janet.'

'She knows as well. No point in covering things up.'

'Perhaps, perhaps not. These are not matters about which we would normally expect girls of her age to know.'

'I didn't want to know them,' said Janet, suddenly and with passion. '*I don't want to know*.' It was the most spontaneous thing she had said since it happened.

'Of course you don't, dear. So when you come back to school, let's do what we can to ensure that there shall be no idle gossip. Christine was not a girl who was amenable to the particular type of discipline we have to offer, but she was one of our pupils for a while. There will of course be a wish, among those who remember her and among your own classmates, to express sympathy and to pray for the repose of her soul. That is perfectly proper and no more than we would expect. But you will help them, and help yourself and your parents to put this sorrow behind you, if you let well-wishers know that you do not wish to discuss the circumstances of her death.'

Sandy put in gently, 'They'll probably know already.'

'They may know something, Mr Toms, but they probably won't know as much as they think they know. Nothing kills a rumour more quickly than silence, be the rumour true or false. Do you understand what I am saying?'

It seemed clear enough to me. The price to be paid for Janet returning to the convent was silence. One indiscreet word and she would be packed off to Bleswick Grammar. Perhaps it was none too bad a thing. You didn't get over something like this by endlessly talking about it. In any case, Janet had shown no sign of wanting to talk. As she had just said, she didn't want to know.

At the time, of course, she had demanded the facts; and of course we had given them to her as honestly as we could. She had cried a bit but the worst seemed to be over. She was being sensible and looking to the future, which was what we all must do. If Janet didn't want long discussions with us her parents, it seemed unlikely that she had a great burning desire to unburden herself at school. The rule of silence would impose no hardship.

'I think we understand, Reverend Mother,' I said. 'Don't we, Janet?'

'Yes.'

'Thank you all for sparing the time to come in. Janet, I shall look forward to seeing you at the beginning of term.'

She said huskily, 'So will I, Reverend Mother.'

When we got home she cried and said, 'I don't want to go to school.'

Her tears nearly set me off. 'But darling, you *said* – '

Sandy intervened briskly, 'If she doesn't want to go back there, she doesn't have to.' He liked having a problem to solve. 'Whatever you want is fine with us, Janet. Where's it to be, Bleswick Grammar?' He would have got on the phone there and then if it hadn't been too late in the day. 'You could show them a thing or two.'

'I don't want to go anywhere.' She wouldn't look at us. 'I don't want to go to school.'

'Ah,' he said. 'I know the feeling. Beginning-of-term-itis.'

I tried to sound comforting. 'You'll feel better when the time comes.'

'I won't.'

'Try it for a term or two,' I suggested. 'If you're not happy, perhaps we could move away?' I glanced at Sandy but he was looking at Janet.

'You've got to go to school, old thing.'

'Why?'

'A because it's the law, and B because you've got a brain in there.' He tapped her head. She laid it on his shoulder and he cradled her like a baby. 'How do you expect that school to run without you as form captain? Hm? It'll be chaos.'

'Eva can do it.'

'And Eva can snap up all the prizes I suppose.'

'I don't care.'

'*I* care. That girl's had enough of your prizes as it is. Suppose you didn't go back to school. What would you do?'

'We could go round the world,' she said.

He laughed sadly and stroked her hair. 'What, now?'

'You always said we would one day.'

She wept on his shoulder. He looked hopelessly at me over the top of her head. I knew what he was thinking: this was what came of giving voice to your fantasy in front of a literal-minded child. You had your bluff called. The child wanted to know why you didn't stop talking about it and do it. A family called the Moss's had done it. We had read about them a couple of years ago in the *Sunday Express*. He was a merchant seaman, she was a yachtswoman who had been a teacher. She educated the children herself as they went along. When they came home, both children got into university.

We had cut the article out and pinned it to the door of the airing cupboard. *We could do that*, we had said, safe in the knowledge that we could not, because of Christine.

She was no longer here to prevent it. All that prevented it was me. I was not a teacher. I was not even a competent sailor. And I might be pregnant.

55

The coroner called my daughter, 'A sad and foolish teenager, a casualty of the times. A tragic victim of the live-now-pay-later attitudes to sexual morality which have grown up with the post-war generation.' He gave his verdict – Death by Misadventure – and released the body for burial.

All the Toms's turned up for the funeral. So did Christine's old friend Stella, weeping with her mother. Wreaths came from the convent and from Bleswick County Girls, from the Godards in France, and from Adam in hiding.

Charged with statutory rape, he had broken the terms of his bail and disappeared. Sandy said he was not surprised. He invited the police to inspect the wreath for clues as to where it had come from. It was home-made, in the shape of a ban-the-bomb symbol. The card said, *For darling Chris, all my love for ever, Adam*. 'The depths of that fellow's want of taste,' said Sandy, 'are yet to be plumbed.'

Secretly I hoped that Adam would stay hidden. I didn't want to give evidence at his trial. I didn't want him to go to prison. What would be the point?

•

The brothers carried the coffin into the church. Seeing them together, I kept expecting horseplay to break out.

Something else happened. It was most peculiar, I couldn't tell whether it was a hallucination or my eyesight or what. Their four separate faces seemed to become one face.

Each brother's characteristic feature – Rutherford's beard, Humphrey's nose that turned up at the end, Kennington's chicken-pox scar, Sandy's marvellous bone structure – seemed to be slipping away, like icing spread too soon on a hot cake.

For a split second, they were all the same man. His face – which was the face of all of them, and yet not really of any of them – was handsome and haunted. His mouth turned down at the corners. His eyes were blank but dry. He was sad and shocked but in command. He was always in command. He was strong enough to carry himself. He was strong enough to carry the coffin on his bowed, black-coated shoulders.

He was strong enough to set it down. A sigh went round the church, barely audible. It might only have been mine. The brothers separated and moved to their pews. They stood at the ends as if guarding their separate families. What from, I wondered. Death? Christine?

We sang 'Abide with Me' and 'The Lord's my Shepherd'. These were the hymns that were sung at Daddy's funeral in India. I remembered Mummy writing to tell me about it.

Outside, the brothers lowered the coffin into the grave. Again their faces seemed to come together, to become the face of one man. The man let the ropes go, inch by inch. He looked as if he had done it before, he looked as if he had been practising.

The vicar said, 'Forasmuch as it hath pleased Almighty God of His great mercy to take unto Himself the soul of our dear sister here departed, we therefore commit her body to the ground.'

Next to me, Janet shuddered. It must have been the words *our dear sister* that did it. Christine had been her sister, nobody else's. I squeezed her shoulder to buck her up. We were doing so well, it seemed a pity to break down now. So far the only person to break down had been Stella, and she wasn't family.

Grandma Toms stood with the family of Rutherford, her eldest son. Her descendants and in-laws thronged at the graveside. Mummy stood with us. In losing Christine, she had lost half her grandchildren. But she might forgive me, if another was on the way.

In November I knew for sure. I told Sandy first.

He said, 'How come?'

'How do you think?'

'I mean, what about the doings?'

'Must have had a hole in it.'

'Suppose so.'

'Aren't you pleased?'

'Dunno,' he said, ruffling his hair. 'Thought we were a bit past that sort of thing.'

'Evidently not.'

'How's Janet going to take it?'

'She'll be pleased,' I told him. 'She's having a difficult term.' There had been an influx of new girls into her class, some of them very bright. She was having to struggle to stay at the top. 'This will cheer her up.'

'Maybe.'

'Why shouldn't it?'

'Dunno,' he said again. 'She's got this bee in her bonnet about us selling up and going round the world.'

'Still? That was a joke.'

'Was it? It wasn't without its appeal.'

'It seemed like a good idea at the time,' I said. 'We were in shock. We've got over it now.'

'Have we?'

'It wouldn't have been practical, Sandy. Baby or no baby.'

'Course it wouldn't. That's what would have been such fun.' He grinned at the thought of it. 'Imagine the *talk*. "Sandy's lot have finally gone round the bend." "What about that poor child's education?" "They needn't beg from us when they come home penniless with parrots on their shoulders."' This in Rutherford's voice. Sandy stopped joking and looked wistful. I could almost see the seascapes in his eyes. One of the first things I had ever loved about him was his capacity for enjoyment. I was hopeless at enjoyment until I met him and discovered his power to carry me along.

His face shone, and stopped. I remembered a poem from school. 'The Old Grey Squirrel', by Alfred Noyes. About a boy who dreamed of becoming a sailor and became a clerk instead.

He is perched upon a high stool in London.
The Golden Gate is very far away.
They caught him, and they caged him, like a squirrel.
He is totting up accounts and going grey.

I used to cry at that poem. I used to wonder who caught him, who caged him. Now I knew.

Sandy was saying, 'We could have cut our losses. I mean, face it, Jo. When it comes to semi-detached family life, we haven't exactly won all the gold medals, have we?'

'It wasn't our fault.'

He looked as if he might be going to argue. I panicked. Argue what? That we were to blame? I was, of course I was, but what guilt was weighing on him, what might he be about to confide? That he thought Christine's death had been in some way a product of his affair with Pam? I didn't know about his affair with Pam. I never would know. I said, 'It's over, let's not talk about it.'

Janet came in. 'I've got some news.'

'So have we,' I told her. 'Is yours good or bad?'

'Bad.'

'Ours is good, so let's get yours over first and then we can cheer ourselves up.'

'The half term marks have come out.'

'Who's top?'

'Guess.'

'You?'

'No. Eva.'

'You're second then.'

Janet lowered her eyes. 'I'm twenty-second.'

I said quickly, 'That's all right.'

Her voice cracked as she said, 'Mummy, it's *seventh* from the *bottom*.'

'Well? You've had a big upset.'

She made a noise in her throat that could have been the beginning of a word. She abandoned it, exasperated, as if there were no point in speaking.

Sandy said, 'It's the six below you who should be worried.'

The atmosphere was so awful that I decided to throw caution to the winds. 'You're going to have a new sister or brother.'

'You're *joking*.'

'That's what I thought,' Sandy said to her, as if I were not present. 'But she ain't.'

Janet said, 'You can't do that. You can't just take someone's place.'

'We're not.' I stopped. It might be better if Janet thought we were. Others might think the same, which would be all to the good.

Christine had still been alive when I decided to conceive this baby. I had conceived in order to patch up my marriage. But since officially I did not know that my marriage had ever needed patching up, it would be much better to have people conclude we were replacing Christine. It was a not uncommon response to the death of a child. I had heard an episode about it on 'Mrs Dale's Diary'.

56

A work contact of Sandy's came round to do estimates for a new boiler and a new bath. He embodied everything about builders that made me tremble. He violated my home with his rigid metal tape measure, his masterfully expert eyes, his hard knuckles rapping my walls. I had no choice but to acquiesce. He was here as my husband's agent. I had invited him in.

Timidly, I said, 'Will it make a dreadful mess?'

'Nah. My lads, you won't know they're here.'

'When . . . will it be?'

'Not before Christmas,' he said.

I squinted viciously at the boiler. *You've got one more Christmas*.

It was our turn to go to Humphrey and Sue's for Christmas. I rang Sue to get started on the rotas and to ask what she would like me to bring.

'Nothing,' she said. 'Just get yourself here with Janet and that idle husband of yours. He can pull his weight this year, you are going to spend the whole time by the fire with your feet up.'

Sandy wouldn't hear of it. For the first time in living memory, he cancelled a traditional Toms Christmas and said we would stay at home. I thought it was a lovely gesture. I heard him explain to his brother: 'There's a lot of work involved in these big get-togethers. Christmas should be a holiday for everybody.'

'Of course, my dear chap,' said Humphrey. 'Quite understand.'

In the second week of December, a card came from Pam MacLeish, airmail from America, addressed to 'Sandy and Jo Toms, Chrissie and Janet'.

Sandy flinched and so did Janet, but I was thrilled to bits. It was proof positive that the little bitch was completely out of touch with our family. The postmark was San Francisco, California, about as far away as she could get without dropping into the

Pacific. I read the message aloud: 'All the best for Christmas and 1964 and love from Rusty and Pam (still of no fixed abode but soon to return to New Zealand and become Mr and Mrs Nayle!)' I beamed from ear to ear. 'Isn't that nice?'

Sandy shrugged. 'If you say so.'

Janet said forlornly, 'Can I see?'

'If you want to, I think it's a bit on the vulgar side myself. Taste was never Pam's strongest point, was it, Sandy?'

'Taste? In an Australian?'

Janet glared at us and examined the card. 'I wish we could write back and congratulate her.'

'Me too, only there's no address.'

Sandy said, 'I expect we'll be told where to send the wedding present.'

'Daddy, you are horrible.'

'Well. Couple of bums. Sell you five hundred.'

It was no different from the derogatory way he used to talk about Pam in her presence. But before, it had been flirtation. It had been a way of pulling the wool over my eyes. This time he meant it. He had come to his senses. He was learning to see that hateful little cow for what she was, just as I was learning to be lovable. He couldn't have her, but my triumph was that he didn't even want her.

He wanted me. He loved me, he was proud of me. He took me up to the rugby club to show me off, but he wouldn't let me stand on the touch line. He had a chair brought out. Afterwards, he sternly forbade me to help with the teas. He got the wives who were doing the teas to serve tea to *me.*

He was proud of me; I was proud of him. He was the oldest father at the childbirth classes, and the best-looking. Not that he actually attended the classes, only the rather wet husbands did that, but when the other women's husbands came to meet them I was able to make a comparison. Sandy came to meet me when he could. Once or twice he happened to be having a driving lesson and was able to pick me up in the car.

He couldn't do enough to please me. How ungrateful that sounded. Of course he could do enough. For me, anything was enough. The simple fact that he was trying to please me was enough.

For Christmas he gave me a lovely bed-jacket to wear in hospital. He took me and Janet out to the Fox atte Bleswycke for Christmas Dinner, and when Sue and Humphrey and their family came over on Boxing Day as a surprise, they brought cold turkey with them so I hardly had to do anything.

With the New Year, I kept expecting the contractors to turn up with the bath and the boiler but they didn't. 'I can't really get on with anything till they do,' I said.

'So I see,' said Sandy, surveying the chaos, the heaps of clobber. I wept. I had had such high hopes, but the house was like a delinquent child, it was beyond my control. 'I'm sorry. I know I'm hopeless, I make plans, I make resolutions, but – ' I didn't know how to explain. He would say he got on with his job and I should get on with mine. 'I never catch up with myself. There's never a moment when everything's done and I can stop. If I could start from scratch somewhere . . .' I couldn't speak any more, I was crying too much.

He waited for the tears to stop. He said quietly, 'Finish your sentence, Jo.'

'What?'

'If you could start from scratch, *what*?'

'I'd be – ' I searched for the word.

'Happier?' he offered.

'More organised.'

'Happier? Would you be happier? That's all I'm asking.'

I didn't know how to answer. He went on reproachfully, 'Not much point in shelling out on a brand new bath and a boiler if what you really want's a new house.'

I felt guilty and bewildered. I thought I had been saying for years that I wanted a new house, but if this was the first time he had heard me, perhaps I hadn't.

'Can we – ?' I began.

'Afford it? Don't you worry about that, we'll manage. We'll look around for somewhere that'll be easier for you to take care of.' I stared. He loved me so much that he was going to buy me a house. Was there a catch?

'You've had a rough year,' he mumbled.

'So have you.'

'Never mind about that. We can make a new start.'

'Yes. Yes, we can.'

'If moving house will make you happier, we'll do it.'

That was the catch. I had to be happier. I panicked at the responsibility. I didn't know if I were equal to it.

I put us on estate agents' mailing lists. It couldn't hurt to look.

Couldn't it? Brochures poured in. Sandy went through a few with me, telling me what the words really meant. 'If it says "needs some modernisation" don't touch it with a bargepole.' I didn't need telling. 'If there's something you like the sound of, go and see it for yourself. Tell them your husband's a Fellow of the Royal Institution of Chartered Surveyors. Don't even ask where the bog is without saying, "Subject to contract."'

I had thought it couldn't hurt to look but it could. The more obviously these modern houses were designed for easy housework – for some paragon to whisk round before setting off for her evening class or to be a Brown Owl – with their smooth worktops, their fitted this-that-and-the-other, their lack of awkward corners, their central heating fired by snowy white wall-mounted gas boilers with fingertip controls – the more terrified I became. What would I do all day?

What if what I did all day was get into a muddle and eat too much? What if we moved somewhere completely different and I turned out to be exactly the same? Sandy's rage would be nothing compared with mine. He would leave me of course, but whom could I leave? Moving would represent an end to all excuses, an end to all hope.

79 Manor Road gave me hope because it was my excuse. It was a preposterous house. No one would buy it with a bath that a girl had died in and the boiler that had heated the water. Sandy thought I was going to see places, but I wasn't. He asked if there were anything I wanted him to look at. I said, 'No,' or 'Yes, but somebody's just bought it.' I procrastinated.

57

I prayed for it to be a boy, if you could call it praying.

God, I make no bones about it. I'm not a good person – You of all people don't need telling that. You hardly ever see me in church. I think it's more important to provide a nice Sunday dinner for my family. If that's wrong, I'm wrong.

But You're supposed to answer the prayers even of sinners if what they ask for is for their long-term good, aren't You? So could it be a boy, please?

When I put it in those terms, I didn't see how God could refuse. How could it not be for my long-term good to have a boy? Sandy wanted one. If he didn't admit it, it was only because it would be humiliating to ask for something he had no power to bring about. He left the asking to me. I wanted what Sandy wanted. God believed in family life. A son would complete our family. A son would make it symmetrical, complete. A son would close it, seal it off from intruders.

I got quite excited. 'I know it's a boy.'

'Good show. He can join the Colts.'

'He can jolly well clean his own boots.'

'He can bring the coal in.'

'And take that task off your shoulders?' I laughed. 'I don't think.'

'I'll put him down for Flexbury.'

I had a cold feeling. He wasn't even born yet and we were sending him away. 'Would he have to board?'

'Course.'

'Oh.'

'What's wrong with that?'

'I always swore I never would, that's all – send a child of mine to boarding school. Don't know why. Mine was great fun. Have to be different from my own parents, I suppose. I had a lovely childhood. It's just, why have children if you don't want to look after them?'

Sandy said, 'Sending a boy to public school *is* looking after him. He'll make contacts that'll stand him in good stead for the rest of his life. He won't thank you for depriving him of that.'

All of a sudden I wanted a girl.

My doctor insisted on a hospital delivery because of my great age – which, being thirty-nine, was nearly twice his – but it was completely unnecessary. My waters broke one sunny morning in April while I was in the garden, squatting down to thin out the early lettuces, and quite honestly I felt I could have stayed there and done the two jobs at once.

But I was a good girl and rang the hospital. While I was waiting for the ambulance I rang Sandy at the office and told him it had started.

'Jolly good,' he said. 'Keep me posted. Chin up.'

Chin up indeed. I had no truck with that sort of talk. Everything was perfectly straightforward, as I had known it would be. One thing I had never understood – as a nurse, or as a mother – was why people made such a fuss about childbirth, a perfectly natural process. There was no point in weeping and wailing. You just got on with it. The female body *wants* to give birth and should be allowed to do so. I knew that the doctors and midwives appreciated my attitude, and by the following morning I was all stitched together again and not too woozy from the anaesthetic to be the thoroughly proud and happy mum of Miranda.

I was the oldest mother in the ward. There was an unmarried girl of about sixteen who gave me a bit of a pang, because she could have been Christine. Give or take the odd month, Christine and I could have had our babies simultaneously. I could have told her what to do.

The girl in the ward was giving up her son for adoption which was obviously sensible but a bit sad. I hatched a plot to adopt him myself, secretly, and bring him up with Miranda as twins. Knowing that he was not flesh of my flesh, I might not mind so much when he was sent away to boarding school. I joked about my scheme with the League of Friends Volunteer who came round the ward with the afternoon tea. 'Good idea,' she said. 'When your husband rings up, we'll tell him you've had twins.'

Full of beans, I took Miranda home and started a grand tidy-up in preparation for the christening. 'Oyez, oyez,' I said. 'Take note, Toms's far and near. The Sandringham Toms family are out of the doldrums.'

'Are we?' said Janet.

'Of course we are. Life goes on, and here's Miranda to prove it.'

'When will the baptism be?'

'We call it christening.'

'When will it be? People keep asking.'

'Who does?'

'Oh, people. Sister Nicholas, Reverend Mother. Eva.'

'I like their cheek,' I said. 'They'll be asking for invitations next.'

'I don't think that's the point,' Janet sighed. She sighed a lot these days, I didn't know why. It was time to stop weeping and wailing over Christine, now that we had Miranda. At thirteen she was too old to be jealous of her new sister, and much too sensible.

Sandy said it was probably teenage blues, but I said, 'Teenage stuff and nonsense.' Teenage blues were like teenage spots: an invention of the teenager industry. Solutions lay in fresh air and common sense. I thought it was much more likely that she was disappointed with herself for not yet regaining her rightful place at the top of her class. She still tended to come only third or fourth. She hadn't had any of her writings published lately either. And at Speech Day she had been awarded something called the de Montfort Shield for Effort, which I thought was an insult.

But there was plenty of time for her to recoup her position before 'O' and 'A' levels and university applications came along. And she was working hard and striving hard to please the nuns, even to the extent of preaching Roman Catholic beliefs in our house.

'Baptism's a sacrament, Mummy. It's got nothing to do with painting the bathroom.'

'What they believe is their business, Janet. What we believe is ours.'

'What *do* we believe?'

'We believe in living a good life. Daddy's relations have been very kind to us, and giving a jolly good party is going to be our way of saying thank you to them. I suppose you think we should have the christening tomorrow?'

'Of course I don't.'

'If we had it tomorrow, it would be a farce and a fiasco!'

'Mummy, there's no need to shout.'

'I'm not.' I didn't shout any more, I had made a firm resolution not to. 'I'm *emphasising*, because this is something I feel strongly about. I don't want to believe in a God who thinks mumbo jumbo is more important than simple things like giving proper hospitality and kindness to people who've given hospitality and kindness to you. If that's a mortal sin, send me to hell.'

Janet had no answer. She sighed again and made for the door. 'I only asked when it's going to be so that I can tell people when they ask.'

'I've told you. When I've got the house straight.'

'And when will *that* be?'

'I don't know, Janet. I'm not a fortune teller.'

58

What I needed was a damn good kick in the pants. It came from where I least expected it, the Roads and Highways Committee of Bleswick Council. Aided and abetted by the Ministry of Transport, they announced plans to turn Manor Road into a motorway.

Number 79 was to be compulsorily purchased. There was something almost sexually thrilling about that word *compulsorily*. The stated aim of the project was to enable more and more cars to move between London and the West Country at higher and higher speeds, but all I could think of was that Number 79 was destined for the ultimate blitz, to be administered by burly men with bulldozers and throbbing drills.

We chose a brand new house called Ravine View. Apart from the silly name – ravines being a bit thin on the ground in Bleswick – it was my dream home. It was handy for the rugby club, the sailing club and shops. It was in a quiet street and had a safe garden for Miranda. It had central heating, fitted milky-coffee carpets and an award-winning kitchen.

All I had to be was an award-winning housewife. I wasn't bitter. I didn't begrudge the kitchen its award, on the contrary it seemed to me to be well-deserved. I wasn't going to know myself with all those acres of unscratched worktop, not to mention two sinks for me to fill up and a rotisserie, also a twin tub and a dishwasher. I doubted that the dishwasher would get things clean, so I continued to sterilise everything with a briskly boiling kettle.

I had long ago come to the conclusion that the secret of successful housewifery was storage space – as long as you had enough cupboards, you could think straight. From now on, I declared, if anyone left clobber lying around, I would toss it into the nearest cupboard. There would be no warning. This was the warning. If the owners of the clobber didn't like having their possessions manhandled, the solution would be in their own hands.

We combined Miranda's christening with her second birthday party, so it wasn't too bad. She was a bit on the big side but she was able to join in with the responses, which seemed more sincere somehow. And as I said to Janet, 'God can't blame us for the compulsory purchase order.'

She was godmother. The other was Lindsay Bixwell, wife of one of Sandy's rugby chums. Lindsay was a pleasant little woman, though downtrodden and childless. You only had to look at her great lardy lump of a husband to know why he had never managed to get her pregnant. Never mind pregnant, she would have been steam rollered. I had been very lucky.

Such were my irreverent thoughts as I waited for the christening to start. But perhaps they weren't as irreverent as all that. I *had* been lucky. Sandy had been promoted, had given up playing rugby and was studying to be a referee; I had managed to be a good girl for three months on a terrific new diet; Miranda was thriving; and Janet was back near the top of her class where she belonged, although she seemed to have lost interest in writing which I thought was a pity.

We were going to have to draw in our horns a bit to pay for our new house, but who cared? I had never been a great spender of money. That was one thing even Sandy would say in my favour. I wasn't likely to start rushing out buying things for myself now. I would be too busy getting Ravine View straight.

The church filled up with Toms's, Sandy's relatives and therefore mine. I remembered the funeral, when all was greyness and gloom. Now my sisters-in-law and their daughters wore spring colours and flowery hats, even flowery stockings and the odd rather daring miniskirt. The men and boys squired them in, talking easily but quietly among themselves, relaxed but respectful. They followed the women into the pews. They leaned forward, not actually kneeling, and pressed the tips of their fingers to the fronts of their foreheads. They closed their eyes. I wondered what they were praying for. They looked as if they expected to get it.

I had heard Sandy and his brothers talking about God as if He were a rather important chap they were on particularly good terms with. Admittedly they didn't go to church very often, but neither, they reckoned, did He. I felt in my bones that this confidence of theirs came from healthy family life, and that was the reason I had not got it.

No, that was not what I meant. I glanced quickly at Mummy, in case she had heard. She was on her own in her pew, casting a swift spit-bullets look at Grandma Toms with her glorious sons. Well, that was the point. Mummy had only had me. So she couldn't expect a huge family to surround her adoringly in her old age.

Not that I blamed her. Having only one child was probably the best solution, in view of all the travelling Daddy had to do. And I did have a marvellous childhood. Daddy being such an educated man, he saw to it that I was only sent to schools that he knew about personally. I had a terrific education, or rather I had the *opportunity* of one. If I chose not to take full advantage of it, if I chose to be lazy and get bad marks, then that, as Daddy said in his letters, was my hard luck. I could have gone to university if I could have been bothered.

I hadn't had a normal family life, whatever that was, but I had one now. I was very, very fortunate. Lots of people in the world were worse off than me. Apart from the odd day when I still felt a bit down in the dumps about Christine dying, I wasn't badly off at all.

The question arose of what we were going to tell Miranda about Christine, and how, and when. Sandy believed in speaking the truth to children, as he believed in speaking it to everyone, and I agreed with him. However, he didn't think a toddler needed to be told what an abortion was, and I agreed with that as well.

When she was three, she found a family photograph with Christine in it. This was something of a rarity because in Christine's day photograhs tended only to be taken on the boat, and therefore of necessity *sans* her. 'Mummy, who's that?'

'That's Christine. Your sister.'

'Janet's my sister.'

'Your other sister.'

Miranda examined Christine. In looks, the two of them were not unalike. They had the same dark hair, and similar bone structure. Slighter than Janet, they had angular little faces and watchful, shadowy eyes. But Miranda had a pleasant disposition. Christine glared up at me with her I-have-been-forced-aboard-this-boat-against-my-will-and-I-refuse-to-enjoy-it look.

Miranda said, 'I like her,' and gave her a kiss.

'We all loved her very much.'

'Where is she?'

'She's dead, darling.'

'Why?'

'She had an accident.'

'Did she wee on the floor?'

'Not that sort of accident.'

'Did the accident hurt her?'

'No.'

'Will I have an accident?'

'No.' I took her on my lap. 'Daddy and Janet and I will always look after you and keep you safe.'

'Did you look after Christine and keep her safe?'

'Isn't it time for "Listen with Mother"?'

It wasn't, but by the time we had found that out the other matter had been dropped.

When Sandy came home I told him about this incident. 'It's all very well for you to preach truth telling. You don't have to answer the questions.'

He snapped, 'And do you want to do *my* job?'

I thought this was uncalled for. It was what he used to say when I complained about my housewife's lot, but with my new labour-saving house I no longer had anything to complain about. Complaining was the last thing I was doing now. On the contrary, I was bringing up an issue of importance that Sandy and I ought to resolve together as parents.

'If we don't tell her it was Christine's own fault,' I pointed out, 'she'll think it was ours. She'll think it might happen to her.'

'At three?' He turned on the television.

I turned it off. 'Sandy, you're not listening!'

'I can't help listening when you shout like that.'

'I am not shouting. I'm emphasising.'

'And I'm emphasising that this is a mother's responsibility.'

'Everything bloody well is, isn't it?'

'Except paying the bills.' He turned the TV back on, then looked in the *Radio Times* and the *TV Times* for the programmes. I didn't know why he bothered, he would fall asleep in front of anything.

Tonight he stayed awake for 'Panorama', because as it happened the subject was abortion. A bill was going through parliament to make it legal. A bishop was saying that it would mark the beginning of the end of family life. Sandy scoffed. 'Family life. Don't know what they're bloody well talking about. Of course it should be legal.' He was thinking of Christine. So was I. I said, 'I agree with you,' and we made our peace.

59

'I seen her,' said Miranda.

'"I *have* seen her." Who?'

'Christine.'

She was in bed. We had just had our story, *Little Black Sambo*. The man-eating tigers had melted into ghee and been turned into pancakes by Sambo's mother. I supposed that was a bit on the gory side, enough to give an imaginative child nightmares.

'No you haven't, darling.'

'I have.'

'Where?'

'Here.' She pointed to the room. Her tone was casual, matter-of-fact. It didn't bother her so it didn't bother me. But I was curious to know more about the dream. 'When?'

'In the night. When you're asleep and Daddy's asleep and Janet's asleep.' Miranda's voice dropped to a whisper. 'She comes on tiptoe.' She got out of bed, went over to the door, peeped round it and demonstrated.

I entered into the spirit of the thing and whispered back, 'What does she do?'

This stumped Miranda. She had to think. She made a gorgeous sight, deep in thought. She screwed up her dark, angular little face. She looked intense and endearingly adult. 'She gives me sweets.'

'What sort?'

'Toffees.'

'I hope she tells you to clean your teeth afterwards.'

'Yes.'

'Then she's reformed since I knew her.'

'What's "reformed"?'

'She's a better girl.'

'Was she bad?'

'Sometimes. Like you.'

'Did Daddy smack her?'

'Only if she deserved it. What else does she do?'

'She takes me to a magic cave.'

'What's that like?'

'It's dark and mysterious.'

'That's a big word.' She had probably picked it up at the pre-school playgroup I took her to on Tuesday and Thursday mornings. Some of the young mothers were university graduates, and, when they weren't making me feel totally inadequate by urging me to join the National Housewives' Register (where would I find time for that? and what would I say when I got there?) were very good at developing the children's vocabularies.

'What do you do in the magic cave?'

'We find treasure.'

'Why don't you bring it home? Then we'll be rich.'

'I can't.'

'Why not?'

'Christine doesn't let me.'

'Well, make sure Christine brings *you* home in time to get up in the morning.'

'All right.'

'And give her my love.' It choked me a bit to say that. I wanted Miranda to reply with something like, *And she sends her love to you*, but how would she think of it? It wouldn't be fair to prompt or ask. It was better to keep things light.

Even so, I thought it wouldn't hurt to mention it to Dr Noonan, the paediatrician who popped in now and again at the playgroup. I didn't want Miranda to develop a complex, whatever that was.

Dr Noonan was in her mid-twenties and didn't wear a wedding ring, but she was very nice. I waited until everyone else had finished with her and said, 'May I have a word? It won't take two ticks.'

'Of course, Mrs Toms.'

'I'm Jo Toms, Miranda's mother. It's probably nothing.'

'Do sit down.'

'It's just that she's having these odd dreams. She thinks she sees her sister. Only her sister's dead.' I laughed.

Dr Noonan gave me an unnervingly steady look. 'You lost a daughter?'

'Oh, years and years and years ago.'

'How come?'

'Only an accident.'

'How long ago?'

'Four years.'

'That's not long.'

'We've all got over it. Except, funnily enough, Miranda, who never met her.' I told Dr Noonan about the toffees and the treasure and the cave.

She said, 'Does it seem to trouble Miranda? Does she have nightmares, is her sleep disturbed?'

'No. It just seems a bit macabre.'

'Children's fantasies often are. Have you read *Grimm's Fairy Tales* lately? It's not unusual for a child of Miranda's age to have an imaginary playmate – '

'What, a dead sister?'

Dr Noonan smiled. 'The unusual thing is for a child of her age to *have* a dead sister. Unusual in this country, I mean. Which is a triumph for the good old National Health, but not so nice for families who *do* lose a child, because it leaves you rather isolated.'

What did she mean, *you*? It was Miranda we were supposed to be talking about and she was over in the sand pit.

I didn't feel isolated, I felt conspicuous and embarrassed and guilty. As Dr Noonan had said, in poor countries it wasn't at all unusual for a family to lose a child. And even here in the playgroup, we had a little boy with psoriasis and a mother who had had a breast off. She didn't make a fuss, and neither did he. And here was I, getting in a state over one of Miranda's games.

'Dr Noonan, I've taken up much too much of your time.'

She said, 'You seem to be troubled by these fantasies of Miranda's? Perhaps more troubled than she is?'

'I think "troubled" is rather too strong a word.'

'What word would you use?'

'No word, really,' I said. 'I haven't got any troubles.'

'That's unusual.'

'Not what I'd call *troubles*. We've got this marvellous new house that I'm just beginning to get on top of. Janet – my other daughter – is doing her 'O' levels. She'll be going to Oxford. And Sandy's just been promoted into a very senior position. I'll tell you one silly little thing: I wish he could pass his driving test. It seems funny, doesn't it? A clever man like that.'

'Some people have a block against it. Do you drive?'

'Good gracious no. I've got my bike. It's just that he has to go away a lot and he can't always get back. Macabre,' I said, 'that's the word I'd use, the word I used before, *macabre*.' Dr Noonan drew back. I said, 'Sorry, did I spit?'

'No.'

'I must have emphasised, then. I'm rather an emphatic person, I'm afraid. My husband accuses me of shouting.'

'You didn't shout, Mrs Toms . . . Would you like to come and see me at the hospital? Ask your GP to refer you.'

'I will if Miranda gets any worse.'

She said, 'I meant you, you yourself.'

'What on earth for?' I laughed, suddenly realising how young Dr Noonan was, and how little she knew. She wasn't even married. 'It's Miranda who has the dreams,' I reminded her, 'not me.'

60

I kissed Miranda goodnight. Under her strict supervision, I then kissed Teddy and Golly, Mrs Mabel Merryweather, Fairy Thistledown, Bert the Rabbit and Steve the Dinosaur in the prescribed order. She said, 'Give me a kiss for Christine.'

For some reason, I looked over my shoulder. 'Where is she?'

'She's not here yet,' said Miranda, with pity for her simpleton mother.

I kissed her delicious toothpastey mouth. 'You give that to Christine when she comes.'

'She's cold,' said Miranda.

'What do you mean?'

'She's a skeleton.'

'Where did you learn that word?'

'I've forgotten.'

I looked closely into her calm eyes. 'Is it nice when she comes?'

Miranda thought about it. Again she said, 'She's cold.' She didn't seem bothered about it but she kept saying it and that bothered *me.*

I hugged her. 'If she frightens you, shout out loudly and Daddy will come.'

'You come,' said Miranda. 'Not Daddy.'

'Daddy's better. He's big and strong.'

'Not Daddy.' For the first time, she looked anxious. 'You.'

'Why?'

'I don't like him.'

'Go on with you. Of course you do. Why don't you?'

'He gets cross.'

'Only when you make him cross. And he works very hard for us, to pay for all our lovely things.'

'He smacks me.'

I laughed. 'So do I, when you're naughty. It's *because* we love you that we sometimes have to punish you.' Miranda looked sheepish and I jollied her along. 'I don't hear all this about you not liking Daddy when he takes you out or gives you pocket money. Poor Daddy. You love him. Don't you?'

'I hate him.'

'No you don't. Little girls don't hate their Daddies.'

'Christine does.'

'Miranda, what do you mean?'

'Christine hates him. She told me.'

This was obviously serious. I didn't mention it to Sandy because I didn't want his feelings hurt. I dumped Miranda with her godmother Lindsay Bixwell and cycled up to the hospital.

I said, 'I'd like to see Dr Noonan.'

'Have you an appointment?'

'No, but could you tell her it's Mrs Toms from the playgroup and it's about Miranda.'

I admired my nerve. If I were in charge of the appointments system, I would hate people like me, swanning in like Lady Muck. But that was what came of being married to Lord Muck. We Mucks get what we want. We have the nerve to put our own children before other people's, and we have the power of command. The receptionist came back and said, 'She'll see you, Mrs Toms, if you don't mind waiting.'

'No! Not at all!'

I did, actually, I hated waiting. Waiting was the thing I hated most in the world, it was such a terrible waste of time. It didn't get you anywhere. I often thought of all the extra time I would have if all the time I had ever spent waiting (for buses, for repair men, for appointments, for Sandy to come home) could be put together and handed to me in a block.

Another thing I didn't like about waiting was that it was when I was waiting that I did most of my naughty eating. And even here in the waiting room where they ought to know better, the Friends of Bleswick Hospital had a trolley offering fizzy drinks and Milky Ways. 'The sweet you can eat between meals without ruining your appetite.' I wished something *would* ruin my appetite.

I decided to have some tea at least. To keep my mind off the

Milky Ways while I was queueing up, I read a Friends of Bleswick Hospital leaflet. 'Volunteers are needed,' it said, 'to help with a hundred and one little jobs to make patient life more comfortable, on and off the wards.'

'Tea, love?' said the woman. 'Are you interested?'

'I ought to be, oughtn't I?'

She looked surprised. 'I wouldn't say that.'

I wondered how she managed to be here, and whether she had children and a husband and a house to look after. I felt she was reproaching me so I gave her something to reproach me for. 'I used to be a nurse,' I explained. 'I gave it up because I was in love. I didn't even finish my training. Wasn't I a fool?'

'That's more your line, then,' said the tea lady, pointing at a poster on the wall. *COME BACK TO NURSING. Full-time, part-time. Details of re-training from Personnel Office.* 'Milky Way or anything?'

'Get thee behind me, Satan,' I said. 'Yes, please.'

'Good morning, Mrs Toms,' said Dr Noonan. 'I'm so sorry to have kept you waiting.'

'Well, I'm sorry for barging in without an appointment.'

'Please sit down. Has something happened?'

'Miranda's been talking about Christine again. But it's not a game any more. It was morbid. It was all bones and skeletons. Christine frightens her. And she said she hated her father.'

'Sorry, you've lost me. Miranda said that she herself hated her father? Or that Christine did?'

'Both.'

'Is there a problem between Miranda and her father?'

'She adores him. And he thinks the world of her.'

'What about your husband and Christine when she was alive?'

'Oh, the same. He was heartbroken.'

'And you?'

'Of course. But you just have to get on with things.'

'Will you tell me about the accident? What happened?'

I looked at the floor in shame. 'It was an abortion.'

'I'm sorry.'

Why should she be sorry? Her compassion made me cringe, I didn't deserve it. 'It was my fault.'

'Yes, I expect you blame yourself.'

'I am not "blaming myself". I'm saying it was my fault because it was.'

'Does Miranda know how Christine died?'

'She's not particularly interested in the details.' I laughed to ease the atmosphere. 'Skeletons are more her line.'

'Are you sure?'

'We told her it was an accident. Or is that wrong too?'

'Not *wrong*, but I think you may be mistaken if you believe she's not interested. It sounds to me as if she's very interested indeed.'

'All right, you tell me how to explain what an abortion is to someone who's not quite four.'

'It's tricky, I agree. I'll have a word with a colleague of mine who has a special interest in bereaved families.'

'What a funny thing to have a special interest in.'

'He runs a group – '

'Everyone seems to these days, don't they?'

'Pardon?'

'Oh, you know. Housewives' Register. Friends of the Hospital. Bereaved Families.'

'Miranda obviously realises there's some sort of mystery, and that might explain why she's having the fantasies. Which, as I said before, are probably quite harmless to her as long as they're not frightening her. What they're doing to *you*, Mrs Toms, is another matter.'

'They're not doing anything to me.'

'I expect your family keeps you pretty busy, but do you have any outside interests, hobbies – ?'

'Oh golly yes,' I said. 'Sailing in the summer, rugby in the winter. Yes, you can smile, I've said myself to Sandy ours must be the only all-daughter family in the world to have rugby as a family hobby, not that the girls and I play, of course.'

'Of course.'

'But you'd be surprised how it does encroach.'

'I'm sure.'

'And then there's the playgroup. I've promised to get involved in the committee, though I haven't got around to it yet.'

'Miranda won't be in the playgroup for ever. What are you going to do when she starts school?'

'I get it,' I said. 'You think I'm half way round the bend now, and when I haven't got Miranda to fuss over I'll go the whole way round it.'

'On the contrary, but – may I ask how old you are?'

'Certainly. Forty-three.'

'And with the age gap between Christine and Miranda you must have been looking after children on and off for – what? – the better part of twenty years?'

I shrugged. 'My husband says that's what I signed up for.'

'Does he indeed?'

'And I agree with him.'

'You mentioned yesterday,' said Dr Noonan, 'that your husband had just got a new job.'

'He's South-East Regional Property Manager for Holland, Murray, Walters.'

'Is that something completely different from what he was doing before, or a sort of continuation of his career to date?'

'Yes. A continuation. Except he travels more.'

'He's moving on.' She shrugged. 'Quite right too. But perhaps you can do the same.'

'I'll tell you about moving on, Dr Noonan. When Miranda's grown-up and Sandy retires, we're going to buy a boat and sail round the world. But in the meantime, being my husband's wife and my daughters' mother is quite enough for me. It's all I've ever wanted. I'm not sending Miranda to school with a latchkey round her neck and I'm surprised to hear a person in your position say that I should, when – ' I stopped. I had been going to say, *when you hear about the terrible things that can happen*, but in our family we hadn't had to hear about the terrible things that could happen, they had happened to us.

'All I'm saying,' she said, 'is that within the next two or three years you're going to have a lot less to do at home than you have now – '

'Don't you believe it!'

'Janet'll be at university, Miranda'll be at school and you should be thinking about something for yourself.' She paused delicately.

'My colleague,' she said, 'has occasionally found a tendency among mothers who've lost one child to be over-conscientious with the others.'

'Over-conscientious! Me! I can't wait to tell Sandy! "Guess what, darling, I'm over-conscientious." Do you know who you remind me of? Christine. She used to go on and on at me about going back to nursing. Perhaps that's why she's started appearing to Miranda. So that she can use you as a way of going on and on at me from beyond the grave.'

'Do you really think that?'

'And he used to go on and on at me about *not* going back . . .'

'And you?'

'Oh me,' I said. 'I'm just hopeless. I go with the tide.'

'And what if the tide turns?'

Janet

61

I didn't get into Oxford, but I was offered a place to read English at the University of Northburgh in Scotland, the Oxford of the North. In the middle of a dark, chilly night at the beginning of October 1970, my family saw me off at King's Cross.

Miranda, who was six, crumpled up her face and wept. She nearly set me off. My mother said to her, 'Janet doesn't want to see tears! She wants to see nice bright smiles!' Daddy said, 'Nice bright smiles!' in a Joyce Grenfell voice. 'Nymphs and shepherds!' He finished loading my luggage into the sleeper, gave me a pound to pay for a porter at the other end and switched to a Scottish accent. 'Och aye the noo. Is that everythin', hen?'

'Yes. Thanks.'

He burst into song. 'We'll keep a welcome in the hillsides, we'll keep a welcome in the dales, we'll keep a welcome in the hillsides when ye come home again from – sorry. Wrong country. Ye tak the high road, and I'll tak – '

'Mummy,' I said. 'Get rid of him.'

'Yes, come along, Sandy,' she said. 'Don't spin it out.' She hugged me. 'By golly, I envy you.'

'Don't forget to write,' he said. 'Give my love to Aunty.' This was a traditional valediction among the Toms brothers, it meant nothing, there would be no aunties in Northburgh, there would be nobody.

Miranda said, 'I envy you too.'

Daddy took me in his arms and whispered in my ear, 'I envy *them*.'

'Who?'

'Them as whose gain is our loss. Fare thee well. Haste ye back. Och aye the noo.'

'See you at Christmas.'

'See you at Christmas.'

*

The compartment was a double but I had it to myself. The air was blue and stuffy. I felt like an insect in a killing bottle. The bottle was being shaken. Soon the lethal gas would spread. The more I thought about the insect, the more I envied it. For an insect in a killing bottle, the future was certain.

I lifted the blind a few inches. I only meant to take a quick peep but the blind snapped out of my hand and shot up. There was no escaping the awful sight of North London passing me by at relentlessly increasing speed.

North London was unfamiliar to me, but at least it was London, and Bleswick was almost West London, so it was still home. I wasn't ready to let go of home yet. Perhaps in the morning I would be. Perhaps.

The sombre domes and weird glittery turrets of Alexandra Palace added to my sense of being in a nightmare. That was all right. I quite liked being in a nightmare. From a nightmare I could wake up, at home in Bleswick. I would be in about Form Four.

I pulled down the blind. Unable to see the speed at which we were travelling, I felt calmer. I stowed my luggage on the bottom bunk and prowled around the compartment reading notices. A leaflet urged me to press the bell for the steward should I feel like a nightcap. I liked the sound of a nightcap – both grown-up and cosy – but somehow the offer of one didn't seem to apply to me. I felt that if I sent for one, I would make a fool of myself in some way. I would ask for the wrong thing and be snubbed.

I unzipped my holdall. I wanted to look at something familiar, something that would reassure me that I was loved. Miranda had drawn me a picture of our house so that I would not forget it. Two 'Good Luck at University' cards had come from Salthaven with five pound notes attached, one from Grandma Toms in her adapted bungalow and one from Gran Woolgar in her warden-assisted flat. My mother had made me a Guinness cake. Daddy had bought me six sherry glasses.

My Northburgh folder confirmed beyond all doubt that this really was happening to me. Here was my acceptance letter from UCCA, my offer of a place in a hall of residence (sharing a room with somebody called Gillian Glenn), my Student Handbook, my receipt from the university outfitters for eight guineas for my gown, my street map (presented with the compliments of the Clydesdale Bank) and my programme for Wuzlet Week. A wuzlet was a first-year student. It came from the French *oiselet*, meaning a young bird. The female form was wuzlette. As from tomorrow morning, I was a wuzlette.

Until then, I was a novelist. If I was going to be miserable anyway, I might as well work. I got out my exercise book, climbed the little ladder to the top bunk, took all the pillows from the bottom one, arranged a blanket round my legs and made myself as comfortable as I could. I was on page 203, about two-thirds of the way through, I reckoned.

The novel was called *Off-Ration*. I had begun it on the day I left school and had been writing it all summer. Before *Off-Ration*, it had been years since I had written anything apart from school essays and unavoidable letters.

As a child I had wanted to write novels. I had written several, and short stories, and poetry. I had won prizes with them, and in one glorious moment a real, genuine publisher's reader had mistaken my eleven-year-old jottings for the work of someone of sixteen. But I had stopped making things up out of my imagination when Christine died.

I was writing when the news came. We were on holiday on the Norfolk Broads and I was working on a novel called *Cornelia*. Christine was supposed to be in the South of France, and I had been thinking she should go to the South of France more often. I had been wondering why it had to be Pam rather than Christine who was leaving England forever.

Being an only child would suit me fine, I had thought, especially if I had Pam nearby as a sort-of sister, sort-of friend.

Cornelia was about an only child. It was set in Victorian times. At twelve I reckoned I knew quite a bit about Victorian times, having read *Nicholas Nickleby* and *The Water Babies*, and having listened to *The Woman in White* on the radio. My eponymous heroine lived with her parents on a trading wherry on the Norfolk Broads. She didn't go to school, which didn't matter because she was naturally clever, and now and again a kindly old clergyman came aboard to give her lessons. Most of the time the little family plied up and down in their wherry and did their trading (I glossed this over, I didn't know much about trading) and had various adventures.

I would think of the adventures during our day's sailing, and write them in the evenings by lamplight, when my parents went to the pub.

One evening while I was sitting on deck writing, Uncle Rutherford loomed up out of the darkness with a torch. He asked where my parents were. I said, 'The pub.' Without another word he strode off towards it.

When he brought my mother and father back they had white faces and news for me.

I remembered thinking how funny it was that I had been writing about being an only child and now I was one. Then I thought how funny it was to use the word *funny*, and I tore *Cornelia* in pieces and gave up writing stories.

Now, though, I thought I was starting to get the hang of it again. I wrote for two hours, then nodded off. When the steward woke me at 5 am, I was still in my clothes. He brought me tea and a shortbread finger wrapped in cellophane. He was Scottish. Last night's steward had been English. I felt abandoned.

62

I looked at the shortbread with disgust, but I knew I was going to eat it so I did. I drank my tea, washed my hands, face and teeth, and rolled deodorant around my armpits. Beyond the window of my compartment, a cold grey dawn was coming up over a racing, rugged, granite-faced wilderness, with bent-backed trees and occasional glimpses of wild sea. Suburbs with yellow street lamps reached into the wilderness, grim and regular as barracks.

The suburbs became the stony city of Edinburgh, towering black against the ice blue sky, graceful enough but forbidding. The train stopped and I dragged my luggage on to the platform.

There were no porters, only students everywhere. I realised that my train must have been full of students and that they had probably been making friends with each other in the cattle trucks while I lay in state in the sleeper which Daddy had insisted I should have.

Still, at least I had done some writing. Nothing was too bad if you could write. I followed the throng to the Northburgh train. It only had two carriages, and the guard made everybody put their luggage in his van. My cases vanished beneath an indiscriminate heap of rucksacks, guitars, rugs, record players, brown paper parcels and bikes.

The journey took an hour. I stood all the way, dividing my fellow passengers into three categories, depending on the way they added to my gloom. There were the ones who stood silent and immobilised by misery and reminded me of myself. Then there were the ones who already knew people and so obviously would not want any new friends. I didn't blame them but I resented them anyway. Finally there were the people with the guts to introduce themselves to strangers, along the lines brightly drafted by my mother in one of her pep talks. ('Make a joke of it!

Say, "I'm Janet Toms and I'm wondering if I've made a terrible mistake!" Chances are they'll say "Me too," and bang! You've got a conversation going!')

Medieval domes and spires and the thick grey city wall showed why Northburgh was called 'the Oxford of the North'. In the station forecourt, coaches were waiting with cards behind their windscreens showing the names of halls of residence. I climbed aboard the one for Elizabeth Blackwell Hall.

It turned out to be a converted Gothic Victorian hotel which looked as if it had escaped from Salthaven. You could make out the faded letters of its old name on its red brick front: Queen's Cliff. Beyond was a golf course and the sea.

Two porters in brown overalls came out with trolleys to help with luggage. The air smelt of breakfast; the time was about eight fifteen. Senior-looking Scottish girls with purple undergraduate gowns hanging down majestically over tweed skirts and cashmere jerseys, checked names on lists. 'Janet Toms? You're with Gillian Glenn.'

'I know.'

'She's already gone up. Room 376.'

Room 376 was large with a sea view. Gillian Glenn was small and pale, from the north. Or the south, as I supposed it was now. The north of England. She said, 'Which bed do you want?'

'I don't mind. Which do you?'

'This one.'

'All right.'

I smiled to cover my annoyance that she had got the sea view. That was my bed, anyway. It had my parcel on it. She tossed it over. The label said, 'A. J. Strammington and Son, Suppliers of Academic Dress to the University of Northburgh since 1632.'

I unwrapped my gown and put it on, doing up the hooks at the neck. The deep purple wool, the gold silky lining, the velvet collar and the graceful way the gown hung from my shoulders gave me a certain professorial dignity. I supposed that was the idea. The gown was warm too, but at eight guineas it ought to be. It was a special offer price, for wuzlets who ordered in advance.

Gillian said, 'Can I try it?'

Crossly, I let her. She clowned around in front of the mirror. 'Catch me going round looking like this.'

'I think we have to,' I said.

'Says who?'

'It's in the Wuzlet Week programme.'

'The what?'

We went down to breakfast. I watched the Scottish girls closely to see if it were true that they ate porridge with salt. They seemed to prefer sugar and milk. Bacon was served with fried slices of grey suet pudding with sultanas in it, and there were fresh, doughy rolls, white or wholemeal. All naughty foods, as my mother would say.

I found out the names of a few more girls and we went as a gang to the Principal's Welcome in Fraser Lamont Hall. The Hall was behind a quadrangle with cloisters. Several hundred of us sat in rows, half boys, half girls, half wearing gowns, and half not.

'Welcome to university,' boomed the Principal from the stage. His gown was black with a fleece collar that looked as if it could have been made out of his own tufty white hair. 'Welcome to this very special university. When I travel to other universities and meet my fellow vice-chancellors, they frequently say to me, Principal, what *is* it that makes the University of Northburgh so special?

'When I ask them what they mean, they say, Principal, what we mean is, how has it come about that over the past couple of years, when *our* universities – when virtually every other university in the United Kingdom, nay, the Western world – has suffered upheaval and lawlessness within its student body, the University of Northburgh has remained peaceful and harmonious?

'I have three answers for those who put this question. Tradition, tradition and tradition. If any of you have it in mind to start marching round the town for "student power", save your shoe leather. "Student power" is already a reality at Northburgh, and has been so since the middle ages.' We clapped. It seemed expected. Gillian whispered, '"Big happy family". Bet you.'

The Principal continued, 'There is no need for you to "sit in" in my office. Would you "sit in" in your father's office? It would be a rather peculiar family if you did. If there is anything you would like to discuss with me, please make an appointment through my secretary.

'Another important tradition may be found sitting in this hall this morning; it is the calibre of our students.' He held out his arms as if to embrace us. 'We accept only the finest young men as undergraduates. But let me add a note of caution. Some of you have come to us from schools, or if you will forgive the pun, pools, where you were big fish. At Northburgh, you will be surrounded by other big fish. You may have to come to terms with the discovery that you are not the cleverest young man in the world.

'If you find yourself struggling or in difficulties – in your academic work, or any other aspect of your life here – please, please, please do not allow the problem to get out of control before you seek help. Northburgh is a friendly place and full of people who will be only too pleased to help. You are going to meet some of them this morning.'

The first was the President of the Students' Association. He explained that he represented us on the Senatus Academicus and was in regular consultation with the Principal and the Master on matters of student concern. He moved on to the history of the Northburgh undergraduate gown, and the correct way to wear it.

'As wuzlets,' he said, 'you're probably feeling a bit nervous and uncertain, and those of you who've come up from England – you've perhaps heard that this is the Oxford of the North? Actually it's the other place that's the Northburgh of the South – ' The Scottish students cheered. He held up his hand. 'As I was saying, you probably aren't used to the cold. So you wear your gown like this. Annabel?'

A girl came slinking on to the stage like a fashion model with her gown done up to her neck. Underneath it she had on a very short skirt but you could only just tell. Her legs were slender, her stockings patterned. The boys wolf-whistled. 'In your second year,' continued the President of the Students' Association, 'You can undo the hooks.'

'More! More!' bayed the boys as Annabel undid her hooks.

'Wait for it,' said the President. 'As you move into your third year, you're half way through your time as an undergraduate so you wear your gown off one shoulder.' Annabel's shoulder poked out. 'And finally, in your Senior Honours year, you hardly wear the gown at all.' Annabel trailed the gown down her back, winked and slunk off the stage. The boys stamped their feet on the floor of the hall in a frenzy.

'Thank you, Annabel,' said the President. 'And in case any of you were getting any ideas, Annabel isn't just my Deputy President, she's also my girlfriend.'

Gillian turned to me. 'Have you ever had the feeling that you've made a terrible mistake?'

63

The President of the Students' Association was followed by a local bank manager who told us all to open bank accounts, preferably but not necessarily at his bank, to pay in our grant cheques immediately and to avoid getting overdrawn. 'Your bank manager is there to help you,' he said.

Also there to help us were the two chaplains and the rabbi, who followed on the bank manager's heels. They stressed that their help was available to all students, whether of their faith or not. At this point the bank manager chipped in and jovially declared that the same applied to him as far as those of us were concerned who chose to bank with his competitors.

The convenor of Wuzlet Week reminded us of the programme for the rest of the day: Wuzlet Week Fayre, Matriculation, meetings with Deans of Studies and this evening a Gaudie. 'Northburgh is like a family,' he said. 'And, as with all families, we look after each other. Each of you is entitled to a Senior Woman – no, be serious for a moment, please. Each of you is entitled to a Senior Woman and a Senior Man who will guide your first, faltering footsteps and teach you everything you need to know. Perhaps not quite everything.

'When you meet a third- or fourth-year student whom you would like to be your Senior Man or Senior Woman, all you have to do is ask. Men, that is. With girls, in this as in so many things, it's traditional for you to wait to be asked. Don't worry, though, most of you wuzlettes will be beseiged with offers, if the view from where I'm standing is anything to go by.'

I turned to ask Gillian if she would go to the Wuzlet Week Fayre with me. She seemed to have left the hall. I tagged along with another group but once we got to the Fayre itself we were soon separated because of the crush.

On the French Society stand, a girl with *Bonjour* on her

sweatshirt was handing out bits of buttered croissant. The Debating Society had a list of forthcoming motions: *This House Would Join the Common Market; This House Regrets the Discovery of America; This House Supports the Reintroduction of the Scold's Bridle.* There was a Hobbit Club, a League of Northburgh Gourmets, Amnesty International and a Women Students' Prayer Circle. There was also a sailing club, which I joined at once because I knew Daddy would ask, and something called SLUG. At the SLUG stand, a man with long auburn hair, a pall-bearer's coat, a trilby hat and sleep in his eyes handed me a duplicated sheet.

'*SLUG.*

'*Noun.*

'*1. Slow, lazy fellow, a sluggard, slothfulness. 2. Piece of lead or other metal for firing from a gun; a roughly formed bullet. 3. A hatter's or tailor's heating iron. 4. Slow-moving, slimy gasteropod in which the shell is empty or entirely absent.*

'*Etc . . .*

'*5. STUDENT LITERARY UNDER GROUND: the society to blow your mind; the best five bob you ever spent; the perfect antidote to the English Syllabus.*'

I asked the man with sleep in his eyes, 'What is it?'

'It's . . .' he seemed to drift off and come back. 'SLUG.'

'Is it a sort of literary society?'

He found my question funny. 'Is it a *sort of literary society*? Sort of yes, man. Sort of.'

'I mean is it for people interested in writing?'

'Writing. You mean like – ' he mimed holding a pen. '*Writing* writing?'

'Do you have meetings?'

'You want meetings, we'll have meetings.'

I moved on.

My eye was caught by a rail of purple gowns, on sale at six and a half guineas each. I picked one up to see if it were second-hand. It seemed new. It weighed the same as mine. The fabric felt the same. A voice said, 'Why don't you try it on?'

The voice was deep but quiet and pleasantly resonant. Its owner looked as if he had just got back from an athletics tour of somewhere sunny. His skin was golden, his hair was reddish-blond. He wore a suit. He was short-haired, clean-shaven and in his late twenties. 'Try it on,' he repeated, as if he were suggesting something slightly naughty.

'I've already got one,' I pointed out.

'So you have. May I be very rude and ask what you paid for it?'

'Eight guineas.'

'From?'

'Strammington's.'

'Strammington's.' He said it with me, nodding that it was just as he had thought. 'I suppose you ordered it in advance.'

'Yes.'

'I suppose the order form came in the post with all the other official papers and you didn't realise you had any choice?'

'Yes,' I said again. 'I mean no. Sorry.'

'*I'm* sorry, for your wasted money. I'm embarrassed, and it's not even my fault.'

I thought it was kind of him to be concerned, but I didn't know what to say. I was hopeless at meeting new people. I hadn't been a new girl since I went into Kindergarten One, aged four.

Meeting people was one of the things university was supposed to be good for. Everyone had said, *You'll meet lots of people*, particularly my parents. They meant boys. I had never had a boyfriend, apart from occasional members of the Colts with whom I had smooched at rugby club hops. Daddy had stressed that this was not my fault. The Colts were all very well but they weren't really our sort of chap.

'I'm Godfrey de Salis. Small d, capital S.'

'Janet Toms.'

'Would you like to join the Conservative Association, Janet?'

I hadn't realised it was the Conservative Association. I looked up and saw the Union Jack. On their table they had leaflets and books for sale with titles like, *Ian Smith of Rhodesia: Hero and Statesman – Everything Must be Sold: The Final Solution to Council Housing* and *Equality and Mediocrity: The Bright Man's Burden*.

I said, 'I don't know anything about politics.'

'You know about being charged eight guineas for a six and a half guinea gown.'

I nodded. He said, 'It's British industry in microcosm. Monopolies, leading to restrictive practices, leading to inflated prices.'

I didn't know what he was talking about, but he didn't seem to expect a reply other than, 'Yes.'

He said, 'When this country has a Conservative prime minister – '

Now I had to speak. A political ignoramus I might be, but even I knew who had won this year's general election. 'We've got one.'

'We've got Edward Heath,' he said, as if he were sorry he had to correct me.

'Isn't he – ?'

'He's a traitor.' Godfrey de Salis smiled sunnily. 'Would you like to buy a ticket for our social? Even the Labour Club admit it's the party of the year.'

'How much?'

'Free to members, ten shillings to non-members.'

'How much is it to be a member?'

'Five shillings.'

I joined. It was a way of meeting people. I thought Godfrey de Salis might offer to be my Senior Man but I was out of luck. On my way out I bought a copy of *Nuts*, the student newspaper. The front page report was about how the government and the University Grants Committee were trying to make the university expand, and the Principal was resisting because it would spoil the family atmosphere.

64

Lunch at Elizabeth Blackwell Hall consisted of gigot of lamb with mashed turnips and boiled potatoes, followed by arctic roll with golden syrup out of a jug. Breakfast had been help yourself, but now we sat at table and were served by waitresses in black dresses and white aprons. Those of us who had gowns wore them.

The conversation was all 'Have you got a Senior Man?' and 'What have you joined?' Quite a few people had joined the Conservative Association (they called it the Tory Club) as a way of meeting people.

My room mate Gillian said, 'What kind of people?'

In the hope of being on good terms with her I said helpfully, 'If you haven't got your gown yet, you should get it from the Tories.'

'I wouldn't have a Tory Club gown as a gift.'

'Why not?'

'They give me the creeps.'

'Gowns?'

'Tories. *Both*. I was talking to a girl in the Labour Club. They're no ordinary Tories here, you know. They've got some very nasty people and some very nasty policies.'

Gwen, one of the girls who had joined the Tory Club to meet people, said, 'What do you expect the Labour Club to say?'

'They're fascists,' said Gillian. 'Guess who they had speaking at their annual dinner last year?' We couldn't, so Gillian told us. 'Enoch Powell.'

'Enoch Powell only says what a lot of people think.'

'Speak for yourself, Gwen.' Gillian was getting quite worked up. 'Northburgh Tories are even more right-wing than the government. Twenty years from now they'll probably *be* the government.' She spooned gloomily at her arctic roll.

Somebody said to me, 'I expect you're sorry you brought the subject up.'

I shrugged. 'I just thought Gillian might like to save some money on her gown.'

'I can save even more by not buying one.'

A second-year girl told her, 'You have to have one.'

'What for?'

'Formal meals in Hall.'

'I'm not wearing one now.' Gillian looked round. 'The place hasn't burst into flames.'

'This isn't a formal meal.'

'You amaze me,' said Gillian.

'It's a tradition,' said the second-year girl. 'It gives a sense of belonging. If you don't want to belong, you shouldn't have come here.'

It was the sort of thing Daddy would have said. After lunch, Gillian and I went to our room and finished our unpacking. We were fair in our sharing out of space, and meticulously polite with our 'Which side of the basin do you prefer to keep your toothbrush?' and 'Do you mind if I plug in my coffee pot?' but we didn't talk about anything else.

I thought she was probably as scared as I was of finding out that we couldn't stand each other. I didn't understand why she had to be so indignant about everything, so intense. It was embarrassing, ill-mannered, like criticising your host. She in her turn probably thought me dull, narrow and ill-informed. I wondered if I would ever have the room to myself.

I had never shared a room before. I wasn't worried about it from the point of view of academic work – I knew from school that I could study in a full classroom or a crowded library – but writing *Off-Ration* was different. It was my novel, my fiction, mine. It was private. It came from my imagination. For years I had kept my imagination locked up. Now it poked forth painfully and grudgingly, like a hard, slow, smelly bowel movement. On better days it flowed like the flowing limbs of an elegant and graceful dancer, preening herself naked. But I didn't relish having an audience for my nakedness and vanity any more than I did for my going to the toilet.

*

In the afternoon we had matriculation, which meant standing in a queue to sign a long Latin oath with a short English translation. After that we were given our grant cheques. We also had interviews with our Deans of Studies to arrange our timetables. These were followed by afternoon tea at Elizabeth Blackwell Hall.

A silver urn was put out in the common room, together with a trolley-load of scones and cakes, for us to help ourselves. It was only four o'clock and only October, but in this northern latitude evening was closing in. The sun dipped into the choppy grey-and-white sea. The air turned navy blue, clouds were black-edged. Wind rattled the windows.

Somebody turned on the lights. I went back and back and back for more food. It was exhilarating to have it there, to be allowed to eat it, to be expected to eat it. When my mother made cakes at home she always warned me of the regret I would feel if I ate them.

Again and again and without remorse I loaded my plate. This wasn't greed, it was an emergency. I was far from home, uprooted, rootless. I could die at any time. I was hungry, empty, hollow. I had to have the sweet, floury scones, the crisp, thin triangles of shortbread, the light sponges with tangy jam. I ate them, though I knew they would never fill me. Perhaps nothing would. Down went the sweet food into my void. After tea we had a library tour, and then dinner: Chicken à la King, mashed potatoes and chips, green beans and lemon meringue pie.

The evening event was a gaudie – community singing – in Fraser Lamont Hall. In candlelight we sat on the floor in our gowns with *The Student Song Book*. A friendly man with a guitar led us in 'The Bonnie Lass of Fyvie', 'Banks of the Ohio' and 'Shoals of Herring'. Then gangs of boys and men started to arrive with carry-outs. The guitars and the master of ceremonies became less and less audible under catcalls, roaring and songs like 'Roedean School' and 'Caviare Comes from a Virgin Sturgeon'.

I felt homesick for Daddy and decided to phone home. I told the operator I wanted to reverse the charges. She asked for my name, and I heard her getting through. She said, 'I have a call from Northburgh in Scotland from Miss Janet Toms. Will you accept the charge?'

What if they say no? I thought. *What if they say 'Who?'*

'Of course,' said Daddy, as if he had never heard such a ridiculous question. 'Hullo, chum. Och aye the noo? Is this a Mayday call? Want us to send in the choppers?'

'No, it's lovely.'

'She says it's braw and bonnie up there, Jo. Mummy says she told you it would be and oooh she envies you. Shall I put her on the train? You don't have to answer that. What have you been doing?'

Eating, I thought. 'Learning about traditions.'

'Jolly good. Any work yet?'

'Starts on Monday.'

'A likely story. Now she's saying, have you met lots of people?'

'Hundreds, can't you hear them?' I held the phone towards the singing.

He said, 'Sounds like the rugger club on a Saturday night.'

'I know.' I blinked hard. 'I miss you.'

'I say. Well, I'm just the same when the Royal Marines play *Heart of Oak*. Lump in the throat. Probably get worse before it gets better. Mummy wants a word.'

She said, 'Hello, darling, did you get there all right? Daddy's rolling his eyes and saying, "No, of course she didn't."'

'Yes. How's Miranda?'

My mother laughed. 'I think she's forgotten you ever lived here.'

'Oh.'

'Are you having a wonderful time?'

'I want to come home.'

'Go on with you. Throw yourself into things.'

65

'WOMEN STUDENTS! Are you fed up with this male-dominated university, with its patronising "traditions" and unfair practices? DID YOU KNOW that only one lecturer in eight is a woman, and she is likely to be earning about two-thirds as much as her male counterparts? There are NO WOMEN PROFESSORS. DID YOU KNOW that as a woman you are only allowed in the Beer Bar of YOUR OWN STUDENTS' UNION on Saturday nights? (The rest of the time it is a Male Preserve. Why? Well, because it's A TRADITION of course!) DID YOU KNOW that male students living in Halls of Residence get their beds made for them? DID YOU KNOW that the Appointments Board aids and abets employers in discriminating against women graduates? Did you know that if you marry during your course, your grant will be REDUCED but your husband's will be INCREASED? DID YOU KNOW that the so-called Charities Queen Contest is in fact a Cattle Market?

'If you would like to discuss these issues, and consider forming a Women's Lib Consciousness Raising Group, affiliated to the Women's Liberation Workshop in London, come along to the reading room in the Union at 8:00 pm on Tuesdays.

'Further information from Gillian Glenn, Elizabeth Blackwell Hall.'

She put the leaflet on my desk. I said, 'Good idea.'

This pleased her. 'You'll come then?'

'Not this week,' I said. *Not any week*, I thought. The good idea was the idea of Gillian being out of our room on a regular basis, which might give me a chance to get on with writing my novel.

The only other time when I could rely on having the room to myself was on weekday mornings between nine and ten, when she had a lecture and I didn't. But almost invariably that was the time the cleaner chose to dust the room and hoover it (though not to make our beds). And even when she didn't come in, the chance that she might was enough to spoil my concentration.

Off-Ration demanded terrific concentration, much more than essays, with which I kept more or less up-to-date, getting more or less good marks. An hour in the morning wasn't enough for *Off-Ration*. Sometimes it took that long to build the concentration up and then let go of it.

I listened inside myself for the voices of Emma and Elaine. They were my main characters and, childish though it would sound if I told anybody (so I didn't) they had voices and they told me their stories.

I didn't feel as if I were making anything up. I was being told. But I had to listen deeply inside myself. It was like listening to the movement of blood along the blood vessels of my own ear. Sometimes what I wanted to hear was blocked out by the very sound of my listening.

There were days when I would get into a state of concentration so intense that it would be hard to emerge. Going to my lecture I would feel as if I had turned myself inside out. My internal organs were exposed to the cold gritty air, while my outer skin and senses were engaged in deep contemplation of themselves and each other, and would not be distracted.

In that state I wrote my novel. It was fine for novel-writing, but I couldn't go around like that. I couldn't study like that, or be a convivial room mate. I didn't want to be any kind of room mate. On the evening of Gillian's meeting I bade her goodbye and hoped that it would go well. I wasn't sure what would constitute *going well* for a women's lib meeting (I didn't think she knew either) but I hoped that whatever it was it would take a nice long time.

I closed the curtains, put half a crown in the electricity meter and turned on one bar of the fire. I made myself a cup of coffee, stirred in the Marvel, wrapped myself in my gown for warmth and set to work.

*

Off-Ration, the title of the novel, the phrase, came from a joke Daddy used to make when Christine was alive, about the difference between our two personalities. She had been born in 1948. The war had only been over for three years, Labour were in power and everything was rationed: food, fuel, sweets, furniture, everything. Christine was hungry and resentful, bitter and twisted. Her first words (according to the joke) were, *I want*.

I, on the other hand, was supposed to have popped out of my mother's womb in 1952, realised that the Conservatives were back in power, embraced the prosperity they had brought with them and declared, *That's mine*. I was an off-ration baby, hence my cheerful disposition and tendency to succeed at everything I did.

The novel came indirectly from all that. It was about a pair of twins, Emma and Elaine. They were younger than Christine would have been, older than I was. Emma had been born just before midnight on the night rationing ended. Elaine was born just after. Elaine was the off-ration baby. Emma was the hungry one, who cried, *I want*.

I wrote in the first person, switching, chapter by chapter, from Emma's version of events to Elaine's. I followed them through their schooldays and their first romances, or (in Emma's case) lack of them.

Emma hung around with boys but you couldn't call that romance. She was too hungry for romance. She wanted too much from boys. She gave them too much. They took what they could and then walked off. They pretended to despise her for being too easy but that was only part of it. She scared them. They preferred full, contented girls like Elaine. Elaine knew what belonged to her and what did not. Emma got confused, and so confused others.

The evening Gillian went off to her women's lib meeting, I was writing the episode in which Elaine was having her first period. She didn't exactly tell her sister about it but she made sure she knew. She left packets of sanitary towels lying about and made it clear that she was unable to participate in household chores.

She put her hand lightly on her stomach and assumed a faint, wise, martyred expression. She dissolved aspirins in glasses of water with a great deal of fuss and said she couldn't go swimming.

When her twin asked why, Elaine said, 'You'll understand when you're older.'

Emma had never had a period. Emma's breasts had never developed. Her body was too hungry and too bitter to flourish into puberty. It dared not shed its own blood when it might not get any more. It refused to accumulate tissue that would secrete and store milk for some hungry stranger. Why should it, when Emma was hungry herself? It – Emma's body, Emma – had never been properly nourished. Why should it nourish somebody else?

One problem in writing the novel was how to make it clear that these were only metaphors. I didn't want to suggest that Elaine and Emma's parents made any difference between them, or deprived Emma of food or of anything, because obviously parents wouldn't do that. Somehow I had to show the difference between what was actually happening, on the one hand, and, on the other, what were the bitter, twisted fantasies of the I-want baby, and the difficult adolescent she became. Emma became difficult through no fault of her parents, who loved her and always did their best for her. It was the way she turned out.

I was struggling with this when the door opened and Gillian came in in her coat, followed by four girls also in coats and with very cross expressions. Gillian said, 'Janet, I'm really sorry, but the rugby club sat in at our meeting and wouldn't budge so we've had to move. Would you mind if we had it in here?'

66

In the Elizabeth Blackwell common room a party was going on. In our library, seniors sat studying for their Finals, broody as spiders, one at each table. There was a girl called Kathy. I had noticed her before. She had a habit of plucking hairs from her head one by one in a kind of agony as she translated Anglo Saxon. I would be studying Anglo Saxon next year.

It was ten o'clock. The main library would be closing, the Union would be noisy. There was nowhere else. I went out into the night, holding my novel and my pen. I was still wearing my gown. I considered going back to my room for my coat or another jersey, but I didn't dare. Gillian and her friends were angry enough already – with the men of the rugby club, with men in general – and now they would be angry with me. They would think I was making a gesture.

My gown would have to be enough. I hugged it round me. The air was dark and salty but unusually still and mild for November, as if a storm were on its way. The flat sea swelled slowly, half-heartedly, and flopped, and became flat again. There was a bright white moon.

I went to the beach, and sat in a shelter next to a boarded up ice cream stand. I wrote by moonlight. I felt romantic and martyred. I glanced back towards the turreted town and the chunky bulk of Elizabeth Blackwell Hall. Gillian and her women's cohort were inside. I was outside. Why? They were the ones who were out of step. They were the ones who were angry. I accepted. They wanted. They were difficult. I was good. I was writing in the middle of the night, and I didn't even have to. I counted lit-up windows and found my room.

That's mine.

But you can't have it.

*

Footsteps approached. Two sets. Male and female, quietly talking. Easy talk, not lovey-dovey, but relaxed, going-for-a-walk-at-night talk.

I recognised the tall, elegant silhouette of Godfrey de Salis from the Tory Club, sauntering this way with a girl. Her purple gown flowed behind her in the style of a final-year student; his was the black gown of a postgraduate. She was nearly as tall as he was and equally elegant. They held hands. I froze. They would think I was spying on them. What excuse could I make?

He said to her, 'Let's sit down for a bit. Oh.'

I said, 'Sorry.'

'Not at all.' He inclined his head and his white teeth flashed. 'You were here first.'

'I'm just going.'

'Not on our account, I hope . . . It's Janet, isn't it?'

'Yes.'

'Are you all right?' I didn't answer. He said to the girl, 'This is Janet Toms. Janet and I met,' he told her, 'during Wuzlet Week.' *He feels he has to explain*, I thought. 'She'd just bought this from Strammington's.' He touched my gown with the tip of his finger. *He remembers that too.*

The girl said, 'Oh gosh. Bad luck.'

Godfrey asked me, 'Do you live round here?'

'Elizabeth Blackwell.'

'This is Diana Foster-Lee, our treasurer.' He bowed slightly. 'Our *treasure*.'

'I say, Godfrey. Don't overdo it.'

'How do you do.'

She shook my hand. Under her gown she wore a white mohair jumper, tailored slacks and good brogues. Her legs were long, her face was aristocratic. The moon cast soft shadows between the outlines of her delicate bones. She aroused a kind of despair in me. Her voice was plummy. Daddy would call her *almost a lady*. He would approve of her. He would approve of Godfrey even more, were he ever to meet him. I longed to take home a boyfriend of whom Daddy would approve. *Almost a gent, our type of chap*. Someone who would accompany him to rugby matches, as his brothers' sons accompanied *them*, and understand what was going on, and take the place of the sons Mummy had never given him.

Diana looked at her hand that had shaken mine. She said, 'You *are* cold.'

Godfrey touched my other hand. It was a light gesture with the back of his right index finger, testing my temperature as he might test bath water. He moved his finger away. He said, 'Frozen stiff. Is something the matter?'

Diana said, 'You get peculiar people along here sometimes.'

'I was writing.' I put my exercise book into the inside pocket of my gown. 'I'm going back now.'

Diana said, 'We're going that way, aren't we, Godfrey?'

Godfrey said, 'Perhaps Janet will allow us to walk her home.'

I walked between them. She was half aunt, half hostess. 'Are you a wuzlette?'

'Yes.'

'Settling in all right?'

'Oh yes.'

'Essay crisis tonight?'

'Not really. I'm trying to write a – ' I couldn't say *novel* – 'story.'

Godfrey said, 'That's very enterprising of you. Is it a novel?'

'It might be. In about a hundred years.'

Diana said, 'Do you get inspiration in the moonlight?'

'There's a women's lib meeting going on in my room.'

'Golly.'

'How come?' said Godfrey.

'My room mate.'

'Who's your room mate?'

'Gillian Glenn.'

'Labour Club,' said Godfrey automatically.

Diana laughed. 'Honestly, Godfrey. You'll have Janet thinking you keep files on who's a member of what. He's got a capacious brain, Janet.'

'Full of useless information,' said Godfrey. We all laughed. 'It's not very good though, is it? If you're driven out of your own room. Shivering on the beach in the middle of the night. Can't you find a different room mate?'

'Everyone's settled.'

Diana said, 'I remember my first room mate. Extraordinary girl. Kept her bike on her bed.'

Godfrey ignored her. 'You don't really want a room mate if you're trying to write. You want a room of your own.' He looked at me with tender concern.

'There aren't any singles for first years.'

'Have you asked? Explained to the warden what the problem is?'

'It's not really a *problem*. I mean, you have to give and take.'

'Normally I would agree with you,' said Godfrey. 'But there are limits.'

'It seems so selfish,' I said. We reached Hall. 'I can't ask you in, it's after hours.'

Godfrey said, 'Have you read *The Virtue of Selfishness* by Ayn Rand? Di, does Ayn Rand ever come to Britain? We ought to get her up here to speak. I'll lend it to you, Janet. If you can't face the warden, get your Senior Woman to put in a word for you.'

'I haven't got one,' I said, ashamed.

'That's a pretty poor show,' said Diana. 'I'd better be yours.'

Godfrey said, 'I expect she's got an entire platoon of Senior Men, so there's not much point in me asking.'

67

North Crag Cottage belonged to friends of Godfrey and Diana's, Professor and Mrs Lincoln of the Department of Political Economy. They had been saying only the other night that it was a shame not to let out their spare room, and they were grateful to Godfrey for drawing attention to my clear and serious need. I was to call them Alex and Babs.

The house was as it sounded – cold and old, granitey and high up. Night and day seagulls swooped and cried around its roofs and precarious-looking chimneys. My room had three outside walls. It was up its own short flight of stairs, over the front door, separate from the rest of the house.

It had a sloping ceiling, and small leaded windows through which you could look straight down a hundred feet of sheer cliff face. It had a desk, a wardrobe, an electric fire (for which a shilling meter was promptly fitted) and an enormous double bed, which made Diana giggle and say, 'Gosh.'

There were no facilities for cooking. Wuzlets weren't allowed self-cooking accommodation. I would continue to eat my meals at Elizabeth Blackwell Hall, half a mile away down the steep and bumpy cliff track. I bought a bike. Technically my room was now an annexe of the hall, which meant I was supposed still to be subject to its rules, but Babs gave me my front door key and said, 'Do whatever you like as long as you do it quietly.'

When Gillian realised that I meant it about moving out, she was stricken with remorse. 'Please, Janet. Let's try again.' She made it sound as if we were a husband and wife in the closing stages of our marriage.

I said, 'It's not your fault. Honestly.'

'It is! I was totally selfish over that meeting. I was so pissed off with the rugby club that I didn't think about you.'

'It's not just that.'

This made things worse. She said, 'What else have I done?'

'*Nothing*.'

'We'll draw up a contract,' she suggested. 'We'll have agreed hours of silence and lights-out time. We'll draw a line down the middle of the room.'

'It's better if I move out.'

'*Why*?'

'I'm trying to write something.'

'What?'

I said, 'A novel,' so that she could dismiss me as peculiar and stop feeling guilty. But she said, 'Now that I know, I can be quiet.' She made it sound as if I had an illness.

'That wouldn't help.'

'I don't understand.'

I didn't tell her that it was because she didn't understand that I had to move out. I didn't tell her that even I didn't understand the special quality of the silence and the separateness that I needed to write *Off-Ration*.

She reconciled herself to my going. She told everyone that I was writing a novel. I could have done without them knowing, but I supposed she had to save face.

She came with her new room mate to my room-warming party, and admired the room, though not my Tory Club guests. Most of them were my academic brothers and sisters, which was to say that they too had Godfrey and Diana as their Senior Man and Senior Woman. Gillian spoke with teeth-gritted politeness to Diana and the other girls, but refused to say a word to Godfrey.

If he came near her, she moved away. This meant her cutting off her nose to spite her face and going without a drink for much of the evening; for he had volunteered to be (in addition, he joked, to being my Senior Man and my accommodation agent) my wine waiter, and was pouring out the reasonably priced South African sherry that he had helped me to choose.

In my chilly annexe I seemed to find the silence and separateness I needed to finish my book. I was productive. At night I went to sleep with my gown over my pyjamas, cuddling a hot water bottle; I woke at around six, shivering between sheets like slabs of ice. I boiled a kettle, refilled the hot water bottle, made tea, took it back to bed and wrote till seven-thirty.

I was aware of the sounds of the family getting up but they were nothing to do with me. The children – Brenda aged four and Simon aged two – were under instructions from their parents not to enter my part of the house unless I invited them, a thing I was usually too busy to do.

I went to lectures and the library and wrote essays all day; I wrote my novel again in the evenings, unless the Lincolns were playing host to a meeting of the Tory Club, in which case attending it seemed the least I could do.

The rest of the time I lived apart from them. But I liked to hear their noises and to know they were around. I liked carrying on my life on the edge of a family. It helped me to imagine what things were like for Elaine, the off-ration baby for whom everything had always been there for the taking; and Emma, the difficult one, who cried, *I want*.

When I flew home at Christmas (Godfrey drew my attention to the night flight from Edinburgh to Heathrow with the student discount) *Off-Ration* was more or less finished. All it needed was tidying up and typing.

Daddy met me at Heathrow. I was unprepared for the emotions aroused in me by seeing him again after our ten-week separation.

After puny undergraduates, he astonished me by being so large. He looked fitter than many students I could think of – cleaner too. His face was square, his moustache neat. His wrinkles were subtly-drawn, formalities, imposed on him, as it were, for reasons of fairness so that he should not have too much of an unfair advantage over other fifty-year-old men. And although his pale hair had streaks of grey, and although faint glimmers of his scalp could be made out under the harsh lights of the Domestic Arrivals Terminal, his hair was not an old man's hair. Curls gathered round his collar, and he had not made Mummy snip them off as he once might have. The curls were his one concession to the changes that had been made in men's hairstyling fashion since the end of World War Two.

No such concessions had been made in his clothes. He looked

tonight as if he had come straight from work, or perhaps from dinner with a client. He smelt faintly and pleasantly of alcohol. He wore his dark, double-breasted Crombie overcoat and carried his trilby and his *Daily Telegraph*. His shirt was white, his tie was RNVR, his trousers had wide turnups. He had a waistcoat on, and – I would have been prepared to bet on it – braces.

I felt suddenly tearful. It wasn't just the sight of him. It wasn't simply that he had come on a cold December night to meet me with the minicab that he could just as easily have sent on its own. It wasn't only the possibility this hinted at – that he was as impatient to see me as I was to see him. It was the suddenly overwhelming realisation that *I could come back*. I was not aware that I had ever consciously doubted this; but it dawned on me that homesickness, of the kind I had suffered in my early days and weeks was no more than the fear that, having gone away, I could not come back.

I could. He let me. I could leave him but I did not have to give him up.

I could travel north through the night on a sleeper, get myself a Senior Man, write a novel, go to lectures and learn things that Daddy would never conceivably know or possibly understand, fly home like a jet-setting film star, and *he would be here*.

He would always be here. I could betray him by not needing him any more, but he would still stand around in arrivals terminals in the middle of the night clutching his trilby, reading his *Daily Telegraph*, not caring whether or not I needed him to be there, allowing me to take my own time to discover that I did need him and always would.

Carefully and with embarrassment we disentangled ourselves from our hug. He gave a little bow. He said, 'Lady MacMuck, your carriage awaits,' and carried my case to the minicab.

At home my mother was up a ladder in a black satiny dressing gown and old flannel pyjamas, fixing Christmas cards to bits of glittery string. She tore into sticky tape with her teeth and said, 'Welcome home, darling.'

I said, 'Thanks,' but she didn't mean me. She descended the steps at a terrifying pace, hugged Daddy and kissed his mouth. I got a peck on the cheek and a pat on the back. 'Have you had a marvellous term? Have you met lots of people?'

'A few.'

'Tum-tum-te-tum?' said Daddy enquiringly, to the tune 'Here comes the Bride'.

'Of course not.'

'I do envy you,' said my mother.

'Why don't you join the Open University, then?' I suggested.

'It's not as simple as that, Janet.'

Miranda came careering down the stairs at high speed in her nightie and bare feet. She hugged my legs and climbed up me. She was six. She had grown taller since I left, and wirier and, in her own odd, intense, wizened sort of way, prettier. 'Welcome home, Janet! Welcome home, Janet!'

Daddy said to me, 'You are honoured. I never get any of this fuss. Why aren't you asleep, young lady?'

'I wanted to see Janet.'

'You want to see Daddy too,' said my mother. 'Give him a kiss.'

'In a minute. I want to show Janet something.'

'Let her get in the house first.'

'She *is* in the house.' Miranda dragged me upstairs to my room which had been adorned with dead twigs dipped in glitterwax and dolly-peg angels with fixed grins.

'Miranda, you are kind! Thank you.'

Downstairs my mother was yelling, '. . . might have let me know, that's all!'

'For Christ's sake, woman! I was meeting Janet.'

'You said you'd be coming home first! I've made you a cauliflower cheese!'

'Cauliflower ear? Again?'

'It's *your* bloody relatives we've got coming for Christmas and I'm the one who's stuck with all the preparations!'

'You've got nothing else to do.'

'Oh haven't I? You watch out, mate. One of these days, the worm may turn.'

I made a face at Miranda. She said, 'Mummy always says that. "The worm may turn!"'

'Oh dear.'

She said, 'It's only one of their usual rows.'

She sounded adult and tolerant. I said, 'Go on with you. They don't have rows.'

'They do,' she said.

'They don't.'

'They *do* Janet. All the time.'

'Those aren't real rows.'

68

I woke next morning at six o'clock, my usual time. I lay still for a while, working out where I was. I could hear cars outside, but no seagulls. The central heating ticked; the air tasted dry and scorched. I was too hot.

I got out of bed, sat at my desk in my nightie and took the cover off my typewriter. It was the old Imperial that Pam and Daddy had bought me as a reward for passing my eleven-plus. I remembered my hopeless desire for the elegant little Japanese portable; and their insistence, that this was the more sensible purchase. Certainly it had lasted. But then I had not made much use of it, once I gave up writing.

The day they bought me the typewriter was the day Pam met Rusty, or rather met him again. Years before they had been boyfriend and girlfriend in New Zealand, and then he had turned up at Bleswick Rugby Club. I remembered the evening, like the morning with the typewriter, as a time of yearning and hurt and puzzlement. Why couldn't I have what I wanted? Or who I wanted? Why did it hurt so much? Another thing I remembered was the dreadful row Christine had with Daddy when we got home. She was really cheeky. I couldn't remember what the row was about, but she swore at him and he had to smack her. She ran out into the street in the middle of the night. I dashed to my room and buried my head and in the morning everything was back to normal.

It was a different room in a different house. It was a different time. Pam had gone, and apart from that one Christmas card which had included Christine among the addressees and so shown how lost she was to us, and we to her, she had never contacted us again.

I didn't want to think about her. I didn't want to think about anything to do with that time. I wanted to finish my novel. I got my handwritten exercise books out of my holdall, fed paper and carbon paper into the rollers and started work.

At seven o'clock my mother came in with a cup of tea slurping in its saucer. 'Must you make that noise so early?'

'Sorry.' I stopped typing. 'I'm used to nobody being able to hear me.'

'I don't mind for myself but you woke Daddy.'

'OK. I'll wait till he's up in future.'

'It's not really fair to him.'

'Mummy, I've said I won't do it again.'

She said, 'I hope you're not becoming selfish now that you're so privileged.'

I sighed with exasperation. I wasn't used to this. She seemed to resent my being at university, even though she was always the one who wanted me to go there. She had urged me on to university with even more enthusiasm than Daddy, who said he himself knew a great deal more than a great many chaps he could think of with letters after their names.

I had always known that I would go to university, but until this term I could not have told you what university was. I had seen it vaguely as the next stage, where you went after the sixth form. It was the seventh form, the eighth form, thc ninth form, the tenth form. It was where you met people, including our kind of chap. It was a way of bringing honour to the school. Girls who got into university always had their names read out first at speech day. Student nurses and trainee teachers were clearly second best.

There had never been any possibility of Christine going to university. University (I had gathered) was not open to girls who cheated in their eleven-plus and got sent to the secondary modern in disgrace. After her death I had held tight to the assumption that I would go to university, as if to prove that I was different from her and would not go down her road. Yet now my mother was behaving towards me with such irritability and perverse determination to pick a fight that I might *be* Christine.

She said, 'What are your plans for the vac?'

I cringed a little, nobody I knew said *vac*. 'I've written a novel. I've got to type it.'

'So there's no point in my asking you to help me get ready for Christmas.'

'I didn't say that.'

'I don't hear you offering.'

'You asked me what my plans were and I told you. What would you like me to do?'

'It's not as simple as that,' she said. 'I can't tell you exactly.'

'When you've thought of something, tell me and I'll do it.'

'And in the meantime you'll get on with your novel?'

'Yes, if that's all right.'

'How bloody typical!'

She slammed out and cooked Daddy his breakfast. Later, though, she was as nice as pie. She said, 'I wouldn't dream of letting you waste your time on my housework, you've got something much more important to get on with.' She even tried to stop me taking Miranda to see Father Christmas. She said, 'Write your novel, Janet, *I'll* take Miranda to see Father Christmas!'

I said, 'But *I* want to see him,' so we all went together. Afterwards we had knickerbocker glories (to be precise, Miranda and I had our own knickerbocker glories; Mummy had black coffee and spoonfuls of ours) and she asked me what the novel was about.

In between mouthfuls of cold sweet cream I tried to explain about *I-want* and *that's-mine*. It was difficult; having worked so hard to write it, I felt imposed upon and belittled by being expected to summarise it, explain it and speak it. I did my best for my mother. I wasn't sure that she understood, but she seemed to like hearing me talk about it. And when Humphrey and Sue and my cousins and their fiancés arrived for Christmas, she seemed proud to be able to say, 'Janet's writing a novel,' as if that made up for my failure to acquire a mate. She said, 'I'm awfully afraid it's going to have me in it.'

Daddy said, 'I should bloody well hope it's got me in it.'

'It hasn't got either of you in it. It's not autobiographical, how can it be? It's about a pair of twins.'

I finished on the day before I was due to go back to Northburgh. I went to Bleswick Library and looked up the D section of the list of publishers in the *Writers' and Artists' Yearbook*.

Delbarco and Wilde were still in existence. I thought the address was different from the one to which Pam had taken me, but the first name in the list of company directors was still Miss Monica Delbarco (Managing). I stared at the name for a long time, remembering. I hardly believed that she would remember me. But I had to start somewhere. This was the only publishing company with which I had a connection, however tenuous.

I drafted a covering letter.

'Dear Miss Delbarco,
'I don't know if you remember me, but in 1963 when I was eleven I was introduced to you by your former secretary, Miss Pamela MacLeish. You said that if I wrote a novel when I was older, you would be interested in reading it.

'I am now nineteen and in my first year at Northburgh University. I have just completed *Off-Ration*, which is a fictional account of the lives of two contemporary teenagers, and I am submitting it herewith for your consideration.

'Yours faithfully,
'Janet Toms (Miss).'
'PS. I enclose a stamped addressed envelope.'

The enclosing of stamped addressed envelopes seemed to me to be a loathsome custom, barbaric and brutal, like expecting the condemned man to provide his own rope, but it was what you were supposed to do. I posted my novel. Next day I set off back to Northburgh thinking of all the ways in which I could have written it better.

69

I had given Bleswick as my return address and told my parents to forward anything immediately. A few days after I got back to Northburgh, catastrophe struck.

The postmen went out on strike. Throughout Britain, nothing was delivered, nothing was collected, and everyone said it would go on for weeks. Post boxes were sealed. Sorting offices were locked. Some, it was said, had packages and letters inside them, but you weren't allowed to go and see if any of them were yours. You would just have to wait.

The Tory Club tried to take the Northburgh branch of the postmen's trades union to court for interfering with Her Majesty's Mails. When this didn't work they set up their own local postal service. Godfrey organised this, and got his wuzlets and wuzlettes to help. I didn't mind doing deliveries around the town but they were no help to me. My manuscript was somewhere between Bleswick and London.

I was in limbo. This was worse than rejection. When I tried to make pictures in my head of an ageing Miss Delbarco reading my manuscript, they were totally unconvincing. Her smiles were as false as her frowns. She probably hadn't even received it yet. Still, I was anxious. I resented my anxiety. Worrying would be bad enough if I knew that she was at this moment reading, assessing, judging. To worry without even that knowledge was like wearing myself out running a race, only to be told that I had not yet reached the starting block.

I was fidgety and restless. I was used to having something to write, but I couldn't start another novel when I didn't know what was happening to the first.

Godfrey suggested that I should join the staff of *Nuts*, the student newspaper. 'It's a terrible rag,' he said. 'You might improve it.' He introduced me to the editor, David Cunningham, a pale, whippety third-year with a checked cap down over his eyes, who said I should come to a news meeting.

I was one of five people, and the only girl. The men – second and third years from the way they wore their gowns – introduced themselves as Stuart, Colin, Gordon and Ronnie. David Cunningham sat with his cap on his head, a cigarette in the corner of his mouth and his feet on the desk. He pulled a sheet of paper out of a tray and said, 'The Exec of the NSA are voting this week on whether to pull out of NUS because of the NOLS takeover.'

Colin said, 'Christ! That could mean the end of cheap flights.'

David said, 'You want to do that one? Gordon: decimalisation. Three weeks to go. Talk to local shopkeepers, ask if they're ready and how they feel about it. Ask the catering people in the Union. What are bacon rolls going to cost in the new money?'

'Big stories this week, Dave.'

'Wait for it. Women's lib.'

'Women's what?' said Ronnie. David read in a grand voice from a sheet of paper. "Northburgh Women's Liberation Press Release. We will be mounting a picket – " '

'Lucky old picket,' said Stuart. 'I don't think.'

David smiled lazily, winked at me under his cap and put up his hand for silence. ' " – A picket outside the Charities Office in the Students' Union to protest against the Charities Queen Competition. This so-called charitable event is no more than a beauty contest, a – " What's this? I wish they'd clean their typewriter – "cattle market in which first-year women students are pressured to compete for male approval, and we protest against – " '

'The sourness of the grapes?' suggested Ronnie.

'You want to do this one, Ronnie?'

'Hell no.'

'Perhaps you're right. It needs a woman's touch.'

Stuart said, 'Some of those bitches have never had a man's touch. That's their problem.'

'I don't want to touch 'em,' said Ronnie. 'Do you?'

David Cunningham looked as if he and I were the only rational adults in the room. 'Think you can handle this one for us, Janet?' He gave me the press release.

I felt marked by it. The anger and contempt in the office would come to me. No one had nominated me for the Charities Queen contest. If they had, I would have assumed they were being satirical – I was not beautiful. For Charities Queen girls, beauty was off-ration. *That's mine*, they said. The rest of us must want humbly, and in silence. I said, 'I'd rather do something else.'

'Perhaps you're right. It is a bit on the petty side. Are you interested in gowns?'

'Yes, very.'

The story was that Strammington's, the university outfitters, were threatening to take the Tory Club to court under a Town Statute of 1632 which, said Strammington's, gave them the exclusive right to supply academic dress to the university 'in perpetuity'. The Tory Club – or rather, Godfrey – said in return that if there were indeed a law preventing them supplying students with the gowns they wanted at a price they could afford, it was a bad law and any Conservative Government worthy of the name would repeal it. 'Freedom of choice in a free market will be the watchwords of the 1970s and 1980s,' he said. 'A new economic dawn is coming!'

In my article I quoted the comments of both Godfrey and Mr Strammington – not to mention Gillian Glenn saying, 'I don't see why we have to wear gowns in the first place.' It appeared on the front page under the headline 'GOWNS RUMPUS, by Janet Toms, our special correspondent'. It was the first time I had seen my name in print – prefaced with that potent little word *by* – since a short story won me ten shillings from the 'All Your Own Work' page of *Elizabethan* in 1963.

I thought I would prefer anything, even the rejection of my novel, to this silence. It was a safe thing to think as long as the postmen were on strike. Shortly before Easter, they went back to work.

At home, in Bleswick, my package awaited. The rejection slip said, 'Delbarco and Wilde thank you for the opportunity of considering the enclosed manuscript but regret that it does not meet their current requirements.'

I read it over and over, hoping I might have missed something. I looked on both sides for a signature, initials, a fingerprint, an ink blot, anything. I held it up to the light. I found no sign of life.

Being at home, having an audience – however well-meaning – for my disappointment, made things worse. My mother sang, 'Pick yourself up, dust yourself down, and start all over again.' These days she was working one afternoon a week as a Friend of Bleswick Hospital, and I wondered if she had the same advice for people coming round after a general anaesthetic.

Daddy took me out for a drink and talked to me man to man. 'Get back on your horse.'

'What horse?'

'Try another firm.'

'No point.'

'Janet, it is a well-known fact that all great authors collect a drawerful of rejection slips.'

'It's an even better known fact that so do hopeless ones.'

'You're not hopeless,' he said.

'I am according to Miss Monica Delbarco.'

'Probably wasn't even her. Probably dropped dead years ago.'

'She is *still there*.' Did he think I was stupid? I had looked up Delbarco and Wilde in the *Writers' and Artists' Year Book*. I *wasn't* stupid. If my book was no good, I didn't expect her to publish it just because she had patted me on the head when I was eleven. But I had thought she might have the manners to write a letter. Sending a rejection slip was like turning your back and walking out of the room while someone was talking to you.

Daddy said, 'What do you expect from a company that employed a bum like that MacLeish girl? They're probably no great shakes.' But memories of Pam made the rejection even harder to bear, because Pam had rejected us too.

70

It was a modern office block near Ludgate Circus. The strong sunlight of the July afternoon glittered from the brass nameplate: Mervyn Chilcott Books. I was dazzled. The time was two minutes to three. I went inside.

The reception area was air-conditioned and hushed. The sweat on my body chilled and dried to what felt like a cold and crusty slime. The walls around me were adorned with pictures of authors looking wise. I thought I ought to whisper.

'Could I please see Mr Sutton?'

'Have you an appointment?'

'Yes.' I hunted unsuccessfully in my bag for the letter that proved it, but she seemed to believe me. She picked up the phone.

'What name?'

'Miss Toms.'

'Take a seat, please.' She dialled. 'Hilary? Claire at Reception. A Miss Toms to see Julius.'

Julius Sutton, Publishing Director was the signature on the letter. I waited, turning the pages of catalogues: *Chilcott Academic 1971, Chilcott for Children, Chilcott Spring Fiction*.

A blonde vision in a cool cream minidress said, 'Miss Toms? I'm Hilary, Julius' secretary. Will you come this way?'

Feeling grimy and oversized I lumbered after her into the lift.

'Phew,' she said 'hot today.' I said, 'Yes.' We stared at ourselves and each other in the silver walls. Two of us, about the same age. So unalike we could be twins. I-Want and That's-Mine. Which was which? She was lissom, leggy, sweet-featured; I was a frump. But I had a letter in my bag from Julius Sutton, Publishing Director, inviting me to call; she had only typed it.

*

He was about forty-five, short and balding and pleased. He wore a light grey suit and a bow tie. He took my right hand in his right hand, pressed his left hand on top and shook gravely for a long time with a slow, swaying motion. 'Thank you, Janet, for sparing the time to come and see me.'

He led me into his office and gestured me to a soft-backed grey chair beside his desk. On the desk was the manuscript of *Off-Ration*, and also a framed photograph of a pretty woman with a baby. I thought of the scene in *The Bell Jar* when the heroine thinks that the reason her psychiatrist has a picture of his wife in the surgery is to discourage her from getting any ideas herself.

He said, 'To repeat what I said in my letter, this is just an informal chat. I'm not ready to make an offer for *Off-Ration* at the moment.' He gave me a smile that was tantalising but oh-so-fair. *I might make an offer one day*, it said. *But if I don't, you will have no cause to reproach me*. 'You understand that, don't you?'

'Yes.'

'Nevertheless, it interested me a lot, and as you live not too far from London I was curious to meet you. Have you been writing for long?'

'I used to write stories when I was little.'

'And?'

'And then I stopped.'

'Why?'

I said quickly, 'I don't know.'

'But you started again and that is the important thing. Are you in fact a twin?'

'No.'

'But you have sisters?'

The conversation was making me uncomfortable. I wasn't here to discuss my sisters. 'One.'

'Close to you in age?'

'She's seven.'

'You surprise me.'

'Why?'

'One naturally assumes that a first novel has autobiographical content – '

'Why? It hasn't. How can it? It's about twins and I've just told you I'm not a twin.'

Now he'll kick me out, I thought.

He said, 'Let's ask Hilary to get us a cup of tea.' He pressed his buzzer. Hilary?'

'Yes, Julius.'

'Would you be kind enough to make me and Janet some tea?'

'Will do. Oh, Julius, while you're there – '

'Yes?'

'I phoned Delbarco's to arrange your lunch with Monica – '

'Thank you, Hilary,' said Julius. 'Is there a problem?'

'Not really. I talked to Pam, she said the fourth or the fifth would be fine but could we let her know which as soon as possible because she's trying to make arrangements for Monica's trip to New York.'

Julius looked in his diary and said, 'The fourth.'

Hilary said, 'Fine, I'll let Pam know. Two teas coming up.'

The tea came, and Julius Sutton talked to me about my manuscript. I was so flabbergasted by what I had just heard that I found it hard to concentrate, even on the compliments. 'Such a neatly turned metaphor,' he was saying, 'for the so-called Swinging Sixties and the more uncertain decade in which we now find ourselves.'

'Yes.'

There must be hundreds of secretaries in London called Pam. Thousands. There was no reason why one of them should not work for Monica Delbarco.

'And some lovely ironies, and edgy writing.'

'Thank you.'

It was not all that much of a coincidence that years ago Miss Delbarco had employed a temp called Pam and had offered her a permanent job.

'. . . holding something back,' said Julius.

'Pardon?' I replied.

'Sometimes your writing collapses. Loses that tight quality, becomes cautious, flabby. As if there's something you don't want to tell.'

'It's not autobiographical.'

'I mean something you don't want to tell in terms of the story.'

I shrugged. 'Such as?'

'The parents, for one. They're rotten to the bad sister.'

'It's her own fault,' I pointed out.

'Maybe not. But let the reader decide. You could have a lot of fun with those parents if you'd let yourself go a bit, just write what they're like and stop protecting them. Another thing you're coy about is sex. Don't you think? I don't mean you need steamy scenes but I think the day of the row of asterisks is gone.'

I felt like shouting, *I've never had sex, I've never been anywhere near it* but that would be to hoist myself with my own petard because I had already said the novel was not supposed to be autobiographical. Everything in the book was made up, so why shouldn't I make up some sex? I knew the theory.

'I've got to go,' I said.

'Sorry if I've offended you.'

'No, it's not that, it's just that I've got to see somebody.'

'I bet it's another publisher,' said Julius. 'And for the rest of my career I shall reproach myself for not sticking my neck out and signing you up right away.'

It was four o'clock. Outside the Chilcott building the hot day was turning into a sticky, breathless evening. The air stank of burning rubber, melting bitumen and failed underarm deodorant, my own and other people's.

I found a call box. Its directories were torn up so I phoned Directory Enquiries. I got the number but I had no two and a half pees. I bought an *Evening News* and asked for two and a half pees in the change. The man said, 'They're still sixpences to me, luv. I'm an Englishman and proud of it.'

'Sixpences then.'

He gave me one and I dialled.

'Delbarco and Wilde, Good – *pip-pip-pip-pip-pip* – '

I pressed in the coin. The pips stopped. The voice said again, 'Delbarco and Wilde. Good afternoon.'

I opened my mouth wide like a fish.

The cracked mirror reflected my eyes, staring like a fish's eyes. I didn't know what to say.

I put the receiver down and leaned against the sides of the call box. My breath came in short gasps. I should have thought this out. A man opened the door. 'Are you using that phone?'

'No. Sorry.'

I stepped outside and he went in. He handed me the envelope containing my manuscript and Julius' notes on it, which I had left on the shelf.

His call went on and on. He was probably listening to the Test Match commentary. I loathed him. He finished and I pushed past him. Again I dialled.

'Delbarco and Wilde, good afternoon.'

I swallowed hard to unstick my throat. I started to speak. 'Does a Miss Pam – ' I stopped again.

When Pam went away, she was engaged to be married. What was that fellow's name? Rusty. A nickname to go with his surname. Rusty Nayle, that was it, Nayle.

'Does a Mrs Pam Nayle work there?'

'No one of that name, caller.'

'Sorry, I mean Miss Pam MacLeish.'

'Yes she does. Putting you through.'

71

I didn't want to be put through. Had I asked to be put through? I had asked if she worked there. She did. Fine. I fled.

What did it mean?

Did I want to know?

What could it mean?

She was still single. So what? She had come back to London. She was entitled to. It hurt that she hadn't been in touch with us, but we had moved house. She might have been trying to find us.

Now I would find her.

In a bookshop I found a Delbarco and Wilde book and copied down their address. It was ten to five. I took a taxi. I arrived as she was descending her office steps with a handful of letters. She headed towards a post box. I watched from a doorway.

I wondered whether I would have recognised her if I had not been expecting to see her. She was shorter than I remembered her, or perhaps it was that I was taller. She had the same slightly bowed shoulders that Daddy used to blame on her fondness for hitch-hiking with a rucksack.

Now she did not look like a hitch-hiker. She looked like an ordinary Londoner, tired at the end of a day in a hot office. She was wearing a skirt of lime green linen, a blouse with short sleeves and high-heeled leather shoes which matched her handbag. Her hair was redder than I remembered it, curly and short, lightly permed perhaps. Pam with a perm! She must be nearly thirty-five. I remembered her with bunches.

She posted her letters and headed for the tube. She queued at a ticket machine. I queued behind her, then followed her on to the train, a non-smoking carriage on the Bakerloo Line going north.

She got out at West Hampstead and made her way along West End Lane. I waited while she chose peaches and oranges from boxes outside a corner shop and went inside for groceries. Sweat was running off me. I still hadn't said hello. I still didn't know why. I had a sense of keeping something in reserve. I didn't know what for. I didn't want to. I felt shy, excited, afraid. Still, I followed her.

She turned a corner and let herself into a Victorian mansion block. The block was U-shaped, with a communal garden. The garden had a bush of delicate white briar roses, clumps of blue lupins, and beds of dazzling marigolds. There was an ornamental pond and one rusty seat. I flopped in the seat and wondered what to do next. Then I saw Daddy.

He was sauntering along the path towards her door. He carried his jacket over his shoulder, and his briefcase, and a bottle of wine wrapped in purple tissue paper.

The silvery gold of his hair and the whiteness of his shirt added to the dazzle in my eyes. Was he real? It had been a very peculiar day. I walked towards him. He was pressing one of the doorbells. He turned his ear to the entryphone, saw me and dropped his bottle.

It smashed on the doorstep. Wine fizzed on the hot stone and splashed his trousers. He yelped. 'Shit! Bloody hell!'

'Language, Daddy.'

'What are you doing here?'

'What are *you*?'

'This is one of the blocks we manage.'

'I don't believe it!'

'Are you calling me a liar?'

'No, it's the coincidence,' I said. 'Do you realise who lives here?'

'I don't know all of the residents personally.'

'Pam's back in London and she lives here!'

'Not that bum from horse-trylia? How do you know?'

'Julius Sutton's secretary knows her.'

'We must be getting slack if we let *her* in.'

The entryphone clicked and a female voice said, 'Yes?' *Yiss*.

'Wrong number, sorry.' He backed away. He pointed at his wine-soaked trousers. 'Can't go calling on residents in this condition.'

The voice came again. 'Stop pratting around, Sandy. I'm in the shower. Come on up.' The door buzzed and swung open.

He went into the building ahead of me. It was very cool and smelt of polish. He climbed the stairs with an official tread.

Her pleased voice floated down from above us. 'Hello, sweetie.'

She didn't mean me. I wasn't sweetie. But I lifted my head and said, 'Hello, Pam.'

She was wearing a black kimono. She looked fresh and damp and absolutely appalled to see me.

He said quickly, 'Ran into Janet outside. Remember Janet? We were just talking about what a coincidence it was that I should take over the management of a building and find you living in it when you're supposed to be in horse-trylia. Now, what exactly is the problem with the windows that's brought me traipsing out here?'

'The one in the bathroom,' she said. 'It sticks.'

'Where's the bathroom?'

She showed him. I waited in the hall. It smelt of flowers. There was a fawn fitted carpet, old but clean.

Daddy fiddled with the bathroom window.

'Probably didn't shut it properly. I know you're not used to windows where you come from.'

'Watch your manners, mate, or I'll have a word with your boss.'

The two of them were the same as ever. Making each other laugh with their insults. Making me laugh. Making me remember how it felt to be nine, ten, eleven, in the time before the bad things started to happen. In the time when I had this extra mother, this extra big sister, making up for the shortcomings of the real ones.

He fixed the window and said, 'Janet and I'll be off. Mustn't be late home to the ever-loving.'

We got on the tube. He said, 'Suppose you'll mention this to Mummy?'

'Any reason why I shouldn't?' My voice was small and shaky, a frightened child's voice, I couldn't understand it.

'Might be kinder not to. I'll tell you why, and you can make up your own mind. Why do you and I never have dinner together these days? Let's stay aboard to Charing Cross and see if Rule's can find us a table.'

Rule's was leathery, velvety, chandeliered, hushed and formal. It was how I imagined a gentleman's club. I felt so little that I asked for whitebait. Tiny fishes, a nursery fantasy. Daddy ordered steak and kidney pudding and told me everything.

'Goes back a little way. When was it you had your book rejected by the Delbarco woman? Easter vac, was it?'

'Yes.'

'Whenever it was. Broke my heart to see what that did to you, Janet. I've brought you up to be a good sport and not to sulk when you lose. And you didn't sulk. By God you didn't. But you didn't fool your old dad either. I knew how cut up you were.

'And frankly, so was I. I suppose every father thinks his own particular goose is a swan, but it wasn't just my opinion. You'd won enough prizes for your writing when you were little, and you'd always been a great one for essays. Thought to myself, she deserves better than this. So I decided – rightly or wrongly – to give Miss Monica Delbarco a ring and find out what's what.

'Wrongly, you're obviously thinking. You may be right. Like arguing with the referee. None of my damn business anyway. Still, that's what I did. Meant to do. Wasn't going to make a meal of it, just introduce myself and then say, look, I don't expect people outside my profession to question my judgement and I'm not questioning yours. I'm asking you: do you think she's got any talent or not? Straight out, yes or no?'

'What did she say?'

'Never got through to her. Phone was answered by old Waltzing Matilda.' He jerked his thumb in the direction of West Hampstead. 'She said who's calling, I said Sandringham Toms, she said Strike Me Vitals With a Didgeridoo or some other antipodean expression of being taken aback, after that it was all cracks about bad pennies and small worlds. She'd got fed up with New Zealand – they always do after they've been over here for a while – dropped the Delbarco woman a line to find out if her offer of a job was still open after all these years, and got sent a one-way ticket to London by return of post. Which seemed to be a hint that it was, so she packed her rucksack.'

'And you've been friends ever since.'

'Yep.'

'So when you said that was one of the blocks you manage – ?'

'It wasn't strictly true.' He raised his great honest chin as if he expected me to punch it, and it was no more than he deserved. 'Sorry, old thing. I was trying to protect you.'

'What from? And why can't we tell Mummy?'

'I'm coming to that,' he said. 'I'm coming to the difficult bit.'

I thought we had already had the difficult bit. But the difficult bit was worse than anything I could have imagined.

72

July dawn over the rocky turrets and neat rooves of Edinburgh was forget-me-not blue with mauve and grey and silver edges. The train stopped and I carried my luggage from my sleeper – misnamed, because I had not slept.

The Northburgh train was signalled, but my way was blocked by a pair of trousers, cream slacks with a neat crease up the front of each leg, and a checked shirt with an open neck, a smooth and hairless neck; a square, closely shaven jaw, and a smile full of clean, bright teeth, and bright eyes.

'Good morning, Janet.'

'Godfrey! What are you doing here?'

'Driving you to Northburgh.' He took my suitcase.

'You didn't have to do that.'

'Of course I didn't, but what's a Senior Man for?'

'Does that still count? I'm not in my first year any more.'

'It's for life.'

He loaded my luggage into the boot of his white MG. He drove me through the waking-up city and out into the green and heather-purple countryside. 'In all seriousness I was worried about you,' he said. 'You sounded upset on the phone.'

'Me? Oh no.'

'You don't have to explain, but I'm happy to help if I can.'

'This is a help,' I said, meaning the lift. 'And for finding me the room. Where is it, by the way?'

'Wait and see.'

'Thanks anyway.'

'It's nothing. Fixit is my middle name.'

'That's what I thought. That's why I rang you.'

After what Daddy had told me, I could not stay under the same roof with him and Mummy. I needed to live on my own for a while, to get over the shock and to work out what I felt.

Northburgh was the obvious choice. There were summer jobs because of the tourists. And it was the only place I felt at home, apart from Bleswick. The only place I felt at home.

Godfrey said, 'And there was me thinking you rang for the pleasure of hearing my voice.'

'That as well,' I told him. It was easy to flirt with him because I didn't kid myself he meant it.

The room he had found me was actually a flat, a granny annexe at the back of a house belonging to Professor and Mrs Hanwell of the Department of Genetics. It had a kitchen and a bathroom on the ground floor and a bedsitting room up a flight of stairs.

The place was clean, the rent was low. There was one slight hitch: the granny in question was spending the summer with her other daughter-in-law. They didn't always get on, and Granny might return at any time. In that event, I must accept two days' notice and leave without argument . . . unlike the student they had had last summer who had tried to claim his rights under the Rent Act. 'Iniquitous,' said Godfrey. 'Janet won't do anything like that.'

Once again I was living on the edge of a family. But now I was self-contained. I would have to buy my own groceries. I would cook them here, and eat on my own. I had never been self-contained before. It was alarming. What if I couldn't manage it? I knew from my mother what a difficult business housekeeping was. She often wept from the sheer difficulty of it, great moaning sobs with her head on the kitchen table, dwarfed by heaps of flotsam and jetsam that never seemed to go down; or dry-eyed furious shrieks when I or Miranda, having been sent out with a shopping list saying 'cauliflower', or 'coffee', came home with the wrong cauliflower, the wrong coffee.

The problem couldn't be forestalled by asking her in advance to specify what kind of coffee, what kind of cauliflower, for she would shout, 'How do you expect me to know?' Or she would snatch the list and cycle off at high speed to buy the things herself.

Perhaps it was part of her depression.

I hadn't realised, until Daddy told me, that she still suffered from depression, brought on by the death of Christine. It was under control most of the time, he said, but the slightest reminder of Christine's death could push her over the edge, and then he would not be answerable for the consequences.

That was why she must not know that Pam was back in London.

Not only did memories of Pam belong to the time when Christine was alive. Pam had been instrumental in bringing about her death.

This was 'the difficult bit' that Daddy had been reluctant to tell me. Over coffee and liqueurs at Rule's I had finally got it out of him.

'Don't know how much you remember about the police enquiries.' He was mumbling as if it hurt him to say these words. 'Bit young, maybe.'

'I remember people talking about it.'

'Lot of head scratching about where she got those tablets from.'

'Ladies' Irregularity Tablets.'

'That what they were called? Fancy you remembering. Anyway, they never found out. Assumed it was Adam, but he wasn't man enough to stay around and face the music . . . Didn't matter all that much, Christine was just as dead wherever she got them. Point is, though . . . turns out . . . the thing we've got to keep from Mummy . . . is that she got them from Pam.'

When I said, 'No,' it was without expression or passion. It was a straightforward denial of a matter of fact. It could not be true. Simple as that, as Daddy would say.

He was saying, ''Fraid so. I'll explain as best I can, and then you can decide what's for the best. Back to the beginning. There's me ringing up Delbarco's to interfere in what's none of my business, and Pam answers the phone. "Christ, you old bugger, how are you after all these years . . ." dum-de-dum, all that. We arranged to meet for a drink. That's not a crime, I hope? Most natural thing in the world. Old friends. First thing she said to me was – of course – how are the family, how are Jo and Janet and . . . Christine. Chrissie. Because of course she didn't know. How would she know?

'So I had to tell her. And she had to tell me something that nobody ever realised. Something that never came out at the inquest because she'd hopped it to *terra incognita*. When Christine flew back from France, she didn't go straight to Bleswick, as we all assumed. She went to Earls Court. To Pam. Natural enough. She couldn't come to us. We were gadding about on the Broads. We'd have stood by her but we weren't there to stand by her. So she went to the next best person, a damn good friend who gave her damn good advice which she chose not to take.'

'What do you mean?'

'Those pills were perfectly above board, Janet. Pam got 'em from a doctor. They wouldn't even have been dangerous if Christine had taken them properly. They were only a test, but she took it into her head to swallow them all at once and mix them with gin. If she'd done as Pam told her, she'd be walking around today. Probably married with a family of her own. Pam's pretty cut up about it. Gets depressed, blames herself. It's one of the reasons why I pop round now and again, to cheer her up – but it's not her fault.' He paused and sipped his Cognac. 'Mummy might take a different view.'

'We wouldn't have to tell her.'

'We don't have to tell her *anything*, Janet. You know how I feel about any sort of dishonesty, but there's such a thing as witholding information for a person's own good. How's Mummy going to feel, coming face to face with the last person to see Christine alive?'

'She wouldn't have to know that.'

'*We'd* know it. You and me. Mummy's always had a soft spot for Pam, and if she hears she's back the first thing she'll do is invite her round. We'd have to see them together, knowing what we know. Are you sure you wouldn't let something slip? I wish I could be. And when – if – Mummy does find out, isn't she going to reproach herself for not being there when her first born child needed her? I do, and I was only her father – for a mother, it's something entirely – ' his voice broke. He finished his drink and paid the bill. We took a taxi to Paddington and got the last train to Bleswick.

We told Mummy that we had been out to celebrate the

encouraging response of Mervyn Chilcott Books to my novel. She said, 'That's all very well, but why couldn't you have let me know?'

I said, 'We forgot. I'm sorry, it was the excitement. Blame me.'

73

It was all so sordid. Gin and bathwater. Drains, wombs, sperms, inquests, irregularity tablets. Misadventure, statutory rape. Grubby words, like grey shreds off an old mop, blocking a plug hole, gathering slime, stinking out the drain.

Sordid. My sordid sixties sister, reaching out her skeletal finger to give this cleaner, saner decade a poke in the eye. Doing her own thing. Making sordid under-age love with a ban-the-bomb beatnik, dying a sordid death. Only it wasn't her own thing now. She was out of it and we lived on and we lived with it.

Daddy lived in fear that my mother might have a nervous breakdown. Pam was tortured with guilt over something that was never her fault. On and on it went. Daddy struggling to accommodate with his honourable heart the many contradictory demands that were made of it.

He had lied. I had lied with him and for him. Lying violated us. Yet I would do it again, and so would he, to protect Mummy. Why should we have to? What gave Christine the right to rule from beyond the grave that Pam's return to England and Daddy's and my friendship with her were matters for shame and secrecy?

Why could she still cast this sordid shadow? Unspeakably sordid. *Unspeakable* was no exaggeration. I could not speak of it.

Godfrey pressed me to tell him what had brought me back to Northburgh. 'A trouble shared . . .' he smiled, mocking himself for the cliché, whilst insisting on its validity.

I denied that there was any trouble. On the contrary, I said, *Off-Ration* had received an encouraging response from Julius Sutton, Publishing Director of a very reputable firm. He had made no promises but he knew what he was talking about. He had suggested certain revisions and I had come back to Northburgh to work on them. 'If you knew my family, you'd understand why I can't write at home.'

I meant to imply that (dearly though I loved them) they were too noisy, hedonistic, philistine in their tastes to understand the austere and disciplined life that a novelist must lead. This was true. But my words took on a different meaning as I came to realise that not only could I not revise *Off-Ration* at home, I couldn't do it here either.

I read Julius' notes. I recalled our conversation. I opened my manuscript. It was alien. It was dangerous. It was a nest of snakes into which I would poke at my peril. Two girls, good and bad, light and dark, I-want and That's-mine. Which was me and who was the other one? Why ask, why find out, why know? At twelve I had honestly thought that my fiction might have killed Christine. I had given up writing it until I was old enough to know that fiction killed nobody. But it might drive my mother mad.

Julius had accused me of holding something back.

Sometimes your writing collapses. Loses that tight quality, becomes cautious, flabby. As if there's something you don't want to tell.

What if there were indeed something I did not want to tell? What if he forced me to tell it? What if I wrote something that brought back maddening memories to my mother?

The parents, for one. They're rotten to the bad sister. You could have a lot of fun with those parents if you'd let yourself go a bit, just write what they're like and stop protecting them.

Why shouldn't I protect them?

It was my duty to protect them.

One naturally assumes that a first novel has autobiographical content.

Why?

What if everybody assumed the same and started asking questions about my bitter, angry sister, my non-existent twin? What if my book came out and some thoughtless old friend popped up saying, *I knew Janet Toms before she was famous. I knew her sister too, she died of an . . .* The most sordid of words. And yet it was everywhere. On and on went women's lib. You couldn't pick up a paper, you couldn't turn on the radio without hearing, Free Contraception and Abortion on Demand. Sex, sex, sex.

Sex should be beautiful, for people who obeyed its rules. People who didn't harp on about it, people who kept quiet and got married and had wedding nights and honeymoons and babies, people like my parents who were faithful and constant. People who protected each other, as Daddy protected Mummy.

Another thing you're coy about is sex. Of course I was. I felt like saying, *My sister died of it, or don't you want to know that?* The trouble was, I felt Julius would want to know. He would be fascinated to know. This, he would say, is what you have been holding back. Put it in your novel and we will publish it at once. And I would be unable to resist. He would force me to let Christine into my novel. And the pain of seeing her there would drive my mother mad.

In the mornings I tried to write, to rewrite. It was hopeless. Nothing was happening. My words didn't look as if they meant anything. I read my work aloud but I couldn't hear it. Sometimes I got into a spitting rage. *He's got his own words*, I thought. *He's a powerful man. People pay attention to his words. What's so special about my words that he wants to claim them for himself, own them, change them? If he's got a story to tell, let him tell it. Why does he want me to tell his story, why should he make me say things, his things?*

In the afternoons I went to the Monk's Head where Godfrey had found me a job as a waitress. I served afternoon teas and bar snacks and suppers. Sometimes he drank in the bar with local Tory councillors or friends from the Federation of Conservative Students, or, once, an MP, whom he introduced as the fiancé of Diana, my Senior Woman.

The MP was an ordinary-looking fellow, and it was hard to imagine anyone preferring him over Godfrey. Godfrey drove me home. He kissed my cheek. He said, 'Thank you for your company, Janet. I'm sorry if I'm a little preoccupied at the moment.'

'What about? A trouble shared . . .'

In the summer sky a sultry moon glowed in the darkness that was never really dark at this time of year, this far north. I thought he would open his heart about losing Diana, and perhaps I might offer some comfort, but he said, 'Professor Blanchard has agreed to speak at the dinner.'

'Oh,' I sighed, wondering if it were good or bad.

'The question is, can we rely on the lefties and the women's libbers to behave themselves? He's got a heart condition, and after what happened at Essex . . .'

I grasped the nettle. 'What did happen at Essex?'

'He was shouted down and forced to leave, Janet. In the United Kingdom in 1971, a man was prevented from expressing his honestly held opinions. Does that shock you? It does me.'

Half way through September, he said he wouldn't be around for a few days as he was going down south for Diana's wedding. While he was away, David Cunningham, the whippety-looking former editor of *Nuts* came scuttling into the bar with his checked cap over his eyes. Without preliminary he said, 'What hours do you work here? Mine's a Special, and have one yourself.'

'Afternoons and evenings.'

'So you're free in the mornings. Great. Better than nothing anyway. We're in a spot. You know Ronnie, the editor elect. He's failed his resits and he's not coming back. Frankly there's only one other person on the *Nuts* staff who's capable of editing the paper – '

I blushed with pleasure, for the editorship usually went to a third-year student.

' – but I'm doing finals,' said Dave. 'So what I'm going to need's a damn good assistant. Think you can handle it? See you in the office tomorrow morning at nine. We'll have to write the first issue between us.' He gave me a key to the Students' Union, which was still locked up for the summer, and another for the office. 'I'll teach you everything I know,' Dave Cunningham promised. 'And next year, you'll be editor.'

74

I abandoned *Off-Ration*. I was glad of the excuse. I couldn't get it right.

I didn't even know what right meant. Right for Julius Sutton? What business was it of his? Why should he change my words? Why should anyone change anyone's? Why did anyone want to?

The important thing was to tell the truth. Fiction was pointless. The events in my novel never took place. The twins never existed. Why write about them? Why bother to make them up? Why think about them again? Why ask what they meant? They would only cause trouble. I became assistant editor of *Nuts*. I reported the facts.

I reported that Professor Blanchard would be speaking at the Tory Club dinner. I quoted Godfrey. 'It would not be too much of an exaggeration to say that Professor Blanchard is coming out of hiding to visit Northburgh. It is a tribute to the moderation for which Northburgh students are rightly famed that he has felt able to accept our invitation. We are confident that even those students who disagree with his views will acknowledge with their usual good manners his right to express them.'

He meant it as a compliment, but the Labour Club, the Overseas Students' League and women's lib set up the Radical Alliance of Northburgh Students Against Fascism (RANSAF) and threatened to picket the dinner. They would bring supporters in coaches from universities all over Scotland and the north of England, and drown out the Professor's speech with their din.

I reported the facts. The facts were that a group of university students intended to silence a man because they didn't agree with what they thought he was going to say. They intended to take away his words.

They would have done the same to *Nuts* if they could. They wrote furious letters saying we should not publicise the visit in advance, or report it afterwards. We should give no platform to fascists.

Slogans appeared on Northburgh's ancient walls. BLANCHARD OUT. NO PASARAN. The Principal issued a statement reminding all students of the university's long, proud history of moderation. Was this to be thrown away in a single night of excess?

It was not. Godfrey outsmarted RANSAF and changed the date of the dinner. It was held one night earlier than advertised. Professor Blanchard came, spoke and went away while RANSAF was making its last-minute plans to silence him.

When *Nuts* published the full text of his speech – whose theme was 'The Challenge of Greatness' – RANSAF announced a boycott of the paper. The Labour Club were particularly enraged by Professor Blanchard's ideas on trades union reform, but I remembered the postal strike and was on the professor's side.

David Cunningham said the boycott would blow over. He considered the whole affair to be a bit of a joke, particularly the proposals in the speech about selling nationalised industries to private investors, because who would be fool enough to buy them? I was more interested in the professor's comments about the family as a bastion of liberty.

On Sunday mornings I cycled to David's cottage – an old farm labourer's dwelling, with flagstones and a wood-burning Aga – and we did the layout on the kitchen table.

When I arrived the sink was full of dirty dishes and he looked as if he had been up all night. He sat at the table, surrounded by manuscripts, photographs, typing paper and carbon paper, glaring at a sheet of typescript. His short pale hair was greasy, and there was stubble on his sunken jaw. Through holes in his brown pullover I could see patches of greying vest; through holes in the vest, glimpses of ribs and sparse flesh. He was counting words. '. . . 247, 248, 249, *don't say anything*!'

'Right, I won't.' I picked up a typed sheet headed, 'SEX VICARS HIT OUT IN PILL RUMPUS'.

I sighed with distaste. 'We've had three Rumpuses this term already,' I pointed out. Besides 'FASCIST' PROF RUMPUS, there had been MIXED RESIDENCE PLAN RUMPUS and RUMPUS OVER NO-LAMP BIKE FINES.

He waved his arm in an impatient gesture. 'If you don't like it, think of something else. Would you prefer to call it "Joint Chaplains' Statement of Concern on Sex and Morals within the Student Body?" What have you got?'

I took out my folder. 'Strammington's are cutting the prices of their gowns to seven guineas. GOWNS PRICE WAR?'

David said, 'And has Godfrey de Salis been rushed to hospital suffering from terminal smugness . . .?'

'You don't like him, do you?'

'. . . raving deliriously about triumphs of free competition? Dislike him? Janet, as a newspaper man I have no opinion of the unctuous creep. He is a student at the university, and as such has a right to express his – I suppose he *is* a student, and not just a hanger around? Has anyone ever seen him studying anything?'

'I've heard your tutors ask the same about you, Dave.'

'That's different.' He took the typescript out of my hand. 'I mean, fine, chaplains get paid to issue Joint Statements of Concern, but listen to this thing. "A spokesman – " guess who? – "for the Northburgh Social Policy Study Group – " aka the Tory Club – "said, 'We have reliable reports that the Student Health Service is dishing out free birth control pills like Smarties.' He'd know. "The proponents of permissiveness cannot have it both ways." Eh? Which ways does he want it? Oh, I see what he means. "If private morality really is private, there is no reason why private *immorality* should be financed out of public funds." '

I shrugged. 'Makes sense to me.'

He said, 'I'll tell you what makes no sense at all, and that's the number of times Godfrey de Salis ends up on our front page.'

'If the Tories have all the good stories, and bother to tell me about them . . .'

He said, 'Why don't we call it the *Godfrey de Salis News* and be done with it? Is it true? Do they dish them out like Smarties?'

'No idea.'

'You could find out.'

'So could you.'

'I could find out what they *say*,' Dave said. 'But you could be an undercover reporter. You could pretend you want to go on the pill.'

'I don't.'

He looked at me sadly. 'Don't you?'

'No.'

'Not at all?'

'No.'

'Never?'

I shrugged. He said, 'You could pretend.'

'I don't pretend.'

'Neither do I then. The time has come for me to declare myself.' He pushed back his chair and walked round the table. 'I have a vested interest in you going on the pill. I fancy you like mad.'

'Shouldn't we be getting on with this?' I pointed at the papers, the layout sheets.

'You're so damn professional. It's sexy.' He growled and gave me a light dry kiss on my lips. 'I'm not just the hard newspaper man, Janet. I have strong emotional and sexual needs – which are not being met. And I bet you have too.'

'I don't think I have, actually.'

'Everyone has. Yours are waiting to be uncovered.' He gave me another kiss but it didn't make me feel as if I had anything waiting to be uncovered. His face was rough, his mouth tasted sour, his tongue made me squeamish. The kisses Godfrey gave me – the kisses he gave girls generally – were like the ones I got from my uncles or Daddy; but there was no avoiding the sex in David's kiss. Over his shoulder I saw the sordid sink full of dirty pans. 'Not now, David.'

'I'll wait then. But I don't know how long for. I have – '

'Strong emotional and sexual needs?' I laughed.

He glared at me. 'Yes. But you're right. Let's get back to work. Stick with good old clean-living Godfrey, he won't make any indecent propositions, all he's got between his legs is a rolled up House of Commons order paper.'

Jo

75

She was the last person I would have expected to see. I hadn't set eyes on her for years. She belonged to the past. But now here she was, shivering on the doorstep in the dark January evening.

Not that I recognised her. She had to say what her name was, and even then I had to rummage around a bit in what remained of my grey cells before the penny dropped.

My mind was elsewhere, elsewhere being the State of Emergency. Nothing new about any house under my charge being in a state of emergency, but this time it wasn't just me, it was the country as a whole. The coal miners were on strike, the Arabs were at war and we were having an energy crisis.

Back in November it had looked as if it might pass me and Sandy by. Then, it was just petrol pumps with EMPTY signs and motorists having to register for ration books. I said, 'Good job we haven't got a car,' because I thought he was still a bit sensitive about never having managed to pass his driving test. I thought it just went to show that even in 1973 you could be a successful executive without, particularly if you were adaptable and didn't mind staying away from home now and again . . . and your long-suffering wife could be trained not to make a fuss about it.

They could keep their petrol coupons, I had a perfectly good bike. But it didn't stop at petrol coupons. Power cuts followed, and, shortly before Christmas, Mr Heath had announced to parliament that he was putting everybody on a three-day working week, everybody apart from housewives, that was.

Now you couldn't switch on the wireless or the television without some MP or other getting up on his hind legs and telling you to turn down your central heating, cook stews in a hay box, keep to a minimum your use of electrical appliances, and make sure your elderly neighbours didn't freeze to death or set themselves alight during power cuts.

This evening Sandy and I were calling the government's bluff. We thought it would be rather fun if I cooked up some of the old recipes from the war years and invited the Bixwells and some other friends round for a State of Emergency supper. Miranda, being a very up-to-the-minute nine-year-old, thought we were completely insane, but appeared to write it off as yet another example of the sort of thing you had to expect if your parents didn't have you until they were in their dotage. She was keeping well out of the way, up in her room with her television on and all lights blazing.

The Bixwells had actually given her her own portable television for Christmas. Sandy and I despaired, but what could we do? As Lindsay said, 'She's my god-daughter, Jo, and I haven't got any children to spend money on, so why shouldn't I?'

I had had to abandon plans to serve Snoek Piquante. One of the blessings of peace was that there wasn't snoek to be had for love nor money in Bleswick Tesco's, and there was a marked shortage of those other indescribable tasting fishes that the Ministry of Food used to inflict on us, such as saith and ling, not to mention good old whalemeat. And I had decided it would be unworthy to go out hunting for sparrows, thrushes or blackbirds to bake in a pie. But I had dredged up some other recipes from the Jo Toms Repository of Useless Information, otherwise known as my brain, and was reminiscently slicing potatoes for Cheese and Potato Custard and listening to the six o'clock news while Trench Meat Pudding *à la* Jo Toms was steaming over a low heat, when the doorbell went.

At first I thought it might be Sandy, coming home early to help me get ready for his friends. Stranger things had happened. I checked that I hadn't left evidence of any of my snacks lying around and went to the door.

She was pale and slight and she had on a military greatcoat and a home-knitted woolly hat. She looked waifish and appealing in the way of tiny little girls in big men's clothes. It was a trick I would have loved to try, but I had never had the build for it.

She might have been a student with the Christmas post, except that Christmas was over and she had not got any post, just a cloth shoulder bag with tiny bits of mirror that caught the light like eyes with tears in them.

'Mrs Toms?'

'Yes?'

'Do you remember me?'

I wasn't sure whether I did or not. 'I'm sorry.'

'I'm Stella. I was at school with Chris.'

Stella, Stella, Stella, I thought. Then I remembered. *The grubby mint*. It was what Sandy used to call her, because of her muddy complexion. He said she looked like an unwrapped Polo that you found in your pocket, and he was absolutely right.

I remembered her as a nice enough girl, a bit on the pert side, slightly common and a tarty dresser, but as I said to Sandy at the time, what do you expect at that school? Christine could have done a lot worse in the best friends department. In fact, given her penchant for annoying her father, it was surprising she didn't do worse on purpose.

I dredged around in the Repository for Stella's surname.

'Stella Henderson?'

'That was it,' she agreed.

'You're married now?'

'Divorced.'

This shook me. Christine would be twenty-six, so Stella couldn't be much older. Just because I knew that divorces could be had for the asking these days, didn't mean I necessarily wanted to know, or approved of people who got them. Easy divorce injected an element of uncertainty into life that my generation had not bargained for.

Divorcee used to be a shameful label, and an unusual one. Now there were so many of them, they didn't even get called that. Women like me didn't need girls like Stella rattling around, knowledgeable, cynical and free. How dare she be divorced? Not only that, she was interrupting my supper preparations and would probably be as scornful of them as Miranda was. But I had been a Toms wife too long to turn away a visitor. *Hail fellow well met* was the family motto. 'Come in, Stella. It's nice to see you.'

*

I helped her with her coat. It was like taking the shell off a snail. The coat felt stiff and heavy and practically stood up on its own. Without it, Stella had a raw look. She wore black tracksuit bottoms and a lilac coloured top made out of a tarnished glittery fabric.

I would have said she was too skinny, if there were such a thing as being too skinny. And she had hungry eyes, heavily mascara'd, but no other make-up that I could detect. The mascara might have been in place for days.

As she pulled off her hat, her whitish blonde hair tumbled down in plaited rats' tails. At the end of each rat's tail was a coloured bead. A single huge gold earring stretched her left lobe, which didn't look as if it had enough flesh to bear its weight. I looked away.

She said, 'I hope you don't mind me dropping in like this.'

I'm trying not to mind, I thought, realising that what I minded most of all was that, divorced or not, she was alive. Why should she be, when my daughter was dead? What was so special about Stella?

76

'I was afraid you might have left the area,' she said.

'We thought about it, but we never got around to it. And Janet was settled at school – '

'Little Janet! What's she doing now?'

'Little Janet's engaged.'

'Yeah, but what's she doing?'

'She's at university. She'll be getting her MA this summer, at the same time as her MRS.'

Stella looked around. 'Nice house.'

'You mean nicer than the other one? Even this one was nicer before I got my hands on it. Housekeeping's never been my strong point.'

'Why should it be?'

'You'd better come through,' I said. 'Would you like a cup of coffee? I'm about due for another cup of coffee.'

'If you're having one.'

'I'm always having one.' In my head, Sandy's voice said, *If it's after six, offer people a drink, Jo.* Mummy chimed in. *Have a bit of social grace.* I said, 'You can have a drink if you prefer. Why are some drinks called drinks and some not? You'll have to help yourself, I never know how much to pour.'

'Mrs Toms, all I really want is a photograph of Chris.'

I practically dropped the jar of Nescafé.

'Sorry,' she said. 'I've got a cheek, I know. I didn't stay in touch after the funeral, I rode off into the sunset and now I turn up asking for favours.'

'It was very sweet of you to come to the funeral and why should you stay in touch? I expect you wanted to forget.'

'I couldn't forget Chris. Wouldn't want to. We'd had this big row because she wouldn't leave school with me. I moved away. I kept meaning to write to her but I didn't and next thing I heard she was dead. And I haven't got any photographs of her and I thought you probably would have.'

'What for?'

'I'll show you.' She reached into her bag with the little mirrors and brought out a newspaper that looked as malnourished as she did. *Atalanta, a Women's Liberation Magazine.*

I said, 'I'm not burning *my* bra, I'd be too jolly uncomfortable without it, with my droopy old boobs,' but I had a quick flick through. There were articles in different coloured inks about battered wives and why the Equal Pay Act wouldn't work unless there was a Sex Discrimination Act to go with it, and why if you had facial hairs you shouldn't necessarily pluck them out.

Stella said, 'I'm doing a piece on the Cresswell Bill.' She seemed to think I knew what this was. People often made the mistake of imagining me to be well-informed, probably because of my emphatic voice. I sounded like the sort of person who might get invited to give a talk, only I had nothing to say. 'Stella, you've obviously forgotten that I'm a complete nitwit.' I started coring cooking apples. 'Excuse me doing this, it's for Victory Apple Cream. I concentrate better if I'm doing something with my hands. Start from the beginning and explain slowly.'

'It hasn't had much publicity, that's the trouble. People would be up in arms if they knew. They're hoping to slip it through under cover of this business with the miners. Do you mind if I smoke?'

'I mind for you, but not for myself.'

She got out a plastic pouch and some papers and rolled herself a grubby tube with about three threads of tobacco in it. 'It's a bill to make it more difficult to get abortions. Reduces the time limit, limits the grounds, and makes it easier for doctors and nurses to refuse to do abortions on grounds of conscience. *Conscience!* It's an attack on the 1967 Act. Most of us reckon it's the first stage in abolishing it.' She smoked furiously. I thought she would suck the cigarette in and swallow it. 'If the '67 Act had been in force in '63, Chris would be alive today. If the Cresswell Bill goes through, there'll be more dead Chris's.' She nibbled the end of her little finger. 'I want to say that. I want them to know what it means; real people, dead. People's friends, people's daughters. Write an article about her. And have a photograph to show how lovely she was, how alive. I want to use her story in our campaign. Is that all right, Mrs Toms? It wouldn't upset you too much?'

Before I could answer, the lights went out.

I could have amputated my thumb. 'Bloody miners,' I said.

'Bloody government,' said Stella, her cigarette glowing in the darkness. 'Shall I do anything?'

'Sit still, I don't want you falling over all the clobber in here. There's a torch somewhere.'

It wasn't where it was supposed to be, which meant Miranda had helped herself to it. If I had told her once about that, I had told her a million times. I opened the door to yell up at her, but she was already there, scared of the dark but fooling around, shining the torch up into her own angular little face, flaring her nostrils, rolling her eyes and making soft *whoo-whoo* ghost noises.

Stella let out a terrified shriek. 'Who's that?' This started Miranda off. She screamed and climbed up me. 'Who's she?'

'*Calm down, both of you!* Grow up, for heaven's sake!' There were times when it helped to have an emphatic voice. I flashed the torch around and lit candles. 'Have a look at each other, you're both human beings. This is Stella, she's an old friend who's dropped in to see us. Stella, this is Miranda, my daughter.'

'Daughter?'

'Didn't I say we had another daughter?'

Miranda said, 'Don't mention me, Mum. I'm just the afterthought.'

Stella said, 'Isn't she like Chris? Made me jump. Sorry, Miranda, I used to hate it when people told me I was like people.'

'I like being like her.'

'How old are you?'

'Ten in April.'

I imagined Stella counting the months back on her fingers under cover of the power cut, in the way we used to do when people had babies too soon after their weddings, in the days when that mattered. She would work it out that Miranda was conceived in the month Christine died, and therefore must have been intended as a replacement for her.

It was fine with me if people thought that. I didn't particularly want it known that the conception of Miranda had nothing whatever to do with Christine (who was alive when it happened, for all I knew) and everything to do with the long-lost and unlamented Pam MacLeish.

Pam had had her fill of Sandy that summer, and then buggered off with Rusty. Sandy was grieving. I was trying to make it up to him, trying to reclaim him. That was why I had Miranda. It had worked, too. Apart from that one tactless Christmas card, Pam MacLeish had not been heard of since. Why should I bring the subject up? Let people think what they wanted.

I said to Miranda, 'Stella was at school with Christine.'

'My school?'

'Which is your school?'

'Convent of the Forty f – '

'*Miranda*'.

' – flipping Martyrs, I was going to say.'

Stella laughed and laughed. 'Chris hated that place.'

'So do I.'

'No you don't.'

Miranda gave me her I-shall-pretend-you-do-not-exist look and said to Stella, 'What school did you go to with Chris? Is that what you called her – Chris?'

'Chris, yes. Bleswick County Girls. BCG, like the injection.'

Miranda said, 'I want to go there.'

'You can't,' I told her. 'It doesn't exist any more, there's just Bleswick Comprehensive.'

'I want to go *there*.'

'You don't, you want to stay at the convent like Janet and go to university.'

Miranda leaned across the kitchen table on her elbows, peering at Stella through the candlelit darkness. 'Do you know Janet?'

'I knew her a bit, when she was little.'

'Do you know Godfrey?'

'Who?'

'Janet's fiancé,' I explained. 'Godfrey de Salis.'

'No, I don't know him,' said Stella.

'You're lucky,' said Miranda.

'Don't you like him?'

Miranda made a vomiting noise. I said, 'Don't be silly, of course you like him.'

Miranda said to Stella, 'What was Christine like? Chris, I mean.'

'She was my best friend.'

'Was she? Really? What was she like?'

'She was great, Miranda. I've come round to see if your mum can let me have a picture of her.'

'What for?'

'For my magazine.' She showed it. '*Atalanta*.'

'Never heard of it.' Nevertheless, Miranda deigned to pick it up. I thought Stella should have realised that battered wives weren't a very suitable topic for a nine-year-old, but fortunately there wasn't enough light for reading, and Miranda seemed more interested in the pictures of ladies with beards. 'Is Chris going to be in this?'

'Hope so.'

'Why?'

'To remember her.'

'I remember her.'

'You don't.' I said. I explained to Stella, 'She used to have dreams about Christine when she was little.'

Miranda shrugged in the despairing way she always adopted when anyone told her she was mistaken about something. She said to Stella, 'Is this your magazine?'

'Yes, but you can keep it.'

'How much?'

'Nothing, I'm on the collective.'

'Is it women's lib?'

'Yes.'

'Are you women's lib? Was Christine?'

Stella said, 'We didn't really have it in those days. But I think she would have been, don't you, Mrs Toms?'

'I wouldn't be surprised.'

'I'm women's lib,' said Miranda. 'I have to be with a dad like mine.'

'This week she's women's lib,' I told Stella. 'Next week she'll be Arsenal.'

77

Stella's request put me on the spot. We hadn't got any late photographs of Christine. This wasn't anyone's fault. If we had known Christine was going to die we might have taken some photographs, no, not *might*, we definitely would have, but you don't make preparations for the sudden death of your fifteen-year-old daughter. And it wasn't as if we used to say to ourselves, Aha, let's only ever take family photographs in the boat and then Christine won't be in them. That was just the way it turned out. If we had forced her to come in the boat so that she could be in the family photographs, that would have been wrong too.

Another problem was Miranda. Sandy and I still hadn't told her exactly what her sister died of. Not that we had lied. We had told her it was a drowning accident, neglecting to mention exactly where the drowning took place. And *neglecting* was the word. It was a sin of omission rather than commission, if sin it were.

It was our old bugbear, procrastination. If procrastination had always got us into trouble we might have given it up, but it had served us well in the matter of moving house. If we had got around to selling 79 Manor Road on the open market, Sandy did not reckon that we would have got as much for it as fell into our laps in the compulsory purchase deal. And we had been spared a great deal of inconvenience. We had just upped and moved. Problem solving by inactivity, he called it. I agreed with him, or at least I did in the matter of the house. In the matter of Miranda, I was less sure.

But Stella's visit turned out to be the equivalent of the Manor Road motorway scheme. It forced the issue. To get rid of her, I told her I would look through the family photograph tin and send her what I found. There might be the odd snap. It would be less embarrassing to slip it into an envelope than to give it to her face to face. I might just conveniently forget.

When she was gone, and Miranda and I were still in candlelight, and I was trying to rescue what I could of my cooking with the help of a spirit stove and the hay box, I said to Miranda, 'Did you understand what Stella and I were saying about Christine?'

'Some of it.'

'The reason Stella wants a photograph . . . Look, Christine didn't drown in an ordinary way. She was trying to have an abortion. That means she had a baby in her uterus and she wanted to get rid of it. In those days you couldn't just go to the doctor and have a little operation to take it away, like you can now. In those days you could only do it by hurting yourself. Christine hurt herself and died.'

'I didn't know that.'

'Daddy and I didn't tell you before because we wanted to protect you. It's not the sort of thing that little girls can understand.'

Miranda shrugged. 'I would have.'

'It's frightening for them.'

'I'm not frightened.'

'But you would have been, if we'd told you before. That's why I'm telling you now. Stella's going to write an article about Christine, saying that if girls need an abortion they should be able to get it from the doctor. They shouldn't have to hurt themselves, as Christine did.'

'I agree with that. Don't you, Mum?'

'I do, yes. And so does Daddy.'

It's funny the way a subject comes up by chance and suddenly it seems to be on everybody's lips. I was going into the hospital to do my Friends stint when I saw a small group of people handing out leaflets. I'm always interested in what people have to say, so I took one. It had a colour photograph of a magnified human hand holding four tiny fingers and a thumb, with the caption, 'ABORTION IS MURDER'.

I said, 'Thank you very much,' and made my way to the cloakroom and the Volunteers' locker. I picked out a clean white overall and a starched hat. There were kirbigrips too, in a communal box, but I preferred to bring my own kirbigrips.

I folded my cap and crammed it down on my head, using plenty of kirbigrips to tuck away my hair. Even though I wasn't a proper nurse, I sometimes thought that I was the only person in the hospital who knew what a nurse's cap was *for*. It was for hygiene, not glamour. Hair is unhygenic stuff, it falls out and carries germs, in the presence of food or sick people it should be kept covered.

I made my way to Women's Surgical and tapped on Sister's door to let her know I was here. She was having a cup of coffee and going through her dangerous drugs.

She was a pretty little thing, she looked about fourteen. You could hardly see her cap in the puffed out cloud of her hair. And to my ancient eyes her ways seemed very slapdash. In my day, for example, you did not eat or drink while handling dangerous drugs. You didn't have anything to do with dangerous drugs, for that matter, without having someone else there to double check on everything you did.

I put my hands behind my back. 'Volunteer Auxiliary Toms reporting for duty, Sister.'

She waved. 'Hi, Jo. Nice to see you.' Anyone would have thought she was giving a party, and my turning up was a pleasant surprise.

Of course I had turned up. I always turned up. I may only have been a volunteer auxiliary but that made no difference. You can't run a hospital if people don't come in when they say they will, from the most eminent consultant surgeon to the lowliest orderly.

'What would you like me to do, Sister?'

'Give me a hand with this,' she said. 'I'll say the names, you tick them off. 200 tabs Allobarbitone 50 mg.'

Strictly speaking it should have been a qualified person doing this, but in my day the ward sister was the captain of the ship. I ticked the list. 'Yes, Sister.'

'100 tabs Barbitone Sodium 400 mg.'

'Yes, Sister.'

'90 tabs Pentobarbitone Sodium 100 mg. You got past Rentacrowd, then?'

'Yes, Sister.' Without appearing too prim, I tried to indicate that I would prefer *either* to check the contents of the drugs cupboard, *or* to have a private conversation, but not both.

'Quinalbarbitone Sodium,' she says. '100 mg. It's being blown up out of all proportion.'

'How many tabs?'

'Seventy. You heard about it.'

'Sister, with great respect, I've never been very well endowed in the grey matter department, and I find it a bit difficult to concentrate on two things at once.' I was looking at the drugs register as I said this, but she took it to mean that I wanted her to stop talking about drugs and tell me about the demonstration.

'It's been blown up out of all proportion,' she said. 'There's this abortion bill going through parliament, and its supporters are latching on to every little bit of scandal they can find.'

'The Cresswell Bill?'

'You know about it.'

'What's the scandal, Sister?'

'Oh, it's nothing much. They were doing a termination upstairs, and the products turned out to be a bit more developed than they'd expected.' Sister stopped talking suddenly and wound her watch with frenzied energy. 'The patient got her dates wrong, and the fetus, well, it moved apparently. It made a noise.'

She stared at me with eyes that were trying not to show anxiety, and I saw how young she was. I wondered why she was telling me all this. No sister in my day would have spoken of such things to someone like me. Perhaps it was because I was fifty this year and didn't belong in the system.

'Or so they say,' she went on. 'I haven't met anyone who actually *saw* anything. Only now it's turning into a tale under which we make a regular practice of leaving fully developed babies to suffocate to death in kidney dishes. It'll blow over, but it upsets the students. Particularly the Catholics. They say they don't want to work with termination patients.'

'Don't talk to me about Roman Catholics,' I said. 'My daughter goes to a Roman Catholic school. I don't mind working with termination patients.' I hated to see anyone unhappy. I liked to find a solution that would cheer them up. I wasn't all that keen on the idea of termination products myself, but I knew what the alternative was. 'Of course, I know I can't do *everything* – '

'No, Jo. You can't. But thanks for the offer. And now would you mind cleaning the sluice?'

'Right away, Sister.' I cleaned it thoroughly. I polished bed pans to mirror brilliance, and used my fingernails to scrape up gunge from between the tiles on the floor. When it came to sluice cleaning, I had received a training second to none.

In my day, student nurses were drudges. Not only did we clean the sluice, we washed sheets and scrubbed bed frames once a week with carbolic soap. This didn't happen any more, and the patients survived, by and large. Those who didn't survive seemed to succumb to something unconnected with the failure of student nurses to scrub their beds with carbolic.

In my day, bed scrubbing was probably thought to be character-forming. The powers that be hadn't worked it out that it made no sense to hand pick bright young women (and a lot of them were bright), exhaust and excite them with a training at once intensive and expensive, and then waste their expertise and wear them out with tasks that could be done by any half-witted domestic.

I've timed my life all wrong, I thought. *Started as a student nurse, ended as a half witted domestic. The time to be a student nurse is now.*

At coffee break I went to Matron's office.

'My name is Mrs Toms,' I said, 'and I want to complete my training.'

78

She was an old-style matron, plump and solid; Hattie Jacques. I had a feeling she was going to put me through it. But she said, 'I've heard good reports of your work with the Friends, Mrs Toms.'

'I just fill vases.'

'May I ask how old you are?'

'Forty-nine.'

'Oh dear. That's four years too old for the SRN course.'

At the words *too old* I felt a pang of regret. Not regret. Regret hurt too much. Regret was too strong a word for it. So was grief. It was nothing really. Yes it was; it was guilt. Guilt felt right. I was used to guilt.

I had missed the bus through not getting up on time. So what else was new? It was more than four years since Miranda's paediatrician had told me to go back to nursing. It was more like seven years. Procrastination wasn't just the thief of time, it was the thief of everything. If I had done as I was told then, I might be a ward sister by now. But I had put it off.

I stood up to leave, smiling at Matron to show there were no hard feelings. It was probably a very wise policy. A person who couldn't organise herself to apply for a job whilst she was young enough to do it would probably not make a very good nurse. You couldn't have old age pensioners staggering about the wards in nurses' uniforms. It was my own fault. I had nothing to regret, no reason for grief. It was just that I couldn't really imagine being too old for this, or for anything. I felt young. When people said 'the younger generation' I still assumed they meant me.

It's the same for everybody, I thought. *There's nothing unfair about it. We all get old at the same rate, one year at a time. It's part of the human condition to find one day that you're too old for this, too old for that, then one day you're too old to live and that's your lot.*

‘On the other hand, for State Enrolment,’ Matron was saying, ‘which is a more practical course, less academic, we accept women up to the age of fifty. When is your birthday?’

‘October.’

‘Just in time then. The next course you could apply for starts in September. I’ll give you an application form.’ She opened a drawer of her impeccable desk. ‘And the leaflet with details of all the allowances and everything.’

‘I won’t need an allowance.’

‘Mrs Toms, if you are offered a place on the course, the allowance is automatic.’

‘But I’m married.’

‘Most of our SEN trainees are. They find the money comes in useful to pay for help in the house.’

I opened my mouth to argue. Fortunately I remembered who I was. Arguing with Matron would have been a fine way to begin a career as a student nurse.

I had never had help in the house, notwithstanding Mummy’s little campaign (begun when I married and not yet abandoned) for me to have a daily woman to do the heavy cleaning. This would give her the opportunity to talk to her friends about her daughter’s servant. I wouldn’t dream of having help. Why should some old woman go down on her knees in my kitchen to make up for my shortcomings? ‘My house practically looks after itself, Matron. I’ll give it a grand blitz once a week. I’d be happy to donate my allowance towards the Kidney Machine Appeal.’

‘That’s very generous – ’

‘Directly, I mean. So it doesn’t come to me at all.’

She said, ‘Administratively, that would be a little difficult to arrange.’

‘Why? If I want to give it?’

I heard myself arguing again. I put my hand over my mouth.

She said, ‘Why don’t you want the money to come to you?’

‘My husband.’ I didn’t know how to put this. Lindsay Bixwell said he was one of the original dinosaurs (she could talk! with that husband of hers), Miranda called him an MCP, but he was what he was, an old-style gentleman with strong ideas on what was proper and what wasn't. Who was to say that he was wrong? Wrong or right, he was mine and I loved him. 'He's not exactly Germaine Greer's greatest fan, let's put it that way.' That was the way to put it, with a little laugh, to signify that the conversation didn't really count.

'Germaine who?'

'Isn't that her name?'

'Are you saying that your husband wouldn't approve of you doing the course? Have you discussed it with him?'

I noticed that she was not wearing a wedding ring. I became aware of my superiority and knowledge. 'Matron, after nearly thirty years of marriage there are some things you don't have to discuss. You read each other's minds. You can sit in silence for hours and know what the other person is thinking.'

It was never my intention to deceive him. Lying to Sandy was out of the question. Quite apart from it being wrong, I would never get away with it. After thirty years of his family's Honourable Heart code (which I agreed with) I had no more talent for deceit than he had.

But, thanks to the mature mutual understanding that we enjoyed, I thought I knew that his main objection to my doing the course would be his worry that I would not get my housework done. In my heart of hearts I agreed with him. The onus was on me to forestall the objection.

What I decided to do, therefore, was to set the wheels in motion, and, between now and September, run my life *as if* I were on the training course. Between 10 am and 3 pm on weekdays I would do no housework at all. I would study nursing books. I would jolly well force myself to get my housework done before and after my study periods. Then, when the time came to ask Sandy's permisson – *if* the time came; there was the small matter of applying and being accepted – if he said *What about your housework?* I would be able to reply with perfect truth that it was under control.

I filled in the application form. I had to give two references, both of which had to come from people who were not relatives and who were in a 'professional or other responsible position'.

Sister provided one. She showed it to me. She had put that I was, 'Reliable, punctual, conscientious, thorough, good-humoured and popular among staff and patients alike.' I said, 'Sister, are you sure you're not confusing me with somebody else?'

The other reference was more difficult. The only non-hospital people I knew who were in responsible positions were Sandy's friends. One possible exception was Lindsay Bixwell, who ran her own kennels. She was the wife of one of Sandy's oldest friends, but whether she was still Sandy's friend was open to question.

I used to think of her as downtrodden, but since Bixwell's heart attack (and it wasn't for me to say that anybody *deserved* a heart attack) she had rather come into her own. Perhaps because the alternative was to be stuck in the house all day with her husband (he had taken early retirement) she had set up her business in the garden, with pens and runs and a caravan for the office.

Sandy disapproved. He said he thought it was a pretty rotten show when a chap became ill through no fault of his own and his wife responded by turning their home into a twenty-four-hour thoroughfare for doggy men and their bitchy wives with you-know-what on their shoes.

He said this to Lindsay's face. He made no bones about it. She said, 'Sandy, you'd have been against us having the vote.' He said, 'I most certainly will be, if anyone's fool enough to suggest it.'

It was all quite good humoured – it had to be, if only because Miranda adored her godmother and her dogs, and practically lived there in the holidays, and this, together with Sandy's visits to his friend ensured the continuance of some sort of diplomatic relations between the two families – but I knew I could rely on Lindsay to keep my secret and write me a reference.

'Sure, Jo. What shall I say in it?'

This rather took me aback. 'List my good points, I suppose.'

'Right. Will do.'

'If you can think of any.'

'Don't be silly.' After a short pause for thought, she said, 'I'm a bit pushed at the moment, why don't you do it yourself?'

'What do you mean?'

'You write it, I'll sign it.'

It was the hardest thing I had ever done. Singing my own praises was totally foreign to my nature. I forced myself. I had to. Fortunately Sandy was away on business so I had two free evenings in which to come up with, 'I have known Mrs Jo Toms for twenty years, during which time we have served together on the Tea Rota at Bleswick Rugby Football Club. I have always found her honest, hard-working and good with people.'

I blushed as I wrote it. My hands shook. *When did your trumpeter die?*

Lindsay called in one of her kennel-maids to type the reference on headed paper. It didn't take up much space. Lindsay's signature filled what remained of the page: *Lindsay Bixwell, (Mrs) (Director)*

'Good for you, Jo,' she said vaguely, before moving back to business of her own. 'Give yourself a bit of independence from your oafish husband.'

Her tone was patronising. I said, 'He's not an oaf and I don't want independence.'

Lindsay laughed.

79

I never did get around to looking out those pictures for Stella. So it was a bit of a surprise when *Atalanta* arrived in the post one Saturday morning in May with a photograph of Christine on the cover, and the headline 'NEVER AGAIN! MY FRIEND DIED IN A BACK STREET ABORTION. See Inside.'

It was the sort of photograph you occasionally saw in the newspapers, of a child who had been kidnapped, or some other person whom disaster had suddenly made famous, but of whom nobody had ever bothered to take proper photographs. It was a blown-up snap, taken, I reckoned, when Christine was about ten. In spite of its blurred, grainy quality the sulky expression was unmistakable. *I have been press-ganged aboard this vessel. I'm damned if I'm going to enjoy myself.* But as Sandy said, flicking through the pages of *Atalanta*, most of the women whose pictures it contained appeared to be sulking about something.

No women's libber he, but he had strong views on abortion. For obvious reasons he thought it should be free, on demand. So he wasn't particularly put out to see the photograph, or the article; in fact he seemed rather moved. And he quickly solved the mystery of where the photograph had come from. 'Miranda, you're looking shifty.'

'Well. I knew Mummy wouldn't get around to sending it.'

'Isn't that what I always say, Jo? If you put a job off for long enough, somebody else will do it.'

Stella's article was a simple account of her friendship with Christine. There wasn't much in it that we didn't know already – apart from the number of times that Christine used to pretend to be having tea at Stella's when in fact she was in detention. Sandy said affectionately, 'Little fibber.'

The article ended with the words,

'The Cresswell Bill fell with the fall of the government after the miners' strike. The immediate threat to abortion rights has passed, but we cannot afford to be complacent.

'Already the anti-abortionists are regrouping for another attack on the 1967 Act. We are mobilising for a mass demonstration in its defence in the autumn. Women MPs, women doctors and their sympathetic male counterparts will be there. Trades unionists will be there and so will celebrities from the world of entertainment, including the Dole Busters.

'One person who won't be there is my old schoolfriend Chris Toms.

'I'll be there for her, and for myself, and for you.

'Where will *you* be?'

Miranda breathed ecstatically, '*The Dole Busters*.'

Sandy gave me a questioning glance. I said, 'I imagine it's a pop group.'

'I expect you're right.'

Miranda said, 'I love Cyril.'

'Oh, so do I, don't you, Jo? Good old Cyril. Who's Cyril?'

'The one with the ring.'

'The ring where?'

'On his finger. Can we go?'

Sandy said, 'I'm not having you going on marches, Miranda. You'll be crushed underfoot in mass hysteria.'

'You mean like when we go to rugby matches?'

'Don't be cheeky.'

'Please, Mum, can we?'

'I agree with Daddy.'

Miranda started to sing. The tune was 'I belong to Glasgow'. The words were:

'I agree with Daddy,
'I agree with Dad,
'There's nothing the matter with Daddy,
'It's just that he drives you mad.'

Again he said, 'Don't be cheeky.'
I said, 'Where did you learn that?'
She said, 'Nowhere, I made it up.'

Stella rang. 'Did you get it? Did you like it?'
'We were all very touched, Stella.'
'You liked it.'
'Perhaps "liked" isn't quite the word.'
'No. Sorry. "Sensitive"'s not my middle name. Look, I want to ask you something else. You know the demo? The one in the article?'
'In the autumn.'
'Some of us were wondering if you'd like to be on the platform.'
'What platform?'
'In Trafalgar Square,' she said. 'Sort of "My daughter died in a back street abortion, that's why I'm defending the right to choose," type of thing.'
'You want me to *say that*? To thousands of people? In Trafalgar Square?'
'It would be fabulous,' breathed Stella.
'I'd be absolutely terrified.'
'Everyone is, the first time. Well, the first few hundred times actually. Bring Miranda, she can hold your hand.'
'I don't know, Stella. It's not me at all.'
'How do you know what's you if you don't try it?'

It was a fair question. Not so long ago I would not have thought it *me* to be accepted, without Sandy's knowledge, for a training course to become a State Enrolled Nurse. Not so long ago I would not have thought it *me* to live a double life, getting ready for September when the course would start.

As soon as Sandy and Miranda were out of the house in the mornings, I flung the breakfast things into the dishwasher. For years I had meant to get rid of the dishwasher. I had never got around to it. Once again, procrastination had paid off. I used to suspect that the dishwasher did not get things properly clean. Now that it had to, it jolly well did. I felt like apologising to it for my earlier mistrust, which belonged to the time when I had nothing better to do than hold glasses up to the light and pick microscopic crustings off plates with my fingernails.

While the dishwasher was doing its stuff I rushed upstairs to make the bed. This took longer than it need have because Sandy drew the line at duvets, but I wasn't planning to make an issue of this. I didn't want him asking what I had against good old English sheets and blankets after all these years.

The aim of this, my secret dry run, was to prove to him, and to myself, that I could be just as good a housewife with a job as without one. Luckily I had nothing much to live up to. Between the hours of ten and three, housework took a back seat. If I wasn't doing one of my extra Friends stints at the hospital, I read textbooks from the preparatory reading list.

Sandy showed no sign of noticing that anything had changed. *Just as well for him it's only nursing*, I thought. *I could be having an affair.*

Miranda said, 'Mum, you're always reading.' She seemed, on balance, to approve, but I didn't want her drawing her father's attention to my bizarre new hobby. I planned to come clean with him and tell all in June, when he and I would be going up to Northburgh for Janet's graduation and a short holiday. In the meantime, to put Miranda off the scent, I made a joke of it.

'My brain cells are rotting,' I told her.

'How do you know?'

'I know because I'm a nitwit. Any organ that isn't used, atrophies. Look it up.'

On another occasion she said, 'What's that book about?'

'This? Oh, nursing, I think.'

'Why are you reading it?'

'So that I can be slightly less useless at the hospital than I am at the moment.'

'It looks hard.'

'It's not hard for the proper nurses. It's a bit hard for a nitwit like me.'

'Why do you always say you're a nitwit?'

'Because I am.'

'You're not. It's only Dad who says you are.'

'He's only teasing. You have to learn to take teasing.'

'Why?'

'Because it's part of life.'

'You said you were a nitwit yesterday and now you've said it again today.'

'Goodness,' I said. 'Have you been taking notes? It's like having a barrister in the house. Does that conclude the case for the prosecution?'

80

Janet got a 2:1. Not for worlds would Sandy and I have let her know how disappointed we were, so we sent her a greetings telegram. And when the time came for her graduation ceremony, I took a few days off from my pretend job, he took a few days off from his real one, and we went up to Scotland on the sleeper.

We dumped Miranda on the Bixwells. To say I was glad to see the back of her would be putting it a bit strongly, but Sandy and I hadn't had a holiday alone since before we started having babies. I wasn't exactly fed up with looking after children, on the contrary I had always loved having them, even Christine. But there had always been a sense of something more important waiting ahead, namely the time when the children would bugger off and I would have Sandy to myself.

This could be the beginning of that time.

We still had a while to wait before we could really up-sticks and sail round the world. He couldn't retire for at least ten years (my nursing would fill that gap, as I would point out to him when the time came for me to ask for his permission, and it would be useful to have a qualified nurse aboard); but the time for our freedom *would* come, and this night in the sleeper, speeding north to watch our grown-up, engaged daughter being awarded her degree, could be the beginning of it.

We had a wonderful passionate session on the bottom bunk. I started it, but he didn't exactly fight me off, once I had got his balls in my mouth (first one at a time, then both together) and the rim of his penis between my spit-covered fingers. I knew the special place and how to touch it. He lay gasping and giggling with his big, square golden head thrown back and a look in his eyes as if the heavens had opened and revealed something ultimate to him. Then at the last moment he reared up, pushed me over, pressed my shoulders down in the way I liked and thrust into me without preliminary.

I didn't need any preliminary. His penis was already wet from my fingers and my spit, and my vagina was chock-a-block with Ortho-Creme. Anyway, it was a relief when he took over like that and couldn't contain himself. Showed he liked it as much as I did.

Perhaps even more than I did.

Could anyone like it more than I did? I adored it. Why shouldn't I adore it with my husband? I had never even contemplated it with anybody else. Perhaps Sandy adored it more. I hoped so. He deserved extra. I like to think of him being always that little way ahead of me, even in pleasure.

I adored his passion. The man should take the initiative. That way, the woman could always rest assured that she was wanted. I did wonder sometimes whether I was wanted and if so why. I wondered in bed at home when he was asleep and my tummy was rumbling and I seemed to feel my wrinkles deepen, and I sniffed the tang of sourness in the odours of my ageing body. He was maturing like an English russet, richly gold in his late summer, ripe and delicious. Why should he want me? No reason, but he did. Who needed reasons?

He pumped, pumped, pumped with the rhythm of the train.

Silver hammer blows, silver visions.

Silver Jubilee. Silver train, silver engine, silver carriages. What a thrill for a nine-year-old. Being allowed to travel so magically, and all alone. They wouldn't have let me go alone. Would they? Someone must have been keeping an eye on me. The guard. *We're sending you in charge of the guard.* That funny phrase they used, from which it was unclear which of the two of us was in charge, the guard or me.

You hardly felt it move. I could feel this one move. The jolt of the wheels, the jolts of Sandy's sex. Our sex. All alone, aged nine. The Silver Jubilee, from Darlington to King's Cross. My first school, St Hilda's, a good school, Daddy chose it. He knew the headmistress personally. He and Mummy gave me two years to settle in and then came to England on leave. I was put on the train in charge of the guard and sent to meet them. How did I get across London? Someone must have met me. Who would have? They probably paid someone. Somehow I ended up at Oxford, where Daddy was doing his research. I ran along the platform. He picked me up.

Sandy groaned.

In my answering groan was a touch of shrillness, a shred of a dying sigh. A beaten child's whimper when it starts to stop hurting. I hadn't been hurt. I had been worked up and calmed down. I felt full.

I had cried and been comforted. I had been to the edge but someone was there and he brought me back. His arms round me. The little blue carriage rattling us up to Scotland like churns of milk or mail bags. Safely delivered, safe, safe. Was that an orgasm?

Who cared? Even if it wasn't, it would do.

I lay beneath him in a glorious languor, hoping he was asleep. I could sleep under him all night, he would crush me. It would be such a divine way to die, and I wouldn't really be dead. I nibbled his chin. It was all crunchy.

He said, 'Are you comfortable?'

'Mmmm. Are you?'

'No.'

'Sorry.' I wriggled out from under him and climbed the ladder to the top bunk to sleep. He put his hand under my bottom to steady me.

At Edinburgh we changed. The morning was as golden and as chilly as a lolly. He bought himself a paper, passing over the *Scotsmans* and *Glasgow Heralds* with lip-curling dignity. '*Daily Telegraph*, please.'

On the branch train I said, 'I don't know why you want to read the paper with this marvellous view to look at.' Sun glimmered through purple heather, and long-haired sheep grazed between stunted trees and rocky outcrops. Now and again he looked up from reading about the thrilling prospect of us having a second General Election this year and said, 'Bonnie Scotland, och aye the noo.' I agreed with him.

Janet and Godfrey met us at the station in his white MG. She had a cotton frock on, and a cardigan, flat sandals and no stockings. She looked fresh and happy and pleasantly windblown, but nobody could ever accuse poor old Janet of being a great beauty. Nevertheless, she had landed this super man, handsome and charming and rich, with obvious prospects. *Good for you, love,* I thought, kissing her. *Just goes to show.*

It was the first time we had seen Godfrey since they announced their engagement. His eyes glowed. 'Do I get a kiss, now that I'm family, Jo?' He was half little-boy, half flirt, irresistible. I said, 'I should jolly well hope so.' Sandy hugged Janet and said, 'Keep an eye on your mother. She'll have him off you.'

It was too early to go to our hotel so Godfrey drove us to Janet's granny flat for breakfast, 14a Craigmillar Terrace, the familiar address now made real. Northburgh was becoming real, just as Janet was about to leave it. I gaped at the medieval towers in the sunlight, and students on bikes in their purple gowns. 'Oh, you're *lucky*.' I didn't meant to say it aloud. It wasn't addressed to Janet in particular, or Godfrey, but to students generally, students everywhere. 'Lucky, lucky, lucky.'

Godfrey said, 'This is your first visit, isn't it?'

''Fraid so,' I replied. 'We kept meaning to come up but we never got around to it. I'm afraid you'll find that's a theme song of our family, Godfrey.'

'Thanks for the warning, Jo. I won't let Janet procrastinate any longer.' Out of the corner of his eye he gave her a steely, thrilling look. 'Bewitching wench, you will marry me this forenoon.'

'I can't, I've got to get my degree.'

'Degree? What do you need a degree for? No wife of mine will need a degree.'

'Shame on you, Godfrey,' I said.

We all had a jolly good laugh and got out of the car.

81

We left our luggage and went in to the flat, which I thought was absolutely super, whether for a student or for a granny. I said so, but Sandy said, 'Stairs are a bit steep for a granny. Might finish her off.'

I said, 'I suppose you're right.'

'Do for your mother,' he said.

I laughingly retorted, 'Do for yours.' I was imagining living as a student in the flat, young and alone and self-contained. Janet was giving all that up now, to be married. But at least she had had it. I had gone straight from boarding school to nurses' home. No wonder when I married I couldn't keep house for toffee. Now *there* was a peculiar expression. If all it took were toffee, I could have done it with my mouth full of toffee and my eyes shut.

Godfrey took Sandy upstairs to the bedsitter part. I followed Janet into the kitchen. 'What can I do, love?'

'Nothing, Mummy, honestly. Go upstairs and recuperate.'

'I'll make the coffee.'

'Why don't you relax and let me wait on you for a change?'

'Aren't you going to prick those sausages? Oops, sorry. Interfering mother.'

She put her hands on my shoulders. 'Out!'

On my way up to the bedsitter I noticed mud on the stair carpet, at least I hoped it was mud. I sniffed it and it was. Nevertheless, I looked in the understairs cupboard for a dustpan.

There was a pile of newspapers and *Sunday Times* colour supplements and also *Atalanta* with Christine's face on the cover. I had brought our copy up to show Janet, but she appeared behind me and said, 'You weren't supposed to see that.'

'Why?'

'Well. It was a big enough shock for me. There's this girl I know, Gillian. She showed it to mc. I think we should sue.'

'What for?'

'They've got a damn cheek, digging up our private family business. And where did they get that photograph?'

'From us,' I said.

'What?'

'You remember Stella, Christine's friend? She came round and asked for one.'

'You gave it to her?'

'Why not?'

'For this?'

I said, 'We don't agree with everything women's lib stands for, not by a long chalk. But Daddy's all for free abortion, and I agree with him.'

'Well, I'm not,' said Janet. 'I'm for standards.'

'Oh dear. I *am* going to be an embarrassment to you. I'm going to speak at a pro-abortion rally in Trafalgar Square.'

'*You are going to do what?*' She put out her hand to stop me answering. She led me back into the kitchen and closed the door. In the frying pan the unpricked sausages were spitting and bursting as I had known they would. Automatically, I picked up a fork and pricked them.

Janet said, '*Stop that!*' She turned the hot plate down. 'What rally?'

'Janet, please don't worry, your ageing mother is not about to burn her bra and shave her head. The fact remains that if the '67 Act had been in force in '63, Christine would be alive today.'

'That's morbid.'

'Depends what you call morbid.'

'I'll tell you what I call morbid,' said Janet. 'The way bloody Christine goes on messing up my life from beyond the grave.'

'How is she doing that?'

'We weren't going to tell you till later,' said Janet. 'We were saving it. Godfrey's been adopted as prospective parliamentary candidate for a constituency in Glasgow – '

'That's wonderful!'

'Is it? There are a lot of Catholics there, and he's going to look wonderful, isn't he, if his mother-in-law's stomping around advocating free abortion and pills on the rates and goodness knows what else.'

'Janet – '

'Keep your voice down.'

'I wasn't, I was emphasising.' I tried to kiss her but she wriggled away. These spontaneous and apparently affectionate kisses between mothers and daughters that you see in films had never been my strong point. I spoke quietly and calmly. 'I think Godfrey's super, Janet, and I hope he'll be elected to parliament if that's what he wants. And you want. But that is not going to stop me thinking what I think.'

'I'm just surprised you do think it, that's all,' she said.

'Evidently.'

'I'm surprised you give it any thought. The number of times I've been told that the best thing is for you not to think about it. And how I mustn't say anything to make you think – '

'Who's been saying that?'

'Daddy and Pam.'

'Who?'

'Pam MacLeish. Pam from New Zealand, remember?'

I seemed to know how a duck feels when its lower half is immersed in freezing black water while its top half is white and serenely smiling.

'I remember.' I kept my head. I was terrific. I said, 'What about her?' While she was explaining, I assumed a look of polite vagueness and disinterest that was utterly convincing. I knew it was convincing because I surreptitiously checked my reflection on the back of a cereal spoon.

'Let me get this clear, Janet.'

'Yes?'

'Pam MacLeish is in England?'

'Yes.'

'Since when?'

Janet shrugged. 'Three years.'

'And I am not supposed to know.'

'No, because – '

'I understand. Because it would remind me of Christine and upset me.'

'So Daddy thought,' said Janet. 'But he was obviously wrong. You obviously love being reminded of Christine.'

'No. I agree with him.'

'But – ' She waved *Atalanta* with its blurred snap of Christine. 'Why didn't you kick Stella out?'

'I did. Stella, I said, I'm sorry but I want no part of it. Trouble was, Miranda took rather a fancy to her and sent her the photograph herself.'

'Bloody Miranda.'

'Bloody Miranda indeed. Daddy dealt with her, I can tell you.'

'And the rally?'

'Of course I'm not going to speak at a rally, Janet! I mean, I ask you! Is it me?'

'I didn't think so, but you just said you were.'

'That was a *joke*. You're as bad as Miranda. My learned friend. You pick on every word I say.'

She said, 'Ha ha,' in cold tones, but she put the hot plate back on and returned to her frying.

I said, 'Shall I cut up these tomatoes?'

'If you want to.'

'How do you want them?'

'Just cut up,' she said.

'I mean halves, quarters or slices?'

'I don't know, Mummy. I've never thought about it.'

'Daddy's the one who's upset,' I said, in the tone of somebody drifting casually from subject to subject. 'That's probably why he didn't want me to know that Pam was in London.'

'Perhaps.'

I was infuriated by her shrug. It reflected my own air of finding none of this particularly important, but mine was a pretence, whereas she meant it. Somehow she must be made to treat it as important. But she must not be allowed to know how important it was. 'I don't want to make a big thing of it, Janet, but it might be better if Daddy didn't find out that you'd let the cat out of the bag.'

'What cat? What bag?'

Godfrey put his head round the door and smiled his winning smile. 'How are you getting on, darling?'

'Fine.' She put a box of cornflakes down on top of *Atalanta*. It was a quick gesture, quick enough for him but not quick enough for me. It told me that everything I needed to save the situation was in my own hands.

I beamed with relief. I turned the beam on Godfrey. 'Sorry. Are you two getting hungry up there? We've been having a natter.'

'Need a hand?'

'No, we can natter on our own. We won't be two ticks.'

When he had gone I said to Janet, 'Does Godfrey know about Christine?'

'Of course I've told him. It's one of the reasons why he's so anti-abortion. One of the reasons why I am too. But he *doesn't* know she's being turned into a women's lib publicity stunt.' She nodded at *Atalanta*. 'He's not what you might call an avid reader.'

'You scratch my back, I'll scratch yours.'

'Pardon?'

'You look after your man, I'll look after mine.'

'Mummy, you're not making sense.'

'When you've been married as long as I have, you'll know what makes sense and what doesn't. Daddy's deep. He doesn't admit what hurts him, but I know. I don't want Daddy to know that you've broken your agreement with him. I don't want him to know that *I* know that Pam is back in London.'

'Why? Now that you do know, why can't we all be friends again? I'd like to ask her to my wedding.'

'It's up to you, Janet. But if you'll do what I ask, I'll come down on Miranda like a ton of bricks and see to it that there's no repetition of – ' I left the sentence unfinished and dropped *Atalanta* symbolically into the pedal bin.

82

The Principal made a speech in Latin. I used to love Latin. *Bellum, bellum, bellum, belli, bello, bello. Bella, bella, bella, bellorum, bellis, bellis*. And, *fero, ferre, tuli, latum*. I loved that one too.

He switched to English. 'I am happy to welcome all graduands, parents and friends to the university of Northburgh's Fraser Lamont Hall and this happy occasion.' Two *happies* in one sentence. So much happiness. All these happy pairs of parents. *Look happy, Jo.*

It wasn't hard. Oddly enough, I *was* happy. It had been a shock but now it was a relief. I knew. I could take steps.

I had already taken the most important step. I had bought Janet's silence in exchange for not doing anything that would embarrass Godfrey over the abortion business. I knew; but nobody knew I knew, apart from Janet. Janet knew I knew, but Janet didn't actually *know*.

Even apart from that, I had a reasonable amount going for me. To say I was attractive for my age would be putting it a bit strongly, but I wasn't too bad when I made the effort. Take now for instance. I was wearing a new frock with a blue, mauve and white pattern and a flattering waistline, and a hat and gloves that picked out the blue. I reckoned I held my own against the other mothers.

We had a family. That must count for something. Our daughter, wearing a long black gown, was about to go up to the platform for her degree. Our son-in-law-to-be was with us, watching her, sharing our pride. Sandy wouldn't be such a fool as to throw all this away.

I cheered up. I felt calm and confident. My only real sadness was that Daddy wasn't here. *Skipped a generation, I'm afraid, Daddy*, I'd say. *But there she is, there's the clever one!*

Mummy could have been here if she had chosen. She couldn't

say I hadn't given her the opportunity. *You're always complaining that you never see Janet*, I said. *Why don't you book yourself a sleeper on the same train as us?*

She said, *To Scotland! These days it's as much as I can do to get to the post office!* Hint, hint. She could hint on. She wasn't moving in with me and Sandy and that was that. Not now that I had my marriage to fight for.

Up the steps went the graduands, six ahead of Janet, then five, then four . . . They bowed to the Principal, he bowed back. He put collars of silk and fur round their necks, gave them scrolls and spoke to them in Latin. *There she is, Daddy. The clever one.*

I'm cleverer.

I imagined the scrolls containing everything they knew.

Not much for four years.

I know nothing, but I know more than they do. Knowing nothing is the mark of my cleverness.

I felt like standing up and shouting.

Listen, you girls, clever clogs one and all! You think you're so clever, you think you know so much but sometimes the cleverest thing is to know nothing!

When some little tramp is after your husband, the most dangerous time is the first time he has her. When she lures him into her putrid stinking bed. If your marriage can survive that, it's set fair to survive anything.

The second most dangerous time is when the husband finds out that the wife knows. That's the point when people say and do things that they'll regret. A slut's a slut, a bit on the side's a bit on the side, easy come is easy go is the motto of girls like Pam MacLeish. But if he thinks he's got to make a choice, he might make the wrong one.

Easy come, easy go.

She came, she went.

She seems to have come back.

But if I sit tight – if I put off my nursing course for a year or two, and concentrate on giving the house a jolly good blitz and Janet a jolly good wedding – if I'm a good wife, if I'm GOOD – maybe she'll go away again.

*

After the ceremony there was a garden party in the sunny quadrangle with terrible fresh-cream-and-strawberry shortcake. I only had a sliver. Sandy, Godfrey and I took turns to take pictures of each other standing with Janet in her graduate's gown, holding her scroll.

Godfrey had an appointment. He kissed Janet on the mouth, and me on the cheek, shook Sandy's hand and went off. It was the first time the three of us had been alone since Janet's revelation and our agreement. I was nervous. I said, 'Do you know what I think we should all do now? Go for a jolly good walk.'

It was a normal sort of remark for me to make, and it got on Sandy's nerves in the normal way. This in itself was reassuring. He yawned. 'Too hot.'

'Get rid of all those calories!'

'You go.'

Janet said, 'No, come with us, Daddy.'

He said, 'For you, anything, O Master of Arts.'

It was only in fun, but even in fun he never said anything as sweet as that to me.

She returned to her flat to change; I went to the hotel with Sandy. He got out of his suit and I hung it up. He said, 'What shall I wear, what have I brought?' I chose his fawn slacks and his white T-shirt. He raised his arm and said, 'Do I need to wash?' I sniffed his armpit. 'No, you're fine.'

I put on my calf-length gingham skirt with the elastic waist, a short sleeved blouse and sandals. I washed my face in cold water and brushed my hair vigorously. I wondered if Pam still had the rough, outdoor-girl look that he seemed to like so much. *Girl.* What was I thinking of? She must be nearly forty, and still a MacLeish. A real old maid. Rusty must have changed his mind. The man was obviously nobody's fool, more's the pity for me.

We met Janet at the beach. Her jeans were too tight. I said to her as tactfully as I could, 'Those jeans look a bit tight, darling.'

She said, 'I'm slimming down into them, I'm determined to be a size twelve bride.'

'You shall be. I'll race you. Ready, steady, go!' I ran across the hot sand. The tide was out. Everything was so flat, so white and dazzling, that there was no horizon. My feet were running but there were no landmarks, no proof that I was getting anywhere. I had left Janet behind. I called over my shoulder, 'Oy, you're supposed to be racing!'

She trotted up to me. 'I thought you meant racing to get down to size twelve.'

'That too. Get some exercise. And less of the strawberry shortcake.'

We ran a bit but it was too hot. Sandy sauntered coolly over to us saying, 'I shall wear my RNVR uniform to give her away.'

I clasped my hands together. 'Oooh, lovely.'

He said, 'What about dates, Janet? We ought to book the church.'

I said, 'Bleswick Parish Church?'

'You must be joking, Jo. Got my eye on a nice little place in Pimlico. Sixteenth century. Pass it now and again. Often thought, you could have a damn nice wedding there. Bit like that one in Chelsea where Humphrey's girl got spliced.'

Janet said, 'We don't live in Pimlico.'

'Don't think that matters these days, chum. Get married wherever you want. Park a suitcase in the vicarage for three weeks and that counts as residence. I'll have words in the right ears but I'll need a date.'

'We thought the autumn. Everyone's on holiday at the moment.'

'When in the autumn?'

'October the 5th,' she said. 'It's a Saturday.'

I knew it was. My heart skipped. It was the day of Stella's rally in Trafalgar Square. It was perfect. It allowed me to get out of speaking at the rally without anyone questioning my reasons. Not even Stella and her cohorts would expect me to miss my own daughter's wedding.

Without any prompting from me, Janet and Godfrey had picked the perfect date. Luck was on my side. Everything was going my way.

Miranda

83

On 5 October 1974 Janet got married to Godfrey de Salis, don't ask me why. It must go down as one of the bleakest days in the Toms family saga.

Where was her taste? I asked myself. She had never been a great one for boyfriends, but there must have been *somebody* other than Godfrey. Where was her self-respect? She was *my big sister*, for heaven's sake. I had looked up to her all my life (well, I did sometimes) and now this.

My mum was as bad. She came home with Dad after Janet's graduation and went wedding-crazy. She announced a grand blitz on the house. The wedding was still three months away and it wasn't even going to be held in the house, but she didn't let that stop her.

She dashed about like a hamster with rabies, tipping out the contents of drawers and cupboards. She piled everything up in the middles of carpets. That way she would have to sort it all out. She couldn't procrastinate, she said. The die was cast.

Daddy must have a den, she announced one day. 'Would you like a den, darling?' He looked at her as if she were mad. 'When Janet's gone,' she said, 'I'll turn her room into a den for you.' She sounded as if she couldn't wait. 'You can keep all your sailing magazines in it, and your dinky toys. You can have a comfortable arm chair without any ironing on it.'

Dens – other than for lions – sounded a bit American to me. The only Englishman we knew who had a den was Bixwell. I skulked off to Lindsay Bixwell's whenever I could. It was chaos there too, but a friendly, doggy sort of chaos. Bixwell stayed in his den and the dogs roamed free.

Mum gave up her voluntary work as a Friend of Bleswick Hospital. Too much to do, she said.

I thought this was a rotten shame because she used to enjoy

being a Friend. She used to read up about nursing in her free time. Now she read up about marriage. I had thought she might move on from being a Friend and become a proper nurse, but suddenly she wasn't even a Friend, she was a housewife and mother of the bride.

Needless to say, all this giving-up was completely one sided. I didn't notice Janet giving up her summer holidays or her temp job to get ready for her own wedding. I didn't notice Dad giving up his job, or spending anything less than his normal amount of time on his hobbies, i.e. sailing, boozing, going to rugby matches and falling asleep in front of the TV.

When I tried to point out to Mum that this wasn't really fair on her, she said, 'It is.'

'Why? Why should you give everything up?'

'Give what up?'

'Your nursing, for a start.'

'Nursing!' she scoffed. 'Don't exaggerate. I popped in now and again and did the flowers.'

Another thing she gave up was the chance to speak at the abortion rally in Trafalgar Square. I said, 'Well I'm going.'

'You are not. You're going to be chief bridesmaid.'

'I want to see the Dole Busters.'

'They won't turn up.'

'They will.'

'People in the pop world are notoriously unreliable,' said my mother. 'And in any case, your attitude's all wrong. You should go to something because you believe in it, not because of some pop group.'

'I do believe in it,' I said.

'You're too young to know what you believe.'

'*I believe in it. You* said *you* did. You said you'd go to the rally and make a speech.'

'That was before we knew the date of the wedding.'

'Why can't she have her wedding on another day? If she's got to have it at all.'

'Oh, Miranda, you are funny when you get a bee in your bonnet!'

*

They trussed me up from head to foot in pastel cotton chintz, and gave me a bunch of honeysuckle to clutch in my clenched fists. There were three other bridesmaids – the four-year-old daughter of one of my cousins, and two smug little brats dug up from somewhere by Godfrey. I was supposed to be keeping them in order but they behaved better than I did.

They sang along with the hymns, and they didn't roll their eyes or grit their teeth when the vicar said, 'Who giveth this woman?' and my dad (trying his best to look like Kenneth More in *A Night to Remember*) handed Janet over like the supreme champion at Crufts. They kept their eyes to the front and looked sweet. They could afford to look sweet. It wasn't their sister making these hideous promises to this hideous man.

Not that Godfrey was hideous to look at. Give him his due, he was actually quite handsome in a poofy sort of way. (Pity he wasn't a poof, or he might have kept his smarmy hands off Janet.) In a bad light, I might have fancied him. I might have mistaken him for a human being, rather than a would-be Tory MP. Or, with a bit of luck and a touch of common sense from the voters next Thursday, a would-not-be Tory MP.

'. . . and obey,' said Janet.

'. . . I now pronounce that they be man and wife together,' said the vicar.

'*Bbblleeucchhh*,' I thought.

All round the church, Toms's and de Salis's beamed at each other. I needed a bit of sisterly solidarity, so I grimaced at Flick. She was my second cousin, one of Uncle Rutherford's grandchildren. At twelve she was a year older than I was, but we were quite alike.

Flick and I only saw each other on family occasions like this, but we had been in correspondence about our plan. She grimaced back and lowered her eyelids in a secret nod that showed she had not forgotten.

After the service, I didn't want to be photographed with Godfrey. It was against my principles to be seen with a fascist. He might use the photographs in his election campaign. Family man, that kind of thing. Vote for me because I've got this beautiful little sister-in-law.

But I had other fish to fry, and I didn't want to draw attention to myself so I put up with it. I stood and simpered with Janet and Godfrey, then with Janet and Godfrey and Mum and Dad, then with Janet, Godfrey, Mum, Dad, and the Salthaven Senility Contingent, and so on. Ever-increasing circles. I was keeping an eye on the church clock – it was nearly ten to three – and also on Flick who was trying to look casual.

'You ready?' I asked, out of the corner of my mouth.

'Yup.'

'Sure you know what to do?'

'I know what you've told me to do, Miranda.'

'Fine.'

'I'm not so sure it's going to work.'

'What can go wrong?'

'You want a list?'

At last the photographers ran out of film. At this point Kenneth More came into his own and started bossing everybody about and getting them into cars to go to the reception.

He tried to put Gran Woolgar with Bixwell and Lindsay, but this didn't go down at all well. Grandma Toms was being ferried by Godfrey's parents in their Ferrari, and Lindsay's old grey Morris Traveller was full of dogs' hairs.

Umbrage was taken all round. Kenneth More put his hands over his eyes in an I-give-up gesture. I said, 'Don't worry about me, Dad. Flick's got me a lift.'

In the same moment, Flick was saying to her parents, 'I'm going in the car with Miranda.' The two of us then nipped back to the church and into the little room off the vestry, where we set the wheels in motion for phase one of the plan. It seemed very fitting to kick things off in there, because that was where Janet had put the finishing touches to her bridal beauty before doing the dreadful deed.

84

We swapped clothes. Flick had done me proud, turning up in this gorgeous shimmery black-and-mauve skirt and matching jacket, with platform shoes and double-axe earrings. I put everything on and felt as if I might be turning back into a human being. Meanwhile she was turning into a bridesmaid.

I said to her, 'You really look the part.'

Flick bit the end of a honeysuckle and sucked the nectar out. 'If you're going to insult me, I won't do it.'

'Do you think we might be twins?'

'You mean, is your dad really my dad, or is my dad really your dad?'

'I'll settle for your dad being my dad,' I said. 'But we are alike, aren't we?'

'Miranda, you're not going to talk me out of thinking this is the daftest idea you've ever had.'

'Can't fail,' I told her. 'Soon as you've changed you go back outside and hitch a lift to the reception with the nearest lot of de Salis's. Say you're me and they won't be any the wiser. When you get there, keep moving about so that people see you're there, but don't get too close to any of our relations. Concentrate on being charming to his.'

'Are his as bad as him?'

'Some of them might not be.'

'Probably are. He must get it from somewhere.'

'Not necessarily. After all, look at us,' I pointed out reasonably. 'We're Toms's and we're quite nice.'

'I'm too nice,' Flick grumbled. 'Agreeing to something like this. Has it occurred to you that while I'm busy being you, somebody might, just might, remember me, and say, "There's Miranda over there but where's old Flick got to? Hope nothing's happened to her"?'

'They won't, you're only a guest.'

'My mum and dad might,' she said.

'Flick, if the worst came to the worst and your parents found out about this, what would they do to you?'

'They'd go on and on at me. "Damn bad form, Felicity".'

'"Damn bad form, Miranda." Yeah, I'd get that too, but I'd probably get a walloping from my dad to go with it, so I'm risking more than you, right? Please, Flick. You promised. Don't let me down now.'

Outside, the church clock struck three. 'Got to go,' I said.

'Go on, then,' she sighed. 'But you'll be risking a walloping from me if you don't get me their autographs.'

I ducked out of the vestry and round the corner. A rusty purple mini-van was waiting, with ATALANTA stickers and SISTER-HOOD IS POWERFUL, and A WOMAN'S RIGHT TO CHOOSE. Stella was at the wheel wearing a white arm-band marked STEWARD. 'In you get,' she said. 'How was it?'

'It happened.'

'She didn't change her mind?'

'Nope.'

'No last minute hitches? No one rushing up from the back saying, "Godfrey's already married, his wife's in a lunatic asylum"?'

'She'd have to be,' I said, 'to marry him.' Then I remembered that, all joking aside, Janet had just done exactly that. Trust me to have two sisters, one of whom was married to Godfrey and the other of whom was dead. It was like having no sisters at all. Still, perhaps Stella would be my sister and we could be powerful together. She drove off saying, 'Let me tell you what's happening.'

'Are the Dole Busters there?'

'Yes, Miranda, the Dole Busters are there. What we – '

'Is Cyril there?'

'They're all there. I think. How many should there be?'

How could she not know? 'Five,' I sighed.

'I think there are five. Which one's Cyril?'

'The one with the ring.'

'He's there, and he's looking forward to meeting you.'

'Oh!' I was in ecstasy.

'Miranda, could you at least go through the motions of pretending that you're coming to the rally to support the campaign?'

'Sorry.'

'I told them about you and about Chris and about how your mum was going to speak but she couldn't because of Janet's wedding. And I told them about you wanting to sneak off from the wedding for half an hour or so and say a few words – '

'Ooh, you fibber,' I said. 'You were the one who said I had to say a few words.'

'Have you thought any more about that?'

'Yes, I can't do it; honestly, Stella, don't make me.'

'Why?'

'I'm only eleven.'

'So? Got a tongue in your head.'

'I wouldn't know what to say.'

She gave me a piece of paper with a lot of different people's handwriting on it. 'Few ideas from the collective.' There was a lot of crossing out, but I could just about decipher, *Sisters, brothers and comrades. I can't give my name because I'm not supposed to be here, I'm supposed to be at a wedding. Not mine, though. I'm a bit young for that, but I'm not too young to have a view on the importance of free, safe abortion on demand. My sister was only four years older than I am now when she –*

I read to the end. There was nothing wrong with it except that it made me feel sad and wish Christine were here. It's funny how it's possible to miss somebody you've never even met, except in dreams, if those were dreams.

With her, I knew I would be brave enough to speak. On the other hand, it was only because she was dead that I was being asked to speak. And if she hadn't died, I wouldn't even have been born. Mum and Dad had me to take her place.

'You want me to say this?'

'Say whatever you want, Miranda.'

'To thousands of people?'

'Pretend you're talking to me.'

'My voice isn't loud enough.'

'There are mikes,' she said.

'What if there's somebody there who knows my dad?'

'Is that likely? Aren't they all at the wedding?'

'He's got spies all over the place. I can't speak, Stella! I'd die.'

'All right, love, I'm not trying to get heavy with you. You're going to meet the Dole Busters anyway, that's what you want isn't it?' She smiled kindly at me and practically rammed the car in front. 'Bloody men drivers.' We could hardly move for crawling traffic and people carrying banners.

WOMEN'S LIBERATION WORKSHOP SAYS DEFEND THE RIGHT TO CHOOSE.

WORKING WOMEN'S CHARTER.

KEEP IT LEGAL, KEEP IT SAFE.

ABORTION LAW REFORM ASSOCIATION.

NO RETURN TO THE BACK STREETS.

NO REVOLUTION WITHOUT WOMEN'S LIBERATION! NO WOMEN'S LIBERATION WITHOUT REVOLUTION!

SPUC OFF.

Stella said, 'I don't know why they allow these marches, I don't know why they don't shoot the lot of them, that's what would happen in Russia.' She stopped trying to drive the car, swung it into a driveway, parked and told me to get out. 'We might as well walk.'

We ran up the side of the march towards Trafalgar Square. 'What do we want? Free Abortion!' shouted some men very loudly. 'When do we want it? NOW!' I could see about twenty people on the plinth. I didn't recognise any of them. They were too far away.

The square was crowded. I wanted to hold Stella's hand but it might seem babyish. She bought a badge that said FREE OUR BODIES FREE OUR SELVES and pinned it on me. People were selling *Shrew* and *Women's Report* and *Spare Rib* and waving banners.

LABOUR PARTY WOMEN'S SECTION.

POWER TO THE SISTERS AND THEREFORE TO THE CLASS.

GAY MEN IN SOLIDARITY WITH A WOMAN'S RIGHT TO CHOOSE.

KINGSGATE PLACE WOMEN'S CENTRE SUPPORTS THE 67 ACT.

'I do support it, honestly,' I said.

'I know you do.' She took my hand and pushed and shoved. We reached the barriers at the front of the crowd. A policewoman tried to stop us going any closer to the plinth where the speakers were, but Stella pointed to her STEWARD armband and we were allowed through. 'Let's go and see if we can find Cyril.'

85

The lions had banners round their necks like bibs. One said ABORTION: A WOMAN'S RIGHT TO CHOOSE. The other lion's banner showed a cartoon of a nun and a priest. IF YOU DON'T PLAY THE GAME, DON'T MAKE THE RULES.

A woman with a spotted scarf tied at the back of her neck like a pirate was making a speech about 'attacks on the working class'. Behind her, the Dole Busters were setting up their instruments.

Stella said to me, 'Which is your one, Miranda?'

It was the sort of thing my mum would have said. I could have killed Stella. Cyril might easily have heard. He was close enough. I was close enough. I could have touched his checked waistcoat. He wasn't very tall. I could have reached up and put my finger in the hole in his bowler hat. I could have kissed his ring, like the nuns at school when the bishop came. I could have but I didn't do anything. I felt too shy. I said, 'That one but it doesn't matter.'

The pirate woman came to the end of her speech. 'On Thursday, have no illusions! Vote Labour, but struggle for socialism!' She stuck her arm in the air and the crowd cheered. Some of them stamped their feet and shouted, 'General strike, general strike.'

Stella said to her, 'Great speech, Mary.' I thought, *You hypocrite. You weren't even here for most of it.*

Mary swept by saying, 'Was it all right?'

'Would have been,' Stella whispered to me, 'if she'd stuck to the point. Bloody Trots.'

A middle-aged woman with thick legs but nice skin said, 'In a few moments, the Dole Busters! But first a few words from Dr Audrey Bonnington from Women Doctors For Free Choice.'

Stella tapped Cyril on the shoulder as if he were just anybody. 'Cyril? It is Cyril, isn't it?'

How could she ask? I had told her it was.

Cyril fiddled with his drums, rummaged around in a box and said, 'Yeah.'

'This is my friend Miranda who I was telling you about.'

'Hi, Miranda.'

'Hi.'

'Miranda was wondering if she could have your autograph.'

'We're on in a minute. Do it afterwards.'

'She won't be here afterwards,' said Stella. 'She's got to get back to her sister's wedding.'

'Fuck me,' said Cyril.

Dr Audrey Bonnington was saying, 'I remember the days of admitting women to casualty with septicaemia following back street abortions and I don't want to go back to those days.'

Cyril and the other Dole Busters were having an urgent conference about one of Raymond's guitar strings. I ran my tongue into the corners of my mouth to get spit together so that when Cyril came back I could say: 'I really like your music.' I didn't manage, *I really like you*. 'And the rest of the band.'

'Yeah? Cheers, Marianne.'

'Miranda.'

Dr Bonnington said, '. . . five days to go before polling. Pester all your candidates. Let them know where you stand.'

Cyril got his drums right and said, 'Give me that.' He took a leaflet out of my hand and signed it. *Love to Miranda from Cyril.* 'There.'

'Will you do one for my cousin?'

Stella said, 'Maybe that's enough, Miranda. They're on in a minute.'

I said, 'What songs are you going to do?'

'Wait and see.'

'I *can't*. I've got to get back to the wedding. Are you going to do, "Who cares if there's fighting in the streets"?'

'Finish off with that.'

'I'll miss it then. What else?'

' "Don't wanna lock up my woman".'

'I love that one.'

'We'll do it for you.'

'Be better for my sister,' I said with feeling.

'What's your sister's name?' asked Cyril.

'Janet. Janet de Salis.' It was the first time I had said it, or even realised it properly.

Dr Audrey Bonnington said, 'Let us serve notice on the government – whatever colour of government is elected on Thursday – that women's hard-won rights will not be thrown away at the behest of a handful of self-appointed male supremacist – '

Stella said to me, 'Sounds like Godfrey, eh, Miranda?'

'Yeah.'

She explained to Cyril, 'Miranda's new brother-in-law's a Tory candidate.'

'Fuck me. Which one?'

'Godfrey de Salis.'

'Never heard of the cunt.'

'Thank you, Cyril.'

'I mean never heard of the nasty male person. What's a nice girl like you doing with a sister who'd do a thing like that?'

I shrugged. I felt happy and unhappy at the same time.

Dr Bonnington finished her speech. The woman with the thick legs and the nice skin said, 'And now from the world of music, the Dole Busters!' Cameras flashed and a terrific cheer went up. Cyril said, 'Comrades and friends, sisters and brothers. This one's for a great little girl called Miranda – ' he pointed at me – 'and for her big sister who's just made the mistake of marrying a Tory MP.' Everybody in Trafalgar Square jeered happily and whistled. Cyril said, 'Are you listening, Godfrey de Salis?' "Don't wanna lock up my woman".' Cyril hit his drums with a tremendous crash and the number began. Soon everyone in the square was singing, *Don't wanna lock her up, wanna see her run free, free enough to love herself, free enough to love me.*

Stella whispered, 'Think you ought to be getting back? We've been here twenty minutes.'

'Suppose so.'

'No point in pushing your luck.'

I waved to Cyril but he didn't notice. When we got to the bottom of the steps a man in a belted raincoat said, '*Daily*

Chronicle. Is this the young lady whose sister's marrying the Tory MP? I didn't recognise the name, what's his constituency?'

Stella said, 'They got that wrong, he's not an MP, he's only a candidate, excuse us.'

The man said to me, 'We got a nice pic of you talking to Raymond – '

'It wasn't Raymond, it was Cyril.'

' – and we'd like a bit of background. Godfrey de Salis, is that a small d?'

'*Come on*, Miranda.'

'Miranda,' said the man. 'That's a nice name. Miranda what?'

'Toms.'

'*Don't tell him!* Do you want to be in the papers?'

She rushed me to the car, which had got a parking ticket. She tore it up, saying, 'Fascists. Get in.' She told me to keep my hand on the horn and somehow we got through the traffic. She said, 'Does your dad read the *Daily Chronicle*?'

'Course not. It's common. Do you think I'll be in it?'

'Nothing would surprise me,' said Stella. 'It's absolutely bloody typical. Major issue of our times, and all the media are interested in is personalities.'

Jo

86

Sandy had decided – and I agreed with him – that it would make an original touch if we held the reception on board ship. An afternoon cruise along the Thames would have been ideal, but his mother had said, 'I'll be sick as a dog.'

This had brought out smugness in Mummy ('She's getting to be rather a difficult old woman, isn't she?') and, among Sandy, Kennington, Rutherford and Humphrey, gales of filial hilarity. 'We're not going out into the Bay of Biscay, Ma.' 'Packet of Kwells and a stiff Scotch'll see you right.' I tried to be kind and practical, suggesting a mind-over-matter approach, but Grandma Toms stuck to her guns. Any cruise would take place without her.

Mummy said, 'Oh dear, will she miss the reception?' but of course it was out of the question that the oldest member of the family should miss it. As a compromise, the reception was held aboard *HMS Radclyffe*, an RNVR training ship permanently moored on Albert Embankment. Grandma Toms was prescribed special seasickness pills by her GP.

Sandy and I, Godfrey and Janet, stood in the receiving line and greeted our guests. Grandma Toms tottered past on Rutherford's arm, pale and frail but gamely smiling. Sandy said to his brother, 'That girl you're with, is she on the pill?' Janet said, 'Daddy, honestly!'

The three little bridesmaids played near us but Miranda was up on deck. Occasionally my eye caught a flash of the fabric of her frock through a port hole. Sandy thought this was damn bad form. She should be in the receiving line. He was all for going up to fetch her, but I said, 'Don't make an issue of it, darling.' Last time I caught a glimpse of her she had been getting on like a house on fire with some of Godfrey's handsome teenage cousins, and I reasoned that if she could make friends with them it might be her first step on the road to liking Godfrey.

In any case, we didn't want a scene.

I said to Sandy, 'I'll round her up in time for the speeches. She won't want to miss yours.'

Sandy believed in doing things properly so there were only two choices of drink: champagne cocktails or (for children and spoilsports) orange juice. Before the wedding I had blotted my copy book by saying, 'Can we really afford champagne for all those people?'

'Don't be so bloody vulgar,' was his reply. It turned out ('Since you must know,' he sneered – he was obviously deeply hurt) that he had been making provision to pay for his daughters' weddings ever since Janet passed her eleven-plus. He had been putting the equivalent of her school fees into one of Rutherford's firm's endowment funds. 'Sorry, darling, for not trusting you,' I said.

I had tried to see that his action was a sign of a provident, caring father. But it chilled me to know that he could save up so much money without my knowledge. What else might he have spent it on? For what other future plans might he be making financial arrangements in secret?

I reassured myself that he could not make them as secretly as all that. This family – this huge, boisterous competitive family that ate and drank so prodigiously, and took up so much space with their long names and their long limbs and their expansive selves, and left such untidiness in their wake, and increased and multiplied and got on my nerves – nevertheless provided me with some protection.

On matters financial, Sandy invariably went to Rutherford for advice. Rutherford was head of the family and the family had an honourable heart. Rutherford wouldn't stand for deceitfulness or underhand behaviour in his younger brothers. He wouldn't stand for adultery.

He couldn't possibly know what was going on between Sandy and Pam. If Rutherford knew about it, Rutherford would tell me. He hadn't, so he didn't. And if Rutherford didn't know about it, it could not be very important. It must merely be a flirtation or perhaps not even that, perhaps a chance reunion of two old friends. It could not have financial implications. Divorce and desertion had financial implications, particularly if there were an eleven-year-old daughter. Sandy would not leave us high and dry.

He would not leave us at all. What was I thinking of on this happy family occasion?

What was I *knowing*?

I must stop knowing. I knew nothing. That was what was so clever about me.

I did not even know that Pam was back in England. All I knew about Pam's whereabouts was that she was in New Zealand. The only people aboard HMS Radclyffe who knew differently were me, Sandy and Janet. Sandy did not know that I knew, and Janet's lips were sealed. I had kept my promise and stayed away from the abortion demonstration; she would keep hers and not tell Sandy that she had told me. She had promised. She had an honourable heart.

Jonathan, the best man, said, 'Think it's time we started rounding them up for the speeches, Jo?'

'Goodness yes. Have you seen Miranda?'

'I think she's on deck.' I set off to fetch her but he put his hand out to stop me. 'Is your mother-in-law all right?'

Grandma Toms was sitting on a chair with her head against a wall. Eyes closed, she was being ministered to by my sisters-in-law, Kay, Gwen and Sue, with glasses of water and napkins which they shook under her nose like fans.

I went over. Mummy appeared at my side saying, 'I hope she hasn't had too much to drink.'

'You hope nothing of the kind.'

'I'm very fond of her.'

Grandma Toms was saying, 'This is so silly. Leave me. You enjoy yourselves.' Her head rolled around as if she had lost control of her neck. In a faint voice she said something about, '. . . the Ideal Home Exhibition in 1937.'

Sue took her hand. 'What about it, darling?'

'Artificial lake in the middle of Olympia. Couldn't have been more than four feet deep. Five. So silly. Got on to one of their floating stands and – ' she put her hand over her eyes – 'dizzy. Like this.'

Gwen said, 'Do you want to be sick?'

'Wouldn't dream of it.'

'Have you had your pill?'

Kay said, 'It may be the pills that are causing it. What do you think, Jo? You're the nurse.'

'That's a bit of an exaggeration. Fresh air will probably do the trick.' I tried to open a port hole but it was stuck.

Sandy came striding to the rescue with his we're-all-right-the-Navy's-here air. He did look capable and gorgeous in that uniform, as if, having won a war, he could cure a sick mother with his eyes shut. From other directions Kennington and Rutherford hurried across in their morning suits. 'What's going on?'

'Your mother's not feeling very well.'

Sandy said, 'She'll have to take more water with it another time.'

Kennington said, 'Snap out of it, Ma. You'll miss Sandringham's speech.'

'I know, dear. I'm sorry to be a drip.'

I said, 'I think we should get her outside.'

'Hear that, Ma? Nymphs-and-shepherds thinks you should be thrown in the river.'

'Probably the best thing for me.'

'Can you walk?'

'I don't think I can. Oh dear.'

I pushed back Sandy's gold-braided cuffs, got hold of his wrists and made our four hands into a chair lift. Rutherford, Kennington and Humphrey helped to load their mother aboard.

She was light. We carried her with ease, up the steep steps to the sunlight and the crisp autumn air that would surely revive her. And if it did not – if this were the beginning of her dying, as I had an odd feeling that it might be – would he remember and be grateful for the time I helped him bear up his mother? Would he keep it in mind if the time ever came for him to judge me? Her bony old bottom pressed into the backs of my hands and his hands. We clutched each other's wrists under the withered passageway through which he had entered the world. Her head was lolling against my shoulder. *Why not his?* I wondered.

On deck, Miranda sat on a bench with her back to us, holding court to three young de Salis boys. Sandy shouted, 'Off there,

Miranda! Let's have some space for Grandma.' She turned. Her face looked peculiar. At first I thought she was just shocked at the spectacle we made. Then I realised that it wasn't Miranda at all, it was Rutherford's granddaughter Felicity, wearing Miranda's dress.

87

We laid Grandma Toms on the bench. Taking my hand away from under her thighs, I found it was damp with urine. I saw shame and horror in her old eyes, and then I saw nothing at all in them.

She passed out. I undid her collar and her belt and checked that she wasn't wearing any sort of tight corset. She was thin as a rail, but you never knew with these stupid old people. I got hold of her jaw, put two fingers into her dribbling mouth, unhooked her dentures and removed them. Her face collapsed, her skull showed.

Sandy was wiping his hand on a hanky as he watched me. His expression was impassive. He seemed unable to move. He left everything to me. He was in shock.

I pointed at his hanky. 'Give me that.' He handed it over without a word. It smelt of an old woman's wee-wee but I wrapped the dentures in it. It would have been indecent to leave them grinning on the bench next to her, unwrapped. I had a feeling it would be some time before she would wear them again. In the meantime they could be given a jolly good scrub by some Friend of whatever hospital she ended up in.

I tried to hand Sandy the little cloth parcel of his mother's teeth, but he said, 'Why the bloody hell has Felicity got Miranda's dress on?'

'Never mind that, we need an ambulance.' Grandma Toms' breathing had a harsh, squeaky sound, like the teeth of a blunt saw trying to make headway through damp wood. I lifted her left eyelid, then her right. Delicate as tissue paper, they felt as if they might tear. Her wide pupils were as eerie as black moons, bottled up inside other moons. 'An *ambulance*, Sandy. Say it might be a stroke, but that's just the opinion of a person who's not medically qualified.'

He seemed relieved to have something to do. He met his brothers and they had a solemn confab before going to the phone together, shoulder to shoulder like bodyguards round an American president. You couldn't tell who was president and who bodyguard. I remembered how they had looked at Christine's funeral, alike and yet not like each other, more like somebody else who was not any of them.

Kay, Sue and Gwen said, 'What can we do?'

'Get rid of these.'

Gwen put the wrapped teeth in her handbag and said, 'You are marvellous, Jo. With your nursing background – '

'My what?'

Guests were starting to crowd up the steps. It was a bit of a shock to see Janet in white. I had forgotten about her getting married. Mummy was preening herself and elbowing her way to the forefront. You could almost see headlines in her eyes. *Grandma Toms is fallen, long live Gran Woolgar!* I said to Kay, Gwen and Sue, 'Tell them Sandy's got everything under control and they're to go back and enjoy themselves.' By the time they had done that, the ambulance had arrived.

Sandy, Rutherford, Kennington and Humphrey escorted the ambulance men to their mother's side. The brothers were their old irreverent selves again. 'She's faking,' they said. 'You can see she's faking. Come on, Ma, you'll miss the speeches.'

'Probably wants to miss 'em. Not daft, either.'

The ambulance men unrolled their stretcher and said, 'What happened, sir?' I explained, though probably not very clearly or helpfully. As they carried Grandma off, we had a quick consultation as to who should go with her. Sue was chosen. She took the teeth. She promised to report back as soon as there was any news, so that seemed to be the end of that. We had done all we could. We went back down to the saloon for the speeches.

Sandy got out his notes and said quietly to me, 'I think the keynote is thanks for your concern but she's an old lady and life goes on, don't you?'

'I agree with you.'

It could have been awkward, but I thought he handled his toast to the bride and groom awfully well. It was probably his naval training.

Godfrey took his cue from Sandy and was brief, charming and to the point as he toasted the bridesmaids.

'Last but not least, Miranda,' he said. 'Miranda and I haven't always seen eye-to-eye on all matters, have we, Miranda? But I've enjoyed this afternoon's truce just as much as I know I'm going to enjoy crossing swords with you again when it ends.'

I looked to see if she were accepting the tribute in the generous spirit in which it had been offered.

What I saw was not promising. Whatever masquerade had been going on earlier in the afternoon – with her and Felicity swapping clothes – was now over, and Miranda was back to normal. Which was to say she had on her pretty frock of floral print and an expression which ranged between thinly disguised pity for Janet and undisguised contempt for Godfrey.

'Ladies and gentlemen,' he said, 'please raise your glasses to the bridesmaids!' Miranda muttered something behind her hand to Felicity and the two of them smirked. I resolved to speak to Miranda at the first opportunity. A joke was a joke but you could not exist in a state of permanent warfare with your own brother-in-law just because he was a Conservative and you were a radical feminist or whatever Miranda was calling herself these days.

By a stroke of luck I seemed to have hit on the right diagnosis: the doctors at the hospital said that Grandma Toms had suffered a massive haemorrhage to the left side of her brain.

Sue phoned round the family on Sunday morning with the latest bulletin. Grandma had been unconscious all night, but she had just opened her eyes and taken a little liquid.

I said, 'Is her speech affected?'

'Everything's affected, Jo. She can't move at all down her right side.'

'What do they, er, say?'

'Her heart's strong. She's not in any immediate danger. But it's too early to know whether she'll get her speech back, or any other movement.'

'Doesn't sound too good,' said Sandy when I told him.

'Oh come, come, don't get down in the dumps. It could be a lot worse.'

'Could it? How?'

'She could be dead.'

'Might be the best thing,' he said.

'Don't say that!'

'For her, I mean. What a life, eh? Imagine being a Toms and not being able to talk . . .' I was pleased that he was able to see the funny side, and to encourage him I laughed. He went on, 'Having to have everything done for you.'

'Oh yes, I know how much you Toms's hate that.'

'Why do you seem to think that if you laugh in that irritating way of yours when you make bitchy comments about my family, they don't count as bitchy?'

'Sorry. You're worried, I know.'

'I think we should all be worried,' he said. 'There's more and more of this sort of thing with our wonderful socialist National Health that we pay into all our lives. They don't keep paralysed old women in hospital indefinitely, and who's going to look after her?'

88

Godfrey had suggested that the honeymoon be restricted to spending Saturday night in a swish London hotel, so that on Sunday they could get back to their Glasgow constituency for the last few days of the election campaign. Janet had agreed with him.

So it was a bit of a shock when she turned up on Monday night in Bleswick. She arrived out of the blue, shortly before midnight, shortly after Sandy, who had been at a function.

He was in the kitchen. He was supposed to be getting ready for bed but this was as far as he had got. I was just wondering if he were making himself one of his outlandish midnight snacks, and whether it might be quicker in the long run for me to go and do it for him when the doorbell went. He gave no sign of hearing it so I ran down the stairs in my pyjamas and dressing gown.

'Goodness! It's Mrs Godfrey de Salis!'

'Hello, Mummy. Can I come in?'

'As if you had to ask! Where's your gorgeous husband?'

She did not reply, so we went to look for mine.

He was sitting in his big pine armchair with his head and arms slumped across the table. Around him were dirty plates, a broken cup and a tube of glue, a shopping list pad with my doodles on it, a final demand, toothpicks, and (for some reason) a packet of paper-chains, all the dull old flotsam and jetsam of my day.

In spite of being so tired, he raised his head. His hair was in his eyes. His voice was slurred. 'Good God. Janet. Left him already? What did the bounder do to my little girl?'

She was tired too, and sharp tongued, which was unusual for her. 'Shut up, Daddy.'

He looked hurt. 'Only asked.' He looked down at his chest. One of his buttons was undone, showing part of the lovely golden fleece of his chest hairs, and his tie had come loose. I had often thought what horrible uncomfortable things tight ties must be. He talked to himself. 'Close trap, Toms. Keep trap closed. Best thing.'

'I agree with you.' My tone was half severe, half laughing. I guessed he had possibly had one or two drinks, which, even if they had made him funny and amenable, obviously hadn't done much for his tact. 'What's wrong, Janet?'

'This.' She got out a newspaper cutting.

> 'LITTLE MISS MILITANT!
>
> 'An exciting moment for Miss Miranda Toms (above) as she meets her idol, Cyril Rathbone of the rock group the Dole Busters at a pro-abortion rally in Trafalgar Square last Saturday.
>
> 'Meanwhile, Militant Miranda's elder sister Janet was getting married to the Tory candidate for the Arrancraig district of Glasgow, Mr Godfrey de Salis, 31.
>
> 'Mr de Salis is well-known for his anti-abortion and anti-women's lib views, but, says Miranda, "We still manage to be good friends. He's marrying my sister, after all."
>
> 'At Miranda's request, the Dole Busters sent a special wedding day message from the rally to Mr de Salis by playing their smash hit single, "Don't wanna lock up my woman".'

My spine seemed to have turned into an icicle – cold, painfully sharp, and disintegrating before the heat of my anguish.

I had failed. I had lost. The precise thing that I had promised Janet would not happen had happened. I had not kept my word. Now I would be punished. The final irony. I had given life to Janet, and she was about to destroy me.

I needed to plead with her.

I needed to get her alone.

How?

Sandy peered at the cutting as if he were having difficulty focussing his eyes. In a voice full of wondering indignation he said, 'The little cow. So that's what she was up to.'

Janet said, 'You *knew*?'

'Knew she was cooking up something.'

'Why didn't you stop her?'

'Because,' said Sandy righteously, 'my poor old mother was practically dropping dead at the time.'

'Daddy was looking after her, Janet.'

She nodded and sighed and sat down.

I said, 'You and Godfrey haven't – ' I dared not say *parted* 'quarrelled over this, have you?'

'He's been very decent about it. He doesn't blame me. But it's an embarrassment and I want to know why it happened.'

'We'll bloody well find out,' said Sandy. He hauled himself upright and lumbered to the door. '*Miranda!*'

Yes I thought in panic. *Blame Miranda. Punish Miranda.* But Janet seemed to change her mind. She took the door handle out of his hand, closed the door, put her arm round his shoulder and escorted him back to his chair.

In her hands, he was meek. She said, 'Leave Miranda for now. There's something I want to sort out with you two. Something I want to get into the open.'

'No!' I said. 'No! Get Miranda! Get her down here!' She would be a distraction at least. She would be a change of subject. She would give me time to think. 'It's her fault. Let's hear what she has to say for herself!'

Janet said, 'Quiet, Mummy,' and I saw why Godfrey had married her. She would be marvellous at dealing with demented constituents, and chairing committees. She said, 'I want to say something that you both know, but neither of you knows the other knows, or rather one of you doesn't know that the other doesn't know that – you see how *complicated* it is? And it's quite unnecessary. Pam MacLeish lives in London. She's got a flat in West Hampstead. I've been there, Daddy's been there. We're friends. All right? I've said it within the hearing of both of you, and the ceiling has not fallen in.

'Now, Daddy, I know you didn't want Mummy to know because you thought Pam would remind her of Christine and that would upset her. But I told Mummy by mistake. And she didn't want *you* to know that *she* knew because *she* thought that *you* would be upset. So I did a deal with her that I wouldn't tell you if she wouldn't speak at the rally, and that would save Godfrey from being upset. Wheels within wheels within wheels.

'We're supposed to be the ones with the honourable hearts, but we've got all these secrets. And it doesn't even work because the best laid plans *et cetera et cetera* and Miranda does a thing like this. If Miranda's going to go around making a spectacle of herself in the women's lib movement, and turning my husband into a laughing stock, we're all going to be reminded of Christine whether we want to be or not, because we all know that those are exactly the sorts of things *she* would be doing.

'I've travelled all the way from Glasgow today so that I can say two things to you personally. One, could you *please* stop Miranda doing things like this, at least until she's old enough to know what she's talking about. And two, Pam is not a ghost from the past or a harbinger of misfortune, she's a perfectly nice and normal person and it's ridiculous if being friends with her has to be treated as some sort of crime.' Janet smiled tiredly. 'Here endeth my speech.'

In the long silence Sandy hauled himself once more to his feet. '*Miranda!*'

I said wearily, 'Don't, Sandy. It's too late.'

'I don't give a toss how late it is. MIRANDA!'

Janet said, 'Daddy. Perhaps in the morning.'

'Morning be damned.' He was furious. 'Important enough for you to come all this way. Important enough to find out what the hell that little bitch thinks she's – *Miranda!*'

Miranda called sleepily, 'What?'

'Get down here.'

'What for?'

'Or I'll come and get you.'

'Do I have to, Mum?'

'Do as Daddy says. Put on your dressing gown and slippers.'

Janet was saying, 'Look, Daddy, I honestly think it would be better if you wait until you're not so – '

'Not so what?'

'Tired.'

Miranda appeared in the doorway, yawning. Her face lit up. 'Oh hello, Janet.'

'You haven't said hello to Daddy,' I reminded her.

'Hello.'

'I'll give you hello. What is your explanation for this?'

He showed her the cutting. She went pink as she read it. She said, 'It's not true.'

'It's an impostor, is it? Perhaps it's Felicity. Whose father is going to be informed, I might add.'

I said, 'Miranda, you might as well tell the truth or you'll only make things worse for yourself.'

'They're the ones who aren't telling the truth!' She pointed at the cutting. '"We still manage to be friends". As if I'd say that! That's crap!'

He grabbed her. She fought but he managed to give her three quick slaps on her backside. It was the best place, with its nice thick coating of flesh and no delicate organs nearby to be damaged. She screamed, 'I hate you, I hate you,' but she was only putting it on. The blows were little more than taps. She could hardly feel them.

89

When the Convent of the Forty Martyrs saw the photograph of Miranda standing in front of a banner-sized cartoon of a nun and a priest, and the slogan IF YOU DON'T PLAY THE GAME, DON'T MAKE THE RULES, they asked us to find her another school. I couldn't say I was surprised. Roman Catholics took themselves so seriously.

I thought Sandy might punish Miranda again, but he was too busy punishing me. 'I have been protecting you from knowing. But now that you've found out – ' he made it sound as if it were my fault. As if I had been listening at keyholes, sniffing through his pockets, inspecting his underwear. I had been doing the opposite. I was doing the opposite now. Walking away from keyholes, averting my eyes as I sorted the laundry, not seeing, not hearing. But he insisted that I hear. 'I have a car,' he said.

'What? *What?*'

'It's a Rover.'

'I don't give a damn what it is.'

'I keep it at the office. Or at Pam's.'

'You can't drive.'

'I can. She taught me. It seemed kinder not to tell you. You'd only have worried. And you preferred your bike.'

'Yes.'

'No point in keeping it secret any longer, though,' he said. 'We'll need to be popping down to Salthaven a lot. Fact, you might like to learn yourself.'

'Yes, I might.'

'Pam's offered to be on the rota,' he said. 'She helped look after her own father.'

'How marvellous of her!'

'Don't be bitter, Jo. It doesn't help the situation.'

'What *is* the situation? Are you saying you don't love me any more?'

'Yes, Jo.' There was ambiguity in his answer. I clung to it but he clarified. 'I am saying that I don't love you any more.'

Any more. Some hope, then. 'You loved me once?'

'Once, yes.' He seemed as relieved to be able to give me that as I was to receive it. One good thing about loving a man who could only tell the truth was that you always knew exactly where you were.

He said, 'I am going to leave you and start a new life with Pam. We have to be sensible about this. You have to start making sensible plans.'

'I made a sensible plan thirty years ago, Sandy. I got up in a church full of people and promised to stick to it.'

'That was another era.'

'Not for me. Not for Janet. I didn't hear anything about other eras last Saturday when you were all dressed up like Lord Muck – pardon me, Lieutenant Commander Muck – *giving your daughter away*!'

'Probably not too late for you to go back to nursing,' he said.

'What? What?'

'Properly, I mean. Once Ma's . . . Once that situation's sorted itself out. They're crying out for people, and you've had the experience. Give yourself a bit of independence.'

I remembered Lindsay Bixwell saying the same thing. I said to Sandy what I had said to her. 'I don't want independence.'

'You're "emphasising" again, Jo.'

'I'm not, I'm shouting.'

'It's one of the things I dislike about you. Your aggressive voice.'

To me it did not sound aggressive, just lonely, in our empty house.

Miranda was at the Bixwells, helping Lindsay with the dogs. Janet was married. Was marriage a place? People spoke as if it were. *Where's your daugher these days? She's married.* What sort of place was it? *What does she do? Oh, she's married.* As if the one were the answer to the other. It would have been, once.

By now our house should be empty – and our lives full. Other couples who married and risked and went without in the war, and contributed babies to the post-war bulge, now had themselves to themselves, each other to themselves. They were taking up new interests, looking forward to retirement, making their plans to sail round their worlds. He said, 'There are special courses for women in your position.'

'Special courses? For women about to be ditched?'

'I mean special hours so that you'll be in when Miranda gets home.'

'What about Miranda?'

'Miranda's interests,' he replied, slowly and deliberately, 'are of paramount importance. She is entitled to grow up in a normal, stable home.'

'I agree with you. So what?'

'I shall not be leaving you – '

I gasped, I waited.

' – until she is sixteen.'

My gasp became wild laughter. Miranda wouldn't be sixteen until 1980.

'I've explained this to Pam,' he said. 'She doesn't like it, but she accepts it and is prepared to wait for me.'

I noted the hint of conflict between them. I noted hope.

I had lots of hope. Buckets and buckets full of it. I had experience. I was an experienced married woman. I was a mother. I had Miranda. He didn't want me – he *thought* he didn't – but for Miranda he would stay. Not for my sake but for hers he was giving me a five and half year reprieve . . . A stay of execution, during which time the execution might be called off. He was giving me until the eighties.

Miranda

90

Godfrey phoned from the hospital to say that Janet had had a little girl and the two of them were fine. Mum took the call; Dad was in a coma, watching an assessment of Margaret Thatcher's first year as Prime Minister and who could blame him?

Mum woke him up, shouting, 'Oy! Grandpa. It's a girl.'

He muttered, 'Better luck next time.'

'Ooh!' she tittered. 'Did you hear that, Miranda?'

'No.'

Of course I had heard it. It was said for my benefit. At sixteen I was the second favourite spectator sport of the men in my family, after rugby. My dad, my uncles, my male cousins and my brother-in-law went out of their way to make gratuitous sexist comments. (Not that they needed to go too far out of their way, mind you.) They did it to see how I would react. I tried not to, but my mum always said, *Ooh! Did you hear that, Miranda?* and *Now there'll be fireworks!*

The new grandmother hugged the new grandfather, and then the new grandfather went back to sleep. For me it was a solemn moment and the beginning of a lifetime's responsibility. How was I going to protect my new niece from the awful lumbering patriarchal juggernaut that was her extended family?

Janet and Godfrey decided to call her Margaret. I suppose I shouldn't really have been surprised.

When notification reached us that Janet and Margaret were home from hospital, Mum packed her bags and set off to Cheltenham for a couple of weeks, to be a tower of strength and take over the housework. Well, you couldn't expect Godfrey to take it over, could you? He was a busy man with a country to run.

This left me with the choice of staying at home alone with my dad, or going to Penny's. Naturally I went to Penny's. Penny was my best friend and blood sister. We had mingled our blood in a dish and sworn eternal fidelity to each other and to the cause of women. I won't tell you what kind of blood we used. Another good thing about Penny was her brother Louis.

Louis was seventeen and weird. He had very short hair and very long legs. He wore big round glasses held together with Blue-Tack and huge boots that always seemed to be covered with mud, which was funny because he never went anywhere muddy. He generally looked as if he had been put together out of old bicycle parts. He was the sort of bloke who you'd take one look at in a train carriage and pull the emergency cord right away, just to be on the safe side.

You'd be wrong, though. Louis wouldn't have hurt you. He was more interested in telephones. He was obsessed with telephones; also computers. He got as worked up about computers as I wished he would get about me. He kept one in his bedroom. He stared at it and fingered it for hours.

He kept getting the sack from Youth Opportunities for using the phone. He once told me a whole string of numbers to dial if I wanted to get through to Australia for 5p. When I said I didn't know anyone in Australia he gave me some other numbers which I could use to make local calls free. He made me swear not to write them down because if the GPO found out that I was using them I could get life imprisonment, and so could he, for aiding and abetting.

I nearly said I wouldn't mind as long as we could be in the same cell, but I held it back. I wasn't sure how he would react to me making the first move.

It wasn't that he was unliberated, he'd have a fat chance of that with Penny for a sister and Brenda for a mother, but I had a feeling he might be shy and easily scared off. Just because we were equals, it didn't mean I had to behave like a sexual and emotional blunderbuss. On the contrary, I was determined to be a tender and considerate lover.

I was eating my California Revival and having a gloomy discussion with Penny and Louis over how we could possibly persuade Janet and Godfrey to change the poor little thing's name, when in came

Brenda with the morning post. Most of it was computer magazines, but there was some normal post as well. 'One for you, Miranda,' she said. 'And one for me.'

I wasn't expecting post. Nobody knew I was here. And I certainly wasn't expecting a letter from my dad. I was only three streets away from home, and letter writing was strictly women's work.

This was a special occasion. In his own personal handwriting on blue Basildon Bond he had written:

> 'Dearest Miranda,
>
> 'I have 'opped it, as they say. Gone, flitted. Your old dad has done a bunk.
>
> 'You won't need telling that things have been pretty bad between me and Mummy over the past couple of years or so. And I don't think it'll come as too much of a surprise that Pam and I are very much in love. We have decided to share a life together before I get wheeled off into the old folks' home.
>
> 'Mummy and you are provided for. She'll need a bit of propping up over the next month or so until she admits to herself how lucky she is! Prop her up if you can. I am leaving her but I am not leaving you, I'll be in touch once the dust has settled, and Pam and I look forward to inviting you to our new home.
>
> 'Lots of love,
>
> 'Da.'

I focussed and refocussed. *Da?* What was *Da*?

I had never called him *Da*, unless it was when I was six months old and had the good sense to spit rusks at him.

If he thought his name was Da, where the hell did he think he was going, and why was he telling me to look after Mummy? People whose names were Da and Mummy should be looking after me.

Perhaps he had simply got bored with writing the word, as he seemed sometimes to get bored with speaking. Particularly when he was drunk, he would abandon sentences half way through, and say, '*Et cetera, cetera, cetera,*' or even just, 'Dum-de-dum,' and leave you to work out what he meant.

A million miles away, through a sort of mist, Penny's mother Brenda was saying, 'Miranda – '

'It's from Da,' I said.

Perhaps he had meant to write *Daddy* or *Dad* but somebody had knifed him in mid-word. *Lots of love Da – aaaaaargh!*

Brenda was saying, 'Just like that, eh?'

What was she talking about? I hadn't told anyone yet.

She had a letter too, on the same sort of paper.

She said, 'I'll show you mine if you show me yours.'

We swapped.

> 'Dear Brenda,
>
> 'I'm afraid that after a number of stormy years, Jo and I have reached the end of the road and have decided to make a clean break. Call me a fool at my age, but I am going to have a try at starting a new life with Pam MacLeish, a friend of our family whom you may have met and who has recently become a bit more than a friend.
>
> 'Miranda will probably be rather upset, though not (I console myself) unduly shocked. I fear she has been well-placed to witness the death throes of her parents' marriage.
>
> 'If you can mop her up a bit and hang on to her until Jo gets back from Cheltenham, I shall be eternally grateful.
>
> 'Many thanks,
>
> 'Cheers,
>
> 'Sandringham Toms.'

Brenda said, 'I love his timing.'

Penny said, 'What's going on?'

'My dad's left home.'

'Alleluia.'

Brenda said, 'Penny, *shut up*.'

'It's alleluia for me too,' I said.

'Maybe. I bet it's not for your poor mum. Do you want to phone her?'

The phone rang on her words. Brenda picked it up. 'Hello, Janet,' she said, as if everything were normal. 'Congratulations. How are you? How's little Maggie? Margaret, sorry. Yes, she is.'

Brenda handed me the phone and ushered Penny and Louis out of the room.

'Miranda?' Janet's voice sounded tense. I could hear the baby crying. 'Have you had a letter from Daddy?'

'Yes. Have you?'

'Where is he?'

'How should I know?'

'You've got to find him,' said Janet. 'He can't do this.'

'What am I supposed to do?'

'What am *I* supposed to do? I've got a baby to look after.'

'I know.' I was wondering whether all new babies made that heart rending, agonised, wailing noise that sounded as if they were being tortured and set my teeth on edge. 'I can hear her crying.'

'That's not Margaret,' Janet said. 'That's Mummy.'

Mum came on the line, sobbing. 'Miranda?'

'Yes? Hello?'

'It's a joke, darling. You're not to worry. Daddy's joking.' She tried desperately to laugh. The laugh rose and fell to the rhythm of tears. Her tone became coaxing. 'Pop round on your way to school.'

She might have been asking me to fetch a lost cardigan. 'What for?'

She wept. 'Tell him to change his mind!' The sound of her beseeching was hardly human. It was the wail of a run-over dog. I wanted to cry myself, but only because she was crying. She was in so much pain that I wanted to share it; but I was over the moon at the news, so how could I?

91

Penny was putting on her blazer. She gave me an embarrassed look and said, 'Coming?'

'Where?'

'School.'

'Oh, that.'

Brenda said with concern in her voice, 'Do you want to go to school today, Miranda?'

'I don't know.' I felt rather peculiar. Not ill, exactly; just vague.

Brenda said, 'I'll send a note. Tell them what's happened.'

'I want to go home.'

'Now?'

'Yes.'

'For good?'

'I don't know.'

Penny said, 'It's half past eight and it's French.'

'*Allez-vous en*, then,' I told her.

Brenda said, 'Do you want someone to go with you?'

'I'll be all right.' I knew she had to get to work. I put on my blazer and took my Adidas bag so that I could go to school afterwards. *After what* I wasn't sure.

Louis said shyly, 'Shall I come?'

I didn't know if I wanted him to or not. I didn't know what to expect: the house like a tip, or stripped bare; Dad in it, or about to depart, or lying back in an armchair laughing. 'Ever been 'ad?' Perhaps Mum was right, and it was a joke.

Mum was not right. It was not a joke. It was practically unheard of for him to write two letters. He meant to go all right. If he hadn't gone yet, would I try and stop him? I ought to, for Mum's sake. I didn't know if there would be a scene, or, if so, what kind. I didn't know what I expected, or wanted. I stalled. 'Aren't you going to work?'

'Got the day off,' said Louis.

'Oh yeah?' said his mother.

He put on his greasy green anorak and we set off. His feet in his enormous boots clomped supportively on the pavement beside my school casuals. At the pelican crossing he made me wait for the green man to flash. 'No point in killing yourself.'

'You can say that again. This is the start of a new life.'

'Think he means it?'

'Bloody well hope so.'

'Your mum won't say that.'

'That's what's so lousy.' The thought of her sorrow and shock and whole predicament made me feel sick with bitterness. 'She's fifty-five now. I mean, he can swan off, but it's a bit late for a woman to start a new life, isn't it? If she'd known a few years ago that this was going to happen she could have gone back to nursing or something.'

'Any wife of mine will have her own career. Who is Pam anyway?'

'Friend of my parents. She helped look after my grandma when she was dying.'

'How long ago was that?'

'About six years.'

'And d'you think that's when she and your dad – ?'

'Six years ago? Don't be daft, Louis. He'd never have got away with it for that long. My mother's not that stupid.'

I saw at once that the car had gone.

That was another thing that happened six years ago, apart from both my grandmothers dying and Janet getting married: out of the blue, Dad had passed his driving test and come home in a dark grey Rover. I didn't even know he was having lessons.

The car had some uses, most notably when he drove me over to Lindsay's to help with the puppies, but most of the time it gave us nothing but trouble. It put him in complete charge of where the family went, and not only that, he drove when he was drunk.

Mum always denied this, but she had lessons herself to save him from being breathalysed. Everything she did, she did for him, and now he had left her.

I shivered to remember something else about the car, something that had happened a year ago. He was driving off somewhere and she was trying to stop him. I watched from the window as she wept and pleaded with him and tried to snatch the ignition keys.

I remembered her red, desperate face. She was beside herself. 'Please don't go, darling, please, please, please.' He started the car. She held the door handle, ran with it. She fell in the gutter. He zoomed off. I went to her. I said, 'Mum, what's the matter?'

She said, 'Daddy and I were playing.' She limped home and put a dressing on her knee. She wouldn't let me help.

At the time I didn't understand. But now I thought perhaps I did. Perhaps he was going to an assignation with Pam, and perhaps Mum knew.

Was it possible that she had known for as long as a year? She might have started to suspect. I thought miserably of her being burdened with that knowledge, that suspicion. She had been alone with it. Why hadn't she told me?

Had she thought that I would be no help, hating Dad as I did? I did sometimes wish that I could love him, not for his sake but for hers. She loved him and I loved her, so I ought at least to be able to like him.

I opened the front door with my key. I called, 'Hello? Dad?'

There was no reply, so I prowled around. Louis walked a few steps behind me, like Denis.

On a scale of one to ten, the state of the house was five or six. Mum had done one of her blitzes before going off to be a tower of strength, so it had been pretty terrible then; but Dad had taken a lot of junk away with him. There were no sails in the hall, rugby magazines in the loo or framed photographs of naval engagements on the sitting room walls. In his den he had emptied his desk, including his pornography drawer. In the bedroom, his wardrobe was empty and the bed was made.

I wondered who by. And were the sheets clean?

I burst out, 'How *can* she?'

Louis said, 'How can who what?'

'Pam. Go off with *him*. He's nearly *sixty*.'

'How old is she?'

'In her forties, but she's still quite attractive.'

'He's probably her father substitute.'

'Ugh.'

I looked in the linen basket. He had even taken his dirty underwear. 'She's a *feminist*,' I said. 'Well, I thought she was.' But why had I thought that? Wishful thinking, probably. I didn't even know her all that well. When she came to our house she tended to involve herself in activities that left me stone cold, such as rugby matches, sailing trips and boozy do's with the Toms uncles and aunts. 'She was always capping his jokes and telling him where to get off.'

Louis said, 'Flirting, probably. Putting up a smokescreen.'

'Ugh.' The sound was all the more disgusted because I thought he was probably right. 'To hear Dad talk, you'd think he hated women like Pam. Far as he's concerned, any woman who can hold a job down is a formidable, castrating bitch by definition. Maybe that's a smokescreen too.'

'Wouldn't be the first time,' Louis said. 'And Pam wouldn't be the first woman to – '

'To what?'

He looked down at me from his skinny height, like an immense strange fruit on a tall, bendy tree. 'Pretend to be a feminist but secretly want a man with machismo. Say all the right things, but despise wimps.'

I said shortly, 'I never say "wimp".'

'You think it though.' He stopped being a fruit on a tree and bent towards me like a sad-eyed bullock. 'You think I'm a wimp.'

'I do not! I just think you're not interested.'

'Try me.' He held out his arms.

92

Anyone who thought Louis was a wimp – or even that he wasn't interested – was in for a big surprise. He practically raped me.

No he didn't. I shouldn't use that word lightly. I wanted it. You'd better believe I wanted it. But he was a bit quick and I wasn't ready.

I had been planning to seduce him over a period of weeks. Days, anyway. Getting him used to the idea, bit by bit. In the meantime, I was supposed to be stretching my hymen – getting *it* used to the idea – by sticking extra fingers in when I masturbated. But I hadn't got around to it. The old family vice of procrastination had me in its grip.

To cut a short story even shorter, I found it quite exciting but I didn't come or anything, and there was blood on the skirt of my school dress and also on the counterpane of my parents' bed.

Louis took his glasses off, mopped his brow and said, 'Oh, Christ, Miranda, I'm sorry.'

'I'm not.'

'What if something happens?'

'Something just did. Didn't you notice?'

'Get up and jump about.'

'Eh?'

'Then it'll all run out of you.'

'I want a cuddle. I'll be embittered against men for life if you don't cuddle me.'

He folded me in his lanky arms. I took his shirt off, followed by his vest. His flesh had a yellowish tinge, like the stem of a plant grown in a cupboard. His shoulders were covered in tiny white scars as if he had once been spotty. I couldn't make up my mind whether the earthy smell was an expensive macho deodorant, a friendly sort of BO or something to do with computers. He said into my ear, 'I want you to be embittered against men, apart from me.'

'Have you fancied me for long?'

'All my life.'

'Liar.'

'What about you fancying me?'

I said, 'What makes you think I do?'

'You've got your hand on my prick.'

He was so serious normally, it turned me on to hear him using a word like *prick*. I said, 'Have you done this before?'

'What do you think?'

He wouldn't tell me so I wouldn't either, only in my case he could probably work it out from the blood. It was only half past nine in the morning but we shared a can of lager to celebrate.

We lay on the bed drinking. Louis tightened my fist round his cock. It was like holding a tiny, long balloon while somebody blew it up.

The phone rang. He murmured, 'Don't answer,' and I shouldn't have.

'Miranda, this is Mummy.' Her voice had the ghastly brightness of sun on new snow. I froze.

'Hello, Mum.'

'Could I speak to Daddy?'

I let go of Louis' prick at once. 'He's not here.'

'Tell him the joke's over and we all think it's jolly witty but now I'd like a word.'

'Why do you think Dad's here, Mum?' This was as much for Louis' benefit as anything else. I had never seen anyone move so fast. He jumped off the bed and pulled his trousers up.

Mum said, 'Where else would Daddy be?'

It was funny and then it wasn't funny any more. She said, 'He's not at the office. They say he's on holiday, but I told them they were quite wrong, we're not due to go on holiday until August. Allow me to know, I said.' The grief in her voice went straight to my heart. I tried to feel her humiliation, her despair, to take some of the burden off her, but I was too happy, starting out on my long life of love, just as love left her bereft. I was too selfish.

I said, 'I've been all round the house, I haven't seen him.'

'He's probably just popped out.'

In as gentle a voice as I could manage, I said, 'He doesn't live here any more. All his things are gone.'

'They'll turn up.'

'Mum. How long . . . has it been going on? Dad and Pam?'

'No time at all,' she said briskly. 'Nine-day wonder.'

I was late for school, but nobody said anything until after break, when I got a message to go to the headmaster's study. He wasn't there. In his place was a Black man of about thirty with a roll-neck shirt and very short hair.

I had never seen him before, but that wasn't particularly significant. Bleswick Comprehensive was so huge that you never knew anybody, unless you chose to get to know them; and nobody knew your business unless you chose to tell it. This was better than the convent, where you were constantly under surveillance by some nun or statue or crucifix.

He said in a posh voice, 'I'm Malcolm Hilaire, the school counsellor.' He was making a big deal about not sitting at the headmaster's desk. He was sitting on his chair but he had moved it round to thc side. 'Do you know what a counsellor is?'

'I know we've got one, sir.'

'You don't have to call me sir. Call me Malcolm.'

I shrugged and wondered whether he fancied me. I quite fancied him. He said, 'I thought we could have a little chat. I hear you've had some rather upsetting news.'

'No.'

He looked puzzled. 'About your father?'

'That? I'm not upset, I'm celebrating.' *And how*, I thought, wriggling my tingling fanny on the seat. 'How did you know?'

'He's written to the Head.'

'Wish I had shares in Basildon Bond.'

'It's useful for the staff to know,' said Malcolm Hilaire, 'if you've had some kind of upset at home.' He was earnest and well-meaning but he had something wrong with his ears. He obviously hadn't heard me when I said I wasn't upset.

'Can I see the letter, sir?'

'It's private to the Head.'

'Have you seen it?'

He wouldn't answer so I knew he had. I said, 'Have you or haven't you?' I guessed I had a reasonable amount of leeway for cheeking him and it was good practice for when I became a barrister.

He thought a bit, shrugged and handed the letter over.

> 'Dear Mr Lees,
>
> 'You will probably hear about this from other sources, but I thought it best to inform you myself.
>
> 'My wife and I have reached a point in our relationship at which separation is the only course open to us. It is a symptom of the troubled times in which we all live that you will not lack precedents for dealing with this sort of thing, in fact I understand that a substantial proportion of even very young pupils at your school are from what I believe are now known as "one-parent families" and that you are divorced yourself.
>
> 'I therefore leave Miranda confidently in your care . . .'

It was the usual self-justifying garbage but Malcolm Hilaire said, 'He seems very concerned about you.'

'Ha ha ha.'

'You don't believe him?'

'Look, sir. Malcolm. He's always made this big thing about telling the truth, but for things to go this far, he must have been lying to my mum for ages.'

'How long, do you think?'

'Don't know.' I felt furious with Dad for fooling us. 'But I'll find out.'

'And how is your mother taking the news?'

'She's shocked. She's staying at my sister's.'

'To get over it?'

'To be a tower of strength. My sister's just had a baby.'

Malcolm Hilaire looked relieved at being able to hear something nice. If he didn't like bad news, I wondered why he was doing this job. He said, 'What's the baby's name?'

'Margaret.'

'That's nice.'

People always say *That's nice* when you tell them the names of new babies. If I ever have a baby, I'm going to call it Snot or Carcinoma, just to see if anyone will be honest enough to say, *Ugh, horrible.*

'Will you be seeing your father?'

'Only if I don't shut my eyes in time.'

'You're very angry with him.' Malcolm's voice had a caressing quality. I wouldn't have minded a real caress from his nice black-and-pink hands (was his prick the same?) but the voice was embarrassing, put on.

'What about my mum? That's what I'd like to know.'

'You're probably feeling protective towards her, Miranda, but you don't have to take sides, you know.'

'There's only one side to take.'

'Why do you have to take any side?'

'I hate him. He's a male chauvinist. That's right, laugh.'

'I wasn't,' said Malcolm, who was smiling as if he thought male chauvinism was a bit regrettable but not serious enough to make a reasonable person hate their father.

I said with heavy sarcasm, 'Can I go now?'

'You're free to go any time you like. And to come back, if you want.'

'Thanks, sir. Malcolm.' I gave him the eye. 'See you.'

93

After school Louis was waiting for me. His long, weird, sensuous fingers were coiled round the wheel of a rusty green mini that looked as old as I was. 'Get in,' he said.

'As the actress said to the bishop.'

'Get in, Miranda.'

'Oh, very masterful.' He didn't laugh, so I obeyed. 'Where did you nick this from?'

'Borrowed it.'

'"My client borrowed it, your honour".' I opened the glove compartment, and found a supermarket bag of bite-size Mars Bars. 'Did you borrow these too?' I didn't wait for an answer, I started eating ravenously. I polished off two of the Mars Bars, then gripped one end of a third between my front teeth and tried to push the other end into his mouth.

'Miranda, lay off!'

'All right, all right. Where are we going?'

'To get you fixed up.'

'You did that this morning. Good and proper.' I kissed him. 'Good and improper.'

He said, 'We were very stupid.'

'Speak for yourself.'

He seemed to know where he was going. He parked in a seedy street and took me through a door marked 'Prudence Laburnum Youth Advisory Centre'.

I said, 'I bet this is where you come for your Intermediate Treatment.'

He was not amused. He got hold of my wrist and dragged me up a long flight of stairs towards a poster of a man with a gormless expression and a six-months-gone stomach. 'IF *YOU* WERE THE ONE WHO GOT PREGNANT, WOULDN'T YOU BE MORE CAREFUL?'

'See that, Lou?' I goosed him.

'Why do you think I've brought you here?'

We climbed three more flights and went through a pink door. The waiting room had pastel coloured walls with pop and reggae posters, a coffee machine and anti-smoking slogans over the ash trays. There was a huge picture of a hand with its fingers crossed. 'THERE ARE SEVEN RELIABLE METHODS OF BIRTH CONTROL. THIS ISN'T ONE OF THEM.'

A cassette recorder was playing 'Hit me with your rhythm stick'. About seven people were waiting, all girls, sitting on bean bags and foam sofas. They were all quite sharply dressed, and cast pitying glances at my school uniform.

There was one really scruffy girl, so I guessed she was a member of staff. She was wearing patched jeans, a cheesecloth top and odd socks. She changed the cassette to 'Sharin' the night together' by Dr Hook and the Medicine Men and said, 'Hi! My name's Kathy. Have you got an appointment? Doesn't matter if you haven't.'

Before I could speak, Louis said, 'Yes, we have. Louis Gilmour and Miranda Toms. We're seeing Dr Darcy at half past four. That's in a minute and a half.'

Kathy said, 'We're running late.'

Louis said, '*We're* not, we're on time.'

'How old are you, Miranda? We have to know because if you're under sixteen there may be legal complications. If you're sixteen or over, no probs.'

'I'm sixteen.'

'Thought so. Fantastic.'

We sat down. Louis looked at his watch and drummed his feet.

I said, 'Calm down.'

He said, 'It's urgent. What's the point in making an appointment if people who don't make them are allowed to push in?'

He was getting on my nerves so I ambled over to look at an exhibition of contraceptive methods.

The sign said 'PLEASE DO TOUCH!' otherwise I wouldn't have dared, it might have looked perverted to start fingering those weird bits of plastic and rubber. I had never seen them before, but I recognised a Dutch Cap, a Copper 7 and a neat little pill box with slots for each day of the week.

I knew all about it in theory. It was funny, this feeling that it had nothing to do with me.

I picked up what could have been a sausage skin. 'Hey, Lou. Is this what I think it is?' He looked as if I were about four and a great trial to him and he must have been mad to bring me on a grown-up outing.

The sausage skin made me giggle, like his car, or like Beatles music played on the Radio Bleswick Goldie Oldies hour. The other customers saw the funny side. I said, 'Hey, catch,' and we threw the thing around.

Instead of telling us off, Kathy seemed pleased that we were being so uninhibited. She wrinkled her nose. 'I don't know why they go on making them, really.'

One of the customers said, 'They give boys a chance to take a bit of responsibility.' She was glaring at Louis as she said this, and all the other girls nodded and glared too. He picked a copy of *Spare Rib* off the pile and skulked behind it.

I gave him an encouraging smile. He was a lot more responsible than I was. And he needn't worry that I would expect him to put one of those horrible sticky slimy things over his beautiful pink prick.

A dark, skinny curly-haired man of about twenty-five, wearing a T-shirt and tight Farahs over jutting hipbones said, 'Miranda Toms?'

Louis stood up. 'I'm coming with her.'

'I'd like to see Miranda on her own first,' said Farahs.

Any time, I thought, imagining those hard hipbones grinding into mine.

In a little green room, Farahs said, 'I'm Simon Darcy. Simon. I'm one of the doctors.'

He sounded surprised, and a bit embarrassed too, so I said, 'You can't help that,' and laughed, to put him at his ease.

'Er, no. Was that your boyfriend out there?'

'It was, yes. Still is, I hope.'

'Do you want him to come in with you? I always like to check with the girl first.'

'I don't mind.'

It was good with Louis there. He did all the talking, so I didn't have to worry about what words to use.

'Miranda and I had unprotected sexual intercourse this morning. Now we need post-coital contraception.'

'Oh right, fine, fantastic, no probs,' said Dr Darcy. I called him that to myself, I didn't want a doctor called Simon, though I wouldn't have minded a lover called Simon.

'When was your last period, Miranda?'

I sighed inside and worked out that it was two weeks ago and he said, 'Oh dear, gosh yes, you may have taken a little bit of a risk.'

He asked a few more questions and wrote me out a prescription. 'You take two a day for five days. They'll bring on your period and bob's your uncle.'

Louis said, 'What about side effects?'

Dr Darcy said, 'There may be a spot of queasiness, Miranda. Any probs, come back and see me. Come back anyway when you've finished the course, and we'll pop you on the pill, the proper pill. This Morning After Pill is strictly for emergencies, you don't want to have to go through this every time you make love, sex should be spontaneous and without regret, it's there for you to enjoy.'

He smiled into my eyes as he said this and I wondered if he fancied me. All day I had done nothing but fancy people. Boys in my class, boys not in my class, teachers, men walking past the school. I was looking at them with new eyes.

I felt like somebody who had never eaten a particular kind of food, fruit, perhaps, and then someone gave them an orange. The orange was so delicious that they couldn't wait to try apples, grapes, bananas, pomegranates.

94

In the nightmare I was running alone across a dark field. I was late for something. The wind stung my skin, but it wasn't hot or cold, just raspingly dry. It wasn't any particular time of year. I didn't seem to be wearing a coat.

The grass was short. The field was a never ending playing field and I was going to a party in the club house. Two great white Hs loomed out of the night: rugby posts. I realised I was at Bleswick Rugby Club, and I was going to one of its parties. In real life I never went near the place, but in the dream it seemed quite normal to be going to the party.

It seemed quite normal until I got within earshot. Then I stopped and stood still, by myself in the dark windy field. I couldn't see its edge. It had no edge. It went on forever. It didn't reach a road or a cliff edge or the sea or anything. It went on. I couldn't see a thing except the lit-up club house.

It throbbed with boozy bonhomie. I didn't want to go to the party. I didn't think I did, but if I didn't, why was I running to get there?

I dreaded it. I knew what it would be like – men guffawing at nothing, women poking their heads of out the kitchen to giggle at the same. Stupid remarks that you had to laugh at. If you didn't laugh, it showed you had no sense of humour, so they made the remarks again. Insults that you weren't allowed to object to. Sexist cracks, sexist songs, followed by, *Hear that, Miranda? Now there'll be fireworks*!

Another one was, *You are looking nice, Miranda. Or aren't we allowed to say that*? The trap. The nice remark to lure me, followed by the goad with the cattle prod.

Everyone treating me as a spectator sport. *How come you're not in the kitchen with the other girls, Miranda*? Winding me up. *Better not say that to Miranda! Burned your bra, Miranda? Anyway, old boy, we've got this dollybird in the office, whoops, sorry, Miranda! I mean, secretaryperson*!

Goading me to see what I would do. Why should I be their spectator sport? Why give them the satisfaction? Why give them *me*? I was worth more. Why shouldn't I withold myself, stay outside?

No reason. Except that I knew – in the dream, and later when I woke up shivering with terror – that if I stayed outside I must stay outside for ever.

Alone. In a field that went on to infinity, a field that contained nobody but me. Everyone else was at the party.

If I went inside to join them, I must stay inside for ever.

The choice was mine, and it would last for all eternity. There could be no changes of mind, no turning back. I must remain interminably at the party; or interminably outside. The H-shaped goal posts stood for Heaven or Hell. There was only one way of finding out which was which; and by then it would be too late.

I didn't know which choice I made. The dream ended, and I awoke in a panic in my unfamiliar bed at the Gilmours' house.

This reminded me that the previous day, my dad had gone to shack up with Pam MacLeish. Perhaps my dream was a symbolic way of showing that by behaving so shabbily towards my mother he had put himself outside the Toms family for ever. None of its members would speak to him again.

It was a nice thought, but the dream was about me, not him.

The school counsellor had said something like, 'You're free to go and free to come back,' and dreams sometimes went in opposites so I supposed it might be that. His words were meant to be reassuring, but the dream gave me the creeps.

The most nightmarish thing about it was the thought of making one choice and having to take the consequences for ever. The thought of choosing to be completely, utterly alone, and realising too late that I didn't want to be.

I wanted my mum. I wanted to rescue her.

I needed a car. Louis' borrowed mini wasn't available, but I didn't want her to have to come home from Cheltenham on the train. That was how she had gone up there, leaving the car (of course) for Dad. Off she had set, the proudly beaming new grandmother, the tower of strength, with her thermos of coffee, her knitting and her *She*.

What state would she be in now? How must it feel to go on a journey, to have some ghastly thing happen while you were away and then have to make the same journey back? You would spend all the time thinking of how you had felt when you were going in the opposite direction.

I couldn't face ringing round the family. They might not even know yet about Dad, and I would have to tell them and listen to their words of shock and sympathy.

The same applied to her friends. Not that she had any real friends. She had old schoolfriends and wartime nursing friends, whom she never saw. They exchanged Christmas cards, but she was always too busy running round after Dad to fulfil the promises the cards made. ('This year we really must have lunch!') Apart from them, her friends were the wives of his friends. He imposed himself on everything, even her friendships. And now that it suited him, he expected her to live her own life.

I phoned Lindsay Bixwell. She wasn't exactly a friend of Mum's – Mum said Lindsay made her feel inadequate with her successful business and her spotless house – but she didn't count as one of Dad's friends' wives either, now that her awful husband was dead. And she was my godmother so I was allowed to ask her for things.

One of her kennel lads answered the phone and went to fetch her. She had a staff of four now, and new premises. She had inherited quite a bit of money from her husband, and it was one of Dad's witty quips that she had bumped him off in order to get her hands on it.

She came to the phone and I said, 'This is Miranda.'

She said, 'Hello, sweetheart. You've caught me at a dreadful time. It's a bugger of a day.' In the background, dogs yapped. 'When are you coming to help me again? Get your dad to drive you. Make himself useful for once. Apart from drinking my gin.'

I said, 'He's left home.'

'*Sandy* has?' Even the dogs fell silent. 'Where's he gone?'

'He's run away with Pam MacLeish.'

'That little scrubber from Australia?'

'New Zealand.'

There was a long silence before Lindsay said, 'The lousy, rotten, stinking, two-faced – '

'He is, isn't he?'

'How's Jo taking it?'

'It's awful, Lindsay. That's why I rang you.' I explained about Mum needing a lift from Cheltenham.

She said, 'Poor old Jo. She's tried so hard with Sandy over the years.'

'Does that mean you will?'

'Should have married a country vicar. She'd have been much happier.'

'Lindsay – '

'Miranda, you know how fond of her I am. But I'm running round in small circles as it is. *Pam MacLeish*. I thought she was a friend of your family.'

'So did I.'

'She's been to your *house*. How long's it been going on?'

'Don't know. It could be a year. Or even longer.'

'The *bastard!*'

I was pleased to hear how indignant Lindsay was on Mum's behalf. It showed how women stuck together. It boded well for the support Mum was going to get. I hoped she would take some comfort from it.

95

I took the train to Cheltenham. I had finished my course of Morning After Pills without being sick once and I was bleeding away merrily into a Super Plus Tampax with a fluffy white sanitary towel for back-up just in case, but apart from that I was feeling pretty depressed.

Janet met me in the car at the station. She didn't look all that much slimmer than when she was pregnant, just looser. Her skin was pale and blotchy and she had bags under her eyes. Her hair was pinned behind her ears with kirbigrips. I said, 'How's Mum?'

Janet said dully, 'All right,' and we exchanged one of the quick formal kisses that were our stock in trade. Suddenly, I smelt milk. It dawned on me that, since I last saw her she had given birth. That amazing business I had heard about, when your cunt opened up like a mouth and spat out another person, had happened to her.

It gave her a sort of majesty, and yet I had forgotten about it, and about her baby, my niece, in my concern for Mum, my rage against Dad. The thought increased the rage.

I turned my fingers into a gun and shot myself in the head. 'You're not going to believe this. I haven't brought Margaret a present.'

Janet showed no sign of not believing it. She said, 'I didn't expect you to.' It wasn't clear whether this meant, *I am too well mannered to expect presents*, or, *Why would I expect a present from someone as mean as you?*.

'It's Dad,' I said. 'Distracting me.'

'That's right, blame him.'

'Don't you?'

'There's no point in blaming anyone, Miranda.' She smiled in a distant, martyred way, as if my negligence were no more than she expected, and only one more item on a list of failures by members of our family to rise to the occasion of her starting up her own. She turned on the ignition and said, 'We've all had a lot to think about.'

More than you know, I thought, as I felt myself bleed.

'How's Margaret?'

'Screaming the place down, thanks.'

I did not say, *Taking after her namesake.*

'Is Mum . . .?'

'Mum's in a state,' Janet snapped. 'What do you expect?'

In the pine-fitted kitchen, Godfrey was pacing up and down with Margaret who was crying. He gave me a smug perfect-father look, as if to say, *You'll have to revise some of your theories now.*

Mum was washing tiny garments in the sink. She was crying too, but silently.

Janet said wearily, 'Mummy, do them in the machine.'

Mum said, 'It doesn't get things clean.'

I could have said it with her. She never had faith in any machine whose purpose was to make her life easier. She gave a deep, muscular, cheering-up sniff. 'Hello, Miranda. What news of Daddy?'

Her eyes were glittery with pain. Her face was pink from weeping and effort. At the same time, her face was dead. It made me think of hell. I used not to believe in hell because I couldn't see how you could be dead and hurting at the same time, but looking at my mum I knew you could be.

As gently as I could, I said, 'No news.' I kissed her tearstained cheek and hugged her. I wanted her to wilt in my arms, swoon under my lips. I would raise her up and make her better. Since we last saw each other, I had had sex. She hadn't. I would have it again. I doubted that she would. I ought to share it with her, invigorate her and make her happy with my new knowledge of love.

Now my love embarrassed her. She shook me off, saying, 'Is he back yet?'

I glanced at Janet whose look said, *You deal with it, we've had it all week.*

I said, 'Mum, he's not coming back.'

'Why must you always think the worst of Daddy?'

'Because he's the nastiest person I know.'

'Go on with you.' She gave a little snicker of laughter, as if I were a toddler making an error that was harmless, understandable and quite cute. I decided to introduce myself to my niece.

'Hello, Margaret.'

Janet gave her to me and she stopped crying. Even Godfrey was impressed. I said, 'It was nothing.'

Janet smiled. 'Miranda, you can stay.'

Mum said, 'I won't stay, I've been hopeless.'

'You haven't, Mummy!'

'You haven't, Jo! Thanks for all you've done.'

'But I wanted to do more, for my first grandchild!'

'Yes, well,' said Godfrey. 'She's Sandringham's first grandchild too. He certainly picked his fucking moment.'

I looked at Godfrey in awe. It was the first time we had agreed on anything. Perhaps a beautiful friendship would ensue. He was very good-looking. I wondered what he was like in bed. Masterful, probably.

I wondered what he would say if he knew that I might be having an abortion, now this minute, standing in his kitchen with his baby in my arms.

Janet was saying, 'Don't swear in front of Mummy.'

Mum said, 'I don't mind swearing, but please don't say unkind things about Sandy.'

'Why shouldn't we, Mum? After what he's done to you, to all of us?'

'He is not to blame.'

'How do you work that out?'

'He has done it in the most considerate way possible.' She took one of the blue Basildon Bond letters from her apron pocket. He must have had to buy a whole pad.

Janet said, 'Mummy, please don't read it out again.'

'I wouldn't dream of it, since you refuse to understand.'

She gave me the letter. It began, 'Dear Jo, this is the letter you have been dreading . . .' which seemed a bit funny, almost as if they had discussed it in advance.

The letter informed her that he was leaving and listed the costs of running the house, with figures for electricity, rates, insurance and so on. It also told her how much maintenance he would pay. 'This will tide you and Miranda over for the time being but in the long-term I will have other commitments so you'll have to get a job, or maybe take in a lodger or two. If the latter, make sure you get proper professional advice on drawing up the lease, as the pitfalls are many.

'You probably think that I have chosen a rotten time to make the break, but you go away so seldom and I wanted to spare you from the 'orrible spectacle. At least you are with the family and they will prop you up . . .'

On and on, the same hideous, dead-hearted drivel. I pushed the letter away. Mum commanded: 'Read it to the end!' The end was, *Yours in friendship, or at least without enmity*. She was proud of her love letter.

I said, 'He's right about one thing. You need proper professional advice.'

Godfrey said, 'Yes. Absolutely.'

Agreement number two. I gave him my most winning smile. There was something sexless about his perfect features. But then Janet didn't exactly exude sexuality herself (unlike me) so they were probably well-suited.

He said to me, 'I've given your mother the names of a couple of good solicitors.'

Mum said, 'Who needs a solicitor when I've got a family of lawyers?'

Janet said, 'We're not lawyers – '

'Miranda is. She's always putting me in the dock, cross-examining me – '

'Mummy, nobody is cross-examining you. But when a husband and wife are in dispute – '

'There's no dispute. I agree with Daddy.'

'It's not for the husband to decide how much maintenance he's going to pay. There are laws and precedents on this, and women have rights.'

In my mind I replayed Janet's words, to check. Yes, she had said, *Women have rights*.

Mum was saying, 'I don't want rights. I'm quite happy with a voluntary agreement.'

A song came into my head. It was like one that Christine used to sing in my dreams when I was little and I used to irritate Mum and Dad by singing out loud: *I agree with Daddy*, to the tune 'I belong to Glasgow'.

Now there were a few extra notes.

I'm quite-happy-with-a-voluntary-agreement with Daddy,
I'm quite-happy-with-a-voluntary-agreement with Dad.
There's nothing the matter with voluntary-agreements with Daddy.
It's just that they drive you mad.

96

I took Mum home, where she divided her time between housework, eating, crying and trying to make contact with Dad.

She rang Pam's flat but the number had been changed. She rang his office and was told he was on holiday. She wrote him long screeds with lots of capital letters. She underlined words like *LOVE* and *SLUT* and *LOVE* and *PLEASE* and *LOVE*. She made no attempt to keep them hidden. She wanted me to see them. She leaned forward as I passed so that I could hardly avoid reading over her shoulder. She left the half-written letters lying around. She wrote PLEASE PLEASE PLEASE DARLING all over the envelopes.

She drafted and redrafted. Sometimes I would take her her tea in the morning and find her sitting up in bed scrawling, looking as if she had been doing it all night.

I thought of Jo March in *Little Women*. She wrote in bed too, but she wrote stories, not servile letters. She munched apples, brown russets, proudly and openly, while my mother gobbled sweets and comforted herself with bowls of pappy cereal with cream and brown sugar, and hid the bowl.

She rang his office and said, 'Could you please put me through to Mr Toms urgently? This is the casualty doctor at the Whittington Hospital, it's in connection with a Miss MacLeish.' Then she said, 'Just playing, darling. Sorry for the subterfuge. Please come back to me, please, please, please.'

I divided my time between revising for my O-levels, going to my Young Women's Group and finding opportunities to have sex with Graham.

Graham was Louis' successor. This was Louis' decision. I would have been perfectly willing to carry on with the two of them, but Louis said, 'I won't share you, Miranda.'

I said, 'You didn't own me in the first place.'

Graham was an older man, he was twenty-four. He worked in a bank, and had a lot of sexual experience and a mortgage.

The first time we did it, he knew I wasn't a virgin, but he did it as if I were. 'It's your first time with me. Everything before this is cancelled.' He was slow and gentle, tender and tantalising. It took him an hour even to get my clothes off. Every time he took something off, he looked at the part of me newly revealed beneath it as if he had never seen anything so beautiful. Then he tasted it.

He slithered into me like a snake and fucked in this steady rhythm that was like swinging in a hammock. I relaxed into it. I almost nodded off. I said, 'I feel lazy.' He said, 'Be lazy. This is for you.'

Sometimes it was for him and sometimes it was for me. I liked taking turns, instead of trying to do everything at once. When it was for him, I was very macho. I hurt him. Not badly, just the odd pinch or scratch or bite to make him jump, to let him know I could. When it was for me and I was just lying there, I would feel this great wave of sensuality welling up and breaking. It wasn't coming exactly. Not the way I came from a tongue, or from my own or someone else's fingers. It wasn't even particularly physical. It was raw emotion. I felt like crying. I did cry sometimes, and he comforted me.

It was greedy of me to allow myself to be comforted when I had nothing to cry about. Nobody was comforting Mum.

Two letters came on blue Basildon Bond, one for her, one for me. She danced on the doormat like a child. 'Daddy's sent us letters, Daddy's sent us letters!' She handed me my envelope. I let it fall back on to the mat but she didn't notice. She was tearing open her own.

She read its contents and became a grown-up again. 'Have a look at this, Miranda,' she said importantly. 'It concerns you.'

> 'Dear Jo,
>
> 'What happened at the office yesterday was unforgivable – '

I stared at her in awe. 'What did you do?'

'Nothing. It was only a joke. Don't read that bit.'

I read all of it.

' – Be in no doubt that if your hysterical behaviour makes it necessary for me to change jobs, and/or for me and Pam to find somewhere else to live, we will do so.

'I would take such a step only with the greatest reluctance, as it is my earnest wish to maintain some sort of normal relationship with Miranda, as well as with Janet and the family. You and I must not forget, in our selfish concern for our own difficulties, that they are still our children, and Miranda is only sixteen. Nothing must be allowed to interfere with her final years at school or her progress to university and the Bar.

'Janet has informed me that she prefers me not to attend Margaret's christening because of the risk that you will (as she puts it) "make a scene".

'You will appreciate what a bitter blow it would be to me to miss such an important occasion in the life of our family. Pam thinks you will draw some sort of satisfaction from being able to avenge yourself on me in this way, but I think I know you better than that.

'Perhaps a word with the doctor would not come amiss. He can probably fix you up with some tranquillisers or whatever they're called these days. Then I would like you to reassure Janet that her fears are unfounded and that it will be perfectly in order for me to attend the christening of my first grandchild.

'Needless to say, out of consideration for you, there is no question of Pam accompanying me on this occasion, much though she would like to.

'Love (well, why not?)

'Sandy.'

Mum said, 'What do you think?'

'I love it.'

'I agree with you. And I agree with him. Except about the pills. It's up to me to pull my socks up.'

'God, Mum, I was being sarcastic! I hate it! Look how he puts all the responsibility on to women! Janet's being rotten about the christening, you're hysterical and should be tranquillised, Pam's making catty remarks – '

'Do you have to score feminist points off *everything* Daddy says and does?'

I stared at her. She said, 'What's in your letter?'

'More crap I expect.'

'Open it!'

'I'd rather open a dead dog's bowel.'

'Oh, Miranda, you have such command of language! You're going to be marvellous in the High Court!'

'You open it if you're so interested.'

She read aloud:

> 'Dearest Miranda,
>
> 'Hope the O-levels went all right and that now you've had time to reflect, you're not thinking too badly of your old dad. Pam and I would be chuffed to bits if you would come to lunch at the flat next Saturday. We are so looking forward to seeing you again.
>
> 'Lots of love,
>
> 'Daddy.'

'It's the olive branch,' said Mum.

'And he knows where he can stick it.'

'Miranda! He's your father!'

'Don't I know it. I'm not going.'

She said, 'Please go. I want you to go.'

'What for?'

'Don't you see? He's trying to keep our family together.'

'Who broke it up in the first place? Why don't you go? Eat their food. Drink their drink. Smash up their flat, you'd enjoy that.'

'I'm not breaking bread with that little bitch. And anyway, Daddy would be cross.'

'I'm not going. It would be disloyal to you.'

She touched my arm. 'The really loyal thing would be to go.'

'How do you work that out?'

'Don't you see? He's trying to get back to normal.'

'Where does it say that?'

She laughed softly, knowingly. 'When you've been married as long as I have – '

'Which will be never.'

'Aha, you say that, but we all fall in the end. When you've been married as long as I have, you'll find out that some things don't have to be said in so many words. He's tiring of her already. I can tell. I knew he would.'

'Since when?'

For a moment she looked trapped. Then she said smoothly, 'Since he left me. Accept their invitation, be my spy. There's a lot of unhappiness in these letters . . . Let me know what he's unhappy about. Find her Achilles heel.'

'Maybe she hasn't got one.'

'Every woman has one. No woman is good enough for Daddy. But we're all inadequate in different ways, and if I can just get him to see me as more, well, adequate in my inadequacy than – '

'*Mum*! Please stop this and tell me how long it's been going on!'

She turned away in bitterness. 'The wife is always the last to know.'

'OK, I mean how long have you known about it?'

'Since he told me. Since I was in Cheltenham and that letter came – the one that she made him write – ' her face began to crumple at the memory.

'Why did it say, "This is the letter you have been dreading"?'

She looked startled. 'Did it?'

'You know it did. You've read it enough times.'

'Why would it say that? Why would I dread what I didn't know about?'

I said, 'Where is the letter?'

She said, 'I've thrown it away. I haven't got time to stand here nattering.'

'Mum – was that honestly and truly the first time you knew?'

'Of course,' she said. 'Do you think I'd have let her get away with it for all those years?'

'All what years?'

'However many – how should I know?'

'Honourable Heart, you didn't know before that? You didn't even suspect?'

'Honourable Heart,' she replied. 'Am I allowed out of the dock now, my lord? Can I go back to my cell?'

97

As I climbed the stairs to Pam's flat, she and Dad were waiting in the doorway, hand in hand.

They were sickeningly sexy. I had seen them together before, but this was the first occasion on which they had allowed their sexiness to show.

His left thigh was pressing against her right, a lot more closely than the narrowness of the doorway required. They almost stank of sex. What they actually stank of was soap mixed with fingers. I knew without being told that they had been soaping each other.

I thought of how I would like to soap somebody, and be soaped. It was one thing Graham and I had never done. I might mention it to him, or to Alex, a friend of his whom I had my eye on.

Pam's and Dad's bodies reeked with the odours of deodorant – I imagined them taking turns to roll the wet plastic ball in each other's armpits – his, golden and bristly, hers satin smooth. They were decorously dressed in my honour – her summer frock, his open-necked fawn shirt and matching slacks were fresh from the laundry and crisp from the iron – but I knew that they had not been dressed for long. Her thick, auburn rinsed red hair, the thinning grey blond curls that clustered around his collar, had been hastily combed into place after heaven knew what kind of disarrangement. Heaven was the word. For them it had been heaven. On the left tip of his moustache glistened a droplet of saliva – hers, I would bet. Sex gleamed in the slime of their eyes like the rainbows made by oil in a muddy puddle.

'Do I get a kiss?' said Dad to me. 'Or not?'

'Not.'

'Well said, Miranda,' said Pam. 'We don't expect you to accept us at once. Take your time.'

Dad said, 'Hear hear. We regard it as an honour that you've come to see us. Don't we, Pam? We want you to think of this flat as your home. Your London *pied à terre*. Don't we? And you can start by hoovering the sitting room. That's a joke.'

Pam said pleasantly, 'Sandy, it wasn't a joke when I asked *you* to hoover the sitting room half an hour ago.'

'I was just about to do it when the buzzer went.' He sounded aggrieved. 'I suppose you'd have preferred me to leave Miranda on the doorstep?'

'Just get on with it, darling.' She spoke through sweetly gritted teeth.

As soon as she had disappeared into the kitchen, he said playfully to me out of the corner of his mouth, 'Wanna drink?' He mimed holding a glass to his lips, in case I didn't know what a drink was.

I was on the point of saying, *Why don't you do what Pam asked?* and then I thought, *No. Since I'm here as a spy, why don't I be a spy and see how long this goes on? I might even try my hand as an agent provocateur.*

I relaxed on the sofa. 'Gin and tonic, please.'

'Coming up.'

He poured two and gave me one. He said, 'Cheers. Good to see you.'

'No ice? No lemon?'

'Ah.'

'Bad form not to offer ice and a slice, old boy.'

He cast a nervous glance in the direction of the kitchen. 'If I go in there she'll tell me off for not hoovering the carpet.'

'The answer's in your own hands.'

'You're dead right.' He took my glass and headed for the kitchen.

She said, 'Now what are you doing? I asked you to hoover the bloody sitting room.'

'Don't nag, Pam. You'll remind me of my wife.'

'Jo never worked. I do, so I expect you to pull your weight at weekends.'

I listened, enchanted.

He came storming into the sitting room. 'Fraid you can't have a drink, old chum. Pam says not.' He sat in an armchair and read the *Daily Telegraph* in a tremendous sulk.

Pam stood in the doorway, staring at him in disbelief. She said quietly, 'Miranda, please help yourself to anything you want. Sandy, if I have to hoover this carpet myself I swear to God this is the last time we have your bloody family here.' I must have flinched or something, because she added, 'You're not included in the "bloody", Miranda.'

'Who, then?'

Before she could answer, the entryphone buzzer went.

He dived for it. 'Saved by the bell. Yep?'

The microphone rumbled and harumphed. 'Rutherford.'

Dad gave a cry of joy at the sound of his brother's voice, pressed the button, went to the front door and stood waiting.

The buzzer went again. Pam answered. My aunt Sue's voice trilled, 'It's me and Humphrey.'

I said to Pam, 'I didn't know it was going to be a big family party.'

She sighed. 'Isn't it always?'

My three old uncles trundled into the flat, heavy footed yet frisky, roaring with laughter (I hadn't heard any jokes) and slapping each other on the back. I wondered why they didn't kiss and be done with it, they were so obviously in love with each other: grey bearded Rutherford with his brand new hip joint, Kennington with his polished bald head and thick lensed glasses, and snub-nosed Humphrey. Snub noses should turn down with age, I decided. Schoolboy features made old men look even more ridiculous than they were anyway.

In the wake of the brothers came their wives, Aunts Gwen, Kay and Sue. Unlike their husbands, they noticed my presence. They gushed over me a bit but seemed slightly embarrassed and glad to move to action stations. They dashed headlong for the kitchen crying, 'What can we do, Pam? What can we do?'

'Nothing, please sit down.'

'Oh, but there must be something!'

My father was saying to his brothers, 'Got here just in time, we were about to have a major domestic incident, weren't we, Pam?'

'No. But I still want you to hoover the sitting room.'

The uncles fell about.

'Sick of him already, eh, Pam? Don't blame you.'

'Told you not to let him move in. Better women than you have tried and failed.'

'Do as the lady says, Sandy, you old bugger. Hoover the carpet or she'll send you home to Jo.' Humphrey's tone changed. '*I say*, it's Miranda! Didn't see you hiding there! Don't give me that disapproving look, I'm on your side.'

'Which *side*?' I enquired.

'Woman's lib. I just told him to hoover the carpet. You heard me.'

My aunts were making a fruitless search of the flat, trying to find some housework to do. Hearing mention of hoovering the carpet, they raced for a cupboard near the front door. An unseemly scuffle ensued, out of which Aunt Gwen emerged breathing heavily but in triumphant possession of the hoover. 'I'll run it over in two minutes,' she said. 'No, Miranda, there's no need for you to help.'

'I wasn't.' I placed myself between her and the electric point so that she couldn't plug the hoover in. 'I want to ask you something. How did you know where the hoover was? How many times have you been here? How many of these parties have there been?'

Nobody answered. Dad said, 'Now, Miranda. We're having a lovely day, let's not spoil it, of course I'm going to do the hoovering.'

I ignored him. I had read an article somewhere about how teachers imposed their will on unruly schoolchildren. The secret was to pick on the leader. 'Uncle Rutherford. How long have you been coming here? How long have you known about Pam and him?' I jerked my thumb in Dad's direction.

'I say, Miranda! No one told me you'd been called to the Bar already! Thought you were still at school!'

'Don't patronise me, please. How long have you known?'

'Objection, my lord! Counsel must not brow-beat the witness!'

'Is anybody going to give me a straight answer?' I looked from uncle to uncle, aunt to aunt. One by one they avoided my gaze. 'How long, Uncle Rutherford?'

'I don't know off-hand, Miranda.'

'Weeks, months or years?'

'Well – '

My father said, 'Does it matter? Honestly?'

'It does, actually. *Honestly*. You see, I've got a mother. Her name's Jo. She used to give parties like this. She used to knock herself out, giving them. You've all enjoyed her hospitality, and I think she'd be a bit upset to think you'd been laughing at her behind her back.'

Aunt Gwen said, 'Nobody's been laughing at Jo, Miranda. On the contrary. It's been very difficult for us, trying not to take sides.'

I said, 'Don't you think covering up for him *is* taking sides?'

'It was none of our business,' said Sue. 'We were trying to protect Jo.'

'Trying to protect *you*, Miranda,' said Gwen. 'You weren't old enough.'

'It seemed kinder to keep quiet,' said Kay.

'Until it was too late, you mean? How long's this been going on? I bet it's years and years, I bet you've all known about it for years and years. My mum's been left high and dry. She's fifty-five, she's never been anything except a housewife, what's she expected to do? If she'd known this was going to happen – '

'She did know,' said my father.

I turned on him. 'Dirty liar.'

'I gave her fair warning. When you were ten, I told her that I would leave her when you were sixteen.'

'She didn't know you were leaving till you left!'

'Miranda, she has known all along.'

'All along what?'

'For as long as it's been going on,' said Dad, 'Mummy has known about it.'

'And how long is that?' I asked, sneering to hide my panic.

'Six years.'

98

She was on her hands and knees scrubbing the staircarpet with a stiff brush and soapy water. Carpet shampooers did not do the job properly.

'You're early,' she said, through a mouthful of something, carefully disguised.

'Yes,' I said.

'How was Daddy?' She finished swallowing and turned round from her scrubbing. Her eyes were misty. 'Did he seem happy?'

I thought of all the vicious things I had planned to say, the accusations I was going to lay at her door. But pity blocked my throat and I said feebly, 'He and Pam had a row.' I was glad to have their row to lay at her feet like a gift.

She clasped her wet, soapy hands in glee. 'What about?'

'She wanted him to hoover the sitting room carpet and he wouldn't.'

'Well, of course he wouldn't. Why should he?'

'Mum – '

'The girl's a fool,' she said. 'He'll be back here before you can say Jack Robinson. It's not interesting conversation that keeps a man. It's not even sex. It's elbow grease.' She polished the air with vigorous circular movements.

It was pathetic. The pathos of it allowed me to speak. Where I dared not accuse her, I could freely give her pity. 'Is that what you thought you could do? Win him back with elbow grease?'

'I don't know what you're talking about.'

'I *know* about it now, Mum.' My voice was gentle. I sounded like a parent myself, telling a child that some secret offence is out in the open and that there is to be no punishment. 'Dad said . . . that you've known for six years that this was going to happen.'

'"Known",' said my mother, 'is hardly the word.'

It was one of her habits of speech. She pounced on words and poured scorn on them for meaning what they meant, for being too strong. Sometimes I thought she was doing the same to me. I wondered if the words felt as guilty as I did. Did they doubt themselves as deeply? They couldn't. Yet I pressed on.

'What is the word then?'

She gave it a lot of thought before conceding, '"Suspected", perhaps. Any wife of any attractive man knows that he is always prey to – '

'He says he told you in 1974 that he would leave you in 1980.'

'He may have mentioned something of the sort. I didn't take much notice. These things blow over in a marriage. You'll understand when you're older.'

'Mum, I've got one more question and then I'll shut up.'

'After that can I go back to my cell?'

'Don't, Mum! Please!'

'You must learn to take a joke at your own expense, Miranda.'

'When in 1974 did he tell you?'

'You want the exact date? The hour? The minute?' She pretended to thumb through a notebook. 'Fraid I don't seem to have written it down, yer honour.' She slapped herself on the wrist.

I said, 'Janet's wedding was in 1974. October. Was it before or after that?'

'I can't remember.'

'You must remember.'

'All right, Miranda; you know, I don't. Why don't *you* tell *me*?'

'I snuck off from the wedding. Do you remember? I went to the abortion demo.'

'Did you?' said my mother. 'Oh yes.' She took her bucket to the kitchen to change the water.

I followed her. 'I thought I'd got away with it. Only he found out. And when he found out, he hit me. Do you remember?' She turned her back and turned the tap on full. I spoke loudly above the rush of the water. 'He called me out of bed in the middle of the night, he made me come down to the kitchen, he was drunk, and – '

'"Drunk" is a bit of an – '

'He was drunk. He hit me in front of you and Janet. He hit me for being in one place when I was supposed to be in another. For pretending. Disguising myself. Lying. Did you know then that he was pretending? That he was lying? Were you covering up for him even then?'

'He didn't hit you hard,' she said. 'He didn't hurt you.'

Perhaps she was right.

I had survived, so I couldn't have been hurt all that much.

Perhaps I should take a leaf out of her book and be a bit more careful of the words I used.

Hurt was much too strong a word for the bewilderment I felt now as I reviewed the last six years.

They had been eventful. Grandma Toms was discharged from hospital after her stroke. She was half paralysed. She wanted to stay in her home in Salthaven. There was a family conference about how she should be looked after. The daughters-in-law formed themselves into a rota. My mum was told that she didn't have to be on it because she still had me at home, but she said she wanted to be on it. I was parked out at Lindsay Bixwell's for days on end while Mum went to Salthaven.

Also on the looking-after-Grandma rota was this old friend of the family, Pam MacLeish. She helped out at weekends. The weekends were when the men went down.

That must have been when it started.

I remembered something else.

At the same time as Grandma Toms was trying to recover from her stroke, Gran Woolgar had a fall and broke her hip.

'Not to be outdone,' said Mum.

Not only did Mum make catty comments about her mother (which wasn't unusual), she totally neglected her. While Mum was looking after Grandma Toms at home, Gran Woolgar lay ignored in hospital, and finally died of pneumonia.

When I asked Mum why she put her mother-in-law before her mother, she said, 'You'll understand when you're older.'

I said, 'I won't! I want to know now! It's not fair!'

'It's perfectly fair. Mummy put me in an institution, why shouldn't I put her in one?'

It sounded fair, but it made me cry.

Now I thought, *She must have known.*
She dared not leave Pam and Dad by themselves.
Not even at his mother's deathbed.

And then there were the times when he came home late.

It would be easier to think of the times when he didn't come home late. Not only were there fewer of them; they were less confusing.

I was always confused by his lateness.

What time are we having supper? I would ask Mum.

Usual time, she would reply.

When's that?

When Daddy gets home.

When's that?

AT HIS USUAL TIME. Stop cross-examining me!

I did not think he had a usual time. But she seemed sure that he had one.

At least, I had thought at the time that she was sure. It never crossed my mind that she would say *usual time*, and go on saying it, year in, year out, whilst knowing full well that there was no such thing.

It was one of a great many things that did not cross my mind, but were crossing it and recrossing it now. It was the dream. The dream where I had to go to the party and stay forever, or stay away and stay outside forever. What if I went in and found that it was her party? And there was no food? 'Not until Daddy gets home! Not until his usual time!' An eternity of waiting for him to get home, of being refused food until he got home. And the person refusing it was the person who knew he would never get home.

Outside in the field there might at least be crusts or crumbs or bits of half chewed gum lurking in the short grass; but in the dream I had made my choice, and I had gone inside and would never be allowed out.

I didn't go to Margaret's christening. Mum said, 'Aren't you being a bit petty? Surely you and Godfrey can bury the hatchet for an occasion like this?'

'It's nothing to do with Godfrey.'

I stayed at home and lay on my bed and read A-level law books. I planned to be half way through the syllabus by the time I started at Bleswick Sixth Form College in the autumn.

Chapter One. Fundamentals of Law. The Nature of Law. Folkways, Mores, Taboos, Custom.

I imagined bearded old men in the mists of history drinking mead round a log table and agreeing on the rules.

Just like my dad and my uncles.

I imagined them at the christening: reverent at the service, pushing and braying and jockeying for position afterwards. How would he behave towards my mother? How would all of them behave? As gentlemen, doubtless; in accordance with the folkways.

Whose folkways? Not mine. Which folk? Not me. I was outside. If this was a family, you could keep it.

One thing, though, I wished I knew where Chris was: inside or out.

I wouldn't mind pacing across an infinite field for a few million years if I thought there was a chance of running into her.

But what if she were at the party? From what I knew of her, she wouldn't choose to spend eternity in the indiscriminate company of our relatives any more than I would. But *what I knew of her* might not be true. She might have changed her mind.

She had been dead for a long time. She might be getting cold.

99

The A-level law course at Bleswick Sixth Form College was taught mainly by Mr Steinem, a former barrister with slinky legs and an actorish manner. I thought he would prefer to be in court. He loved to get us to put on mock trials so that he could be in them, usually as judge, but sometimes as defendant.

'I'll be Othello,' he said. 'I'm charged with murdering Desdemona. Miranda, I want you to defend me.'

'Sorry, sir. I'm not accepting the brief.'

'If the clerk of your chambers gives it to you – '

'My chambers don't do wife murderers, sir.'

'Who are you calling a wife murderer? I'm pleading not guilty.'

'Then you're lying, Mr Othello, sir. It's in the play.'

Mr Steinem appealed to the rest of the class. 'What defences are open to Othello?'

'Insanity, sir.'

'Mistake.'

'Duress.'

'Incitement. Racial harassment.'

'Anything else? Think about it for next week.' He appointed jurors and counsel for the prosecution.

I said, 'Please, sir, couldn't I prosecute?'

'Miranda, the fact that you want to prosecute,' said Mr Steinem, 'is a very good reason indeed for getting you to defend.' I groaned at him, but he launched into one of his PR speeches. 'People outside the profession often ask barristers, How do you defend someone if you know they're guilty? That misses the point. You don't know they're guilty unless they say they are, in which case you must advise them to plead accordingly. But even then *you are still their advocate*. You make out a case in mitigation.'

*

I didn't want to be Othello's advocate. I had my work cut out, being my mother's.

In order to be able to help her, I was doing a special project on Women and the Law. I had made myself an expert on divorce and matrimonial property. 'You have a right,' I informed her, 'to a standard of living as close as possible to what it would have been if he hadn't left you.'

'How can it be? Without Daddy, I have nothing.'

'No court would expect you to take in lodgers to make up for his meanness.'

'"Meanness" is rather a harsh way of putting it, Miranda. It's not Daddy's fault there's been inflation. I think it would be rather fun to have a lodger. Look at this.'

It was one of her letters.

> 'Dear Sandy,
>
> 'This is a business letter, so please don't ignore it as you have all the others. (Just joking, darling. I know how busy you are.)
>
> 'I have decided to take up your excellent suggestion and let out a room.
>
> 'As you yourself have said, letting rooms is full of pitfalls and I will need advice on drawing up the lease etc, so that I do not end up being evicted from our home by someone to whom I have in my dimwitted way given security of tenure in perpetuity or whatever the expression is!!! I am coming to you as I know you will provide the very best advice there is!!! Might as well keep it in the family!!!
>
> 'I have been thinking and I have had an idea. There is no need for us to be enemies. Will you come to supper one evening? I will make one of my super-duper curries and we can discuss the lease and have a chin-wag about the old days. I know Miranda would love to see you.'

She asked me: 'How do you think I should sign off? How can I let him know that for his sake I am prepared to be entirely businesslike even though – ' her voice wobbled and became brave again ' – I still love him and always will?'

'I don't know, Mum.'

I went to my room and re-read the murder scene in *Othello*.

The stage direction was clear enough. *He stifles Desdemona.*

No two ways about it. *I call Mr William Shakespeare*!

I read on and found that Othello's defence was clear enough too, if his counsel chose to use it.

Emilia: O, who has done this deed?

Desdemona: Nobody. I myself, farewell: commend me to my kind lord. O, farewell.

I call Emilia.

Emilia, did the deceased, or did she not, confess to committing suicide?

Did she or did she not refer to him with her dying breath as 'my kind lord?'

Did she or did she not agree with Daddy?

I couldn't face the trial. I stayed away from college. I pretended I had pre-menstrual tension, though my mother briskly declared that there was no such thing and chose that day to spring-clean my room.

A letter came back from Dad's firm, though not from Dad.

It was signed by one of his slaves, to whom Mum's letter had been passed. The slave begged to enclose a model lease and to offer every assistance in finding a suitable tenant and managing the tenancy. With Mum's permission, the slave would visit Bleswick and advise her in person.

She said in a tone of bright wonder, 'Daddy's so busy!'

'Please, Mum, let me take you to see a solicitor.'

'I don't need one.'

'You do.'

She turned on me. 'Are you going short?' She thumped the kitchen table with clenched fists. The cutlery rang. 'Has your standard of living dropped since he went away?'

'No, Mum, you've managed fantastically, but I'll be independent soon, what about *you*? You've got to think long-term.'

'Long-term he'll be back.'

'You ought to have the house transferred into your name,' I said. 'You could sell it and get somewhere smaller.'

'It's his home.' She spoke quietly and simply, as if I were not very bright but even I could understand this; and once I understood it, I would stop saying foolish things.

'He's gone, Mum.'

'You're no help,' she said.

'I'm trying to help!' I was nearly crying.

'Get him back then, Miranda! Get him to come back!'

'I can't, and even if I could – '

'Even if you could, what?' She gripped my wrists with savage fingers. 'Even if you could, you wouldn't! You hate him, don't you? That's abnormal, for a girl to hate her father. You're abnormal. All you're interested in is scoring feminist points. He's always done his best for you and you always think the worst of him. He stayed for you as well as me, you know! He stood up to her! She would have lured him away years ago, but he wanted you to have a normal upbringing! And now you're inciting me to hound him – '

'Mum, I just want you to have enough money.'

'Then I shall get a job,' she said.

'Mum, you're fifty-six and you've never worked! For money.'

'I was a nurse once. Nearly.'

'No court would expect – '

'I don't need a court's permission to go back to nursing, Miranda. I thought you approved of women having jobs!'

What could I say? I sent off on her behalf for details of courses for married women returners; but it was too late. You had to be fifty or under.

'That's ageism,' I told her.

She said, 'You've got a name for everything! I probably wouldn't have been accepted in any case. I'll be a ward orderly instead. No one cares how old they are, as long as they've got strong arms for scrubbing!'

At my Women's Group meeting, I wept. 'Her life's been such a cheat. At every stage of her life, she's been cheated.'

Penny said tentatively, 'Don't you think . . . I mean, she's cheating herself a bit.'

'How?' I snapped.

'Not taking your dad to the cleaners. Becoming one herself, rather than – '

Someone else in the group said warningly, 'Lots of women have no choice about being cleaners.'

'It's Mum's conditioning,' I said.

Another girl agreed with me. 'It's sort of "Stand by Your Man" type thing.'

'Miranda's mum stands by her man even when he's not there,' said Penny. 'I've sworn never to say, "women are their own worst enemies," but – '

'Don't say it then,' I snapped. 'It's all very well for your mum to be so right-on. Mine's from a different generation. Mine was in the war.'

'A lot of women got liberated in the war.'

'And they got forced back into the home afterwards!' I shouted.

'They shouldn't have gone,' said Penny. 'They shouldn't have let themselves be forced.'

Someone else, supporting me, said, 'That's easy to say, Pen.'

'It isn't, but I think there's more to it than conditioning. What's it called when women like being hurt by men?'

I glared at her. 'Female masochism. Only there's no such thing. It's the blame-the-victim syndrome. If you go along with that, you're playing into men's hands.'

We moved on to next business.

An Irish woman, whose husband and sons had been falsely imprisoned on terrorism charges, had sent a petition for us to sign in their support.

The All London Black Women's Caucus was objecting to a planned Reclaim the Night march through Brixton because it implied that black men were responsible for rape.

And some gay men in California who had something the matter with their immune systems were being denied proper treatment and told it was their own fault.

We signed the Irish woman's petition. We argued long and hard about Reclaim the Night. We never got to the gay men in California. I didn't know why we were spending such a long time discussing men's problems anyway. Irish men, Black men, gay men. How had they muscled in? The women's movement should be just that. Women's. Women should always take women's side. Always. No matter what.

100

I studied for a law degree at the LSE. I could have gone to Manchester or Keele, but I didn't want to leave Mum on her own.

I lived with her, and commuted. I paid her a small rent out of my grant and kept an eye on her. I was all she had.

I was her lodger. This was a relief to both of us. She didn't want to share her home with a stranger, and I didn't see why she should have to. When she married Dad for life, it wasn't so that she could be a landlady in her old age, any more than it was in order to be a grey haired ward orderly that she had given up her nurse's training.

More fool her, some might say. But how was she to know that he would leave her when it was too late for her to have a proper career? She had married a man who made a big deal about having an Honourable Heart. How was she to know that he was a trickster?

She had known since I was ten, but even that had been too late for her. She was fifty then, and set in her ways of being a dutiful wife and loving him. She had thought he and Pam were having a brief fling. She had thought she could win him back while I was growing up. He had stayed for me, who did not want him, but not for her, who did. She had bowed her head before the humiliation.

I would not bow my head. I would put a wig on it and speak out for tricked women.

In my final year at the LSE I was offered a place at the Inns of Court School of Law, subject to my degree results. The vocational course would take a year, and then I would be called to the Bar and become a pupil barrister.

In between studying for my finals, I worked volunteer shifts at Paddington Law Centre. It was worthwhile in itself, and a good way to make contacts. I was on the lookout for a radical set of chambers for my pupilage, somewhere where they wouldn't expect me to defend flashers or rapists, wife batterers or runaway husbands who wouldn't pay their maintenance. I would be advocate for the innocent.

The man who came slamming into the Law Centre one Saturday afternoon had wife-batterer written all over him.

He had a Union Jack T-shirt, a gold bone in his left earlobe and a Fuck the Argies tattoo which had probably seemed like a good idea at the time but now had a quaint air. (Had nobody told him?) He was in his twenties, about six foot tall with a build to match, and he thumped the desk where I was on Reception. 'I want my rights.'

I went into Assertively Polite mode. 'We'll try and help you get them.' *If any*, I added to myself.

'She's gone,' he said. 'And she's got my kids.'

'Take a seat.'

'You've sent her to one of them refuges, haven't you?'

I should bloody well hope so.

He was muttering about, 'Fucking lezzies.'

I said, 'We don't *send* anyone anywhere, sir.'

'Don't get lippy with me, bitch.'

'Now look – '

'You look – '

I thought I was in line for a knuckle sandwich but another man came in and said, 'Neil!'

Neil said, 'Orright, mate? Just making a few enquiries.'

The other man was older than Neil – in his late thirties or early forties – and a good deal smaller, but still fairly unsavoury-looking. His jeans were cheap and grubby, his hair was neither short nor long, just neglected, and he had nicotine stains on the insides of his nostrils. Nevertheless, he seemed to be a restraining influence on Neil, and he fancied himself as a smoothie. 'Sorry about that, Neil's a bit upset.'

'So I see.'

'Are you all right?' he was either very short-sighted – he had glasses with thick lenses – or else he was giving me the eye. I gave it back as a matter of routine, keeping my options open, but I didn't really fancy him. Apart from his seediness, he was a bit old for me, and a bit little.

I had never been crawled over by a little man. My sexual preference was to be overwhelmed by someone bigger than I was. *Penetrated.* I hardly dared breathe the word. It was not the done thing. It was unfeminist. Some of my friends went so far as to say it was dangerous. They obviously hadn't been penetrated by some of the pricks I had been penetrated by. I loved being powerfully entered. It felt as if it ought to hurt, but it didn't. I was tough down there. Tough through use. Pricks penetrated, I contained, we fucked. *Pump, thump, pump, thump, whoosh.* The power spent itself. The danger died. That was my power, to make that happen. Who shrivelled to nothing when it was over? Not me.

Neil waved his finger in my face. 'Tell her I won't do it again, orright?'

'Won't do what again?'

His sidekick intervened. 'Are you able to give her that message?'

I replied coolly, 'I can't say. Get him to write his wife's name down – ' I handed over a pad – 'and then if we do know where she is we'll pass the message on.'

'Fair enough, eh, Neil?'

Neil didn't look as if *fair enough* were the phrase that sprang immediately into his mind, if any, but he seemed to realise it was all he was going to get, so he took the pad.

With some difficulty, he wrote 'JANEY DAVIS'. He pondered a bit and drew a heart pierced by an arrow. 'NEIL LOVES JANEY. TRUE.'

The desperation of this reminded me of my mother, though I didn't see why it should. She wasn't a batterer. She didn't go barging into law centres saying *I want my rights*. I wished she would. I hadn't even got her to a solicitor yet. She preferred to wait. *A waiting game*, she called it. Or, *giving Pam enough rope to hang herself.* She was sure Pam's novelty value would wear off, and he would come home. *I'll make it easy for Daddy to come home, Miranda. There'll be no bitterness, now or ever.*

The bitterness was mine. She had been so foully tricked, and she didn't even know it, and she wouldn't fight back, so I must fight for her.

'Those kids are mine,' said Neil. 'Tell her to bring them back.'

I glared at him in disgust. 'We don't tell people what to do. If we know where she is, we'll pass on your message. What she does then is up to her.'

The sidekick said, 'Can we be informed – ?'

'Where she is? No way.'

' – whether or not you've been able to pass the message. Yes or no?'

'Sure,' I said. 'Where can I reach you?'

The sidekick gave me a visiting card that was as grubby as the rest of him. 'LOCKWOOD LEAGUE FOR PENAL REFORM AND AFTERCARE. CASE WORKER, ADAM PRESTON.'

'I'll give you a call,' I said.

'And your name?'

'Miranda.'

'Miranda what?'

'We don't give surnames.' I shot a meaningful glance in the direction of his towering, glowering chum.

'No, of course not.' He looked disappointed nevertheless. *He fancies me* I thought, and felt safe.

My current boyfriend was on the way out. He was a fellow law student. He didn't listen. I kept telling him that I didn't want him to give me orgasms with his fingers. It was something I could do perfectly well for myself, so it was a waste of time him doing it when he could be doing other things, but he went on doing it.

I was looking for his replacement. I hadn't told him yet. I liked to have a new one before the old one was finished. Thc thought of having no one filled me with panic.

If I had no one, I would be like my mother. My mother had no one, apart from me, and I could not be her lover. That was my failure – that, and my dread of being like her.

I ought to want to be like her. How could I be her advocate if I could not feel what she felt, suffer what she suffered? But I dared not suffer her lack of love, her lack of sex. Without love and sex I would die.

I could not give up love and sex, not even to be like her.

Instead, to be like her, I sometimes thought I would share my love and sex with her. I would gather nectar like a bee and carry it home to the queen in her hive. Then she would be happy. That was why I appeared so greedy, I was loving and fucking for two. And why shouldn't I be greedy when there was such abundance? Why should love and sex be rationed? Why were people trying to ration it, with their terrifying stories which could not be true? *Could not.* The freest thing in the world could not be rationed. The most beautiful thing could not be lethally polluted. Ration water, ration air, ration wild flowers and green grass but not that. Nobody had the right. Nobody would dare. Nobody owned it, so who dared ration it? I wanted it. It was mine. Everyone I fancied seemed to fancy me, not to mention all the ones who fancied me when I didn't fancy them, such as this little fellow with the curious eyes, Adam Preston.

Our conversation was over, but he went on staring.

I said, 'You'll know me again.'

He smiled in a puzzled way. 'You remind me of someone.'

'Oh yeah?'

Neil was fooling around in front of the waiting clients. 'See that? Supposed to be my social worker and all he's interested in is pulling the birds.' He got hold of Adam Preston's collar and playfully manhandled him out of the law centre.

101

I asked around the law centre and found that a Janey Davis had been referred that day to Maida Vale Women's Aid with bruising and boiling water scalds on her face and neck. I didn't hurry to ring her with Neil's message.

I dealt with enquiries and proof-read a leaflet called *Greenham Common, the Law of Trespass and Your Rights*. I had helped to write it, but I had never been to Greenham.

This was almost as embarrassing a thing to admit as liking penetration; but the peace campers made me uneasy. Their sentimentality played into men's hands. They set up house and were earth mothers, which was exactly the sort of thing that men wanted women to do.

At the same time, the peace campers were outsiders. Literally and figuratively, they were *outside*. They were wild and shabby. I tried to be stylish. I wore black a lot, because it made me look dramatic and mysterious, and because I wanted to ape the tradition of black for the law. I bought velvet things and lace from Oxfam shops, and wore a lot of silver jewellery.

I had never forgotten the scruffiness of the receptionist at the birth control place where I went for my morning-after pills. I didn't want to be like her. She was old-fashioned, and so were the Greenham women, thinking feminists had to be dowdy outsiders. Those days were gone.

I looked up the number of the refuge, rang it and asked for Janey Davis. Her weepy voice became sharp with panic when I told her her husband had been looking for her. 'You didn't tell him where I was, did you?'

'Course not. I said I didn't know.'

'What are you phoning up for then?'

'I've got a message for you. If you want it.'

'I don't,' said Janey. 'And if he comes in again, tell him to fuck off.'

'Will do.'

I put the phone down, smiling, and finished my shift.

This was my sort of work. I wasn't the type to go out and defend the earth. I would stay inside and defend women.

I finished my shift and walked out into the May evening. In a shop doorway stood Adam Preston, the wife batterer's friend. He seemed to be waiting for me.

I thought I could probably handle him, but I didn't like the idea that his pal might be lurking nearby. I tried to hurry past.

He put out his hand. 'Miranda.'

'What?'

'Can I talk to you?'

'We don't know where she is,' I lied, and I thought of my father's prohibition on lying, his family tradition, his Honourable Heart. And I thought of what a marvellous rule it was, if you were despicable enough to think of it and cruel enough to enforce it: that everybody except you had to tell the truth at all times, and everybody had to believe everything you said. You could get away with anything. You could cheat anybody.

Adam Preston said hesitantly, 'Your surname isn't Toms, by any chance?'

'Who's asking?'

'You remind me of someone I used to know.'

'I'm not surprised. I've got thousands of cousins.'

'So had she. Her name was Christine.'

We were in a street where there had been a market. We were paddling in onion peelings, tissue paper, rotten fruit and plastic box dividers. People were clearing up. We were in the way.

He said, 'She's dead now.'

'I know. I'm her sister.'

'You're not Janet.'

'Janet's my other sister. Are you the Adam who – ?'

'Loved Chris. Yes.'

'That's one word for it,' I said scornfully. 'You ran away.'

He looked at the pavement and at a burst, rotten orange. 'Yes.'

'Why?'

'Why should I go to prison for loving her? Why should I let them say it was a crime? It would have been as much of an insult to her as – '

'Great. She died and you went free.'

'Call that free? She was just as dead wherever I was. The abortion was nothing to do with me. I didn't even know she was pregnant.'

'You should have!'

'I know, I know, Miranda, but she went off to France and she didn't tell me. I don't know what I'd have done if she had, but I wouldn't have let her harm herself.'

It sounded like something he had been saying over and over again since it happened – for longer than my lifetime – though perhaps only to himself.

I believed him. I offered my hand. It seemed the natural thing to do. Our fleshy palms pressed together like thighs. We shook hands for a long time. At first it was our right hands. Then our left hands got involved and suddenly all our fingers were interlocked and we were facing each other, grinning like children in a playground dance.

The market stallholders were sweeping round our feet, cross as housewives. 'Get on with it, mate, are you going to kiss her or not?'

Adam said to me, 'I don't know, what do you think?'

'Don't see why not,' I said. 'We're practically related.'

'How do you work that out?'

'If you hadn't been her lover, she wouldn't have died.' He flinched but I didn't mean it like that. I went on. 'And if she hadn't died I wouldn't have been born. So it's all ended happily.'

'That's one way of looking at it.'

'My parents had me to take her place,' I explained.

I could see him doing his sums. 'Yes, I suppose they must have. I didn't even know you existed.'

'I do.' I kissed his mouth, as she must have.

We walked hand in hand, I didn't know where. I ought to be going home, to work for my finals. I ought to be heading for Paddington and the 6.03 to Bleswick. Mum would have my supper ready. I ought to arrive home at the usual time on my usual train, like the perfect husband of her dreams.

Adam said, 'Cigarette?'

'I don't.'

'That's one way you're different from Chris.' He laughed tentatively, as if he were trying something out to see if it would hurt, and if so how much. 'She smoked all the time. Never bought her own, mind you.'

'It's bad for you. Haven't you heard? Tell me everything about her.'

'Shall we go back to my place? Or . . .?'

'Yes!'

'It's not far,' he said.

I said, 'Have you got a phone?'

'Good heavens no. New-fangled things.'

'It's just that I ought to ring my mum and tell her where I am.'

'Your *mum*!' Adam's face relaxed for the first time and he laughed with a sort of reminiscent delight. 'I remember your mum!'

'Did you like her?'

'I didn't dislike her, I never really got to know her, she was always being towed round the house at ninety miles an hour by a hoover.'

'That's Mum.'

He had a flat in a six-story council block without a lift. 'Hard to let,' he explained, gasping for breath on the steps while I showed off how fit I was. 'So they let it to me.'

'Do you live by yourself?'

'Yep. Always have.'

'You've never been married or anything?'

'No.'

'Because of Chris?'

'You ask a lot of questions.'

'If I can't, who can?'

He let me into the flat. It was untidy, but cleaner than I had expected, with the faint, lonely smell of stale takeaway food. 'Where did you go?'

'Abroad. There were some civil disobedience people in my

CND group who knew about jumping bail and getting passports and things. It was all unbelievably corny.' He spoke as if it had happened yesterday. 'Dyed my hair. Turned up the collar of my coat and got the night ferry over to Boulogne. Felt like Burgess and Maclean. Hitched down to the South of France and got a job in the vineyards. Then I went to Italy and taught English in a language school. All the obvious things. I kept thinking they'd catch up with me.'

'And wishing they would?'

'I was lonely.' He shrugged.

'Is that why you came back?'

'My mum was ill about five years ago – I thought, to hell with it and I came back. I thought some burly hand would settle on my shoulder the minute I set foot on English soil, but it didn't, so I stayed on after she died. I've got a fellow feeling with criminals, so I work with them. There's probably an ageing detective somewhere with a file on me, but he doesn't seem to have opened it so far.'

'If he does,' I said, 'I'll defend you. Chris would want me to.'

'That's the nicest thing anyone's said to me for years.' He took off his glasses and squeezed the bridge of his nose. 'This is so weird.' There were tears in his eyes. 'I can't believe it's happening.'

'All the more reason,' I said.

'For what?'

'For us to continue this conversation in bed.'

He stared as if he had never heard of it.

Perhaps I would be his first lover since Chris.

Perhaps I would feel her on him, taste her.

He said hesitantly, 'I'd love a cuddle.'

He didn't seem in the least bit embarrassed about saying something so childish. I was, but we lay on his bed – a narrow single – and cuddled.

It felt as if we were related. I was still turned on, but it wasn't the wild, hungry turn-on that I knew from other people. I didn't want to go through that business of building up his power so that I could take it away.

That seemed to have been done to him already. By Chris, my sister, my own flesh, my other flesh.

I wasn't turned on as a washing machine is turned on, urgent and noisy and with a cycle to get through, but turned on like a very good music system, giving off sounds of searing sweetness, demanding nothing except that you listen, and even that only if you want to.

We stroked each other through our clothes, and then, eventually, under them. He undid my necklace and my black lace blouse, inserted one finger and toyed with my left nipple, round and round, tickling the tip.

This went on for a long time. I liked it but it made me feel as if I ought to be doing something else. He seemed content in an odd, still, dazed sort of way.

I teased him. 'Don't go too far, will you?'

'Eh?'

'Isn't that what you used to call it in the olden days?' "Going too far"?'

'They're not that olden. Now we call it – '

I put my hand over his mouth. I didn't want to hear. I didn't want to think about it. Urgently, I said, 'Let's do it.'

'We are doing it.'

'You know.'

He said, 'I wasn't expecting you. I'm not equipped.'

'It's OK, I'm on the pill.'

'That's not what I meant.'

I sighed. 'You don't *believe* that stuff, do you?'

'I give it the benefit of the doubt.'

'*What do you think I am*?'

'The sister of a girl who died because I wasn't careful enough when I made love to her.'

There was no answer to that, so we got on with our heavy petting.

102

He licked my spine and my bum and the backs of my knees. I felt like a kitten or a puppy being bathed by its mother.

Or its father. Some male animals nurtured their young. Some male animals liked being parents. Seagulls were one example, I thought. And wolves. Or was it jellyfish? If Adam hadn't had sex with Chris, I wouldn't be here. That almost made him my father, except that I wasn't angry with him. I didn't want to do anything to him.

'Turn over,' he said, and he licked my stomach.

He savoured my taste. He said, 'You're very clean.'

I smiled. 'I am now.'

It almost made Chris my mother, except that for a moment I felt free of the need to scoop up love, or the semblance of it, wherever I saw it. Free of the need to use my cunt like a vacuum cleaner, sucking and scooping up love in case Mum might want some. In case I might have the power to make her happy and, having the power, stand charged with negligently failing to do it.

Beyond the window, between the tower blocks, the summer sky darkened. He said, 'Will you sleep with me?'

'Yes, but I ought to phone my mum.'

He laughed softly. 'Keeps you on a tight rein, does she?'

I retorted, 'She worries if she doesn't know where I am. I'm all she's got.'

'Is your father dead, then?'

'No such luck.'

Adam paused before saying levelly, 'Chris wasn't all that keen on him either.'

'Makes no difference to me,' I said. 'I just think – if he were dead Mum wouldn't mind so much. She wouldn't blame herself. She wouldn't go on hoping.'

'Divorced?'

'No, no. Shacked up with A. N. Other. Keeping his options open. As per. That's what tortures Mum, the hope that he might come back.'

'When did he go?'

'Five years ago but she still won't face it.'

'Left it as late as that, did he?'

'What do you mean?'

'Sorry, I shouldn't speak against him, I should leave that to you.'

'Tell me what you meant.'

'When Chris and I were ... going out, there was this girl always hanging around your family.' He was combing my pubic hairs with an old tortoiseshell comb with missing teeth. It prickled and tantalised. 'Chris and Janet seemed to think she was their friend, but you could see the sexual tension between her and your dad. Fizzing – ' he slid his finger inside me – 'like fireworks. New Zealander.'

'*Get out*!' I moved away from him. 'Her name wasn't Pam MacLeish by any chance?'

'Could be. Yes, I think it was. Why?'

'Why do you think?'

'No!'

'Yes.'

'And he left your mother when?'

'In 1980.'

'So it went on for *sixteen years* before he made the break?'

I said bitterly, 'He's a great believer in leaving things to sort themselves out. He calls it problem solving by inactivity.'

'How did your mother take it?'

'Fifty per cent hysterical, fifty per cent it's-not-happening.'

'It's depressing, isn't it, how people don't change? Even in Chris's day she was pretending not to know.'

The air in the dim bedroom seemed suddenly too thick and sour and hot to breathe. I was choking on the stink of sweat and sex and cigarettes and monosodium glutamate.

'*She knew about him and Pam even in Chris's day*?'

'Sure she knew,' said Adam. 'She made Chris promise not to tell.'

'Not to tell *who what*?'

'Not to tell your dad that she – your mum, that is – knew what your dad was up to. Your mum's theory was – let me get this right – that adultery's all very well as long as the wife doesn't know about it. If the wife allows herself to know about it, and allows the husband to *know* that she knows about it, then she's as bad as the husband for doing it.'

I put my face in my hands. 'Chris went along with that?'

'Course not. She used it to get her way, but she felt the same about it as you do. She'd have spilled the beans eventually. She was waiting for the right moment.'

'But she died instead. How very convenient for him.'

'Chris was a feminist before her time.'

I thought about the awful loneliness of that.

I thought of something else. 'It was convenient for Mum too, wasn't it? That Chris died. She must have been quite relieved.'

Adam looked worried. 'I think that's putting it a bit strongly.'

That's the sort of thing she would say. Blaming words for meaning what they mean.

'Go on,' I said bitterly. 'Defend her.'

I had been defending her. All my life. Making excuses. Campaigning for her rights. Calling it feminism, pretending my concern was for all women, knowing in my heart that she was the one I wanted to save. I was her advocate. Her voice. Putting her case. A false case. Speaking out for tricked women. But the tricked woman was a trickster. The brief was lies from start to finish. I had thought I was defending her from him. But she didn't want to be defended from him, she wanted to defend him. That was what I had been doing: defending her so that she could defend him. Speaking her lies, so that she would speak his.

Speaking Desdemona's lies and setting Othello free.

O, who has done this deed?
Nobody. I myself, farewell:
Commend me to my kind lord –
I agree with Daddy –

'She's a menace,' I said.

She's a woman of a certain generation,' Adam cautiously corrected. 'She hasn't had that many choices.'

'She chose him,' I retorted. 'She chose to protect him. She chose to lie to her daughters and teach us to lie to ourselves.'

'Was it a choice? Really?'

'If people can't *choose*, Adam, then people can't change, and there's no hope for any of us. Women like her will just go on and on, covering up for the husbands and the fathers and driving the daughters mad.'

'Miranda,' said Adam. 'You are not mad.'

'How do you know? But it doesn't matter one way or the other, does it? Mad or sane I must be wrong! It's perfect!' I was shouting. 'Perfect! Patriarchy is the perfect trap! Everyone's in it and there's no way out of it! As long as I'm not mad, I must be wrong! But if I go mad and prove myself right, do you know what everyone will say? They'll say, "Take no notice of anything *she* says, don't you know she's mad?" And I can't even call it patriarchy! It's my mother!'

Was I mad?

How would I know? How could I know? Could a mad brain diagnose itself?

I had to get out of that flat. I was suffocating.

I had to get out of everywhere. Any minute now bolts would be shot home. Wherever I was, I would be there forever.

He said, 'Can I come with you?'

'You want to?'

'Of course I do.'

He sounded hurt. I didn't see why. Why should he want to go anywhere with someone as loathsome as I was? He was probably my last friend. *Call yourself a feminist, Miranda? Making friends with the man who caused your sister's death!* Ironic, yet obvious. *Call yourself a feminist! Putting the blame on your lonely old mother! She's a victim of her conditioning, you've said it yourself often enough!*

Of course I had said it. I had believed it. I had believed her. Now I saw that she was a victim of nothing except her own self-contempt. Upon which point she agreed with Daddy. And I agreed with both of them. Victim? She was a perpetrator. Betrayed? She was a traitor. Lied to? She was a liar. Her lies had seeped into my soul. Even my ambitions were polluted. For as long as I could remember, she used to say, *Are you going to be a barrister when you grow up*? And I had thought she was urging me on to a career, but she wasn't, she was putting me off the scent. Throwing sand in my eyes. The sand of flattery. *You're so clever with words, Miranda! You could argue the hind leg off a donkey! You could argue anything! Sometimes you even seem to be right, but you can't be, because you disagree with Daddy. You only SEEM to be right, because you are so clever at arguing. And because you are clever at arguing I dismiss everything you say.*

I had thought she valued me, but she had been sneering at me for knowing what I knew, casting me off for knowing, making me separate, warning me not to know because the penalty for knowing is to be cast out. Out, out, out, for ever.

I knew everything now, but how could I bear to?

Was this knowledge madness?

If so, did it make itself invalid?

Holding my hand, Adam took me out into the street.

It was about ten o'clock. The pubs were still open. He led me towards one, across the hot dusty road.

I said, 'Not that one.' My voice had gone funny. It was an urgent whisper. 'Not that one.'

'What's wrong with that one?'

'I don't like it.'

'Why not?'

'It hasn't got a garden or anything. It hasn't got any seats outside.'

'You particularly want to sit outside?'

His tone was indulgent. It made me angry. *Sod that*, I thought. 'I am not going inside and that's flat.'

'All right, fine, no problem.'

He obviously did think it a problem. He was obviously ruing the moment he had set eyes on me. He was probably comparing me with Chris and thinking how much saner she was. Not surprising, really. She had had less time to be driven mad.

We found a pub with dusty metal tables and chairs on the pavement under Dubonnet parasols. He said, 'What would you like to drink?'

'Lager, please.'

I watched him go into the pub. Suddenly I changed my mind. I stood in the doorway and called in to him. The pub was crowded and I had to call quite loudly before he heard me. '*Adam*!'

He came running. 'What's wrong?'

'I've changed my mind, I don't want a lager.'

'All right, but did you have to shout like that?'

'I tried to call quietly but you didn't hear.'

'Couldn't you have come in after me?'

'*No*. I can't go inside.'

'What, pubs? Too smoky for you?'

'Anywhere,' I whispered. 'I can't go inside.'

That was why I had said no to the lager. A lager would mean visits to the lavatory. How could I go to the lavatory when I couldn't go inside? How would I ever be able to go to the lavatory again?

He said, 'What would you like instead?'

'Nothing. But it's OK, I'll watch you drink yours.'

He stared at me for a bit, then shrugged and went into the pub. After five minutes he came back with a pint of bitter and two bags of dry roasted nuts.

It was definitely him. He had definitely gone inside and come out again. The Rule of the Dream said that once you went inside you had to stay inside for all eternity. Obviously Adam was not subject to the Rule of the Dream.

'Nuts?' he offered me a packet.

'Thanks.' I put the packet in my handbag, unopened. 'I'll need these.'

'What for?'

I didn't answer. He said, 'Miranda, do you often get claustrophobic?'

'Now and again.'

'Are you staying with me tonight?'

'Not in your flat.' I shuddered.

'OK, OK . . .' he looked anxious, as if I were getting hysterical or something. He said, 'Do you want to go home?'

I wondered about that. I didn't know whether getting into vehicles constituted going inside, or if going inside only meant going inside bui'dings. Obviously I couldn't go into stations to board trains, but I must be careful too about climbing on to a bus only to find that it was packed with my mother and father and all my other relations telling lies to keep the family together and to drive me mad. The driver would drive for ever and I would never be able to get off. I would be stuck inside for ever with the lies.

'I'll be fine,' I said. 'I'll walk.'

'To *Bleswick*?'

'To Greenham.'

'You're going to walk to Greenham?'

'Why not? That's where the outsiders go and I'll never have to go indoors again. Never get trapped.'

He said slowly, 'Weren't you going to phone your mother?'

'If you're wanting to offload me, Adam, go ahead. I'm not your responsibility. You don't have to look after me.'

'I just thought your mother might – '

'Look after me? Yes, I thought that for years. Chris probably thought the same. You'd know better than me about that. Chris is dead. I never met her. Mum only ever looked after Daddy. That's all. For ever. There's nothing she wouldn't do for Daddy. No lie she wouldn't tell. That's what she calls him, you know. "Daddy". "I agree with Daddy." I don't call him Daddy, I call him Dad or my father or Sandringham or That Shit but she seems to think that if she doesn't refer to him as Daddy I won't know who she means.'

Janet

103

When I got the message from Mummy that Miranda had disappeared and was rumoured to be at Greenham Common, Godfrey said, 'She can stay disappeared.'

Margaret passed the message down the chain of command to her dolls. 'She can stay disappeared.'

I said, 'Yes, Margaret, I agree with Daddy too.'

Miranda, after all, was a final-year university student, and, as she was always so fond of telling everybody, her own person. I, on the other hand, had Margaret to look after, and her eighteen-month-old brother Norman, not to mention Godfrey and the constituency. I had my column to write for the *Cotswold Advertiser*, the Women for Family Life Newsletter to edit, and an appointment with Alfred, my psychotherapist.

Alfred did not allow you to cancel. He had explained this on my first visit, a year ago, after I had stopped crying and given him my particulars. 'A few ground rules, Janet, to keep the sessions as productive as possible. Thursday at mid-day is your time now. I have it marked in my diary as that, and you should too. I don't want you to miss a session for any reason whatsoever.'

'What if one of my children is ill?'

'Do you worry a lot about your children becoming ill?'

'I worry more about them thinking I'm ill if I keep bursting into tears for no reason.'

'Let's talk about that next time.'

Not that he could stop you missing sessions – he didn't come and capture you, or at least I didn't suppose he did – but he made you pay anyway. Seventeen pounds an hour to lie weeping on a bed in the home of a complete stranger was hard enough to swallow. Seventeen pounds an hour *not* to lie on said bed would be out of the question. So I kept Thursdays at noon for Alfred and parked the children on my neighbour Marsha Cunningham – oddly enough, the wife of David Cunningham, my old friend and admirer from Northburgh and *Nuts*, editor now of the *Cotswold Advertiser*, hence my column. It was all a bit incestuous.

Alfred was a placid little man with a bald head, a bow tie and eyes that managed to be both faraway and warm. He aroused memories of Julius Sutton, the publisher who, in the distant days of the seventies when I was going to be a novelist, had suggested that I revise some sections of *Off-Ration* and show it to him again.

Alfred gave off the same air as Julius of being totally fascinated by everything I had to say. At seventeen pounds an hour, he probably was.

'My sister has disappeared,' I told him. 'My mother seems to think she's gone to live at Greenham Common.'

'Yes?'

'Miranda is supposed to be doing a law degree. Her finals are this term.'

'And you feel that her going to live at Greenham Common will interfere with that?'

'Yes.'

'And it worries you?'

'People shouldn't give things up. Especially women. I mean, they moan and bellyache about not being allowed to do things, and when they are allowed, they give up. If anyone said women shouldn't do law because they have no sticking power, Miranda would be the first to start jumping up and down.'

'Do you ever give things up, Janet?'

'Me? No, Never.'

'You seem very sure about that.'

'I am. But this isn't about me. It's about Miranda.'

'Go on.'

'I'd better drive down there and find her and straighten her out.' I sat up and put on my shoes.

He said, 'We still have another twenty minutes.'

Five pounds sixty-six pence, I thought. Ever since my eleven-plus I did mental arithmetic on reflex. I lay down again.

'Janet, if we could go back a year to when you first came to see me. What can you remember about that?'

'I remember crying.'

'Yes, I remember that too. You seemed very distressed.'

'I remember thinking what an absolute fool you must think me, and I remember you giving me a box of Kleenex and I remember wondering how many you got through in a week and whether you got a bulk discount or whether your professional association did, and whether you claimed them against your income tax.'

He nodded. 'What else do you remember?'

'You asked me when the crying started, and I said when Norman was born. We talked about that. And then I realised it went back further to when Margaret was born. And, do you know, Alfred – ?'

'Yes, Janet?'

I sat up and faced him like a colleague. 'I think that was the point at which I started to be interested in the therapeutic process. I stopped being sceptical and embarrassed and I realised what was happening. Realised the extent of my denial. Because even after I told you about Margaret being born – I gave you a blow by blow account of every contraction, do you remember? – it took me weeks to tell you what really happened. To get to the *point*. To get past my pain. To tell you that that was the time when my parents' marriage broke up.'

'I think you said your mother was staying with you – '

'*Yes*. Of course she was. I'd just had my *first baby*. Mummy was supposed to be helping me and looking after me but she was in such a state about Daddy that she wasn't there for me in the way I needed her to be. I had to look after her instead. I resented that. Wasn't it horrible of me? And I was so angry with Pam, for choosing this time of all times to take Daddy away. And the other hard thing was – '

'Was what, Janet?'

'Facing up to my own responsibility in the matter.'

'Janet, how can *you* be responsible for your father's adultery?'

'I knew you'd say that, but I had actually known for some time that Daddy and Pam were friends, and I kept it secret, and it was probably during that time that it became more than a friendship.'

'So you feel guilty about your father's sex life?'

'Of course!'

*

I phoned the *Cotswold Advertiser* and asked to be put through to the editor.

'Dave, it's Janet.'

'Hello, love.' He was still a flirt. Now and again we had secret dates together, behind the backs of our spouses, just for the hell of it. 'How are you?'

'I'm going to Greenham Common,' I said.

He burst out laughing. 'That'll please Godfrey. Try and get your picture in one of the nationals, chopping down the fence with a woolly hat.'

'Could we be serious?'

'I am entirely serious. You have hidden depths.' His words reminded me of that time in Northburgh when he said, *you have deep sexual and emotional needs, which are not being met.* Quickly I explained about going to look for Miranda. I said, 'Could I do a story for you while I'm there? Might as well cover the cost of the petrol.'

'By all means, if you can find a local angle. Apart from the presence there of your good self.' He chuckled. 'When are you going?'

'Right away.'

'What a pity,' he said. 'I'd have liked to come with you.'

'They'd eat you alive.'

He groaned a groan of erotic longing. 'Which bit will you eat?'

All Godfrey's got between his legs is a rolled-up House of Commons order paper.

This was completely untrue. Godfrey and I had a very pleasant sex life.

'This is sexual harassment, David.'

'I know, and I'm supposed to be in a meeting. When will you be back?'

'This evening. I'm not sleeping in a tent.'

'Have lunch with me tomorrow,' he suggested. 'Let me know how you got on.'

'I can't ask your poor wife to babysit again.'

'She won't mind. She knows it's business.'

104

The Women's Peace Camp was not what I had expected, though why I should have expected anything, I did not know. This was not my usual stamping ground.

I had imagined a park with rows of tents, through which I could conduct a systematic search. I had assumed that there would be some sort of headquarters, with names on a register.

What I found as I drove slowly round the perimeter of the base in the pouring rain, wishing I had brought my wellies, were acres of thick woodland – in which it would be impossible to find one individual, particularly if she didn't want to be found – as well as heaps of rubbish, signposts marked FIREWOOD and SHIT PIT and random clusters of makeshift temporary dwellings. I peered out at the clusters and at passing groups of tramping women encased in oilskins or wrapped in filthy blankets. I rolled down the window. 'I'm looking for a girl called Miranda Toms.'

'Who? Hey, you couldn't give us a lift round to Green Gate, could you?'

'You don't happen to be going to Yellow Gate, by any chance?'

'You don't happen to be going into Newbury?'

I declined to go to Newbury but I ferried various eccentric individuals between the gates. The gates were named after different colours, apparently, but they all seemed to me to be the same colour, as did the women: mud coloured. Godfrey was going to have a fit when he saw the upholstery.

I described Miranda and asked if anyone had seen her.

They kept saying no, and I wondered if they had rumbled me as a Tory lady or thought I was from the Special Branch. At last someone said, 'That woman who won't go inside the tents, isn't her name Miranda?'

*

She was lying under a tree in a sleeping bag wrapped in polythene. Some women crouched around her, trying to get her to drink tea from a thermos. Half-maggot, half-corpse, she was staring up at the low grey clouds, unflinching as raindrops broke on her drenched white face.

My irritation vanished. She looked so pitiful. She might be about to die. My eyes stung, my throat went into a spasm. *I can't lose two sisters*, I thought desperately. *It's not fair! I'm the middle one*!

I said, 'I'm her sister,' and the women moved a few feet away in a gesture of discreet respect. Sisters had status. I squatted down in my fawn trench coat and Hush Puppies. 'Hello . . .?' It was the tone I might use to a baby, gently waking it in the night to be potted. 'What are you up to?'

'Hello, Janet.' Her voice was flat and hoarse. 'Have you come outside to join us?'

'Oh, definitely. Mummy's worried about you.'

Miranda's face and voice turned vicious. 'She's pretending.' Behind the polythene, inside the top of the sleeping bag, her shoulder quivered in a tiny shrug of contempt. 'Mum always pretends. Always lies. Always has.'

'What do you mean? Can we go inside somewhere? You're soaked and I'm not much better.'

One of the other women said, 'I've been trying to get her to come in my tent, but she won't.' After one look at the tent's sleazy interior I almost saw Miranda's point, but I didn't say anything.

'Come and sit in the car,' I suggested.

Miranda shook her head from side to side in the wet grass. 'I'm staying outside.'

'Just for a few minutes.'

'That's it, though, isn't it? It won't be a few minutes.'

Another woman said, 'She's been like this since she got here. She seems to think that if she comes inside the tents, we won't let her out again.'

'Do you think that, Miranda?'

'It's not them,' she said to me, and then, over my shoulder to them, 'It's not you. Honestly!'

The women said, 'She's terrified of something.'

Miranda said, 'It's the Rule of the Dream.'

'What dream?'

Tearfully, she told me about her dream – about having to go in or stay out, and about it being permanent – and how it had suddenly started seeming real to her.

I said, 'I know someone who'd be fascinated by that. Alfred, my therapist.' That made Miranda sit up – not literally, she remained lying on the ground but she was obviously surprised and impressed that her boring old sister should have a therapist. 'Maybe you should see him,' I said.

'I'm not going to a male therapist.'

'Come and sit in the car, Miranda. I won't start the engine if you don't want me to. If you want to get out, you can get out.' She kept floating off behind her own eyes. I shook her shoulders. 'Miranda, stop blanking out like that! Stop it! This is your elder sister speaking! I'm not going to harm you! I'm Janet, and you're upsetting me!' I was nearly crying.

At last she agreed to sit in the car, but she kept the door open and her feet on the ground outside. She made me give her the keys to hold. She said suspiciously, 'Have you got another set?'

'Not with me, no.'

'Is that true?'

'Yes it's true. Honourable Heart.'

At the sound of our old family promise, Miranda went into a convulsion of disgust. She spat and vomited bile and tea into the grass. She sat back, exhausted, wet with sweat and rain.

'Better?' I enquired.

'A bit.'

After a lot of persuasion she allowed me to drive her into Newbury to get her something to eat. She wouldn't go into a restaurant, but I fetched her a Chinese takeaway which she devoured in the car. Godfrey wasn't going to like that either.

I said as gently as I could, 'Are you going to tell me what all this is about?'

'All what?'

'Aren't you supposed to be revising for your finals?'

'What's the point?' In a cruel parody of Mummy's voice, she said, '"Aren't you going to be a barrister when you grow up?"' Miranda spoke as herself again. 'Mum doesn't really think women should be barristers. She doesn't think we should be anything, apart from doormats. Calling me a lawyer. "Can I go back to my cell now?" I used to feel so guilty when she said that. I thought I was bullying her. Flaunting my abilities and my opportunities in her face when she had neither. Of course she had both, only she'd given them to him. She was torturing me. Making me feel guilty for spotting when she was talking nonsense. Making me think I must be wrong. If I saw through her, I might see through him, and that would never do. So she warned me off. Played on my guilt. Fancy me being stupid enough to take her at her word. That's what having an honourable heart does for you. You believe people. Why didn't I see what she was doing? Do you realise he and Pam were having it off before I was even *born*? They were at it when Chris was alive?'

I brushed aside Miranda's rambling – she was obviously suffering from pre-finals nerves – and helped her back to the point. 'Whatever the reason for you deciding to study law, Miranda, you *did* decide to study it, you're practically at the end of your course, and it's a jolly good qualification to have.'

'Is it?' The food had perked her up. She seemed wild now, hyperactive like a lead-poisoned child. 'I don't know that it is. What's the point of being an advocate for women who only want to be advocates for men? I think a barrister is a pretty shabby thing to be, actually. An *advocate*. One-who-speaks-for. I think people should speak for themselves. Tell their own truths, tell their own lies. I mean, do you realise, Janet, if you're a barrister, some total villain can come to you, and lie his head off – or her head off – to you, and you can know in your bones that they're lying, but as long as they don't actually admit to you that they're lying, you have to go into court and make out their case! You have to speak their words, tell their story, doesn't matter if you believe it or not, it is *your job* to make the jury believe it! Some job! They can stuff it!'

Her words disturbed me, though I was not sure why. I tried to commit them to memory so that I could repeat them to Alfred and work through the emotions they aroused. In the meantime I concentrated on the aspect of the situation that I could handle, the one that seemed simple and clear cut.

'There are lots of things you can be with a law degree other than a barrister. Prime Minister, for example,' I suggested roguishly, to test the water.

'Ugh.'

'You say ugh but if you think she's so terrible as the first woman prime minister, let's see you do better as the second. Let's see Militant Miranda in parliament. Or you could be a solicitor – your woodland chums must need the services of solicitors from time to time. Or go the other way, be a company lawyer. Or you could teach, or go into any job where you have to have an arts degree.'

'I could even be a housewife, like you,' said Miranda nastily.

'You could be a dull old housewife like me. And just think, if you give up your course now – if you chicken out of taking your finals – in a few years' time you might be able to carry on the family tradition.'

Miranda looked at me out of the corner of her eye. 'What do you mean?'

'You might have a daughter of your own, to inspire with the tragic tale of how you were once *very nearly* a lawyer. And who will you blame for the fact that you didn't make it? Mummy? Daddy? Mrs Thatcher? Sexism? Or your own faint heart?'

She thought a bit and nodded, and said softly, 'Yes.'

'Does that mean I can take you home?'

'I haven't got a home.'

'You live at Mum's.'

'I'm moving out,' she declared. 'It's about time Mum let go of me.'

'Or *vice versa*?' I murmured.

105

'Mummy seems to think Miranda's moved in with a new boyfriend.'

'Yes?' said Alfred. 'Shall I take your coat?'

'Thanks.' I lay down. 'It's hard to stay abreast of Miranda's boyfriends at the best of times, but she's really keeping this one under wraps. No one's even allowed to know his name. Still, he seems to have persuaded her to sit her finals.'

'It sounds as if you had a hand in that too.'

'It's not really important who persuaded her, is it? The important thing is that she should get her law degree.'

'Important to *you*,' said Alfred's disembodied voice from behind my head. 'Why is it so important, do you think? It's not *your* law degree.'

'I don't think people should give up on things,' I explained. 'What you start, you should finish.'

'And do you ever leave things unfinished?'

'No,' I sighed. I lost control of the sigh. It turned into a sound that was half way between a sob and the word *yes*. 'Yes. I wrote a novel once. There was a publisher quite interested in it, but he said it needed more work. He was probably right. Monica Delbarco – of Delbarco and Wilde – found it unworthy of comment, but this other one might have published it if I'd done the work. I said I'd do it. But I didn't.'

'Do you know why?'

I lay in silence and tried to remember. All I could think of were the words that Miranda had spoken at Greenham Common, and that had disturbed me so deeply.

I think a barrister is a pretty shabby thing to be. An advocate. One-who-speaks-for. I think people should speak for themselves. Tell their own truths, tell their own lies . . . Some total villain can come to you and lie their head off and you have to speak their words, tell their story.

It doesn't matter if you believe it or not, it is your job to make the jury believe it!

One could pick any number of holes in her argument. Nevertheless, there was something about what she said that I recognised.

It went back to the time of *Off-Ration*. I had discussed the manuscript with Julius Sutton. I had listened to his criticisms – and his compliments – and read his notes. He had put no pressure on me, but I had agreed to make certain revisions. And then I couldn't do them.

Not only could I not do them, I had got into a great rage at the thought of doing them. I had been blocked by rage. Of Julius Sutton I had thought, *He's got his own words. He's a powerful man. People pay attention to his words. What's so special about my words that he wants to claim them for himself, own them, change them? If he's got a story to tell, let him tell it. Why does he want me to tell his story, why should he make me say things, his things?*

Why had both Miranda and I, in our different ways, at crucial moments in our different careers, become afraid of having lies planted on us? Why were we demoralised by terror and revulsion at the idea of our words, our stories, our truth telling, being violated by another person?

Which other person?

In my case, I thought I knew. And the implications were scarcely bearable. I stared at Alfred's ceiling. Someone in his room was moaning. He said softly, 'Janet, what's happening for you at the moment?'

'Nothing.' Quickly I rose to my feet, wiped my eyes and paid him.

He said, 'The session's not up yet.'

I laughed breezily. 'Let's talk about that next time.'

'Janet, we made an agreement, do you remember? Please stay till the end of the session.'

I walked out, though I should have known better. All day I felt deprived and depressed. That evening I needed to talk to somebody, but when I phoned Alfred to make an emergency appointment, all I got was his answering machine.

Godfrey was at Westminster. The children were in bed. I had no number for Miranda.

I tried to reach Dave Cunningham. He could always cheer me up. He might pop round on some pretext or other. As the phone rang, I was rehearsing what I would say if his wife answered – I would pretend I wanted to discuss babysitting arrangements – but the subterfuge was unnecessary. Like Alfred, the Cunninghams had their answering machine on.

I had a fantasy of myself as an answering machine: speaking dead words, planted on me by another person. Words of rejection, words on a rejection slip, words that were nothing to do with me.

There was no escaping the truth.

I had to face up to it.

The time when I was being asked by Julius to rewrite my novel was also the time when I discovered, quite by accident, that Pam MacLeish was back in London.

Not only was she back, she had an appalling secret. She had been actively involved in the death of Christine. She had given Christine the pills that killed her.

Somehow, Pam had persuaded me to keep quiet about all this, and to think of her as a friend.

She had not done it directly, of course. She was too clever for that. She had used Daddy. She had got Daddy to persuade me not to tell Mummy that she, Pam, was back in England.

She had planted some superficially convincing rationalisation into his mind, and he, being such a straightforward person himself, and unable to think evil of anybody, had believed it and passed it on to me, and there we were, violating a deeply held family principle and lying on Pam's behalf!

Their love affair must have begun some time after this.

Miranda could not be right in thinking that it went back to Christine's day. That was absurd, they would never have got away with it for so long, and anyway how could Miranda know such a thing about a time before she was born? This fantasy was clearly part of her breakdown or her brainstorm or whatever she was having, under the pressure of her approaching finals.

If Pam's and Daddy's relationship went back that far, who was to say that Monica Delbarco's rejection slip had really come from

Monica Delbarco? Monica Delbarco might not even have read *Off-Ration*. Pam herself might have intercepted the manuscript and returned it, rather than risk my finding out that she was back in England.

Not that I would put such a thing past a deceitful person like her, but Daddy would not have been party to it. I had been so upset when *Off-Ration* was rejected, and he had been so kind to me. It couldn't have been an act.

No, the love affair must have begun after the lie.

It was hardly surprising. After being persuaded by Pam to tell lies, he must have been like putty in her hands.

He wasn't putty any more. Godfrey and I had given up going to the flat because of the rows Daddy and Pam had, usually about his domestic habits (lack of) and about what time he got in. When I recounted the rows to Mummy, she said, 'I take that as a hopeful sign.'

Hopeful sign or not, I had no sympathy for Pam. As I said to Godfrey, 'Daddy's no angel, but she had time enough to find out what she was letting herself in for!'

These days, when I saw Daddy, I saw him alone. He would ring me and invite me up to London for lunch. He took me to places like Rule's or the Epicure. The lunches were lavish and went on a long time. He was easing himself out of his job and down into a well-earned retirement.

'How about next Thursday, Janet?'

'Thursday's difficult, that's when I see my therapist.'

'Your shrink!' he shouted with laughter. 'Hasn't that charlatan sorted you out yet? My God, I know what hobby I'm going to take up when I retire. Fifteen quid an hour, was it?'

'Seventeen.'

'Forget it,' he said. 'Have lunch with me instead, we can get a damn good bottle of wine for that.'

'Couldn't we make it another day?'

'Only day next week I can manage,' Daddy said. 'And I've got a special reason for wanting to see you.'

'All right.'

It wasn't for Alfred to order me about. It was I who paid him, not the other way round. And in any case, there was no point in going to see him. Why go every week, just for the sake of it? I had not yet sorted out my thoughts on why I had abandoned *Off-Ration*, or whether I would try to write it again. There was no point in going to see Alfred when I had nothing to say to him.

What remained of Daddy's hair had turned quite white, but it still curled roguishly round his collar. 'Cad's hair,' I called it fondly, giving it a gentle tweak. 'Are you a cad, Dad?'

'Hope you won't think so, old chum. Got something to tell you.' He called for two large gins. He said, 'Pam and I have reached the end of the road.'

'Oh dear. I am sorry.'

'Don't be, don't be, it's all quite amicable.' He consulted the menu and the wine list. I seemed to know that he was looking for something costing exactly seventeen pounds. 'Truth is, Janet, I hate to say this, but all those years on her own, waiting for me, seem to have turned Pam into a bit of an old maid. Fussy. Pernickety. Intolerant. You know? She'll be happier having her own place to herself without me cluttering it up.'

I said, 'Does Mummy know yet?'

'No,' he said slowly. 'And I was wondering if you'd tell her for me. She's not the most balanced of people, and it may be a bit of a shock – '

'Daddy, she's going to be over the moon. Why don't you just turn up?'

' – bit of a shock when she hears about me and Lindsay.'

'*Lindsay Bixwell?*'

'Lindsay's been married, you see. Makes all the difference in a woman. Not so set in her ways.'

'I don't know what to say.'

'I told her you'd be pleased. You and she have always got on – '

I said faintly, 'She's always been a friend of the family.'

'Exactly,' he said.

'For as long as I can remember.'

'She's a good girl, is Lindsay.'

'Was that why?' I asked him.

'Was what why what?'

'Was that why she was a friend of the family? Was that why you asked her to be Miranda's godmother? Was that why you were always taking Miranda over there when she was little – to play with the puppies?'

Daddy sipped his gin and twinkled reproachfully at me over the rim of his glass. 'Honestly, Janet. The things you come up with. What do you think I am?'

Afterword

When the circumstances of a character in a novel appear to resemble those of the author, the assumption may be made that the fiction is autobiographical. So I would like to make it clear that, although *Daddy's Girls* was to some extent inspired by events which occured in my own family, it is not an account of them. Any similarities – other than on points of background detail – should be regarded as coincidental.

To be specific . . . I am one of three daughters of a mother who had given up her nursing training to become a housewife, and a father in the property business. My sisters and I attended a Catholic convent school, even though neither we nor our parents were Catholics.

When I was in my mid-teens, during the sixties, a boyfriend told me of his suspicion that my father was having a love affair with a young woman whom I liked and admired. I had always regarded her as a friend of our family, and my friend in particular.

I had no way of knowing whether the allegation was true (and I still don't know whether it was true at the time it was made); but rather than contemplate the possibility, I told the boyfriend that I wished never to see him again. He took me at my word and I never did see him again.

So far, so factual. But facts are only starting points for fictions. *Daddy's Girls* is a 'what-if?' fantasy. It is entirely fictional, and so are all the characters, places and events it contains.

In particular, I am happy to make it clear that both my sisters are alive and well and that neither they nor I cheated in the eleven-plus.

Zoë Fairbairns
London, 1990.

Also available from Mandarin Paperbacks

Here Today

ZOË FAIRBAIRNS

She always knew men wanted her, as wife, secretary or lover. What if they don't?

Antonia's life had been perfect – temp of the year at the Here Today agency and a happy marriage to come home to. Suddenly all that has changed. Her husband doesn't want her and nor, it seems, do the increasingly-automated offices of London. Her home and her health are under threat, and so is her knowledge of who she is.

Antonia's search for answers also becomes the search for Samantha, another office worker and a rumoured victim of sexual assault. Pursuing the truth about Samantha provides Antonia with answers to questions about herself she didn't even know she was asking . . .

'Her most successful novel so far – racy, crisp and yes, very thrilling'

Tribune

'Witty, provocative, ironic and, above all, lots of fun'

Sara Maitland, *New Statesman*

Closing

ZOË FAIRBAIRNS

Four women meet on a sales training course.

Gina: the highflyer who has it all – love, money, success and a career planned to the last detail. But who is doing the planning?

Ann: the mother who has always put her children first. In the bleak world of 80s unemployment, might there be something for her . . . Or someone?

Teresa: who finds that principles don't pay the bills and whose millionaire ex-lover has made her an offer she can't refuse.

and

Daphne: spellbinding, sinister, superb, whose mission is to turn women into sales women.

After a week in Daphne's grip, the women's lives are irrevocably changed . . .

'Witty and perceptive . . . funny and eminently readable.'
Over 21

'Such a pleasure to read, such fun, so intelligent, so perspicacious, so well plotted, so unobtrusively moral, so elating, I find myself in danger of writing an extended quote rather than a proper review.'
Fay Weldon, *Books Magazine*

'A subtly feminist version of the power-sex-and-money sagas . . . highly enjoyable.'
Spare Rib

Stolen

DEBORAH MOGGACH

'Utterly absorbing . . . *Stolen* is a real page-turner'
Daily Mail

'Deborah Moggach captures brilliantly the basic incompatibilities and misunderstandings that arise when two people have little knowledge of each other's culture . . . both funny and moving'
Sunday Express

'A powerful and disturbing book'
New Woman

'A real page-turner; a kaleidoscopic Kramer versus Kramer . . . the novel assumes the tension of detective fiction . . . the mother-child detail is all painfully right. This is a nicely balanced account of marital breakdown in peculiarly difficult circumstances'
Sunday Times

'Compelling'
The Times

Mad About Bees

CANDIDA CREWE

Mad About Bees is a novel about obsession: about a London schoolteacher, Samuel, whose irrational anxieties are dominating his life. A whole series of rituals (including tapping his head twenty-four times when he drinks coffee) has to be observed – or his children will be run over by a bus.

Between acting jobs, his sister-in-law Nell reads Tolstoy to a blind Irish poet. She has a cynical distrust of human nature – everywhere she looks people are deceived by those they love the most – but her sister's life with Samuel seems to her a model of what relationships should be. But then Samuel is a very sane and straightforward man . . .

'funny and achingly sad'

New Woman

Waverly Place

SUSAN BROWNMILLER

To all appearances, Barry Kantor and Judith Winograd are like any other professional New Yorkers. He is a lawyer – she is an editor of children's books.

But the closed doors of 104 Waverly Place conceal a routine of battery, abuse, neglect and drugs that seventeen years and two illegally-adopted children have only helped develop. Too late, the tragic death of a little girl reveals the truth.
Based on fact, *Waverly Place* is a leading feminist's fictional exploration of sexual politics and the warped psychology of enslavement. Not since *In Cold Blood* has a real event been so purposefully reconstructed.

'Barry Kantor is the kind of sleazy fictional character Dickens might have been proud to have invented'

Guardian

'Not a book that is easily put aside, nor a story that can be forgotten'

New Statesman and Society

'A persuasive portrait of New York middle-class life . . . *Waverly Place* is a triumph'

Literary Review

Raj

GITA MEHTA

Born a princess into life as it has long been led in the Royal House of Balmer, Jaya Singh must grapple with history if she is to fulfil her role as the guardian of her people. For momentous changes are sweeping across India as her great civilisation heads inexorably towards the bloody struggle for Independence from the British Raj.

Torn between tradition and the ideals of Mahadma Ghandi, Jaya becomes the politically aroused leader who will guide her Kingdom through a treacherously shifting world until the moment when palace and country can triumph over their destiny.

Not since *Gone With the Wind* have fiction and history been so compellingly interwoven.

'Easily the year's best novel'
Daily Mail

'Mehta's talent is as sharp as a laser beam'
Sunday Times

'The best work of historical fiction from the pen of an Indian writer'
India Today

'Richly decorated and densely worked . . . oversewn like a length of brocade with sex, landscape, polo, politics, tragedy . . .'
Observer

You Must Be Sisters

DEBORAH MOGGACH

'The happiest, saddest, funniest, most perceptive truth about growing up since *The Catcher in the Rye*'
Over 21

'Assured and successful . . . a complex story, with many ironies and surprises, but it is told with touching and unaffected simplicity . . . Altogether a most satisfying and intelligent first novel, and something for the author to be proud of'
Financial Times

'Sensitive and humorous'
Daily Express

'Very readable'
Times Literary Supplement

'This readable, often touching book gives off all the signals of a writer with real potential'
Daily Telegraph

'Sharp and wry'
Spectator

'Warm and witty . . . family life most achingly bared'
New Statesman